The Halversons: Book #1

by

KIMBERLY RAE
JORDAN

THREESTRAND
PRESS

A CORD OF THREE STRANDS IS NOT EASILY BROKEN.

***A man, a woman & their God.
Three Strand Press publishes Christian Romance stories that intertwine love, faith and family. Always clean. Always heartwarming. Always uplifting.***

This is a work of fiction. Names, characters, places, and incidents are a product of the author's imagination. Locales and public names are sometimes used for atmospheric purposes. Any resemblance to actual people, living or dead, or to businesses, companies, events, institutions, or locales is completely coincidental.

Gareth/ Kimberly Rae Jordan. -- 1st ed.
ISBN-13: 978-1-988409-64-1

A broken and a contrite heart,
O God, thou wilt not despise.

Psalm 51:17

CHAPTER ONE

Aria Jensen stared out the window of her car at the two-story building she had parked in front of. The exterior looked nice enough, but it didn't reflect what was in her apartment. She'd lived there for almost a year, but she would never call it home.

To her, home was a safe space. A warm and welcoming place. Somewhere she was happy to be.

She'd had that in the small home she'd shared with her mom. Until she could no longer afford it. Even with a roommate, she hadn't made enough at her current job to pay half the rent.

Aria gripped her steering wheel so she wouldn't scratch at the anxiety that itched beneath her skin. So much had happened over the past year, and Aria wasn't sure if she could handle things getting any worse. Surely, being homeless was better than her present living situation.

Knowing she had no choice but to go inside, Aria loosened her grip on the steering wheel and grabbed her things from the passenger seat. Clutching her purse and water bottle to her chest, she made her way across the cracked sidewalk to the concrete steps that led to the door of the building.

The door swung open, and a slovenly dressed man stumbled out, catching himself on the railing of the steps as he leered at her.

"Well, hello, sweetheart," he mumbled. He reached out a hand, but Aria skirted past him and went inside without responding.

If only he was the worst the building had to offer. With heavy steps, she climbed to the second floor. When she reached the door of the apartment, she paused and took several breaths, praying that the apartment was empty for a change.

Aria gripped the doorknob and twisted it, not surprised to find it unlocked. Whether or not her roommates were home, they never locked the door because they always forgot their keys.

Wrinkling her nose at the smells that assaulted her, she stepped into the apartment. Burnt and rotten food seemed to be a constant in the air, and it made Aria want to gag.

"Ariaaaaaaaa!"

Aria ignored the call and hurried toward her room. Her steps faltered when she saw that her door stood open, the doorknob broken. She swung around to face the woman who came toward her with unsteady steps.

"Why is my door open?" Aria demanded, the sick feeling in her stomach intensifying.

"Is it open?" the woman asked as she bumped into the wall, then just stayed there leaning against it. "I guess you left it open."

"I did *not* leave it open," Aria said.

She hated moments like these. She'd never been good at confrontations, and this one was going to leave her shaken. With her door broken, she had no safe place to go.

"Did you bring food?"

The woman who had seemed to be such an ideal candidate for a roommate initially had turned into a nightmare. And now Aria just wanted to be free of her. Unfortunately, she had nowhere to go.

"No. I didn't bring food." She turned on her heel and went to her room.

Tears stung her eyes as she took in the destruction. They had pulled her clothes out and strewn them all over the room, as if they'd been searching for something in her drawers. The lamp on her nightstand had been knocked over, and her mattress sat at an angle on her box spring. The blankets and pillows were tossed all across the floor.

Aria wanted to scream at Tonya that she'd had no right to go through her things, but she knew she'd just deny it had been her. Turning, Aria closed her door, wishing she could still lock it.

She began to put things back into place, but when she got to her clothes, she paused. There was no way she could keep living there. Her anxiety was constantly high, meaning she struggled to sleep, fearing what might happen while she was unaware. And now, with the broken lock on her door, there was no way she'd be able to fall asleep at all.

Instead of putting her clothes back into the drawers, Aria went to the closet and pulled out her two suitcases. As quickly as she could, she crammed all her clothes into them.

When Tonya had first showed up to view the apartment, Aria had thought she'd make a decent roommate. The woman must have come during a rare moment of sobriety, and she'd managed to pull the wool over Aria's eyes. But since the day she'd moved in, she'd been either drunk or high, and the same was true for her boyfriend, who had become a second roommate that Aria hadn't agreed to.

On top of eating all her food and only giving her part of the rent money they owed, they didn't clean up after themselves. Basically, they were the worst roommates ever. Until they'd broken into her room, Aria had been willing to tough it out. But she was done now. She was better off sleeping in her car.

Thankfully, they had a month-to-month lease, and she'd paid until the end of that month. Let them deal with next month's rent. She'd covered for them for the last two months—at the expense of her food budget—so they could figure out how to pay the next month if they wanted to stay.

With all her clothes and toiletries packed, she went to the kitchen to grab a couple of garbage bags. Tonya and her boyfriend were passed out on the couch, which was just fine, as far as Aria was concerned. Maybe she could get out without them realizing she was leaving for good.

Back in her room, Aria put all her bedding, pillows, and towels into the garbage bags. The bed was hers, but she didn't care about it. She would happily write it off if she could just walk away from the nightmare her life had become.

In just over an hour, she'd packed up everything she wanted to take. Now she had to get it all down to her car without waking the terrible twosome.

Moving quietly, she carried her purse, one suitcase, and one garbage bag out of the apartment. She was breathing hard by the time she got down to her car. Partly from nerves, partly from having to carry a heavy bag down a flight of stairs.

She shoved it all in the trunk of her car, including her purse, which she hadn't wanted to leave upstairs in case they woke up and went into her room while she wasn't there. After locking the car, she went back into the building, praying that she would catch a break and they'd still be asleep. She didn't have a lot of hope, since it felt like she hadn't caught a break in a very long time.

Thankfully, when she walked into the apartment again, they were still dead to the world.

The knot of anxiety began to loosen as she made her way out of the apartment with the last of her things. She didn't care that she was leaving behind dishes and other furniture. All of that could be replaced. What couldn't be replaced was her peace of mind.

Back at the car, Aria's hands shook as she put the bags in the trunk, then slid behind the wheel and started the car. She didn't have a ton of gas, but she had enough to get her away from this place.

That her anxiety was dropping even though she was currently homeless told her how much living with that pair had been stressing her out. Aria knew her anxiety would rise again once the realization of how bad off she was settled in. But for now, she appreciated being able to breathe without it feeling like she had a vice around her chest.

Two years ago, everything had been great. She'd been engaged to a man she'd loved, and she'd had a job she enjoyed. Her mom had been struggling a bit with her health, but they hadn't thought it was anything too serious.

Unfortunately, they'd been terribly wrong. By the time the cancer had been confirmed, the disease had advanced to a point where there was no treatment that would help.

With her mom's diagnosis, Aria's perfect life began to slip away. She had wanted to spend every moment she could with her mom, to the detriment of her engagement. Two months before her mom's death, her fiancé had ended the relationship, leaving her devastated and without a support system for the horrible blow her mom's death had dealt her.

Her grief had swamped her and clouded her judgment. Mired in grief, she'd made some bad decisions. One of which had led to the loss of her job as a nurse.

Without a steady job, she'd lost the home she'd shared with her mom, and she'd had to take a job as a cashier at a big box store in order to afford the living space she'd just left. Because she couldn't afford the apartment on her own, her desperation had led her to accept Tonya as a roommate without a lot of questions or references.

And now, just days into a new year, she was even more desperate.

Aria didn't have a destination in mind as she put the apartment building behind her, but then she steered the car toward the cemetery where her mom was buried. It wasn't that she thought her mom was present there, but it was a peaceful place, and right then, she needed that.

"What am I going to do, Momma?" she asked a short time later as she sat on the grass next to her mom's burial plot. She pulled the edges of her sweater close to ward off the chill of the early January afternoon. "I just don't know how to deal with all of this."

Time slipped by as Aria sat beside the grave. It was peaceful, and right then, Aria desperately needed that. Unfortunately, she also needed a place to sleep.

A friend from nursing school who lived in northern Idaho had a possible job offer for her as a receptionist at her family's clinic that would also provide her with a place to live, but she hadn't heard back from her yet. So, in the meantime, she had to find a place to stay unless she wanted to sleep in her car.

Pulling out her phone, Aria checked her bank and credit card balances. She needed to make sure that if she *did* get the job, she had enough money to pay for gas to get to Idaho. She would get a paycheck in two days, though it wouldn't be a very big one since she hadn't had many shifts recently.

After some searching, she found a motel that she could afford for a couple of nights. If she still hadn't heard from her friend by then, she'd need to look at other options.

As she let herself into the run-down room a little while later, she prayed that her car wouldn't get broken into. The guy at the desk assured her that they had cameras, and it looked like a well-lit parking lot. Aria could accept the less-than-stellar room as long as her car and its contents were safe.

She just had to get through one day at a time. For now, she had a place to sleep and food to eat, even if it was just some bread and peanut butter that she'd picked up on her way to the motel.

She'd deal with tomorrow... tomorrow.

***

Doctor Gareth Halverson clicked his pen, his gaze bouncing back and forth between the other two people at the table. He had an opinion on the subject they were arguing about, but he was going to wait to express it. If it was even needed at that point.

"I promise you," Janessa said earnestly. "Aria will be an asset to the clinic."

"But will she be a *lasting* asset?" Jaylen asked from where he sat sprawled back in his chair, arms crossed over his chest. "We need a receptionist, not another nurse."

"And she's fine with that. Her mom passed away last year, and she's been under a lot of stress. I think she would welcome a job with fewer responsibilities. At least at first." Janessa sighed. "I've been praying a lot about this, and I really feel that Aria is an answer to my prayers. C'mon, Jay. Don't dismiss the idea so easily."

The stand-off between the siblings was nothing new. Gareth had been witnessing them for as long as the pair had been in his life, which was coming up on twenty years. The siblings had joined the Halverson family when Jaylen was nine and Janessa was seven.

Gareth wasn't sure which one was going to win this particular argument, but he had a feeling it was going to be Janessa. Though she and Jay went head-to-head on a regular basis, they usually came to an agreement without any lasting damage to their relationship. That was true of most of the squabbles he and his nine siblings had.

Janessa's brown gaze swung his way. "What do you think, Gareth?"

He met Jay's gaze for a moment before looking back at Janessa. "I agree with Jay."

Jay's bark of laughter showed that he was as surprised by that answer as Janessa was. Her brows rose, then lowered as she scowled at him.

"Come on, guys," she said. "Aria is a good friend, and she's a hard worker. She'd be a benefit to the clinic. I know she would be."

"Why does she want to move here?" Gareth asked, clicking his pen again. "I mean, it's not like Serenity is a thriving metropolis or anything."

"She wants a change of scenery," Janessa said. "And she has nothing holding her in Sacramento. C'mon, guys. She'd be perfect here. I just know it."

Jaylen's dark eyes narrowed, and the stubborn set of his jaw was now aimed in Gareth's direction. Gareth knew what was coming and wanted to shake his head in frustration. They couldn't be making decisions based on taking the opposite stance from each other.

He'd promised his dad that he'd try harder to get along with Jay, but butting heads seemed to be their way of communicating. Gareth was well aware that he was as responsible as Jay was for their sometimes-tense relationship, but both of them had to try if they were going to make any progress.

"Maybe we could give her a trial," Jay said, confirming Gareth's assumption. "Three months or something."

Janessa's huff of frustration was audible, while Gareth managed to keep his inside. He knew that Janessa wanted to give her friend the job without restrictions.

"We can't keep going without a receptionist," Gareth said. "But I think we should go for someone local. Someone who already lives in the area. Haven't we gotten any applications from local people?"

"Sure," Janessa said with a nod. She flipped through the papers in the folder in front of her, then slid one across the table to him. "Check that one out."

Gareth picked it up and scanned the info, wincing as he read the name. "Well, that's a definite no. Why is she even applying? Do people really re-apply to places they've been fired from?"

"Read her comments at the bottom," Janessa said with a smirk.

I promise not to flirt with Jay and to not comment on Gareth's broad shoulders. I also won't try to get either of them drunk by spiking their coffee at nine in the morning.

"Yeah. Because spiking my coffee later in the day would be totally acceptable," Gareth muttered. He crumpled the paper in his hand and tossed it at the garbage can. Unsurprisingly, he missed, making Jay snicker.

"Should've let me do it," Jay said, as he got up to snag the paper. He settled back in his chair, eyed the garbage can—which was further away from him than from Gareth—then managed a perfect shot.

"Show-off," Gareth griped.

Janessa lifted her hands in a stop gesture. "Let's get back to the issue at hand."

"So none of those other applications are any better than Chelsey's?" Gareth asked with a gesture at the garbage can.

Janessa's shoulders slumped. "There are probably one or two, but please, guys. Just give Aria a chance. She won't disappoint you."

Gareth stared hard at Janessa for a moment. "Is there something more you're not telling us?"

"She just really wants to move and start a new chapter of her life now that she's on her own."

Jay's phone dinged, and he picked it up. After reading the message, he said, "Let's get this settled. I have plans."

Gareth did too, but they didn't involve the opposite sex as Jay's likely did. Though he still had reservations about the whole idea, it was essentially two against one, and he knew that his argument against hiring Aria Jensen really wasn't all that strong.

Clicking his pen again, Gareth glared at it as he said, "Fine. I'll agree to it as long as she comes here on a trial basis." He looked up at Janessa, seeing the hope on her face. "Is she going to stay with you?"

Janessa nodded. "I talked to Charli, and she's fine with it. We've got the room, so it's not a problem."

"Not sure living and working together is a great idea," Gareth said. "But I guess it's your life."

"So we're done here?" Jay asked. "You'll let her know?"

"Yep." Janessa smiled broadly. "This is going to work out great. I just know it."

She popped up from her chair, then came around the table to give each of her brothers a kiss on the top of the head. "Thanks, guys."

As she left the room, Jay pushed to his feet. "Bet that hurt."

Gareth knew exactly what he was talking about. "Not really. I'm not going to agree with something that I don't actually agree with just so I'm not on the same side of the issue as you."

"I'm still not entirely convinced this is a good idea. Just for the record. But we need someone, and if Janessa is willing to take on the responsibility of letting her go if it doesn't work out, then I suppose we have nothing to lose. I don't believe that Janessa would bring someone in that she knows would hurt the clinic."

Gareth nodded. "Yeah. I do trust her judgment. I just don't think friendship and business necessarily mix well."

"Kind of like family and business?" Jay asked with a lift of his dark brows.

Pushing back from the table, Gareth click his pen to make sure the nib was concealed before he slipped it into the pocket of his shirt. "I think we do pretty well, all things considered."

"I suppose so." Jay gave him a nod, then headed for the door.

As he thought over the decision they'd just made, Gareth hoped that it turned out well. The responsibility for the clinic weighed heavily on him. Though they all played a role in things, he felt as if any issues that negatively affected the clinic would be his fault. It was why he wasn't altogether certain about bringing in Janessa's friend.

The last thing he wanted was for something bad to happen to the clinic on his watch. But in this particular instance, he was probably overreacting.

Gareth returned to his office, his thoughts shifting to the evening ahead. Thursday nights were reserved for the men's Bible study he was a part of. He and his two best friends co-led it, and it was something he looked forward to each week.

By the time he was ready to leave the clinic and head to his friend's place for dinner before the Bible study, Janessa and Jay had left already. He locked up, then used his phone to arm the alarm on the building.

As he drove out to Wade's place, Gareth let go of the day, shutting off doctor mode for a bit. He'd had to learn how to do that, accepting that it was a switch he could flip back on at any point if he needed to. But he needed to be more than just a doctor.

For much of his life, that was what had defined him the most. Medical school and residency had dominated his life. He'd lived and breathed it but coming back to Serenity Point had allowed him to cultivate a life beyond his role in the medical community.

Pulling up outside the cabin, Gareth spotted Jackson's motorcycle parked alongside Wade's dirty truck. He was looking forward to spending a bit of time with the two guys before the rest of their men's group showed up.

The three of them had been friends since kindergarten, and he thanked God every day for their presence in his life. Even when he'd left for college, they'd stayed in close contact, the two of them visiting him in Seattle as often as they could spare the time.

Climbing out of his SUV, he reached his arms up, stretching out the kinks in his back and shoulders. After making sure he had his phone, Gareth jogged up the steps to Wade's door and walked in without knocking, ready to relax and enjoy the evening.

CHAPTER TWO

Aria was carrying her bag into the motel room when her phone rang. She stumbled through the door, dropping her suitcase onto the threadbare carpet, then fumbled to get her phone out of her pocket. Her heart skipped a beat when she saw Janessa's name on the screen.

"Hello?"

"Hey, Aria!" Janessa's voice held an edge of excitement, and Aria really, really hoped that meant she had good news for her. "Are you ready to move?"

Aria sank down on the bed, her legs giving way. "I got the job?"

"Yes! How soon can you get here? Do you need to give two weeks' notice?"

"I think I can work it out so I don't have to. Vacation days and such," she said, not wanting to let Janessa know that she wasn't working at the hospital anymore. "I can be there in a couple of days."

"That would be wonderful," Janessa said. "I can't wait to see you."

"I'm so thankful for this opportunity."

"Well, I'm really looking forward to you being here. This is going to be great!"

Aria had come to love Janessa's enthusiasm when they'd been roommates in nursing school. She'd always been more low key herself, and lately, she'd been borderline depressed. Scratch that. She'd definitely been depressed and more anxious. She hoped that this change was what she needed to get out of the horrible place she'd found herself in.

They talked for a couple more minutes, then Janessa had to go. Aria sat for a moment on the bed, trying to identify the strange feeling inside of her. It took her a couple of minutes to realize what it was.

Hope.

She'd lost all hope when, one after another, the things that had been important in her life were ripped away. And she wasn't getting any of it back. Her ex-fiancé had moved on. Her mom was never coming back. And she wasn't sure she'd ever find the confidence to work as a nurse again. All of it was gone.

But this offer from Janessa could bring back some stability to her life. A job that would hopefully not be too stressful. A safe place to live. And being close to the one person she'd always considered her best friend—even though there was much she hadn't shared with her about the past couple of years.

Focusing on her cell again, Aria phoned her supervisor to let her know to not put her on the upcoming schedule. She would work her next shift, and thankfully, since she hadn't been scheduled for more, she wouldn't leave them in a lurch.

It was time to focus on her new life.

The drive was longer than what the navigating software said it would be to reach Serenity Point. She'd left Sacramento the previous evening, wanting to get a few hours out of the way since it was supposed to be a fifteen-hour trip. After driving six hours and stopping at a cheap motel, the remainder of the trip had taken eleven hours because of stops she made along the way. It was a relief when she saw the signs indicating Serenity Point wasn't too much further.

Though she'd lived her entire life in a city, she was looking forward to experiencing small town life. It couldn't be too bad a place considering that Janessa had come back after graduating, even though she could have gotten a job in Seattle where they'd both ended up for college.

The winter sun had disappeared hours earlier, casting the road she travelled on into darkness. Thankfully, there wasn't much traffic, so her slower pace wouldn't annoy anyone. She had put Janessa's address into the GPS of her car, and carefully followed it to find the place she'd soon call home. Excitement fluttered inside her.

As the GPS guided her the final distance to the house, Aria gripped her steering wheel and let out a sign of relief. The exhaustion after spending so many hours on the road slipped away as she pulled to the curb in front of her new home.

Aria knew it was the right place because Janessa had sent her a picture of the house. She'd fallen in love with the large two-story home from the moment she'd seen it, and it just made her feel even more like she'd made the right decision.

She'd barely pulled to the curb when the front door of the house opened, and Janessa appeared, hurrying down the wide stairs that led to the sidewalk. Grinning, Aria climbed out from behind the wheel of her car and rounded the car to greet her friend, trying not to shiver as the frosty January air of Northern Idaho hit her.

Though they'd video chatted off and on, it had been forever since they'd seen each other in person. Aria couldn't keep from laughing as she wrapped her arms around Janessa.

"You're here!" Janessa squealed. "You're finally here!"

"I'm here!"

The two of them held on to each other as they rocked back and forth. Finally, Janessa released her and stepped back. "It is *so* good to see you."

"I'm so glad to be here," Aria said. "That was a *long* drive."

"Well, let's unload your stuff so you can crash."

"Luckily, it's just suitcases and bags," Aria told her. "No furniture."

"I've got your room all set up," Janessa said as she pulled one of the suitcases out of the back of Aria's car. "So you can just fall into bed."

Aria made sure to grab the bag she'd packed with her essentials so she wouldn't have to unpack any other bag that night. With the other suitcase in hand, she locked the car, hoping that no one would walk off with the rest of her stuff while she was inside.

As they stepped through the front door, Aria came to a stop, looking around at the foyer area. A glossy wood floor was covered by a large area rug. From where she stood, she could see into a spacious living room filled with overstuffed furniture. Lamps sat on dark wood end tables, casting a warm yellow glow throughout the room. There was also a large, unlit stone fireplace with a wood mantle in the middle of the far wall. It was like she'd stepped into a different world.

"You're upstairs with me," Janessa said as she headed toward a wide set of stairs. "Charli stays down here with her daughter, Layla. They're doing Layla's evening routine already, so you'll have to meet her tomorrow."

When they reached the second floor, there was a spacious landing with four doors opening off of it. The landing area also had a couple of comfy-looking loveseats, and lamps illuminated the space, giving it a cozy feel. Large windows looked out over the front yard and the houses across the street.

"My room is there." Janessa pointed to a door that appeared to belong to a room at the rear of the house. "Yours is over here."

She led Aria to the door she'd pointed to. The door was open, and Aria held her breath as she walked into the room and got her first glimpse of her new home.

"This is beautiful," Aria said as she took in the dark wood sleigh bed covered with a cranberry-colored comforter.

There were navy accents around the room, including the floor to ceiling curtains that were currently closed. This room was way nicer than anything she'd ever had before, and tears pricked at her eyes. She turned away from Janessa, blinking rapidly to clear her vision.

"Charli and I had fun decorating the rooms," Janessa said. "This house used to be a bed-and-breakfast, which is why it's so big." She gestured to another door in the room. "You also have your own bathroom."

"It's just you, your sister, and niece here?" Aria asked as they walked down the stairs to get a second load from her car.

"On a full-time basis, yes. My youngest sister, Skylar, stays with us when our parents are away. The other siblings pop in randomly." Janessa laughed. "I suppose you should know that if you want complete privacy, it's best you go to your room. This place can feel a bit like Grand Central Station at times. Not all the time, mind you, but it can happen without much warning."

Aria knew Janessa's suggestion was made because she remembered how Aria needed her space sometimes. Socialization was something she'd done only when absolutely necessary while in nursing school, and Janessa knew that.

Janessa was a tremendous help in emptying the car, and soon the bedroom held the contents of Aria's life. Unfortunately, there was no way she had the energy to unpack anything that night.

"Did you want something to eat?" Janessa asked. "Charli made supper, and it was delish."

"If you made it, it wouldn't have been?"

Janessa laughed. "No. I'm a good cook, too. We take turns most nights."

"Well, I'm not a chef by any stretch of the imagination," Aria said. "But I can cook the basics."

"The basics are good. Charli is the better cook, but I think that's partly because Layla loves to cook as well, so they're always finding new recipes to try together."

"So we'll sort everything out tomorrow? Like the meal schedule and how I contribute to the food budget?"

Janessa nodded. "Yep. Once Charli and I are home from work, we can have a discussion about it. But just take it easy tomorrow. We're not expecting you in the office until Thursday, so you have a couple of days to settle in."

"Thanks so much," Aria said. "I'm super excited, and I can't wait to get started at the clinic."

"We're looking forward to having you there. We've been without a receptionist for several weeks now, so I'm glad that you're going to take that over." Janessa paused. "You're okay with being a receptionist instead of putting your nursing degree to work?"

"I'm perfectly okay with it," Aria assured her. Beyond okay with it, actually, but Janessa didn't need to know that. "Hopefully, I live up to expectations."

Janessa waved her comment off. "The only expectation we have is that you do your job, which I know won't be a problem."

"Then I'm happy to join you at the clinic."

Janessa beamed at her again. "We always used to say how fun it would be if we could work together. I never imagined this would be how it worked out, but I think it's perfect."

"I do too." It was more perfect than Janessa could ever know. The job and the place to live were more than she had dared to hope for following everything that had happened over the past couple of years.

"I'm gonna let you relax and get some rest," Janessa said. "Oh! You didn't say if you wanted something to eat."

Aria shook her head. "I'm fine. I grabbed some nuggets and fries around suppertime."

"Still with the nuggets and fries, huh?" Janessa asked with a laugh.

"Not as much as I'd like, but it felt like a good time to indulge myself."

"Well, if you get the middle of the night munchies, there is plenty to eat in the kitchen. Did you want a tour tonight?"

"I think I'll be okay."

"If you need anything, just text me or come knock on my door."

With another hug, Janessa left the room. On her own, Aria did another quick tour of the room, then went into the bathroom. Sighing in appreciation of the garden tub that sat in the corner of the room in front of the windows, Aria decided she was going to take a bath to unwind before falling into bed.

First, she went back into the bedroom and found her bag of essentials and carried it into the bathroom. As she waited for the tub to fill, Aria took the time to wander the bedroom again, so in awe of how beautiful it was.

The house she'd shared with her mom had been nice, but it had been fairly basic. They hadn't had a lot of extra money to spend on décor. Most of the things they'd gotten to decorate the apartment had been from the thrift store.

She went to the bed and folded back the thick comforter. Running her hands over the sheets, Aria discovered they were soft. Not at all like the cheap sheets she'd been using on her bed, which had pilled and gotten rough. It looked like she could just leave her bedding in the garbage bag she'd packed it in. It wouldn't fit the bed anyway, since she'd been using a full-size bed in the apartment, and this one was most definitely a queen.

Going back into the bathroom, Aria finally felt like she could relax. Baths were something she enjoyed, but she hadn't taken one in ages because she hadn't been able to relax enough when she knew Tonya and her boyfriend were in the apartment or could return at any moment. But she didn't need to worry about that anymore.

The gorgeous soaking tub was like the icing on top of the cake of her new life. And as she sank beneath the water scented with some bath oils, Aria hoped that she could enjoy this new life without her past encroaching on it.

Her mom would have loved Aria's new home, and how Aria wished she could have been alive to see it. Except that if she had still been alive, Aria wouldn't have lost her job, moved into a trashy apartment, then taken on this job.

Still, she would give up the beautiful new home if it meant her mom was back with her. The hardest part of leaving Sacramento had been leaving her mom's grave. She wouldn't be able to go visit it, but Aria carried her mom in her heart and the memories they'd made together would always be with her.

Aria woke the next morning feeling fully rested, but she didn't rush out of bed. She had nowhere to go, and from what Janessa had said the night before, the house would be empty since she and Charli would be at work and her niece would be at school.

It was nearly ten by the time her growling stomach dragged her out of bed. She wandered downstairs, and after touring through the shared spaces of the house, she ended up in the kitchen. Mindful that she hadn't contributed to the grocery budget yet, she settled for a bowl of cereal.

Once she'd finished eating, she went back up to her room and started to unpack her bags. They were a bit of a hodge-podge since she'd just been cramming things into bags because she wanted to just get it all done so she could leave.

Unpacking was an adventure as she figured out where she wanted things to go. There was plenty of space for everything. More than enough space, really, since she didn't have a ton of stuff.

The most important things that she'd brought with her were the picture frames that held photos of her and her mom and the album that they'd put together during her mom's illness. In addition to the pictures they'd chosen for that book, the importance of that album was the time they'd spent together and the memories they'd created.

Aria set the last photo they'd taken together on the high chest of drawers. Gripping the edge of the furniture, she stared at the picture. "I'm in a new place, Momma. It's so beautiful here. I think you would have liked it. I *know* you would have liked it." She blinked back tears. "It's a new chapter. I'm going to do my best to make you proud. No more bad decisions, I promise."

A knock on her door made Aria jump. Her heart started to pound since she didn't think anyone would be home until later.

"Aria?" The sound of Janessa's voice brought a wave of relief.

She hurried to open the door. "You scared me!"

Janessa laughed, her dark eyes sparkling. "Sorry about that. I just wanted to come home and see how you were doing."

"C'mon in," Aria said as she walked back into the room. "I'm making progress."

"I love seeing you settle in like this. Makes it all the more real."

"It is very real," Aria agreed. "And I'm loving it."

"Did you want something to eat?" Janessa asked. "I'm going to make myself a sandwich."

"Sure." Picking up her phone, she followed Janessa down to the kitchen.

"Sit," Janessa said, pointing to a barstool at the island counter. "What do you want in your sandwich? Ham? Turkey? Cheese?"

"Turkey and cheese would be great."

"Tomato? Lettuce?"

"Both, thanks."

Janessa worked quickly as she assembled sandwiches for each of them, chatting about what had been going on at the clinic that morning.

"Gareth and Jay were getting into it again this morning," Janessa said with a sigh.

"They fight a lot?"

"I wouldn't say it's a fight, necessarily. More like there are certain things that they never see eye to eye on. Jay, the businessman, is always focused on the budget, while Gareth doesn't want to cut corners on anything, even when doing so wouldn't affect patient services. So yeah, another heated discussion on where money was being spent."

Janessa slid the plates across the island, then went to get glasses and filled them with water. "Part of your job will be ordering supplies, so you might get caught in the middle of discussions at times. If you want to please them both, you need to find the best products for the cheapest price."

"Is *miracle worker* part of my job description?" Aria asked with a laugh.

"No, but it probably should be."

"I'll do my best. I've never done anything like that before, since at the hospital, I just got what I needed from the supply room. I never had to order anything with an eye towards cost."

"Yeah. Because we're a small clinic, we have to deal with that ourselves."

Aria hoped that she'd be able to fulfill the role in a way that made both Jay and Gareth happy because, if they weren't happy with her, she wasn't going to last long in the job.

"Oh, and whatever you do, don't flirt with Jay or tell Gareth you like his broad shoulders. And definitely don't spike their morning coffee."

"What?" Aria gaped at Janessa. "Why would I do *any* of those things?"

"Well, one of our previous receptionists did, and she re-applied when the position came open again, even though Gareth had fired her the last time she'd worked for us after he took a sip of his coffee and discovered it had a little *extra* added to it."

"Rest assured, I would never be even remotely tempted to do anything like that."

"The guys will be relieved to hear that," Janessa said with a laugh.

Janessa was unaware of how bad things had gotten for Aria. There was no way she would ever do anything to jeopardize this job opportunity. The last thing she wanted was to once again lose her job and her place to live. Maybe it was a mistake to go into a situation where her employment and housing were so closely tied, but it also felt like it was the perfect answer to the mess her life had become.

"Do I need to fill out any paperwork?" Aria asked. "Should I come in and do that this afternoon?"

"If you want," Janessa said. "But I can also bring the papers home, and you can fill them out here instead."

Aria decided that she'd just stay at the house. "Sounds good. Did you want me to make something for dinner?"

"Charli said she was going to make dinner again tonight," Janessa said. "I'll be back around five-thirty. Charli and Layla will probably be here by four-thirty."

"Okay. If there's anything I can do to help prepare for supper, just shoot me a text."

"I will," she said. "Are you finding everything okay?"

Aria nodded. "I think it's going to take me a while to get used to so much space. And the bathtub... I'm in love!"

"I know, right?" Janessa laughed. "When this place came up for sale, Charli and I decided we wanted it."

"So you own it together?"

She nodded. "Neither of us were planning to get married any time soon, but we were both ready to get out of the family home, so this was perfect. Plus, it's big enough to rent out a room or two if we want. Like with you."

"It really is a beautiful place," Aria said. "I'm looking forward to living here."

"I'm excited to have you here, too." Janessa finished the last bite of her sandwich, then drained her water. Getting up, she took her glass and plate to the dishwasher. "I'd better get back to the clinic."

Once she'd left, Aria cleaned up her dishes, then returned to her room. Over the next couple of hours, she finished emptying the last of her bags. It looked more like her space now that she had little bits of her own stuff spread out across the room.

After everything was done and put away, she settled down on the overstuffed loveseat that sat in front of the windows on the far side of the room. She used her phone to pull up her favorite playlist. It was made up of songs that she and her mom had loved to listen to. Before her mom had gotten so sick, there had been times when they'd danced around to the music, laughing and happy.

She didn't feel much like laughing, and she wasn't sure if she was exactly happy. But for the first time in months, she felt at peace, and there was a spark of hope growing inside her. Hope that she could get back on her feet and maybe find a place to belong once again.

CHAPTER THREE

Gareth unlocked the back door of the clinic and let himself into the building. Before going to his office, he took a quick tour of all the rooms to make sure that they'd been cleaned well.

They'd had too much staff turn-over recently. First the receptionist, then the person who cleaned the clinic after hours. They'd recently found someone to do the cleaning, but since they'd only been working since the beginning of the week, Gareth felt like he had to check and make sure that they were doing what was needed.

Thankfully, it looked like the cleaner was living up to their references. He hoped that would be the case with the new receptionist too, even though she had never been a receptionist before. If she couldn't do the work, it was going to be Janessa's job to fire her.

In his small office at the back of the clinic, Gareth settled into his chair and turned on his monitor. He glanced over the list of appointments for the day, recognizing most of the names.

He enjoyed knowing his patients so well and being able to follow them through whatever health challenges they might face. Before he'd ever gotten his medical degree, his parents had shared with him how they spent time each morning praying for the patients they'd be seeing that day.

It was something that he'd begun practicing as soon as he'd begun seeing patients. His prayers had been more general while he'd been in school and doing his residency. But at the clinic, he could pray for each patient by name, which was what he did, using the appointment schedule as his guide.

He was in the staff room pouring his second cup of coffee of the day—his first had been inhaled on the drive to the clinic—when he heard the back door open. When he heard Janessa's voice along with another female one, he knew that he was about to meet their new receptionist.

"Good morning, Gareth," Janessa called out.

Gareth glanced over at her as he tossed the stir-stick he'd been using into the garbage. "Good morning."

"Gareth, I'd like you to meet Aria Jensen, the new receptionist. Aria, this is Gareth, one of the doctors here, and, of course, my oldest brother."

The woman at Janessa's side was about her height, though she was more slender, almost to the point of appearing fragile. Delicate. She had straight blonde hair that hung almost to her shoulders, and her hazel eyes were framed by dark lashes.

The smile she gave him was tentative as she said, "It's nice to meet you."

"You as well."

"Gareth will be glad to have someone manning the front desk, since I've been struggling with being both nurse and receptionist."

"You've done a good job," he told Janessa. "The clinic is still standing, and we haven't lost any patients."

"I'll still be splitting my time as I train Aria, but I think she'll be a quick learner."

"I hope I am," Aria said, her arms moving to hug herself. "Just let me know if I do anything wrong."

"Oh, you don't have to worry about that," Janessa said with a smile. "Jay and Gareth are quick to point out anything we do wrong. I think they see it as their role as older brothers."

"Don't scare her off," Gareth said. "We need someone on that front desk."

"Don't *you* scare her off," Janessa shot back. "Put the grumpy doctor away for a couple of days. At least until next week."

"I'm not grumpy." Janessa's brows lifted. "Okay. I *can* be grumpy, but only when it's deserved. I'll try my best to keep that under control, but I make no promises."

"Well, we're heading off to start going over Aria's responsibilities," Janessa said.

Gareth took a sip from his mug as he watched them go. What had Janessa been thinking, hiring someone who looked like Aria? Not that he thought they should hire based on looks, but she knew as well as he did that they had someone else working in the clinic who would see Aria one way, and one way only.

Still, he hoped that Aria worked out. That she would be strong enough to stand up for herself. At the very least, he hoped she'd be better than the receptionist who had spiked his coffee.

Regardless, he had a feeling that she was in for an interesting day. The patients would view her as fresh meat, so to speak, and anyone who had a single male relative was going to be circling Aria.

As the morning progressed, Gareth's assumption proved to be correct. Every patient commented on the new receptionist, many asking about her relationship status. Gareth suspected she was single, but he really had no idea, so he hadn't been able to satisfy their curiosity. The queries seemed almost constant, to the point where he felt sorry for Aria if she was dealing with similar queries at the front desk.

"So, is that your new girlfriend at the desk?"

Gareth turned to face the elderly woman, who sat on the chair beside his desk. "Say what?"

"The lovely young woman at the front desk," Mrs. Givens said, a curious gleam in her eyes. "Is she your girlfriend?"

"Nope. I just met her for the first time this morning," he told her. "She and Janessa went to nursing school together."

"Maybe you should ask her out," she said with a smirk. "You need a girlfriend."

Well, it looked like he wasn't going to be able to escape the matchmaking after all. "Why aren't you trying to fix her up with your grandson?"

"Hmph," the woman said with a dismissive wave of her hand. "That grandson of mine doesn't deserve a shot at a nice girl."

"Uh oh. What did he do?"

"He told me he couldn't make it to my family dinner because he had to study for an exam. And *then*, I see pictures plastered all over social media of him out with his friends."

Gareth tried not to grin. "So, are you more offended that he bailed on your dinner or that he thought you were too old to use social media?"

"That I was too old to use social media, of course," she retorted. "He must also be having trouble with his short term memory because he messaged me on one of my social media accounts to tell me he couldn't come."

Gareth didn't bother to hold back his laugh at that. "Well, I hope you've told him that he doesn't get any of your snickerdoodles for at least a year after that stunt."

"A year?" She tilted her head to the side. "You think that's long enough?"

"Eh, go for two."

"That's what I was thinking," she said. "And I'll just bring them to you instead."

Gareth rubbed his hands together. "Well, his loss is definitely my gain. Probably in more ways than one."

"Maybe if you had a little more meat on your bones, the women would snuggle up to you more."

"Uh..."

"My George was like a big teddy bear. Soft and furry, and when I snuggled with him, I never got cold."

It didn't surprise Gareth that the woman had once again rendered him speechless. She had a way of doing that on a fairly regular basis. He'd known her and her husband for as long as he could remember, though her husband had passed away a few years earlier.

"I'll keep that in mind," Gareth said, then decided it was time to get the visit back on track before she ended up really embarrassing him. "So what's brought you in this morning? I'm sure it wasn't just to get a look at the new receptionist."

And with that, she launched into her latest ailment, and Gareth breathed a sigh of relief.

When lunchtime rolled around, he headed for the staff room to see if Janessa had ordered lunch for their first day with the new receptionist. As he neared the door to the room, he heard Aria say, "You know, you could have warned me."

"Warned you?" Janessa asked, her tone far too innocent to be believed. "About what?"

"That every patient would have at least one relative they wanted to hook me up with. I'm beginning to think you all are running a matchmaking service on the side," she said with a laugh that made Gareth smile. "Bring in an unsuspecting employee, then let everyone in town try their hand at matching her with their eligible males."

"Maybe we should do that," Janessa said. "Hey, Jay, that might bring in some more cash. Make the patients pay to put their prospects in front of the fresh meat... I mean, new employees."

"I think Mom and Dad might have something to say about that," Jay replied dryly. "Not to mention Dr. Grumpy."

Gareth rolled his eyes at Jay's nickname for him. He was only grumpy when he had to deal with Jay's constant complaints about the budget for the clinic.

"You have nicknames for each other?" Aria asked. "That's cool! What's yours, Jay?"

"His is Mr. Scrooge," Gareth said as he sat down at the table. "Because he penny-pinches like his next breath depends on it."

"Someone has to keep track of the many pennies you like to spend."

Janessa held up her hands, one palm facing each of them. "Enough. This is Aria's first day here. Let's try to maintain at least a measure of decorum for the first week or so."

"I'm not sure that's possible," Jay said.

"Gotta agree with Jay." Gareth unwrapped the sub sandwich Janessa handed him. "A week might kill us."

Before they could argue further, the back door opened, and a moment later, his parents appeared in the doorway of the room.

"Did I miss a meeting reminder?" Jay asked, pulling out his phone.

"Not at all, son," their dad said as he rested his hand on Jay's shoulder for a moment. "We thought we'd stop by and see how Aria was doing on her first day."

"She's doing great," Janessa said. "Like I said, she's a quick learner."

Their parents joined them at the table, his mom sitting next to Aria. "Are you enjoying working here so far?"

"It's been great," Aria said. "Although the interest in my relationship status is higher than it's ever been before."

His mom laughed. "Oh yes. Didn't Janessa warn you? Trying to marry off my kids has become a favored pastime of the regulars who come to the clinic."

"Did you take anyone up on their offer to introduce you to their eligible bachelor?"

"Thankfully, no," Aria said. "I don't really need the complication. I have enough changes going on in my life at the moment. Definitely don't need to toss a relationship into the mix."

His mom reached over and patted her hand. "I think that's probably an excellent plan."

As his parents talked more to the clinic's newest employee, Gareth ate his sub. They'd been officially out of the clinic for two years, but Gareth wasn't sure that they would ever completely step away from it.

That was likely why they'd showed up on Aria's first day. They'd let him, Jay, and Janessa figure out whether or not to hire her, but they'd want to get to know her, too.

Treating patients in the clinic had been Gareth's goal for as long as he could remember, so being there now was the realization of that dream. After surviving on caffeine and prayer during his residency, he was so glad to be working in the clinic. He enjoyed the more relaxed pace, plus the ongoing relationships with his patients.

The only thorn in his side was Jay's constant harping about the budget. Even though he really did understand that Jay was only trying to make sure the clinic succeeded, it got a little wearisome after awhile because they weren't so close to the edge financially that they needed to pinch pennies quite so tightly. He just hoped that Aria realized that he and Jay didn't really dislike each other.

Aria seemed to converse easily with his parents, and Gareth liked having the chance to listen to their conversation and get to know her a little better as he ate his lunch. He was curious about Janessa's friend, already liking the calm air that surrounded her.

"Was it busy today, Gareth?" his dad asked.

"Fairly busy, but none of the appointments really pushed the others back, so we kept on time."

"I guess Nora's not in yet," his mom said.

Gareth shook his head and did his best to not grimace. "She had a personal appointment this morning but should be in soon."

He wished that they could have gotten away with just him treating patients, but there were those who preferred a woman. Plus, they also helped at the women's shelter in town, and they required a female doctor. His mom had originally taken care of all that, but with her out of the clinic, they'd needed to hire someone else.

Nora had been the only applicant that had worked out. As a doctor, Gareth had no complaints regarding how she dealt with their patients. His major issue was how she related to him. From the moment she'd started working for them, she'd made it pretty clear she thought the two of them would make a great couple.

The thing was, Gareth had often thought that having a wife who worked as a doctor in the clinic would be great. He'd seen how well his parents had worked together, both at home and in the clinic. However, he hadn't planned to hire someone to work at the clinic based on whether he thought they could eventually get married.

Gareth hadn't been interested in Nora the way she was interested in him, and he wasn't going to date her simply because she was a doctor working in his family's clinic. That had made Nora unhappy, but she was nothing if not persistent in her belief they belonged together.

Which was why he was quite certain that she was going to be very unhappy with their new receptionist.

"Are you Nora's nurse on Saturday, Janessa?"

"No. Betsy is working two Saturdays a month to help me out."

"That was nice of her," his mom said. "Especially since she's retired now."

"Semi-retired, apparently. I think she got a bit bored," Janessa said with a laugh. "She was the one who approached me about coming back to work for two mornings a month."

A few minutes later, the back door opened again, and Nora walked into the room. She smiled when she saw them all gathered there. His mom got to her feet and went to the woman.

"Nora, darling," she said as she hugged Nora. "It's so good to see you again."

"How have you been?" Nora asked.

"Very good. How about you?"

"Been keeping busy, but you know I enjoy that."

"We have a new staff member," his mom said. "This is Aria, our new receptionist."

Nora turned to Aria and held out her hand. "Hello, Aria. I'm Doctor Nora Miller."

Aria got to her feet and shook hands with the other woman. "Nice to meet you."

If Gareth hadn't been watching Nora, he would have missed the momentary tightening of her lips before she smiled at Aria.

"I'm sure that Janessa is glad to not have to juggle the front desk and her nursing duties."

"Oh, I am," Janessa agreed.

Janessa and Nora clashed a lot, which led to some tense moments in the clinic. If Nora had issues with Aria, her problems with Janessa would only get worse. Gareth could see already that Janessa was protective of her friend and would likely step in if she felt Nora wasn't treating Aria right.

"Well, we'd better get back to work," Janessa said, crumpling up the wrapper from her sub.

Aria did the same, then got to her feet to throw out her garbage. She said goodbye, then followed Janessa out of the room.

"She seems very... sweet," Nora said as she watched the pair disappear down the hallway toward the front.

"She is," his mom said. "She and Janessa are great friends, so I'm glad it worked out for her to come here."

"Where did they meet?"

"At nursing school," Jay volunteered.

Nora frowned. "And she wants to work as a receptionist instead of a nurse? Could she not hack it as a nurse?"

"I'm glad that she's willing to do the receptionist work even though she's a nurse," Gareth said. "It means that should Janessa need a day off and Betsy's not available, we still have a nurse. Plus, she might be willing to step into the Saturday rotation."

"That's very true, sweetheart," his mom said.

"Are you around for a while now?" Nora asked his mom.

"Nope. We're home for a couple more weeks, then we're headed back to Haiti to help the clinic there."

Nora had never understood his parents' devotion to the medical mission trips they went on. What most people didn't know, because his parents hadn't flaunted it, was that a significant inheritance from his mom's side of the family funded their overseas trips to help people in third world countries and other places that had been struck by disasters.

But their charitable work didn't just extend abroad. For as long as Gareth could remember—even before the inheritance—his parents had made Saturday morning appointments available free of charge to those patients who didn't have insurance.

With a glance at her watch, Nora said, "Well, I guess I'd better get ready for my appointments."

Once she'd left, his mom said, "Everything else okay around here?"

"Yep," Jay said.

Before he started to get into admin details, Gareth got to his feet. "I've got more appointments this afternoon as well, so I'll catch you later."

His mom grabbed his hand and gave it a squeeze. "Love you, sweetheart. Have a good rest of your day."

"Thanks, Mom," he said as he bent to kiss her cheek. "You too. See ya, Dad."

As Gareth walked down the hall, Janessa gestured to one of the rooms, indicating that his first afternoon appointment was waiting. He braced himself for the next wave of comments about their new receptionist.

He wondered if Nora was going to get all the comments, too. And if so, how she'd react.

"Good afternoon," Gareth said as he walked into the exam room Janessa had indicated. "How're you doing?"

And with the start of that appointment, his afternoon was underway, and he happily pushed aside thoughts of Nora to focus on his patients.

CHAPTER FOUR

Aria had thought it rather odd that Janessa had warned her not to make any comments about Gareth's broad shoulders. But then she'd met him. The man did have some nice shoulders. He had just enough muscle to show that he took care of himself without making it seem that he spent hours and hours in the gym.

Jaylen had a similar build, though he was an inch or so taller than Gareth. Aria wasn't sure why Janessa had only warned her off mentioning Gareth's shoulders and not Jay's. It didn't really matter, however, because she had no intention of mentioning something like that about *any* guy.

Shoving aside all thoughts of Janessa's attractive brothers, Aria focused on the job at hand. The work wasn't terribly complicated, but she'd experienced a few moments of panic when someone called in requesting an appointment and her mind had completely blanked on how to use the appointment program. She'd just jotted the information down on her notepad and waited for Janessa to return from the patient she'd been dealing with to bail her out.

"You're new around here."

Aria had originally been keeping a tally on how many times someone said that to her, but she'd eventually tossed that effort out the window because she'd lost count.

"I *am.*" Aria smiled at the middle-aged woman who stood on the opposite side of the check-in counter. "My name is Aria."

"Are you single, Aria?"

"Yes, I am," Aria said. "But I'm definitely not ready to mingle."

The woman grinned. "Well, when you *are*, you just let me know. My son would treat you really well."

If Aria had a dollar for every time someone had said a variation of that to her that day, she'd be able to treat Janessa to dinner.

"It's going to be awhile," Aria warned her. "I'm already dealing with lots of changes in my life, so I wouldn't really be able to give a relationship the attention it deserved."

"Well, now I think you'd be even more perfect for my son." The woman pointed a finger at her. "You keep him in mind."

"Mrs. Whitmire," Janessa said as she came up behind Aria. "Do you want to follow me back?"

"If I have to, I suppose," the woman said with a wink at Aria. "I was enjoying getting to know my future daughter-in-law."

"I thought *I* was your future daughter-in-law," Janessa said.

Mrs. Whitmire waved her hand. "You've been dragging your feet, sweetie. You snooze, you lose."

"Well, that's disappointing," Janessa said, then shrugged. "Oh well. My loss is definitely Aria's gain."

"I agree," Mrs. Whitmire said as she followed Janessa down the hallway leading to the exam rooms.

Aria wasn't sure if it was the small town or that specific clinic, but there were certainly some interesting people coming in for appointments. She wondered how long it would be before they got used to her and stopped trying to match her up with the single men in their lives. Maybe she should ask Janessa about that.

"I need you to print off a requisition for some lab work."

Aria looked up to see Nora standing at the end of the desk. As her words registered, Aria frowned. "I'm afraid I don't know how to do that yet. I believe Janessa mentioned that the doctors usually print those off."

"I *did* mention that," Janessa agreed as she reappeared. "Because that's what the doctors do. You know that, Nora."

"But she should know how to do it if she's going to be working here," the doctor said.

"I agree. However, this is Aria's *first* day here, so we're concentrating on the aspects of the job that she is completely responsible for. I'll get around to teaching her about the requisition print-outs next week. You'll just have to continue to print your own. Like you've been doing since... um... you started working here?"

"Is there a problem?" Gareth asked as he joined them.

"Nora wants Aria to print out her requisitions," Janessa explained. "I told her that's not what we're dealing with today for Aria's training, especially because it's something the doctors usually do."

"But she needs to know how to do it sooner rather than later."

Gareth turned to Nora. "Janessa is responsible for training Aria. If she says that she'll teach her that later, then she'll teach her that later. You can print your own requisitions. Just like I do."

Nora's eyes narrowed at Gareth before she spun around on her high heels, her white coat flapping behind her as she walked back down the hallway.

"We need to hire a new female doctor, Gareth," Janessa murmured. "She barely tolerates me, and you're my brother. She's going to treat Aria even worse."

"I know, but we haven't found a replacement yet. In the meantime, we just have to deal with her."

A patient approached the desk, so Aria turned her attention to her while Gareth and Janessa carried on with their whispered conversation near the hallway. Now she was wondering what the deal was with the other doctor. She needed to start a list of things to ask Janessa once they were away from the clinic.

She had to admit it was nice to see Gareth coming to Janessa's defense. Nora hadn't thought so, though. That had been clear.

After dealing with a couple of phone calls from people wanting appointments, Aria flipped to a new page in the notebook Janessa had given her and jotted down the non-work-related questions. Well, they were related to work, just not to her job.

"You okay?" Janessa asked when she appeared a few minutes later.

She smiled up at her. "I'm fine."

"We'll talk about that situation later."

When Aria handed her the notebook, Janessa read what she'd written and laughed.

"Yep. Just keep adding to it. Anything you might wonder about. Make your notes, and we'll talk about it after hours."

"Will do," Aria said.

"Feeling okay about everything else?"

"Yep. It's going fine. I think. No one has said I've done anything wrong. Well, except for... you know."

"Oh yes, I know." Janessa said with a roll of her eyes. "Anyway, the last patients for today should be coming in the next half hour, then I'll show you how to restock."

Aria was surprised and happy at how quickly the day had passed. She'd been worried about her first day on the job, and now it was almost over. It would be great if every day was as smooth as this one had been, but she knew better than to expect that. Instead, she'd just be grateful for the good days and try to keep a positive attitude for the not-so-good ones. And all the while hoping that the anxiety that she hadn't managed to leave behind in Sacramento wouldn't flare up too badly.

She continued to field phone calls, getting one from a woman who insisted she needed to speak with Gareth. His last patient had left, but Janessa was nowhere to be seen, so Aria put the person on hold, then called the extension for Gareth to see if he took calls like that.

"Gareth here," he said as he answered, his deep voice smooth in her ear.

"Hi, uh, Gareth. This is Aria. I have someone on hold who's insisting on speaking to you. Do you usually take calls?"

"Depends who's calling," he said. "Do you have a name?"

"She said Deborah Barnes."

"Yeah. I'll take the call."

"Okay. She's on line two."

She waited for the flashing light on line two to turn steady before focusing back on her monitor.

"I'll lock the front door," Janessa said when she reappeared. "Then we can go to the stockroom."

Aria began to straighten up the desk, setting the notebook with her purse, so she remembered to take it home. Janessa then took her to a small room where all the supplies were kept, and for the next several minutes, she talked Aria through what they did at the end of each day.

"So how do you feel your first day went?" Jay asked as he stood in the doorway to the stockroom. "Any issues?"

"I don't think so," Aria said, "But maybe Janessa is the better person to answer that."

"She did great." Janessa bumped her shoulder. "I said she would."

"Yes, you certainly did," Jay said wryly.

"Are we having a meeting?" Nora asked as she came to stand next to Jay.

"Just reviewing the day." Janessa turned her back on the pair, directing Aria to a box of gloves while she grabbed a couple of boxes of tissues. "Grab those, and we'll make sure that each of the rooms is well-stocked."

Aria picked up the box, then followed Janessa to the first room. Jay and Nora continued to talk in the hallway, though she couldn't hear what they said. It didn't take long to make sure that each of the four patient rooms had been restocked.

"How do you find working here so far, Aria?" Gareth asked when he ran into them in the hall.

"Aside from the intense curiosity about my relationship status, it went really well."

"You'll get used to it." He smiled at her. "We've all dealt with it. When I started working here after my residency, it was crazy."

"We had people making appointments just to meet him," Janessa said with a laugh. "Jay also had the same issue when he came back after business school."

"Are there that many single people of marrying age in this town?" Aria asked.

"Oh, they don't all live here," Janessa told her. "Some live as far away as Florida, but their mom or grandma seemed to think they'd be happy to move back if it meant they could marry a doctor."

"Are you saying that's my only attractive trait?" Gareth asked, the corners of his brown eyes crinkling as he laughed.

"I suppose women might consider you handsome," Janessa said. "But I'm your sister, so I don't notice stuff like that, even if we aren't biologically related. You could always ask Aria."

"What?" Aria gave Janessa a wide-eyed look as she shook her head. "No. Definitely do not ask Aria. You're my boss. That would be totally unprofessional."

"Excellent response," Gareth said with a nod. "You could learn something from her, Nessa."

Janessa gave an exasperated huff. "Like I'm ever unprofessional. Give me a break."

"I don't know. You like to backtalk to your bosses and tease them mercilessly."

"Maybe they deserve it," she said. "They can be so demanding."

Aria covered her mouth, but it didn't stifle her laugh.

"I'm sure you're really talking about Jay," Gareth said as he shrugged out of his white coat.

"Did you want to come for supper tonight?" Janessa asked. "Charli's cooking."

"As tempting as that is, I've got my men's group. I usually eat with Jackson and Wade beforehand."

"Well, you can come tomorrow night, but I'm the one cooking, and you know there are no guarantees when I'm in charge of the menu."

"I might be willing to take my chances."

"Or maybe you could offer to bring pizza," she said as he walked down the hallway toward his office.

He turned and walked backwards, spreading his arms out. "So you're inviting me for dinner, and you want me to bring it?"

"Yep." She gave him two thumbs up. "Sounds good to me."

Gareth shook his head before swinging back around and disappearing into his office.

"Let's go shut down the stuff at the front, then we can go home," Janessa said.

Back at Aria's desk, Janessa walked her through the end of day tasks. Once everything was done, they returned to the break room where they'd left their personal things earlier.

Though she'd enjoyed the day, Aria was glad that it was over. Starting a new job, even with a close friend training her, was stressful. Her anxiety had spiked at different times throughout the day, but thankfully, it hadn't stayed elevated.

Since they'd lived together before, Janessa knew she struggled with anxiety—though it had never been as bad as it had been over the past year. That knowledge was probably why Janessa had checked in with her frequently throughout the day.

Since Janessa had driven them to work that morning, Aria slid into the passenger seat of her car and relaxed back with a sigh.

"Doing okay?" Janessa asked as she backed out of her parking spot.

"I'm doing fine," Aria said. "Just glad that the first day is over. Should be smooth sailing from here on out."

Janessa laughed as she waved a hand in the air. "Oh, don't expect that."

"Gotta think positively."

The drive home didn't take long, and when they walked into the house, the aroma of dinner greeted them. Layla came skipping out of the kitchen.

"Hi, Auntie Nessa," Layla sang out as she gave Janessa a hug. "Hi, Aria."

After greeting the girl, Aria went up to her room to change into something more comfortable. Once she was in her room, she walked over to the bed and dropped backwards on it, her arms spread wide. Staring up at the ceiling, she blew out a long breath.

Though she'd been determined to be successful at the job, now that she had actually done the work, she felt a bit more confident that she could do it. Still, her anxiety had made her question if she'd be able to handle the expectations of Janessa and her family. She didn't want to let them down.

Knowing that she needed to get back downstairs, Aria sat up. She rubbed at her arms with her knuckles, resisting the temptation to scratch at them, which is what her anxiety often demanded of her.

Peeling out of her work clothes, Aria draped them over a chair to deal with later, then pulled on a pair of leggings and an oversized T-shirt with long sleeves that hung down past her hands. She tugged on a pair of ballet-style flats, then went downstairs.

"How was your first day?" Charli asked with a smile as she looked up from the salad she was making.

"I think it went okay. Lots of people were wanting to set me up with their eligible male relatives."

Charli's expression tightened as she shook her head. "It's ridiculous."

"It seemed a little over the top," Aria agreed. "I hope it dies down soon."

"Just don't buy into any of the glowing recommendations," Charli said, her voice sharp. "They all like to think their son or grandson is an angel, when usually they're nothing of the sort."

"Don't worry," Janessa said as she joined them in the kitchen. "I'm keeping a close eye on her. I won't let her agree to any dates before I vet who it is."

"Oh, I'm not agreeing to any dates," Aria said, waving her hands. "New town. New job. That's quite enough for me right now."

"Make sure to tell Nora that," Charli said, her tone even more sharp. "So she doesn't make your life miserable."

"What's her deal?" Aria asked. "I felt like she was trying to trip me up, asking me to do things I wasn't trained for yet."

"Oh, I'm sure that's *exactly* what she was trying to do," Charli said.

"Nora decided after she arrived here that she wanted to play the role our mom played."

Aria frowned. "As a female doctor?"

"Not just female doctor, but wife of the doctor." Charli handed the salad bowl to Layla. "She thought that she and Gareth could be the next iteration of my parents."

"Gareth isn't interested," Janessa said. "But Nora hasn't accepted that yet."

"She thinks any eligible woman is going to take Gareth away from her."

"Even though he's not interested in her?"

"She thinks she still has a shot, and any single woman is a threat to that," Janessa said as she carried a pitcher of water to the table.

"Is she going to make my life miserable?"

Janessa and Charli exchanged glances, then Janessa said, "She's going to try, but just stand up to her. She can't do anything to you. Only me, Jay, or Gareth have the right to speak to you about your job. And we all know her tricks."

"Why does she continue to work at the clinic?"

Janessa sighed. "We need a female doctor. We have patients who prefer to see one. Gareth and Jay are still on the lookout for another woman doctor, but it's hard to find someone who wants to move up here and work in a small family clinic."

Aria wasn't sure she had the backbone to stand up to Nora, but she would try. It wasn't like she had a choice. She didn't want to make an enemy of Nora, though. Her job would be a whole lot easier if everyone just got along.

The last thing she wanted was to lose this job because so much was riding on it.

CHAPTER FIVE

Gareth hung his white coat up on the rack behind the door, then sat down at his desk. Though he enjoyed meeting with the patients, he also appreciated the end of the day when he could just sit in the quiet of his office, doing all the admin stuff that Jay required of him.

After the brutal demands of his residency, the clinic was a welcome change of pace. He enjoyed having his evenings and most weekends free. The balance of work and life was what he'd looked forward to once he moved back home.

"I guess I'll see you tomorrow."

He looked up to see Nora in the doorway. "Yep."

Though he hoped she was stopping just to say goodnight, she wandered further into his office, settling herself in the chair opposite him.

"Something on your mind?" he asked, even though it was the very last thing he was interested in.

"Just checking in to see how you feel about the newest employee."

Gareth wasn't surprised by the topic, but he frowned at her. "Did Jay or Janessa ask you to check in with me about Aria?"

"No. But since I wasn't part of the discussion to hire her, I thought I'd just see how you felt about her."

"I don't feel any way about her," Gareth said, leaning back in his chair. "She was hired on Janessa's recommendation and has only been here for a day. You're better off asking Janessa's opinion on how things are going since she's the one doing the training."

"Janessa's hardly going to give an unbiased opinion of her since they're friends and that's why she wanted to hire her."

Nora wasn't exactly wrong. However, Gareth trusted Janessa to have the best interest of the clinic in mind, and not do anything that would jeopardize it.

"It's been one day," Gareth said. "I hardly think it's fair to judge Aria just yet."

"You should have hired someone with more experience."

"Like one of the women you suggested?"

"Yes." Nora shifted in her seat. "Either of them would have been excellent in the position."

Gareth leaned back in his chair, clicking the pen he'd been using to make notes. "Jay called both of them."

Nora's brows lifted. "So why weren't they considered?"

"Neither of them were interested in a job that lasted more than six months."

"That would have given you time to find someone more qualified," Nora said, crossing her arms as she lifted her chin.

"There was no need to train someone who would have only been in the position for a few months," Gareth said. "Aria is who we chose."

"Well, I hope you keep an open mind that she might not be the perfect fit for the clinic."

Gareth narrowed his gaze at her. "And I hope you keep an open mind that she just might be a perfect fit for the clinic."

Nora arched a brow at him, then got to her feet. "I highly doubt she'll be *perfect.* No one is."

Gareth laughed. "Except for you, right?"

"Of course," Nora tossed over her shoulder as she left the office.

Things were going to be interesting for a little while. He hoped Nora wouldn't make life difficult for Aria. However, since Nora had made all of their lives difficult at one time or another, it seemed likely she'd do that for Aria, too. Apparently, it was a rite of passage in the clinic.

Lucky for Aria, she had Janessa to run interference for her with Nora. Janessa had perfected that over the past couple of years.

He could hardly wait to share all of this with the guys at dinner. They had liked Nora well enough at first. However, when she'd started in with the *we'll make a great doctor couple,* they'd told him to be careful. It was too bad she hadn't focused her attention on Wade or Jackson. At least then, the clinic would be a tension-free zone, and they wouldn't be trying to find a doctor to replace Nora.

Putting aside his thoughts on Nora, Gareth finished up his work, then changed into more casual clothes before heading out to Jackson's for the men's group.

The next morning, Gareth was once again first in the clinic, but not far behind him were Janessa and Aria.

"Good morning, ladies," Gareth said when they joined him in the break room.

"It's Friday," Janessa said. "And I'm off tomorrow, so yes, it's a goooood morning."

"Ready for your second day on the job, Aria?" he asked as he lifted the mug he'd just filled with coffee to take a sip.

"I think so." She gave him a small smile. "But I'm assuming there will be a whole new batch of patients who want to match me up with someone."

Janessa laughed. "You're learning quickly."

"This is never a problem I thought I'd have," Aria said with a shake of her head.

"I'm not sure any of us thought we'd have that problem," Janessa said. "After all, Mom and Dad were married already when they came to work at the clinic. There was no opportunity to make matches for them."

"It'll die down eventually," Gareth assured her.

"There are worse things that could be going on. I'll be fine."

Gareth was happy to hear that, and he appreciated her attitude. He leaned against the counter as he continued to sip his coffee.

"It's my turn to cook tonight," Janessa said as she and Aria prepared coffee for themselves. "And since you seemed averse to buying pizza for us, I think I'll make it from scratch."

Gareth gave a laugh, then smothered it when Janessa turned to glare at him. "*You're* going to make pizza?"

"Yes. And you are not invited."

"Oh, come on," Gareth said. "I really need to try this pizza that you're making."

"If you have such little faith in my abilities, maybe you should save us all from disaster and buy pizza for dinner."

Gareth shrugged. "Maybe I should."

"If you're going to bring pizza, perhaps we should invite some of the other family members," Janessa suggested.

"Sure. Though I think Mom is planning a family dinner for tomorrow night, so they might not come."

"I'll call a few of the sibs to see what they're up to."

Gareth took another swallow of his coffee, then turned back to the coffeemaker. As he topped up his mug, he said, "Figure it out and place the order. I'll pick it up on my way over."

"Are you bringing the duo?" Janessa asked.

"Not sure that would be a good idea yet," Gareth said, thinking that perhaps it would be okay to invite Wade, but Jackson would likely be annoying.

"I would agree."

Gareth added a bit more cream and sugar to his mug, then said, "I'll be in my office if you need me."

Seated at his desk a few minutes later, he continued to drink his coffee as he reviewed the cases for the day.

"Morning."

Gareth looked up in time to catch the wave of Jay's hand as he walked by his open door. They were supposed to have a staff meeting at lunch, so he hoped it went smoothly. Nora often got a bit heated about something she felt was important, and that might be the case with her feelings regarding the receptionist position. Hopefully, Janessa had given Aria a head's up about the staff meeting and what it might entail.

A couple of his appointments that morning ran long, and because of that, he was late joining the others in the break room at lunchtime.

Once again, Janessa had ordered lunch for them. That day was going to be a bad day eating-wise. He wasn't strict with his diet, but he tried to not eat too much junk food.

"I got you a salad with grilled chicken," Janessa said as he sat down beside her at the table.

"Thanks very much." He said a quiet prayer of thanks for the food, then opened the container. "What have I missed?"

He listened to the others talk as he ate. Aria wasn't participating in the conversation, though that wasn't a surprise. Gareth caught her scratching at her arm, then she seemed to stop herself, curving her fingers into a fist. She was wearing a long-sleeve shirt, so he couldn't see what might be irritating her skin.

Her brow furrowed as she crossed her arms, tucking her hands against her sides. It looked like she was trying to keep herself from scratching again, and Gareth couldn't help but wonder what was bothering her.

Nora and Janessa were in the middle of a debate over something that had happened with a patient the previous day. Aria's gaze ping-ponged between the two, and Gareth wondered what she was thinking. It might take a little while for her to get used to how they all related to each other.

He appreciated that she wasn't rocking the boat too much just yet. But hopefully, she'd come to understand that her opinion mattered too and feel comfortable voicing it.

"Do you have any concerns, Gare?" Janessa asked.

"Nope. Everything's been going smoothly."

"Did you train Aria on printing test requisitions yet, Janessa?" Nora asked.

"No."

"Why not? She needs to know how to do that."

"I am aware," Janessa said, her tone firm. "But that won't be a regular part of her duties, so it's low on my priority list of things to teach her. There are far more important things she needs to learn first."

"Why are you so focused on this, Nora?" Gareth asked. "Janessa explained yesterday why she wasn't teaching her that yet. This needs to be the last time you bring this up. Janessa is in charge of teaching Aria what she needs to know."

Nora lifted her chin. "I'm just trying to help."

"If you have a valid concern, you can bring it to me," Janessa said. "Don't bother Aria. She's still in the learning phase, so it's less confusing for her to hear about issues from just me."

"I agree with that," Jay said, and Gareth nodded.

"You shouldn't need to act as a go-between," Nora said. "If she's not strong enough to take criticism, this might be the wrong job for her."

Gareth sighed. "Nora, Janessa isn't acting as the go-between. She is training Aria, so any issues that need to be addressed during this period of learning should go through her."

"Don't question it," Jay said. "This is what Janessa has asked us to do, so this is what we'll do."

Nora looked like she wanted to argue, but apparently thought better of it. Gareth hoped she'd stop focusing so much on Aria and just do her job. That's what they should all do. Aria would learn the job in due time, and she certainly didn't need four people watching her every move.

And it wasn't as if anything she did was life or death that could end with a patient's health being jeopardized. Any mistake she made could be easily corrected.

"If that's all," Janessa began, "Aria and I need to get back to work."

"Nothing more from me," Jay said.

"Me either," Gareth added.

Janessa didn't bother to wait for Nora's response. She gathered up her trash and dumped it into the garbage. Aria did the same, then followed Janessa from the room.

"I don't think this is going to work out."

"Give it up, Nora," Gareth said. "We're not firing Aria without cause. She'll be given a fair shot at the job."

"Two days isn't a fair shot," Jay added. "So just back off and let Janessa do her job."

Nora glared at them both, then got up and cleared the remnants of her meal away before leaving the break room on her absurdly high heels.

"Is this going to be a problem?" Jay asked as he sprawled back in his chair, crossing his arms.

"I certainly hope not. We need both of them."

Jay nodded. "I just don't want Aria to think that this is a hostile work environment if Nora won't leave her alone."

"I think she'll settle down," Gareth said. "For some reason, she's feeling threatened by Aria."

"For some reason," Jay scoffed. "I think we know what that reason is."

Gareth grimaced. "At least Aria is not spiking my coffee."

Jay stared at the doorway before he said, "What happens if Nora says it's her or Aria?"

He'd kept his voice low, which Gareth appreciated. The last thing they needed to do was give Nora the idea. "I'm banking on her being more professional than that. She has no legitimate reason to offer such an ultimatum."

Jay nodded. "I've begun putting ads out for the position again."

"I would hate to have to fire her, but with such a small staff, we need people who are at least interested in working together. Nora seems more focused on getting rid of Aria than getting along with her."

It wasn't something Gareth liked to point out, but they couldn't ignore it. The only reason Nora hadn't given their previous receptionist any issues was because she'd been married and pregnant. She'd decided to stay home with her baby after the birth, which was why they'd needed someone to replace her permanently.

"Janessa will make sure that Nora leaves Aria alone," Jay said. "But she needs to be able to do her own job without constantly worrying that Nora is going to upset Aria."

Gareth didn't know Aria very well yet, but he hoped that she had a backbone. No doubt she was still feeling some timidity since it was her first few days at the clinic, and she only really knew Janessa. In time, she would hopefully gain some courage as she got to know each of them and found her footing in the job.

"Your first patient is here," Janessa said as she poked her head back into the room.

"Thanks." Gareth had eaten most his salad, so he got up and tossed the rest into the garbage. He washed his hands, then headed to the room where his first patient waited.

The rest of the afternoon passed quickly, and soon, the last patient had left the clinic. Gareth went into his office, pausing to stretch his arms up. He was glad that his week was done. Nora would be in the next morning to handle the appointments at the free clinic. They alternated working Saturday mornings at the clinic, and it was her turn.

He appreciated that she didn't argue about taking her turn at the clinic. It was just one more reason why he wished she'd just lay off Aria and leave him alone. If she did, things at the clinic would be just fine.

A short time later, he left the clinic, locking up before he walked to his car. Janessa had texted to let him know that she'd phoned in the pizza order and all he needed to do was pay for it when he picked it up.

Most the people working at the pizza place knew him, and they called out greetings when he walked in. He talked with them for a few minutes, getting caught up on the lives of the kids who worked there. Some of them were his patients, so he'd seen them a few times in a professional capacity. Others he knew through Cole and Jay.

"You coming to watch the basketball game tomorrow afternoon, Doc?"

Several others chimed in with the name of their competition, which was another nearby high school that had been their chief rival even back when Gareth had been in high school.

"Yep." His youngest two siblings were still in high school, with his brother being on the basketball team and his sister being a cheerleader.

"We're gonna wipe the floor with them," a guy yelled from the kitchen. "Probably should have a doctor there."

Gareth chuckled. "Well, then I guess it's good I've cleared my schedule."

Only two of the workers were actually on the team, but it seemed that anyone that wasn't working planned to be at the game. He hadn't been on the basketball team in high school. Football had been more his speed. Jay, however, had played basketball all four years of high school and had gained a scholarship for it to college. Now he was back in Serenity Point, helping the high school team during practices.

After paying for the pizza, he carried the stack of boxes out to the car. He made a stop at a convenience store and picked up an assortment of sodas.

By the time he pulled up at the house, Gareth was starving, thanks to the aroma of the pizza that saturated the interior of his car. He hooked the bags with the soda on his wrists, then picked up the stack of boxes and headed for the large house. When he reached the front door, he used his elbow to press the doorbell.

The door swung open to reveal Aria. Gripping the edge of the door, she stepped back, opening it wide for him. After he stepped into the foyer, she closed it behind him.

"Can I help you with anything?" she asked.

"I think I'm balanced well enough," he told her. "But thanks."

She flashed him a quick smile, then walked with him to the kitchen. He noticed that she'd changed into a pair of loose sweats and a baggy sweatshirt, seeming to be dressed more for comfort than style. Which was also the case for Janessa and Charli.

"Gare!" His youngest brother, Cole, headed over to him and took the pizza boxes out of his arms. "I hope you brought plenty. I'm starving."

"If there's not enough, blame Nessa. I only picked up the order. She was the one to phone it in."

"Just leave the boxes on the counter," Charli said, then she turned to Aria. "Do you want to grab some plastic cups and paper plates from the pantry? Layla, please show Ari where everything is."

Aria followed Layla into the small pantry that opened up off the kitchen. It looked like Aria was fitting in well with the household. And if Charli felt comfortable enough to give her new roommate orders, that was a good sign.

He greeted his other siblings who had arrived already. Not everyone had come. Two of the family lived away from Serenity Point at the moment, since they were both in college.

"Hey, Sky," he said when his youngest sister sidled up to give him a hug. "How's life treating you?"

"Good. I've worked a couple of extra shifts at the coffee shop this week."

He'd missed a good chunk of Skylar and Cole's growing-up years while he'd been away for med school and his residency. Since he'd been home, he tried his best to keep informed on what was going on in their lives.

As they got ready to eat, Gareth kept an eye on Aria, curious to see how she was interacting with the members of his family who were present. Because she lived with Janessa and Charli, Aria was more than just an employee.

"I hear there's a big game tomorrow," Gareth said as Cole joined them. "Are you both ready?"

"I am," Cole said, his shoulders straightening.

"We've been working on some new cheers," Skylar added.

When he heard the front door open, he glanced over to see another of his sisters walk in.

"Kayleigh!" Skylar skipped over to her and gave her a tight hug. "I didn't know you were coming."

After Kayleigh hugged Skylar, she approached Gareth. He gave her a hug as well. "How's the hotel business?"

"Busy. So busy." She leaned against him for a moment, then straightened, as if she couldn't let herself reveal any weakness.

"Have you met our newest employee?" Gareth asked.

"Not yet."

Gareth knew it was probably something of a baptism by fire introducing Aria to so many of their family at once, but it was probably better that she meet them sooner rather than later. It would also help her understand the dynamics within their family.

If she was going to be around for any length of time, it was important she got to know them.

CHAPTER SIX

Aria struggled to embrace the chaos unfolding around her. She'd had no idea what it was like to have so many siblings. Given that she was an only child, any space she'd shared with her mom had been fairly quiet. The loudest it ever got was when they'd laughed and cheered for one of the reality competition shows they'd enjoyed watching together.

Even her ex-fiancé had only had one sibling, so she hadn't experienced any type of mayhem when visiting his family, either. But Janessa's family... it went beyond anything she ever would have expected. The one good thing was that the boisterous conversations going on around her meant that she didn't have to try to hold a conversation with anyone herself.

A loud whistle pierced the air, then Gareth held up his hand. "Let's say a prayer for the food, then we can all dig in."

Silence descended on the space, then Gareth said a prayer of thanks for the food. As soon as he was done, the conversations erupted around her once again.

Charli was talking with a man who had arrived last, but she handed Aria a plate and gestured toward the boxes of pizza. Aria assumed that was Charli's way of saying to help herself.

As she stepped closer to the boxes, Janessa came to her side. "You'd better take a couple slices of whichever type you like before the others get within grabbing distance."

Aria smiled at her, then put just one slice on her plate. "Where should I sit?"

"Just grab any seat and save the one next to it for me."

Moving slowly, she made her way to the table and walked to the far end of it. She left the end seat open, as well as the one right next to it for Janessa.

"Can I sit beside you, Ria?"

Aria looked over at Layla, her heart warmed at the nickname. "Sure thing, sweetie."

Layla slid her plate onto the table, then climbed up onto the chair. "I looooove pizza."

"I do too," Aria said. "But I like salad as well." She reached for one of the bowls of salad that had been placed on each end of the table. "Do you want some, Layla?"

The little girl stared at the salad with a frown, then glanced over to where her mom stood at the counter talking to one of her brothers. "Nope. No salad with my pizza."

Aria chuckled as she put some of the Caesar salad on her plate. "Okay."

"Do you want a drink?" Janessa asked as she put her plate down on Aria's other side. "Gareth brought a variety of sodas."

"Is there something without caffeine?"

"Probably. Do you have a preference?"

"Not really. Just no caffeine."

"I'll be right back."

While she was gone, Gareth took the seat at the end of the table while the guy that Charli had been speaking with settled into the chair to his right.

"Have you met Wilder, Aria?" Gareth asked as he gestured to the man beside him.

"No. Not yet."

"Well, this is Wilder," Gareth said as he reached over to clap the man on the shoulder. "We also call him Wilder the Wanderer. He's not a fan of staying put for long."

The man shook his head in protest, setting his long curls swaying. "I stay put for most the winter."

"True." Gareth picked up one of his pieces of pizza. "He's a ski instructor at the resort."

"Have you ever skied?" Wilder asked, turning his brown gaze on her.

"No. I've never been a huge fan of winter sports," Aria told him. "Or sports in general, to be honest."

Wilder sighed. "That is just so sad."

"Not everyone is as sports oriented as you, Jay, and Cole," Gareth said.

"I know. But still!"

"I like basketball," Layla announced. "Cause Uncle Cole and Uncle Jay play it."

Janessa set a glass containing clear bubbly liquid in front of Aria. "Do you know anything about basketball?"

"Uh... a little?" Aria glanced at Janessa as she sat down in her chair. "But not enough to pass a quiz on the fundamentals of the game."

"You're going to get a crash course tomorrow," Janessa said. "I mean, if you want one."

"Why tomorrow?" Aria asked.

"Cole is playing in a game against the high school's biggest rival. We'll probably all be there."

"Oh. Well, sure. That might be fun."

"It is," Janessa said. "Skylar is also cheering for the game."

Aria hadn't been into high school sports much. By the time she'd gotten to high school, making friends hadn't been something she'd tried to do much since she and her mom had moved around so often.

The games had seemed like events for groups of friends to attend to cheer on other friends who were playing. Plus, not being an athlete herself, she just hadn't had much interest in going.

"It's lots of fun," Layla said. "I can yell and scream, and Momma doesn't tell me to be quiet."

Wilder grinned. "Yep. The louder, the better, little sprout."

The little girl beamed back at her uncle as she lifted her hands above her head. "We're gonna raise the roof."

Aria couldn't keep from laughing at the expression that Layla had clearly heard from the adults around her.

Cole took the seat next to Wilder. "What are we talking about?"

"The game tomorrow," Wilder said.

The conversation veered off into stats on the two different teams, which left Aria lost. However, she would go with the others to the game the next day, and hopefully it wouldn't be too confusing to understand what was happening. It seemed like even Layla had a firm grasp of the sport.

The others joined them at the table, and Aria noted that there were seven siblings present. Jay wasn't there, and Janessa had said their other two siblings were away at school. Now that the town was her new home, Aria figured that she'd meet them eventually.

Kayleigh was the oldest sister, and she carried herself with poise and a certain elegance. Janessa had said that she worked as a manager at a nearby five-star resort.

It seemed like there was a real assortment of personalities in the Halverson siblings, but none of them seemed overly introverted. At least not to the extent Aria was. Or maybe they were only so highly interactive because they were with family.

"So how are you finding life here so far, Aria?" Gareth asked, drawing her attention from the food on her plate.

Aria set her fork down and rubbed her arm. "It's lovely. A bit colder than I'm used to, though."

Gareth nodded. "We're not as cold as some of the midwestern states, but we get enough snow to keep the snow bunnies happy."

"I'll teach you how to ski if you'd like," Wilder volunteered.

"Nope." Janessa held out her hand. "You're not allowed to encourage our newly hired receptionist to risk life and limb on the slopes."

Wilder grinned at his sister. "Or maybe you're afraid she'll be better on skis than you were."

"I could have been better on skis," Janessa protested. "I just had no desire to spend that much time in the cold."

"Maybe you two need to let Aria make that decision for herself," Gareth said as he flashed her a quick smile.

Aria did not know what to do with the warmth that filled her at Gareth coming to her defense. It was... unexpected. She had yet to see the grumpy doctor Jay had referred to. So far, Gareth had been nothing but friendly and gracious to her, which she appreciated very much.

"I'm really not sure that I'm ready to start the skiing portion of my life." Aria grimaced. "Knowing my luck, I'd break an arm or leg on even the easiest of slopes. I don't need that new experience in my life right now."

"Exactly," Janessa said with a smirk at Wilder.

"There's always next season," he told her. "You might change your mind after realizing there's not much going on around here."

"You mean I'll take up skiing out of boredom?" Aria asked.

"Yep. Wouldn't be the first person to do that."

"Oh, I doubt that will ever happen. When I get bored, I just open up a book."

"No wonder you're friends with Janessa," Wilder muttered. "She'd rather read a book or watch TV than hit the slopes."

Wilder wasn't wrong. Reading was one of many things the two of them had bonded over as roommates. Though, admittedly, Janessa hadn't read as much as Aria. She'd managed to balance her reading with a social life.

Janessa lifted her hand with a grin, prompting Aria to smack it.

"I like to read too!" Layla said and lifted her hand.

Aria smiled at her as she gave her little palm a light smack. When she glanced over at Gareth, he was watching them with an affectionate look on his face.

"Always read, Layla-bug," he said. "It's the most important thing."

"Well, I do like to ski too," Layla reminded him. "I'm not even on the easiest slope anymore. Right, Uncle Wild?"

"Yep. You've graduated from the beginner slope."

"Wow," Aria said, suitably impressed that the young girl enjoyed skiing and seemed to be good at it. "That's great."

"I think you could learn without breaking a bone." Layla's expression was serious. "I've never broken a bone."

"A lot of kids around here learn to ski," Wilder said. "It's a family outing."

Aria didn't know much about what families did together if they were more outdoorsy. She'd just assumed they went on walks or rode bikes.

"Does everyone in your family ski?"

Wilder sighed as he shook his head. "Unfortunately not. Charli does, and so does Zane. Skylar doesn't love it, but she'll hit the slopes every once in a while. Cole and Jay are all about basketball, and neither of them want to risk getting hurt and not being able to play. Gareth only skis if his buddies are hitting the slopes."

"It's not my favorite thing to do," Gareth agreed. "I'd rather hike or ride a bike on the trails or kayak. All summer things. Winter isn't necessarily my favorite season."

None of those were things that Aria had ever really done much of, and she didn't envision that changing. She was glad that Janessa's interests lined up more with hers.

Aria didn't talk with everyone there that evening, but she enjoyed those that she did converse with. It was also nice to see Gareth in a more relaxed environment. He smiled and laughed easily, which made him seem much more approachable.

At the same time, it was odd to socialize with her boss. She'd done a small amount of socializing with co-workers, but that had usually been with nurses or aides. Rarely with the doctors.

This was definitely a whole new experience for her, and she hoped she wouldn't mess anything up.

The next afternoon, Aria left her bedroom, dressed in an outfit that Janessa had approved. Even though she didn't know much about basketball, she found herself excited about attending the game.

"You look great," Janessa said when Aria walked into the kitchen a few minutes later.

"With your help," Aria reminded her.

She knew that a basketball game wasn't an event with a dress code unless you were a player or a cheerleader. Still, she hadn't wanted to stand out because she wore the wrong thing. She was comfortable in the fitted jeans and dark blue sweater with a draped neck that Janessa had chosen from her clothes. Janessa also wore jeans, along with a baby pink turtleneck sweater.

"I'm bringing some water, because if we start yelling, we're gonna need something to drink."

"We're going to yell?" Aria asked.

"You betcha." Janessa grinned as she slipped a couple of bottles of water into a large shoulder bag. "If Cole gets that ball and heads for the basket, we'll all go a little crazy."

"Your parents will be there too?"

"Yep. Most of us try to make any game that family members are playing in. Jay was the star for the years he played at the high school. That's how he ended up with a scholarship to college."

"Are we going?" Layla asked as she skipped into the kitchen, with her mother trailing behind her.

Aria had known the girl for less than a week, but Layla never failed to bring a smile to Aria's face when she was around. She was a little ray of sunshine, and Aria wasn't sure she'd seen the girl actually walk normally anywhere yet.

"Yep," Janessa said. "I think we're ready."

The four of them left the house and piled into Charli's small SUV. Aria sat in the back with Layla, listening as the little girl talked about her hope to be a cheerleader like Skylar one day.

The parking lot at the high school made it clear that this was an *event.* It took a couple of minutes for Charli to find a parking spot. Once she turned off the car, they all climbed out and headed for the doors of the high school. Layla held hands with her mom as she bounced along beside her.

Other people were also walking toward the building and called out greetings to Charli and Janessa.

"Looking forward to seeing Cole win this game for us tonight," one man said with a big grin.

"I'm sure he'll try his best," Charli replied.

They made their way into the building and down a wide hall lined with classrooms and lockers. It brought back memories... not all of them good. She'd spent most of her high school trying to get good enough grades to qualify for scholarships, since that was going to be the only way she could afford to go to college.

There were already a ton of people in the gym, filling the bleachers set against the walls and creating lots of noise. Charli led the way to a section of the bleachers where her parents were seated with Kayleigh. Layla clambered up the steps to sit with her grandparents. Charli and Janessa scooted their way onto the row in front of them where Wilder sat.

The bleacher surface was hard, but no one seemed to notice as they chatted with the people seated around them. Aria shrugged out of her jacket, then laid it across her lap. Janessa sat down beside her and set the large bag she'd brought between her feet.

"Doing okay?" she asked with a smile, as if sensing that Aria was feeling a bit nervous.

"Hey, there," a woman said as she slid onto the row in front of them. "Coming to cheer on your boss's brother?"

Aria tried to place the woman, but she didn't think she'd been one of the patients that had been to the clinic during the two days she'd worked there. Of course, she'd been overwhelmed with the training as well as checking patients in, so she might just not be remembering her.

"Actually, she's here to cheer on her friend's brother," Janessa said. "I mean, she was my friend before she was an employee."

"Ah, so nepotism got her the job." The woman nodded like that clarified something for her.

"No. The reason she got the job was because she was a qualified candidate with previous medical environment experience."

"I had previous experience as well," the woman said. "In that very clinic."

Aria glanced at Janessa in surprise. Well, that kind of explained the woman's attitude.

"Oh, Gareth!" The woman got to her feet as Gareth climbed the steps to where they sat.

He paused with a frown on his face, then walked into the row and sat down beside Aria. Two men followed behind him, both of them wearing big grins as they looked at the woman.

"Hey there, Chelsey," the one closest to Gareth said. "What brings you to the game today? Pretty sure you're not a cheerleader anymore."

The woman—Chelsey—glared at the man. "Shut up, Jackson."

Jackson lifted his hands in surrender. "Just pointing out the obvious."

"You wouldn't know obvious if it bit you on the butt."

"I suppose you *would* be the queen of obvious," Jackson said with a nod. "After all, you've been fairly obvious in your pursuit of first Jay, and then Gareth. Perhaps if you spent less time spiking their coffees and offering to give them massages, you might have had more luck."

"Don't encourage her, Jack," Gareth said with a groan.

Spiking his coffee? Oh! Chelsey must be the receptionist they had to fire. Aria looked at Gareth in time to see him roll his eyes.

"I think you need to go sit somewhere else, Chelsey," Janessa said. "We're just here to enjoy the basketball game."

"I can sit wherever I want," Chelsey said with a toss of her head. "It's a free world."

"Chelsey." This time it was Janessa's dad who spoke. "Do I need to give your mother a call?"

Aria didn't think that was much of a threat, but she was clearly missing something since Chelsey immediately frowned, then got up and walked away.

"What was that about?" Aria murmured to Janessa once Chelsey had left hearing range.

Janessa gave a huff of laughter. "That was Dad reminding Chelsey that she and her parents had agreed that Chelsey wouldn't come around Gareth or Jay anymore."

"It was that bad?"

"Oh yeah. It wasn't just the spiked coffee. Chelsey had a book she'd created to show how much she had in common with the guys."

"Okay?"

"It was filled with pictures of me and Jay," Gareth said. "She had picture after picture after picture showing us going around town. If she had a picture of me coming out of a coffee shop, she'd written next to it what I'd ordered and that she liked her coffee that way too."

"We've known her our whole life. Jay even dated her a couple of times in high school," Janessa said. "But something flipped a switch in her, apparently, and made her start acting really strangely around the guys."

"Seems women lose their mind over Gareth," Aria murmured.

Janessa laughed. "Yeah. First Chelsey, then Nora. I think it has more to do with the fact that he's an eligible doctor than anything about him personally."

"I gotta agree with Janessa," Jackson said as he nudged Gareth with his elbow. "Introduce us, Gareth." Then he held up his hand. "Actually, no. Don't introduce Wade. Just me."

"How about I introduce Wade and *not* you?" Gareth said, bumping his friend back. "Aria, this is Wade, my best friend."

"*One* of your best friends," Jackson corrected.

"Hi, Aria," Wade said, leaning forward to hold his hand out past both his friends.

Aria took it and said, "Nice to meet you."

"And I'm Jackson," the other man said, freeing her hand from Wade's to sandwich it in his. "The other best friend. The best best friend."

"Yes, that's Jackson. My most annoying best friend."

"I second that," Janessa said.

"I third that," Charli chimed in.

They all laughed, even Jackson, as if he was confident in the affections of Gareth's family to know they actually cared for him despite their teasing.

"Now that we've moved past that," Gareth said. "Let's focus on the game."

By that point, the surrounding bleachers had filled even more. Teenage boys in two different colored uniforms had come out onto the floor and were warming up with basketballs. The sound of the balls hitting the hardwood floor echoed in the large gym, increasing the noise level.

Aria felt her excitement building along with that of the other people in the gym. The Halversons were not quiet in their support for Cole, and they yelled and clapped when he neared where they sat. He flashed them a grin and a wave before focusing back on the warm-up.

Aria was so grateful for this family that had welcomed her into their midst, and she desperately wanted to stay in Serenity Point.

CHAPTER SEVEN

Somehow, Gareth ended up being the one to give Aria a rundown on the game. He wasn't sure how it had happened since Janessa was as knowledgeable about basketball as he was.

"Why are they lining up like that?" Aria asked, her shoulder pressing against his as she leaned close to ask her question.

"One of our players committed a foul on a player from the other team, so he gets a free throw. That means the guy with the ball can take a shot without the opposing players interfering with him."

The player holding the ball let it fly toward the net for his free throw, but the ball hit the rim and bounced away. Along with a bunch of other people, Gareth jumped to his feet and yelled, "Rebound!"

Gareth didn't keep standing since he didn't want to block anyone's view. His mom wouldn't hesitate to smack his butt to get him to sit down. Sitting forward on the bleacher, he yelled more encouragement as Cole dribbled the ball down the court.

As he neared the basket, Cole jumped. But instead of shooting, he passed the ball to a fellow player, taking their opponents by surprise. It allowed the other player to sink his shot. All the home team fans cheered and whistled as their team's score went up by two points.

"Good pass, Cole!" Gareth called out to his brother.

Gareth knew that Jay tried to impress on Cole that no matter how good a player he was, he would always be better if he played as a team member rather than a lone star. He was glad to see that Cole was taking those lessons to heart.

The cheerleaders were enthusiastic as they led the spectators in cheers. He could see Aria was getting caught up in the spirit of the game, and she wasn't asking him quite as many questions now. He didn't know if that was because she understood it now, or if she was just enjoying the experience too much to ask.

Gareth hadn't been sure what to expect from Janessa's friend, but he was glad to see that she seemed to be fitting in with the family as well as the clinic responsibilities. She was very easy to be around, which was nice.

At half-time, the home team was leading by four points. The cheerleaders took to the court in a flurry of cartwheels, then they put on a rehearsed cheer that had the spectators clapping along with them.

The acoustics in the gym magnified the noise, adding to the craziness of the event. But that was all part of a basketball game between long-time rivals.

Once the cheerleaders were done, Gareth took orders for food, then he went with Jackson and Wade to buy it. There was only a brief window of time to get food during the half-time, but the canteen was used to the sudden surge of customers, and the staff moved with quick precision.

Back at their seats, the men handed out the food and drinks. It wasn't too complicated of an order since the only food available were hamburgers, hotdogs, small bags of chips and bottles of soda or water.

Aria took the chips and drink she'd requested when Gareth held them out to her. "Thank you."

"You're welcome," he said with a smile.

"Are you enjoying yourself, Aria?" Janessa asked as she opened her chips. "Not too noisy for you?"

"It's great," she said. "I've never been to something like this before. Are there other school sports or just basketball?"

"There are other sports," Janessa said. "Gareth played football, along with Jackson and Wade. I played some soccer."

"I've never been into sports," Aria said. "But this is fun."

"You've definitely had a wild introduction to life in Serenity Point," Charli said.

"It's been great. The most excitement I've had in a long time."

Janessa grinned. "We're all about excitement around here."

Cheers drowned their conversation out as the teams returned to the court. The visiting team must have received a super pep talk from their coach during half-time because they were on fire for the first few minutes of the second half.

"Are they going to win?" Aria asked.

Gareth glanced over to find her frowning as she watched the play on the court. "I can't say they're *going* to win, since this team is a fierce rival of ours. The score always goes back and forth in the games they've played against each other."

"I hope our team wins."

"Well, you're in good company," he told her with a laugh.

When she looked over at him, her eyes were sparkling. "I suppose I am."

A play on the court drew their attention, and Gareth called out encouragement to Cole as he jumped into the air to intercept a shot. This was an exceptionally good game from Cole, and it proved why he'd landed some college scholarships. Gareth couldn't wait to see what the years ahead would hold for his youngest brother.

As the minutes ticked down on the clock, neither team was pulling ahead by much. With a minute left, the teams were tied.

"I'm not sure my heart can handle this," Aria said, pressing a hand to her chest. "I didn't realize it would be so suspenseful."

Everyone was on their feet now, fans of both the home team and the visiting one. As their team got the ball, the cheers rose to a deafening level. With the last seconds ticking down, the player with the ball faked out the guys guarding him, and bounce-passed the ball to Cole. As soon as the ball was in Cole's hands, he went straight up into the air and shot at the basket.

The crowd seemed to collectively hold its breath, and the noise level dropped as everyone waited to see what was going to happen. The ball swished through the net, and a second later, the buzzer sounded.

Cheers erupted in the gym as their team's players spilled out onto the court to hug and high-five their teammates. Jay was out there too, his arm around Cole's shoulders.

Gareth felt a sweep of pride as he looked at his brothers. Though he'd never carried the same passion for sports—especially basketball—that they did, he could recognize the level of talent both Jay and Cole had for the game. Jay went on to have success in his college years, leading his team to several state and national titles in his time there. Gareth hoped that Cole experienced the same, since the teen really wanted to justify the scholarships he'd received.

Next to him, Aria was also on her feet, clapping enthusiastically. For someone who hadn't known much about the game, she'd caught on quickly, and unless she was good at faking her excitement, she'd enjoyed herself.

"How often do they play games like this?" she asked, once again leaning close since the noise level was still pretty intense.

"There's usually a game every weekend, though they're not always at home, and sometimes they're not this exciting."

"This team is one of their fiercest rivals," Janessa said. "So whenever they play, it's always a good game."

"That was just amazing," Aria said. "Thanks so much for including me."

Janessa put an arm around her shoulders. "Thanks for coming with us. I'm glad you enjoyed it."

"And I hope you're planning to join us for supper at the big house," Gareth's mom said as she leaned forward, looping her arm around his shoulders.

Aria glanced at Gareth before looking back at his mom. "If you're sure..."

"I'm very sure. Not everyone will be there since Cole, Jay, and Skylar are going out with the team for pizza to celebrate the win. It's tradition."

"What are we having, Mom?" Janessa asked. "Maybe Aria wants to make sure she'll like the food before agreeing to join us."

"Oh no," Aria said hurriedly. "I'm sure whatever you serve will be just fine."

Gareth's mom laughed as she straightened. "Well, to answer your question, darling, we're having beef stew. It's been in the crock-pot all day, plus I made some fresh rolls."

"That sounds lovely," Aria said.

"Are we invited too?" Jackson asked as he gave Gareth's mom a pathetic hangdog look. "Otherwise, we'll starve to death."

"Now, while I don't believe you'll be starving to death any time soon, you boys are both always welcome to join us."

Jackson and Wade high-fived each other while Gareth shook his head at their antics. People might have said that as men in their early thirties, they should behave more befitting their age. However, given how serious Gareth had had to be throughout most of his adult life, he enjoyed the lighthearted moments he had now with his family and friends. Plus, they both knew when acting a little crazy was acceptable and when it wasn't.

With plans for dinner settled, they all filed down off the bleachers. Cole came jogging over, and they congratulated him on his game. His excitement still lingered on his face, and Gareth was glad he didn't take moments like these for granted.

"Good job passing today," Gareth said as he slapped him on the shoulder.

"Jay's been making us run laps if we hog the ball, and none of us like that."

"I guess negative reinforcement works if positive doesn't." Gareth gestured to where Aria stood talking to Janessa and his parents. "This was Aria's first ever basketball game, and you put on a good show. She really enjoyed herself."

Cole grinned. "Nice to know I can impress the ladies."

"Hah." Gareth punched his shoulder lightly. "Don't worry about impressing her. Think of her like she's your sister."

Cole's brows lifted. "Are you calling dibs?"

"I most certainly am *not*," Gareth said, though he was surprised by the passing thought that maybe he should.

"Maybe if he's not, I should," Jackson said as he bumped his elbow against Gareth's.

Gareth narrowed his gaze at his two friends and Cole. "No one is calling dibs."

Cole just laughed as he backed away. "Gotta go. Talk to you later!"

He spun on his heel and jogged off toward the locker room. People were leaving the gym now that all the excitement was over.

"We'll see you at the house in a bit," his mom said before she and his dad walked off hand in hand.

The rest of them didn't linger in the gym now that the game was over. When the group reached the parking lot, they each went to their separate vehicles.

Gareth drove straight to the big house that had been his home for most of his growing-up years. He hadn't spent the first couple of years of his life in that house, however. Back then, his parents hadn't had plans to have such a big family. But once it became clear that their family was growing by leaps and bounds, they'd built a home that suited their large family.

It was almost too much now, though, since only Skylar and Cole lived at home full-time, and in the fall, even Cole would be gone.

However, Gareth doubted that his folks would sell the house. They still loved to have all the family spend the night for special events like Christmas Eve.

He'd just parked in front of the house when a couple of other cars pulled in beside him. Getting out, he saw that Aria had come with Janessa and Charli, while Jackson and Wade had come together in Jackson's truck.

A deep bark greeted them from the porch where Bella, their golden lab, waited. She was getting up in years, so she rarely bounded down the steps to greet them anymore. Layla, however, was happy to bound up the porch steps to lavish the big dog with lots of love. The rest of them followed at a slightly more sedate pace.

"This is Bella," Layla announced when Aria stepped onto the porch. "Bella, this is Aria. She's really nice. I think you'll like her."

Bella's soft woof in response had them all chuckling.

"We're honestly not sure if the dog really understands Layla," Janessa said. "But it sure seems like she does sometimes."

Aria held her hand out to the dog, allowing Bella to sniff at her fingers before she gave Aria's hand a soft lick.

"Of course she does," Layla said indignantly as she crouched beside Bella with her arm curled around the dog's neck. "She loves me. Don't you, Bella?"

The dog turned her head and gave Layla's cheek a lick. Apparently she did.

"I want to be a doggy doctor when I grow up," Layla announced as she stood up, her fingers still buried in the scruff of Bella's neck. "Just like Uncle Gareth is a people doctor."

"She's a beautiful dog," Aria said, smiling down at the pair.

Layla nodded. "And she can do tricks too."

"How about we go into the house, and you can ask Grandma for treats for Bella," Gareth suggested. "Because we're hungry."

Layla gave a nod, then spun around and led Bella into the house. The rest of them followed behind her, and Gareth inhaled the rich aroma that greeted them. His stomach growled in anticipation of the meal that was to come, even though he'd had a hotdog at the game. After hanging up his jacket and removing his boots, Gareth went to greet his mom in the kitchen and offer his help.

"Why don't you light the fire in the dining room?" his mom suggested. "Your dad got a call that he had to take, so he didn't get that done."

"Sure thing." Gareth kissed the top of her head, then went into the living room, calling for Jackson and Wade to come with him. "Help me carry some wood to the dining room."

"You too weak to carry it yourself?" Jackson asked.

"Have you already forgotten that I'm the brains of this operation? You and Wade are the brawn."

"Dude," Wade protested. "You promised you wouldn't hold our scholastic struggles against us."

"Jack started it." Gareth picked up a couple of logs and pushed them at Wade. The guy scrambled to keep hold of them. "Take them into the dining room."

He and Jackson grabbed some more from the stack next to the fireplace in the living room, then they followed Wade into the dining room. Aria was there with Janessa, and the pair of them were setting the table.

"Nothing better than Mom's stew in front of a roaring fire," Janessa said.

"I've never had that before," Aria replied. "But it does seem that on a cold day like today, it would be wonderful."

Since it was still early in January, the days were short. Even though it wasn't that late, the sun had already set, giving the house a cozy atmosphere. The only thing that made the house even better doing the short winter days was when it was decorated for

Christmas. Unfortunately, his mom had already packed away all the decorations.

"Let me do it, dude," Jackson said, elbowing him out of the way. "You know I'm better at this than you are."

Gareth wanted to argue that he could do it just fine, but Jackson was right. He actually was better at it than Gareth. While away from Serenity, he'd spent a lot of years not building fires, while Jackson and Wade had been building them every day during winter since they both had fireplaces in their homes.

Stepping aside, Gareth crossed his arms and watched as Jackson deftly arranged the logs and, in short order, had a fire going. The scent of burning wood drifted out to compete with the aroma of the beef stew.

"I've never lived in a place with a fireplace before," Aria said as she stood a couple feet away from him, staring at the flickering flames. "This is very lovely."

"There are fireplaces at Charli and Janessa's," Gareth said. "They can teach you how to build a fire."

She glanced at him. "Oh, I'm not sure I could do that."

"Sure, you can," he told her. "Dad taught all of us. Some do it more often than others, but both Charli and Janessa build fires at their place."

Gareth found himself wondering about Aria's past. When Janessa had recommended her for the job, he'd been more interested in if she could do the job. Now that she was there, mixing with the family in social settings, the lines were blurring between employee and possible friend.

He had no problem with that, actually. But if he was going to socialize with her, he'd like to know a bit more about her. That would have to come in time, as he was fairly certain that she wasn't going to be opening up right away, especially with him. He probably could ask Janessa for more details, but he'd wait and see how Aria warmed up to the rest of the family first.

"I did see that there was a fireplace in my bedroom at the house," she said. "But I didn't know it was real."

Gareth grinned at her. "Most fireplaces around here are the real deal."

"I can see why they'd have to be when it's so cold."

"Not much snow where you're from?"

She shook her head. "Nope."

"Well, it sticks around here more often than not."

"Definitely will be an experience for me."

"Did you bring warm enough clothes?" Gareth asked, feeling a bit concerned that she might not have.

She crossed her arms and kept her gaze on the fire. "I think what I have will be okay."

"Layers are great, so if you think you're going to be cold, just add another layer."

"Okay, everyone," his mom called from the kitchen. "Come grab something."

Gareth turned away from the fire and headed to the counter where his mom had been putting the food as she'd dished it up. With so many hands, it didn't take long to get all the food from the kitchen to the table in the dining room.

Soon, they were all seated, and Gareth found himself across the table from Aria, with Jake and Wade on either side of him. Aria had a seat between Janessa and Layla, who looked like she had plenty to say to the new person in her life.

Gareth wondered if Aria would get impatient with Layla, or if she'd embrace the little girl's enthusiastic, curious personality. They'd all gotten used to it, and since there were so many of them, she could spread her conversations out among all of them.

He could only imagine how someone who was an only child must view their family. When he'd been away at school, even people who had siblings were shocked to find out he had nine of them. Or maybe it was eleven, since Wade and Jack felt like brothers.

Once he'd passed three siblings, he'd kind of taken the viewpoint of *what was one more?*

His parents had said they were done with both biological and adopted children, but that didn't mean that they'd say no if another child showed up in their lives needing a family. Gavin admired that about his parents, but he did kind of hope that their family was now complete. Well, except now his mom was after them to give her some grandchildren, so if she had her way, their family would still be growing.

CHAPTER EIGHT

As soon as Aria walked into the church with Janessa, she wished she could turn around and leave. When Janessa had told her the previous night that she left for church around ten-thirty if she wanted to go with her, Aria should have politely declined.

It wasn't that she had anything against church, but she was used to attending in anonymity. When she and her mom had gone, it had always been to a mega-church where they blended in.

Aria had never asked her mom why they hadn't gone to a smaller church or why they hadn't gotten more involved in the bigger churches they'd attended over the years. She'd just accepted that if her mom felt they should attend those bigger churches, she must have a good reason.

And now, Aria was faced with endless introductions to people who would remember who she was while she'd never be able to recall all the names that were being tossed at her. Some of them were people she'd met at the clinic, but the panic she was experiencing had erased their names from her memory.

She didn't know why it hadn't occurred to her that she would be attending a church in a small town where everyone seemed to know her friend and her friend's family.

Rubbing at her arm, Aria tried not to scratch like she wanted to. The urge to get rid of the itch of anxiety beneath her skin was nearly overwhelming.

Calm down. This is ridiculous.

Not one person greeted her with anything but friendly and welcoming expressions.

"Let's go sit down," Janessa said as she grabbed her arm.

Aria allowed her friend to guide her into the sanctuary and to a row that was about mid-way to the front. She would have preferred to sit at the back, but she was glad that at least they weren't sitting right at the front.

"Sorry if that was a little overwhelming," Janessa said softly. "I forget what it's like for someone who's not used to our church."

"It's okay." Aria gave her friend what she hoped was a reassuring smile. "I'll get used to it."

Janessa grinned at that. "It's okay if you don't. I still feel a little overwhelmed by everyone in the church knowing everything about me. There are times I'd like to just blend in and be able to worship. But between who my family is and being a person of color in a fairly white town, I'm never going to blend in."

Aria frowned. It hadn't even occurred to her that Janessa and Jay might struggle with something like that. But as she considered Janessa's words, she knew that it would be so stressful for her if she were in their position. But she wasn't in their position, so she'd never truly understand how it felt.

She reached out and squeezed Janessa's hand. "I'm sorry you have to deal with that."

Janessa shrugged. "For the most part, I don't think about it, and people who know me from the clinic or church don't treat me any differently. But there are days when I just want to hide from the world, and the only way I can do that is to leave Serenity or stay inside."

When they'd been at school together, there had been quite a few other non-Caucasian students around. Janessa had been friends with some of them, but she certainly hadn't limited her friendships to people of one skin color or another. She had befriended anyone who seemed to need a friend.

Aria had definitely fit into the latter group. She hadn't known at first what to make of the friendly young woman who had been her roommate. Janessa hadn't seemed to suffer from the intense homesickness that Aria had. Thankfully, Janessa had been gentle in her interactions with her.

"Did you see who's on the drums?" Janessa said, drawing Aria from her thoughts.

Aria looked toward the front of the sanctuary where people were gathering at the mics and instruments. It only took a second for her gaze to find a familiar figure standing next to the drums with drumsticks in his hands as he spoke to a woman who had taken her place behind a keyboard.

"Gareth plays the drums?" she asked.

"Yep. We all play the piano, and most of us play a second instrument too. Gareth plays piano and drums. Jay plays the guitar, as does Wilder."

"That's amazing." Aria had never had the opportunity to learn to play an instrument, though she'd always wished she had.

Gareth spun one of the drumsticks in his hand before walking to the seat at the drums, which were positioned behind what looked like a plexiglass shield.

"Why is he sitting behind that?"

"It helps to muffle the sound, so that it doesn't overwhelm all the other instruments."

Gareth moved with such confidence without showing arrogance, and his friendly smiles seemed to be genuine, no matter who he was offering them to. With his good looks, he was the total package, and Aria found that to be very appealing.

The past few days had shown her that Janessa's older brother was also as nice as Janessa. He'd been endlessly patient with her questions at the basketball game, and then again later, at the family home, about learning to build a fire.

And now seeing him up on stage added a new dimension to the man she was coming to know. She might have promised not to comment on Gareth's broad shoulders, but Aria was finding plenty else to admire about the man.

There was nothing she could do about that admiration and attraction because he was her boss. Plus, there were a lot of other reasons why she shouldn't let herself get too close to him.

As much as she wanted to just be able to forget everything that had happened in the past year, Aria knew that wasn't possible. At most, she hoped that her recent past wouldn't impact her future, which it wouldn't as long as she didn't tell anyone about the events that had shaken her to her very core. Destroying her belief in herself and her confidence in her abilities.

With a glance at Gareth, the woman at the keyboard began to play. After a few moments, the guitars joined her, then finally Gareth set a light beat. No one sang, but Aria recognized the melody as a song they'd sung at the church she'd attended with her mom.

People were still finding their seats in the sanctuary, and conversations still flowed around her. The musicians' mics must have been turned off because they were talking to each other as they played. All except for Gareth.

Behind his shield, he looked out at the sanctuary. His dark gaze moved across the congregation, and when his gaze connected with hers, a smile quirked the corners of his mouth, even as he continued to keep time with the music.

Aria's heart skipped a beat, and she was sure her cheeks flushed in a way that she couldn't hide as she smiled back at him. His gaze moved on from her, and as she watched him smile at others, she realized that there was nothing special about the one he'd given her. She should have been relieved, but instead, she felt disappointed. Which was dumb. So dumb.

She didn't want a relationship. After her engagement had ended so badly, she'd decided that there were other things in her life she needed to prioritize. And that was still true.

When a man climbed the steps to the stage, the conversations faded away, leaving just the music coming from the instruments. Soon, even that ended.

"Welcome," the man said with a smile once the music had stopped.

Aria tried to focus on the man as he read through some announcements, but her gaze kept drifting to Gareth. His attention, however, stayed firmly on the man who was speaking. After he finished with the announcements, he prayed, then turned the service over to the worship team.

"Good morning," the woman on the keyboard said with a beaming smile. "I hope you're ready to worship God with us this morning."

The woman played as words filled the screens at the front of the sanctuary. Aria immediately recognized the song. She was glad that despite being in a completely new environment, she was at least familiar with the music.

Once again, she had a hard time keeping her eyes off Gareth. Even though he didn't have a mic like the other musicians had, he still sang along with them. He wasn't a flashy drummer like some she'd seen, but it was clear he knew how to balance his drumming with the rest of the instruments.

When the music portion of the service was over, Gareth filed off the stage with the rest of the team and sat down in one of the front pews on the opposite side of the church.

Aria tried to focus on the service, but she was struggling.

The last time she'd been in church had been with her mom, not long after she'd received her cancer diagnosis. She'd sat beside her mom, trying to find peace amidst the worry and fear that filled her heart.

The last thing she wanted to do was break down in tears. For some reason, she hadn't thought that attending church would trigger her grief. But apparently, it had.

She breathed a sigh of relief when the sermon was over. Even the prospect of watching Gareth drum for the final song wasn't enough to distract her from her grief.

"A bunch of us are going to go for dinner at a restaurant here in town," Janessa said when they stood in the foyer a short time later. "You're welcome to join us."

Aria considered it for one brief moment, then said, "I think I'd rather just go home, if you don't mind dropping me off."

Janessa smiled in understanding. "Yep. No problem."

When they'd been roommates, Janessa had always been more likely to socialize than Aria, so she probably wasn't surprised by Aria's decision. Though Aria thought Janessa would stick around to talk to people, she looped her arm through Aria's and guided her out of the church.

When they reached Janessa's car, Aria said, "I'm sorry—"

Janessa held up her hand. "Nope. No apologies. You owe me no apologies or explanations. You know that I'm fine with whatever you decide."

Relief swirled through Aria. "Thank you."

"You're welcome."

Janessa pressed the fob to unlock the car doors, and Aria walked around to the passenger side and got in. Maybe it would be wise for her to start driving herself around so that her friend didn't have to detour from her plans to accommodate Aria.

"Help yourself to anything in the kitchen for your lunch," Janessa said as she pulled to a stop in front of the house a few minutes later. "There is an evening service at the church at six-thirty if you're interested in attending."

"Okay." Aria pulled the handle to open the door. "I'll see you later."

"You can count on it," Janessa said with a laugh.

When Aria let herself into the house, the silence seemed to engulf her. For a moment, she wondered if she should have gone with her friend. But in her heart, she knew she'd made the right decision.

Her struggle with grief had wiped away any appetite she might have had, so rather than prepare herself something to eat, Aria wearily climbed the stairs to her bedroom.

After changing out of the clothes she'd worn to church into something more comfortable, Aria closed the curtains in her room and crawled under the thick comforter on her bed. Then, knowing that she was safe to grieve, she tucked her head down and let the pain over the loss of her mom rip through her in a way it hadn't in months.

The tears that fell soaked her pillow, her sobs draining her. Grief clouded her thoughts, and soon, exhaustion dragged her down into sleep.

When she woke sometime later, Aria fought a sense of disorientation. She lay there for a few minutes, trying to rub away the dull ache in her head. Finally, she reached out to grab her phone to see what time it was.

Just after three. She'd only been asleep for a couple of hours, and she was still tired. The sleep felt more like a reprieve from her emotions than a true rest.

Pushing up to sit on the edge of the bed, Aria felt a strong urge to get out of the house and get some fresh air to clear her head. She still had no appetite, so after washing her face and brushing her hair, she found her runners and a hoodie and left the house.

It seemed that neither Janessa nor Charli were home yet. As Aria stood on the porch, she pulled up the map app on her phone and tried to figure out where she should walk. Serenity wasn't a huge city, so it wasn't likely that she'd get too lost. And if she did, and the map didn't help, she knew that Janessa would come to find her.

Walking in the cold wasn't something she'd really thought through too well, Aria realized a couple of blocks later. She really should have pulled on a pair of sweatpants over her leggings.

Tucking her hands in her hoodie pockets, she bent her head and kept walking along the sidewalk. Once again, her thoughts were caught up in the past, making her wish she'd brought her earbuds so she could have listened to music or a podcast as a distraction.

"Hey there."

The words were spoken about the same time as a pair of hands and booted feet came into her view. Her heart slammed in her chest, and she stumbled back as she jerked her head up.

"Hey. It's just me," Gareth said, concern on his face as he held his hands out toward her.

Aria lifted a hand to her chest. "You scared me."

"Sorry about that." His gaze swept over her. "You looked like you were a little cold."

She balled her hand into a fist and shoved it back into the pocket of her jacket. "It is a little chilly."

"Were you going anywhere in particular?" he asked. "I could drop you off."

"No. I was just going for a walk."

Gareth had also changed out of the clothes he'd been wearing at church. His jeans and thick jacket looked much more appropriate for the chilly day than what she had on.

"Do you want a tour of the town?" Gareth asked with a smile. "I could give you one. It won't take too long."

"Uh..." The thought of being in the warmth of his car was definitely appealing. "Sure."

"C'mon." He nodded his head toward an SUV that was parked at the curb a little way in front of her.

She followed him and slid into the front seat when he opened the door for her. Warmth surrounded her, and she realized that he must have heated seats. The scent of a light masculine cologne lingered in the air. She recognized sandalwood as part of the cologne because it was a scent she really loved.

As Gareth settled behind the wheel, he picked up a pair of gloves from the console between them. "Here. Put these on until your hands warm up."

The gloves were large on her, but they were lined and felt wonderful on her cold fingers. "Thank you."

"I don't want to lecture you, but you really do need to make sure you're dressed warmly enough before you go walking outside."

"I know." Aria sighed as she hugged herself. "I wasn't thinking. I just needed some fresh air."

Gareth guided the SUV away from the curb. "Is everything okay? We missed you at lunch."

The care in his voice touched her. "I... Well, I'm more of an introvert, and I just needed a little time to myself."

"That's understandable. As long as that's all it is."

"Yeah. I'm fine." That wasn't entirely the truth, but Aria had a feeling that if she tried to give voice to everything she was feeling, she'd end up crying again. "Thanks for rescuing me when I didn't even know I needed it."

Gareth chuckled. "You're welcome."

"Am I keeping you from something?"

"Nope. I was heading home." He came to a stop at a stop sign and seemed to debate which way to go before turning left. "Let's start our tour on Main Street."

She'd seen bits of the town while driving around with Janessa, but Gareth was definitely giving her a more thorough tour.

"We've got lots of little shops in the town," he said. "But if you want to visit them, check their hours. The bigger stores keep the usual hours, but the smaller shops aren't open all the days and times the bigger ones are."

He drove down the street slowly, giving her time to appreciate the quaint look of the shops and restaurants. As he pointed out certain places, he filled her in on who owned them. He lifted his hand in greeting to people a couple of times, telling Aria who they were. She knew she'd never remember all the names that had been tossed her way over the past few days, but she supposed she had to start somewhere.

Aria found that she was enjoying her time with Gareth as much as she was enjoying the tour of the town. That wasn't a good thing, but she couldn't be bothered to care right then.

Gareth likely saw her as his little sister's friend and his newest employee, so as long as she kept her feelings to herself, she didn't think it would hurt to acknowledge the little crush she was developing on him.

Actually, Aria was relieved to realize that even after Tim had shattered her heart, it was still capable of feeling something, even if was just a crush. She wasn't sure if she could trust anyone with her heart just yet, however, so a crush was safe as long as it didn't grow into something more.

Or if it did, she couldn't let anyone know about it.

CHAPTER NINE

Gareth wasn't sure what to make of Aria. When he'd spotted her walking down the sidewalk, she had seemed... lost. But not lost as in lost in a new town. She'd been walking with her shoulders hunched and head bent. Her reaction when he approached her made it pretty clear that she'd been lost in thought, not taking in the sights Serenity had to offer.

When Janessa had showed up without her after church, Gareth had just assumed that she'd wanted a break from everything. He understood that. Even though he'd grown up in the town with his large family, there were times when he was over it and needed a break, too.

"So, did you know everyone in your high school?" Aria asked. "Like were the same kids there for every year?"

"There were a bunch of kids who were with me from kindergarten right through until graduation. But there were also plenty of kids who were only around for a few grades." He glanced over at her, noting how she had her gloved hands clenched in her lap. "What about you?"

"We moved around a lot, so I didn't graduate with people who I'd known for years."

"I think school was easiest for me," Gareth said. "I was the first Halverson of my generation to go through the school. The others had to deal with teachers who had already taught me and Kayleigh."

"Was that bad?"

Gareth chuckled. "Well, for the ones who studied hard and were well-behaved, it was fine. For others, like Wilder, it was a trial. He's more of a free-spirit and felt that studying certain subjects should be optional. He got compared to us older kids in a more negative way."

"Oh. Yeah, I can see how that wouldn't be much fun for him."

"Do you have brothers or sisters?" He was pretty sure that Janessa had said Aria was alone after her mom died, but he figured it was a good way to keep the conversation moving.

"Nope. I'm an only child."

"There were a few times when I was younger when I'd wished that was the case for me. Once I left for college, I didn't feel that way as much."

"How about now?"

"Living on my own makes dealing with the antics of my younger siblings a lot easier. Some—okay, mainly Wilder—still drive me bonkers at times."

"Why does he do that? He seems nice."

Gareth smiled. "Wilder *is* nice. He's super nice, in fact. But I struggle to understand how unfocused he can be. He's a drifter. During the winter, he works hard as a ski instructor to the rich, but once the snow melts, he's gone."

"Where does he go?"

"That's the question of the day," Gareth replied with a huff of laughter. "Wilder just heads off and sends a few texts or postcards as he wanders around the country. He's also jumped on a plane and flown halfway around the world."

"How do your parents feel about that?"

"Well, they aren't thrilled because they'd like him to settle on a career or something," Gareth said. "But since they're off travelling too, they can't very well come down too hard on him."

"I can't imagine living life without some sort of plan."

"You and me both," Gareth agreed. "I am happy to put down roots and stay put."

When Aria didn't respond to that, he glanced over to find her staring out the passenger window. His curiosity about what was on her mind was high, but he chose not to pry.

"There's not much else to see around town," he said as he pulled to a stop at a stop sign on a residential street. "Are you ready to head back to the house?"

She turned and gave him a quick smile. "Sure. Janessa might be wondering where I am."

"If she was too worried, she'd be blowing up your phone," Gareth said. "She might not even realize you're gone if she hasn't checked in on you yet. Janessa has always been one to give people their space."

"Yeah," Aria agreed. "I was always so grateful that she was respectful of my need for space when we were roommates. Not space from her. I'm talking about space from other students. She never tried to force me to go to parties or stuff like that. Though she did strongly encourage me at times."

Gareth smiled with affection at the thought of his younger sister. "Yep. That sounds like our Nessa."

It didn't take him long to reach the large house and pull to a stop at the curb in front of it. Gareth hadn't planned to get out of the car, but then the front door swung open to reveal Janessa. She walked out onto the porch and stood there with her arms crossed. Oh yeah, she was definitely wondering what was going on.

With a sigh, he turned off the SUV and got out. Aria closed her door, then walked beside him up the sidewalk to the house.

"Are you missing a friend?" Gareth asked as he reached the bottom of the steps.

She arched a brow at his question. "Perhaps."

"I went for a walk," Aria said. "Gareth spotted me, and when he realized I wasn't dressed for tromping around town in winter, he offered me a ride."

Janessa's gaze flicked between the two of them before she said, "I'm going to need to look through your wardrobe and help you dress more warmly if you're going to go for walks."

"Oh." Aria turned to Gareth as she pulled off the gloves and held them out to him. "Thanks for letting me use them."

His fingers brushed hers as he took them from her. "You're welcome." He tucked the gloves into the pocket of his jacket. "Well, I'd better head for home. See you later, sis."

"Oh yes, you will," Janessa agreed with an emphatic nod of her head. "Drive safe."

"Always," he tossed over his shoulder as he walked toward the car.

He gave a final wave before he drove away from the house. Janessa had definitely been suspicious of seeing the two of them together. He couldn't really blame her, but she had to know that he wasn't going to make any moves on her friend.

***

"Are you doing okay?" Janessa asked as she followed Aria up the stairs.

When she reached the landing, Aria turned to smile at her. "I'm fine. I just thought I'd take a walk. It was a lot colder than I expected."

"You're definitely not in Sacramento anymore. You need thicker pants," Janessa said, poking lightly at her hip. "Don't you have sweatpants?"

"I do." Aria continued on to her room. "I just wasn't thinking."

Janessa flopped down on the edge of her bed while Aria went to her dresser. "Was... uh... everything okay with Gareth?"

Aria glanced over her shoulder as she searched through a drawer for proof she had warmer clothes. "Yeah. Why?"

"I don't know. Just..."

Having found a pair of thick sweats, Aria turned around in time to catch Janessa's frown. "Do you have some sort of concern about me spending time with Gareth?"

"It's not that." Janessa blew out a breath as she shrugged. "It's just that Gareth is a real sweetie, and he doesn't know his own appeal sometimes. Though he can be intense at times, he's super nice, and that's been misinterpreted."

"Oh. You're afraid that I'll think he's interested in me when he's just being a decent human being?"

"Something like that. I just don't want you to get hurt. It happened so often with Kayleigh's friends that she finally told Gareth he wasn't allowed to talk to any of them ever again."

Aria laughed. "Seriously?"

"Seriously. Charli had it happen a couple of times too." Janessa paused, a thoughtful look on her face. "Gareth has an air of dependability that lots of women seem to be drawn to. Being a doctor has also made him a great listener. He focuses on a person, making them feel like what they're saying is valuable and who they are is super important to Gareth. The truth is, in that moment, they *are* important to him, but only as a fellow human being."

Aria understood that. She'd felt that way when she and Gareth had spoken. Even when he'd been explaining the game to her earlier, she'd felt like he really cared that she understood it. However, she didn't dare tell Janessa that she was already a bit too late with her warning.

"He's not perfect, I'm sure," Aria said. "So, what are his faults?"

Janessa relaxed back on her hands. "He can have endless amounts of patience, unless he thinks someone isn't doing what they're supposed to. Laziness aggravates him, and he can't tolerate anyone who tries to make excuses for their own bad judgment or who blames other people for their mistakes. He doesn't get mad often, but when he does, it takes him ages to calm down, and he can hold a grudge forever. Jay is the one who can push his buttons regularly."

"Why is that?"

"I think it's because before we came to live with the Halversons, Jay was used to being the big brother. He was the man of the house since our dad wasn't around. He helped my mom out a lot, especially after she got sick." Janessa sat forward, lifting her legs to cross them and resting her elbows on her knees. "We were both grieving so hard back then. Gareth tried to step into the role of big brother, and Jay just wasn't having it. So yeah, Jay's never really accepted Gareth as his older brother. As his brother, sure, just not his big brother."

"I suppose it doesn't help that they both have fairly important roles at the clinic."

"Yep. They each think that their thoughts on how the clinic should be run are most important. We can all see that they're both right, but they struggle to see that admitting that doesn't mean capitulating. They need each other, you know? The clinic wouldn't be operational if not for Gareth, but it wouldn't run smoothly without Jay."

Aria could see how that might be an issue.

"The difference between Jay and Gareth when it comes to women is that Jay is aware of the attraction he holds. He can be friendly and flirty on purpose. You'll see." Janessa frowned. "Jay likes the attention, so you need to be careful of him, too."

"Any warnings for Wilder?" Aria asked.

Janessa's brows lifted, and she straightened. "Are you interested in Wilder?"

"No. Just wondered if you had a warning for all your brothers."

Janessa grinned. "Not all of them. Also, just know that Jackson is like Jay. Wade is a bit more like Gareth."

"Is there a shortage of single women around here?"

"Not really. Wade's actually been married, but his wife divorced him and left town, taking their daughter with her."

"Whoa." Aria frowned. "That must have been hard on him."

Janessa nodded. "It just about broke him."

"Does he get to see his daughter?"

"Yep. She's almost fourteen now, and she usually spends summers here."

"Fourteen?"

"Dakota got pregnant in their senior year, and they got married not long after graduation. But then she decided she didn't want to be stuck in Serenity Point, and apparently didn't want to be married either. Wade offered to leave Serenity with her, but she wasn't interested. She's since remarried and has a couple more kids."

Aria dropped the sweats she was holding onto the bed next to Janessa. "Will these do?"

Janessa laid her hand on the piece of clothing. "Yep. Just check the temperature before you head out for a walk, and if it's close to freezing, layer up."

"That's what Gareth said too."

"Well, Dr. Gareth will definitely want you to avoid frostbite."

Aria sighed. "It was such a stupid thing to go out walking when it's this cold."

"Not stupid at all, especially considering where you used to live. You just need to learn to dress appropriately."

"Now that I've gotten that lecture from you and Gareth, I don't think I'll step out of the house without doing a layer check."

Janessa bounced up off the bed and brushed her hands together. "My work here is now done." She headed for the door before turning to say, "If you want to go to the service tonight, I usually leave around six. Or I can give you directions if you'd prefer to take your own car."

Aria still wasn't sure if she would go or not, so she just said, "Okay."

Janessa pulled the door closed as she left the room. Aria sank down onto the bed and let out a long sigh. A crush wasn't the same thing as falling in love, was it? Because if it was the same thing, Janessa's warning was coming a bit too late.

As she thought back to her feelings for Tim, Aria frowned. She tried to remember how she'd felt during their first few dates, but everything was so overshadowed by the way he'd ended their engagement. When she thought of him now, there was definitely no positive emotion to reflect on.

Still, she'd take Janessa's words to heart and not let the little crush she had on Gareth turn into anything more.

Deciding that she'd go with Janessa to church after all, Aria took a quick shower, then changed into a pair of jeans and a sweater.

Charli and Layla were in the kitchen with Janessa when Aria showed up. The little girl sat at the island counter with a sandwich on a plate in front of her. The two women were building sandwiches of their own from an assortment of food on the counter.

"Hey there," Janessa said when she spotted her. "Want to make yourself a sandwich?"

"We usually go for light suppers on Sundays," Charli said as she cut through her sandwich, then dumped a pile of chips on her plate.

"Sounds good."

When Charli carried her plate over to sit beside her daughter, Aria took her place. There were plenty of options, and she was hungry, so it didn't take her long to put together a sandwich for herself.

Janessa sat down on another of the barstools at the counter. "Did you grab anything for lunch?"

Aria knew she asked because when they'd been roommates, Aria had often skipped meals. It hadn't been because she was trying to lose weight. Usually, she just had other things on her mind and forgot to eat.

More recently, however, her grief and anxiety had been robbing her of her appetite. She just wasn't hungry a lot of the time.

"No." She didn't bother to give a reason, but she put enough stuff on her sandwich to hopefully keep Janessa from lecturing her.

Once she had her sandwich ready, she stayed standing instead of taking a seat beside Janessa. Lifting half of the sandwich, Aria took a bite.

"Skylar said that she's working with the kids tonight," Layla said. "It's gonna be so fun!"

Charli chuckled. "Yep. Skylar's good at creating fun for you guys."

"The other kids are jealous," Layla announced.

"Why?" Janessa asked.

"They wish Skylar was *their* aunt, but she's only mine."

"You're going to have to share her someday," Charli told her. "I doubt you'll be the only niece for the rest of your life."

Layla wrinkled her nose. "More babies?"

"That's how people start out," Charli reminded her.

"Hmmm." Layla seemed to consider her words. "As long as they're happy babies, that's okay."

"I'm sure they'll be happy babies." Janessa chuckled. "Most of the time."

"I was a happy baby," Layla said. "Right, Mommy?"

"Sure." Charli smiled at Janessa. "Most of the time."

Aria had known that Janessa came from a large family, but she'd only seen her on her own at school. Getting a look at her life through the interactions with her various siblings was eye-opening and fun.

It made her wish that her mom had had a couple more kids, though Aria realized that it would have been a challenge since she hadn't had a steady boyfriend. And honestly, her mom had struggled to be a single mom to one child. Having two or three in her situation would have been nearly impossible for her to handle.

Having a family around to support her mom might have made a world of difference. Charli and Layla were proof of that.

"Well, just make sure you obey Skylar," Charli said. "You need to set a good example for the other kids there."

Layla nodded, her ponytail dancing with the movement. "I will. Promise."

Once they were finished eating, Aria helped clean up, then they left for the church. Charli took her own car with Layla, while Aria once again went with Janessa. She probably should have taken her own vehicle, but Janessa had said that she had no plans to go anywhere after the service.

There was a more relaxed atmosphere at the evening service, and there were also fewer people. That meant that Janessa ushered her a little closer to the front.

Once she'd sat down, Aria glanced around at the people already there. Her gaze immediately landed on Gareth, where he stood talking with a handful of people. His hands were in the pockets of his jeans, and he wore a sweatshirt, unlike the dressier slacks and button-down shirt he'd had on for the morning service.

As if sensing her attention on him, Gareth looked over in their direction. A smile quirked the corners of his mouth, and he gave her a nod before turning his attention back to the people he was speaking with.

Aria's cheeks felt like they were on fire as she dragged her gaze from him, not wanting Janessa to catch her watching Gareth after their little conversation earlier. Thankfully, Janessa was speaking to someone who had stopped beside her at the end of their row and didn't seem to notice what was going on with Aria.

Rubbing her damp palms against her jeans, Aria gave herself a lecture. There was no way she could deal with Gareth at work if she blushed anytime he turned his attention on her. This job—this life—was too important for her to mess up.

He's not for me. He's not for me.

She continued repeating the phrase as she kept her gaze away from the man, anxiously waiting for the service to start and distract her from her thoughts about Gareth.

CHAPTER TEN

Gareth paused in the hallway just behind the receptionist desk, shoving his hands into the pockets of his white coat as he listened to Aria speak to a patient.

"Will this shot hurt?" the boy asked. "I don't like shots that hurt."

"Well, Colby, sometimes shots do hurt, but only for the tiniest moment of time. I bet Doctor Gareth is super good at giving shots, and he'll make sure it doesn't hurt you very much at all."

"I like Doctor Gareth, but I don't like shots," Colby repeated.

"Most people don't," Aria told him.

"Have you had shots?"

"I have."

"Did Doctor Gareth give them to you?"

"Nope. I had a different doctor when I was your age."

"And did the shots hurt you?"

"Only a little bit, but then I got a lollipop afterwards."

"Oooooh," Colby crowed. "I love lollipops. I think I got one last time I got a shot."

Gareth grinned. Lollipops for the win.

"We have a bunch of flavors, so once you've had your shot, you can come choose one." Aria pointed to a basket on her desk.

"Okay. Let's get this done!" Colby held his little hand up, and Aria gave it a light smack.

Turning in her chair, Aria's gaze landed on Gareth, and she startled. "Sorry. Didn't see you there."

"That's fine. I hear that I'm giving a shot to a brave little guy this morning." He grinned at Colby, then looked up at his mother. "Nice to see you again, Joce."

"You, too." She gave him a friendly smile with no sign of flirtation, which Gareth really appreciated. Even though she was a single mom, she'd never shown a bit of interest in him.

"Let's get this done," Gareth said. "So you can get your lollipop."

Colby waved at Aria. "I'll be back." As the three of them walked down the hallway, the little boy said, "She's so nice, and she's pretty like you, Momma."

"Only six and already he's appreciating the ladies," Jocelyn said with a shake of her head.

Gareth chuckled as he stopped at the door to the exam room and gestured for them to precede him inside. "Thankfully, he's got you to teach him to treat them right."

"Oh, most definitely," Jocelyn said with a nod.

Colby chatted throughout most of the appointment, sharing about his love for dinosaurs. They traded a bit of dino trivia since Gareth had also gone through a phase when he'd been fascinated by the animals.

The shot went without incident, and soon the boy was running down the hallway in search of his lollipop. Gareth and Jocelyn followed a bit more sedately.

When they reached the receptionist desk, they found Colby and Aria in the middle of an intense discussion about which flavor was the best. Colby was debating between strawberry—his favorite fruit—or green, which was his favorite color.

"You're not going to like the green one," Jocelyn said. "It's lime."

Colby looked up at her and wrinkled his nose. "But Aria said it's her favorite."

Gareth struggled not to laugh again. Yep. Only six and wanting to impress the ladies. It was kind of sweet to see, especially when a light flush crept up Aria's cheeks.

"I like strawberry too," Aria said. "I think you should go for that one."

"Okay. Strawberry, please."

She held the red lollipop out to him. "There you go. Enjoy."

"Thank you," Colby said, flashing her a big grin. "You're the best."

"Uh... well, you're welcome, and thank you for the compliment. You're the best too."

Colby turned to his mom, his eyes wide. "She thinks I'm the best too, Momma."

Jocelyn reached out and ruffled her son's hair. "That's because you are."

The happy little boy stuck the lollipop into his mouth, then took his mom's hand as she led him to the door. He turned back to wave at Aria one last time before leaving the building.

"You're just sweeping up hearts left and right," Gareth said with a laugh.

She shot him a look before turning back to the computer. "I'm a big hit with the under seven crowd, apparently. It's probably got a lot to do with the lollipops."

"Possibly." Gareth walked to the desk and leaned over to grab the basket of candy.

She looked up at him as he searched through the lollipop for his favorite flavor. "You're going to need to pick up more strawberry and grape ones. They're the ones most kids go for."

"And doctors too, I see," she said when he handed the basket back to her.

"I can't deny it." He grinned at her as he held up the lollipop he'd chosen. "Grape ones are my favorite, so it's possible I'm the reason there aren't many left."

"I'll keep that in mind." Aria tucked the basket under the ledge of the desk, where it was out of sight.

Before he could respond, a patient came in the front door and approached Aria. Not wanting to distract her from her job, Gareth turned and headed back down the hallway.

"What were you doing up at the front?" Nora asked when she spotted him.

He thought about telling her it was none of her business, but Gareth wasn't in the mood to deal with the escalation that would follow. She'd think he was being defensive and hiding something. "I was walking a patient out."

"You don't usually do that."

Gareth couldn't contain his irritation. "Sure I do. Plus this was a six-year-old little boy who just had a shot."

"Or maybe it was because of his mother," she said.

He gave a frustrated huff and turned away from her to go into his office until Janessa let him know his next patient was there. Nora really needed to figure out who she wanted to be jealous of.

The week had been going fairly well, and as long as he didn't spend any time around Aria or any other single woman, Nora was fine. However, it was stressing him out. He shouldn't need to avoid interacting with anyone just to keep Nora happy. That was particularly true when it involved employees at the clinic or the patients that he treated.

It irritated Gareth enough right then that he spun on his heel and left his office for Jay's. He knocked on the door frame, then stepped into the room when Jay looked up.

The man reclined back in his chair, interlacing his hands across his stomach. "What's up?"

Gareth closed the door, then approached the chair across from Jay. He sat down and leaned forward, resting his elbows on his thighs. Jay lifted an eyebrow.

"We need to find another female doctor," he said. "It's getting ridiculous. I can't even go near the front without her demanding why I'm up there."

Surprisingly enough, Jay nodded. Gareth had anticipated Jay joking about it, but perhaps he realized it wasn't beneficial to the clinic to have someone with that sort of attitude working there.

"I've been trying, bro. I'm just not getting much interest." Jay sat forward. "Maybe you need to reach out to more of your connections to see if someone has a suggestion."

Gareth rubbed his hand across the back of his neck. "Okay. I'll make some calls."

"I think we're getting desperate here," Jay said. "We need to explore more avenues."

"I agree," Gareth told him. "I just don't understand why she's acting like this."

"That makes two of us," Jay said. "I mean, you're not *that* great a catch."

Gareth gave a huff of laughter. "Shut up. You're just jealous that she's not wanting your attention."

Jay held up his hands. "No way. She's all yours."

"I'm glad she's been a good doctor, but personally, I just don't like her." Gareth frowned. "I will not get into a relationship with her just so I'm married to a doctor. That's what worked for Mom and Dad, but I doubt they'd want me to marry for that reason."

"That's true. They haven't hidden their thoughts on who we should pursue for a relationship. None of their advice was based on the job a person had."

"I think they'll support us letting Nora go as long as we have someone to replace her," Gareth said. "I'm going to talk with them about the issues we've been dealing with."

Jay took on a surprisingly thoughtful expression. "If it looks like we've found some viable candidates, I think you need to give Nora one more chance."

"What?" Gareth frowned at him. "Why? I've already told her several times to back off."

"I get that, but perhaps if she thinks her job here is truly at risk, she'll smarten up."

"But do you really want her to stay on?" Gareth asked. "Knowing that she could slip back into this jealous, possessive attitude at a moment's notice? None of us want to have to walk on eggshells around her. Already I can see that Aria is wary of her."

Jay nodded. "But the unfortunate thing is that good receptionists are probably easier to come by than good female doctors who want to move to a small town. And like you've said, she does a great job with the patients."

Anger burned through Gareth at Jay's dismissal of Aria. "So you're saying that we shouldn't care how Aria feels? That because she's not a doctor, she isn't entitled to a good work environment here?"

"You know that's not what I'm saying," Jay said. "I don't want her to get pushed to the point where she quits. But when push comes to shove, I have to think about the clinic. Nora's departure without a replacement would certainly affect the clinic more negatively than Aria's would."

Gareth knew Jay was right, but he didn't want to think about Aria leaving the clinic. In the short time she'd been there, he could see that Janessa had been right about her fitting in. Well, except in relation to Nora.

"You're going to be the one to tell Janessa that her friend is expendable," Gareth said as he got to his feet. "I'm sure she'll appreciate your logic."

With that, he opened the door and left Jay's office before they got into an even more heated argument. Janessa spotted him in the hallway and pointed to one of the exam rooms to let him know his next patient was ready.

He gave her a nod before slipping into his office, wanting a moment to settle down so he wouldn't be distracted while dealing with a patient.

Standing in front of the window that gave him a view of the distant mountains, Gareth took a deep breath. He did that a couple of times while thinking of the men's group that evening. Spending time with guys who were willing to support and uplift each other was always a blessing, and he knew that they would continue to pray with him about the situation.

When he finally entered the exam room, he felt calmer and more in control. He knew he and Jay would revisit the subject of Nora a few more times before the situation was resolved. But for that day, it was done.

Gareth walked his last patient to the front door, then stood talking with the elderly gentleman for a few minutes before he left. Turning away from the door, he spotted Aria watching him.

"Everything go okay today?" he asked as he approached the desk.

"I think so." Her brows pulled together for a moment. "At least no one has had any complaints."

"No one?"

Her frowned deepened. "Well, none of the *patients* have mentioned any complaints to me."

"That, I'll believe."

"Gareth." Nora's voice floated down the hallway, and a moment later, the woman appeared. "Are you interested in grabbing dinner? I read an interesting paper in a medical journal that I'd love to discuss with you."

"Sorry." Gareth shook his head. "Thursday night is my men's group."

"I'm sure they could get along without you for one night," she protested as she crossed her arms. "I don't know why you need to get together *every* week."

"Oh, I'm quite sure that they *could* get along without me one night. However, I go because I *want* to be there, not because I *have* to be there. If I needed to miss a night, none of the guys would give me grief."

"So miss this one," she said. "It's important that we have these types of discussions."

"If I want to have medical discussions, I have several people I talk to. This evening, however, I'm more interested in talking about God. So, I'm sorry. You're going to have to find someone else to discuss that paper with."

Nora turned her attention to Aria, scowling at her. "Why are you sitting there listening to a personal conversation?"

Gareth wanted to step in, but he also wanted to make sure that Aria could stand up for herself when he or Janessa weren't around. When she shot him a slightly panicked look, he gave her a small nod that he hoped would encourage her to respond to Nora.

"Well," Aria began. "I was sitting at my desk when you came up here to have this conversation with Gareth. Perhaps if you didn't want me to hear it, you should have waited to talk to him in his office."

The ironic thing was that he was sure that Nora had, in fact, wanted Aria to hear it. She'd probably assumed that Gareth would agree to have dinner with her, especially if she framed it as a *medical discussion.* Clearly, she hadn't been pleased with Aria hearing Gareth decline her invitation.

"You need to be more respectful."

"I'm not being disrespectful," Aria said softly. "You asked me a question, and I gave you an answer, along with a suggestion on how to make sure I don't hear any future personal conversations you have with people in the clinic. Believe me, I have no interest in your personal life."

It surprised Gareth when, instead of snapping at Aria, Nora spun around and walked away from them.

"You never need to be afraid to stand up for yourself," he said. "We all know that Nora can have her difficult moments, and we've had to learn to just calmly respond to her. Usually, it doesn't escalate too much."

"I don't want to upset her."

"I appreciate that, but we don't believe in running a place where one person can make another feel bad or attacked. Let me, Janessa, or Jay know if things are occurring with Nora when we're not around to witness them."

Aria's gaze dropped for a moment before she looked back up at him. "Okay."

Gareth felt a little sick at the thought that there had been events happening, even though he'd suspected that already. She might not have said anything specific, but her reaction told him all he needed to know.

"Talk to Janessa," he said, pointing a finger at her. "If you don't feel comfortable with Jay or I, at least talk to her."

"I will."

"Good." Gareth smiled. "Now go have a nice evening. I'll see you tomorrow."

She smiled back at him. "Yep. See you tomorrow."

At his house a few hours later, Gareth shared the situation with the small group of men who'd gathered for their time of Bible study and prayer.

"This isn't the first time you've dealt with Nora's attitude," Jackson said, being serious for once. "But you hadn't mentioned anything specific about it for a couple of months."

"Aria's presence has stirred it all up again." Gareth leaned back in his chair, legs stretched out and crossed at his ankles. He pressed his chin to his chest, staring at the floor. "And though Aria hasn't said anything to me, I know it's making her uneasy to be around Nora. The woman isn't hiding her dislike for Aria, and she keeps trying to trip her up by demanding Aria do things that Janessa hasn't trained her to do yet."

"That's not good," one of the other men there said with a frown. "Janessa is putting up with this?"

"Not if she catches it happening. But Nora's not dumb. She knows better than to tangle with Janessa."

"Does that mean that Aria isn't telling Janessa what's happening?" Wade asked.

"I'm not sure," Gareth confessed. "I haven't asked Janessa, but I suppose I should. Just so she's aware, in case Aria hasn't said anything to her."

"It's likely that Aria feels dispensable, especially if she's still in training," another man pointed out. "I know that's how I'd feel. Nora has a lot more clout being a doctor in the clinic."

"But that's the thing. She really doesn't. Nora's an employee too. And she was on thin ice even before Aria arrived. If Janessa had her way, Nora would have packed her bags a long time ago."

Jackson laughed. "Janessa is a firecracker. I hope you give her the privilege of firing Nora if it comes to that, since Nora has managed to make her life miserable, too."

Gareth would happily give Janessa that job, except that he doubted that Nora would leave if that directive came from *just a nurse*, as she liked to refer to Janessa. But in their clinic, there was no room for "just a" anybody. Everyone had an important role to play and without each of them, the clinic would function below par. When they hadn't had a receptionist, things had definitely limped along with Janessa trying to do two jobs.

"I'd sure appreciate your prayers that we can resolve this situation," Gareth said. "The most important thing we need right now is another qualified female doctor. Mom would probably fill in if we really needed her to, but I don't think that's her preference since she and Dad are gearing up to leave for Haiti."

The men took time right then to pray about the situation, leaving Gareth confident that it would work out in God's time and in His way.

CHAPTER ELEVEN

Aria breathed a sigh of relief when they locked the doors at the end of the day on Friday. It had been a good week, but not without a few bumps. Janessa had made it clear that she was doing well with her training, which Aria appreciated. It made up for the moments when Nora criticized her.

It wasn't that Aria thought she was doing the job perfectly. She was still making a mistake or two most days, but at least none of them were life-threatening. Janessa had said that there was no mistake that couldn't be fixed. Aria knew that wasn't true in life, but when it came to her current job, she supposed it was.

"Are you two coming to the game tonight?" Gareth asked from the hallway as they were in the stockroom finishing up.

Janessa had let her know earlier that she and Gareth would be working at the free clinic the next day. As part of the services they offered at the clinic, they gave out bags of essentials for patients who needed them. The bags included things like toothpaste, deodorant, and shampoo and soap for kids.

"I plan to go," Janessa said, then glanced at Aria. "But I'm not sure if Aria has decided yet."

When Janessa had asked her about it the previous night, Aria hadn't been sure how she'd feel at the end of the week. But honestly, for a few different reasons, the idea of going was irresistible. "I think I'd like to go. I enjoyed it so much the last time."

"It's out of town this weekend," Gareth said.

"Are you offering to give us a ride?" Janessa asked with a big smile.

Gareth chuckled. "Sure. But if I'm playing chauffeur, you need to feed me."

"I agree to that deal," Janessa said as she held her hand out.

With a grin, Gareth took it and gave it an exaggerated shake. "I'll be at the house by five-thirty."

"Thankfully, Charli said she'd cook tonight since she knew that waiting for us to get home and cook, would be too late."

"Yeah. We're going to have to eat quickly," Gareth said. "We need to leave by six-fifteen if we're going to make it before seven."

Janessa wrinkled her nose. "I really prefer the home games."

"Ah, but it's such fun to beat a team on their home turf. Some of them act so tough until our team arrives."

Aria wondered what it might have been like to attend games as a teenager. But then she remembered that if she had gone to games back then, she would have been sitting by herself.

"Are Jackson and Wade going?"

"Not this time," Gareth said as they walked toward the back of the building. "Wade picked up a side job and Jackson is going to give him a hand with it."

"They didn't need you too?" Janessa asked as she led them into the staff room.

"No. Plus, they know it's important that I go to Cole's games."

Of all the things that Aria had anticipated gaining from the move to Serenity Point, the list hadn't included a family who'd welcome her into their midst socially. She'd figured she'd just hang out with Janessa, since they'd been friends for so long.

But what she'd experienced since arriving went well beyond spending time with Janessa. And she was grateful because it helped her put what had happened in Sacramento behind her. It was even helping her with her grief, keeping her too busy during the day to dwell on her loss. The grief was always at its strongest at night, but that was to be expected.

As they left the clinic, Gareth headed for his car, while Aria followed Janessa to hers.

"Are you sure you're up to going to another game?" Janessa asked as she drove out of the small parking lot behind the clinic. "I don't want you to feel you have to attend just because the rest of us go. You might enjoy some peace and quiet."

Maybe it would get to that point eventually, but Aria didn't feel that way yet. "I'm fine, and I really enjoyed the game last week."

"I'm going to give you a special shirt to wear then."

"A shirt?"

"Yep. When we go to another school for a game, we like to show which team we're there to support. And just wait until you see Layla."

Aria wasn't sure what she meant by that, but she didn't have to wonder for long. No sooner had they walked in the front door, when the little girl came running to greet them.

She was decked out like a mini cheerleader, sporting an outfit that was similar to her aunt's, though she appeared to be wearing leggings underneath her pleated skirt. Her hair was pulled back in a high ponytail with long curls and ribbons that matched the outfit she wore.

"Don't I look beautiful?" she asked as she spun in a circle.

"You do!" Janessa grabbed her hand and kept spinning her around. "I wish I had an outfit like yours."

"You could ask Skylar to borrow one of hers," Layla said with a big grin. "Then we'd be twins... or... What do you call three people dressed the same?"

"Triplets?" Janessa supplied.

"Yep. We could be triplets!"

"Well, I'm not sure I could fit one of Skylar's uniforms, so I'll just have to wear a T-shirt instead."

They took off their winter wear, then went to the kitchen. Before long, the doorbell rang, and Janessa went to answer it. She returned a minute later with Gareth following her. He'd changed into a pair of jeans and a maroon shirt that sported the team name in gold letters, along with the team logo.

"Uncle Gareth!" Layla ran to him and jumped.

Clearly, the man had been expecting the move because he plucked her out of the air and spun her around. "Layla!"

"We'd better get changed," Janessa said to Aria. "Come to my room, and I'll give you a T-shirt to wear. Unless you'd rather not."

"Oh, no. I definitely want it."

Janessa grinned. "Great!"

Upstairs in Janessa's room, her friend went to her dresser and pulled out a folded T-shirt in the same color as the one Gareth was wearing, then handed it to her.

"Thanks," Aria said. "I'll go get changed now."

In her room, Aria slipped out of the black slacks and sweater she'd worn that day, then pulled on a pair of jeans and the T-shirt Janessa had given her. It was a bit long, so she gathered the hem and tied a knot in it in front of her right hip bone. She ran a brush through her hair, then put on a fresh layer of lipstick.

She was excited about going to another game, but she couldn't deny that a big draw was being able to spend the evening with Gareth. Obviously they weren't going to be alone, and that was fine. She was just looking forward to not having to guard her every word or action around him for fear of Nora seeing or hearing something that annoyed her.

Downstairs, Charli and Gareth were setting the food on the table, while Layla twirled around them in her cheerleading outfit. Janessa showed up not long after Aria.

"Let's eat," Charli said, then helped Layla get settled in her chair.

Once they were all seated, Charli said a prayer for the food. The conversation as they ate focused on the upcoming game and also on other family members, some of whom Aria hadn't met yet. She didn't have much to contribute to the chatter, so she just focused on eating since she knew they would need to leave fairly soon.

"Are you riding with us?" Gareth asked Charli as they cleaned up the meal a short time later.

"Do you mind? We'll have to put Layla's car seat in your car."

"You know that's not a problem. I think there will still be enough room for two adults, even with her in the seat."

"Then I guess I'm sitting up front with you," Charli said with a laugh.

Gareth took Charli's car keys, and while the women finished cleaning up, he went to grab the car seat and put it in his car. Once the food was all put away, Aria pulled on her jacket and boots.

Aria was still adjusting to the cold, but it wasn't too bad as long as she dressed correctly, and it wasn't windy. She hadn't ventured out for a walk again after she'd stupidly gone out underdressed for the weather that Sunday afternoon.

Thankfully, when they piled into Gareth's car a few minutes later, it was already warmed up.

"Everyone comfy?" Gareth asked, his gaze meeting Aria's in the rearview mirror since she was sitting directly behind him.

"I'm good," she said.

The other three also confirmed that they were ready to go. Aria relaxed back in her seat, staring out the side window as conversation swirled around her. She would have thought that since she didn't understand much of what they were talking about, she'd feel like an intruder, but no one made her feel that way.

"So are you excited about the game tonight, Aria?" Charli asked.

Aria turned from the window to see that Charli had angled herself to look back at her. "I am. I think it will be even more fun this time, since I have a better grasp of the rules of the game."

"If you keep coming to the games, you'll be hooked," Charli said with a laugh. "We're hoping that the team makes it to state championships once again. They made it last year."

"Jay has been the main reason the team has made it to state," Gareth said. "Both as a player and a coach. He has an uncanny perception of the game and its players."

"He played all through college," Janessa said, leaning forward to look past Layla's seat. "And there was talk of him playing professionally."

"Really? What happened?"

"He was injured his senior year, and though he probably could have still gone on to play, he decided to come home."

Aria thought of the man she saw every day at work and had no problem imagining him playing professionally. "Is he the official coach for the team?"

"No," Gareth said. "But the coach now is the same one who coached Jay when he was in high school. He's been more than happy to have Jay work alongside him with the team. Actually, I'm pretty sure that Jay does more of the work with this team than Coach does. He's more focused on the football team."

"Coach is getting up in years," Charli said. "I think he relies on Jay a lot."

"Would Jay ever want to be the official coach of the team?"

"I'm not sure," Gareth said. "I hope he doesn't decide to give up his work at the clinic. We'd be lost without him. Just don't tell him I said that."

That got laughter from them all.

"Were you in any sports in high school?" Charli asked.

"No. I knew that if I wanted to go to college, I was going to need scholarships, so I was very focused on my classes. I also volunteered a lot. There wasn't much time left for sports, even if I'd been so inclined."

"Being focused on school isn't a bad thing," Gareth said. "I'm sure that Mom and Dad wish Cole was a little *more* focused on school and a little *less* on basketball."

"Yeah, but unlike Jay, Cole's really gunning to play professional basketball," Janessa said.

"If he continues on his current trajectory, I'd say he's got a shot at it," Gareth said. "I guess only time will tell, but you know Mom and Dad want him to have a back-up plan."

"But Cole thinks he's invincible," Charli said. "Even knowing what Jay went through, he seems to think an injury won't happen to him."

When they arrived at the high school where the game was taking place, Gareth pulled the SUV to a stop in front of a set of double doors.

"Save me a spot," he said as the women piled out of the vehicle and helped an excited Layla from her booster seat.

Aria nodded, even though he hadn't been speaking to her specifically. It would probably be better if someone else saved a spot for Gareth. She didn't need to be in that close of contact with him.

Inside the warmth of the building, she and Janessa followed Charli and a skipping Layla toward where the gym was located. They'd clearly been there before because there was no hesitation as they walked.

"Mom said they're already here and have seats for us," Janessa said as she looked at her phone.

The noise level steadily increased as they walked, letting Aria know they were definitely going in the right direction. When they finally stepped into the gym, Charli and Janessa led them off to the side as they looked around.

"There they are," Janessa said, pointing to a section of the bleachers a little over halfway down.

After waiting for a group of people to pass them, they made their way along the gym floor in front of the bleachers, dodging around people walking or standing in their way. When they reached their destination, Charli led them up the bleacher steps with Layla. Janessa went next, and Aria followed her.

It seemed like a repeat of the previous game, with Janessa's parents seated behind them. They'd laid jackets on the bleachers to save sections of the seats. Layla was excitedly showing off her outfit to her grandparents, then she waved frantically as Skylar and her fellow cheerleaders showed up on the gym floor in front of the bleachers.

Skylar came up the steps and scooted into the row in front of them so that she could reach Layla. "Want to come down with me for a few minutes?"

"Yes!" She turned to Charli. "Can I, Mommy?"

"Sure. But you listen to Skylar, okay?"

"Okay!"

Skylar helped Layla over to the steps, then walked with her down to where the other cheerleaders were grouped together, preparing for their part of the game.

As Aria watched, Gareth appeared and stopped to give Skylar a hug and talked to her for a minute. The other cheerleaders clustered around the pair and Layla, smiling broadly at Gareth. Something he said made them all laugh, and Aria saw clearly what Janessa had referred to.

Dragging her gaze from Gareth, Aria looked around the gym that was set up pretty much the same as the one at Serenity's high school, though it wasn't as full. Still, it was good to see that a good number of people had turned out for the game.

When Gareth climbed the steps to where they sat, he didn't even hesitate before sitting down beside her. He gave Aria a quick smile before turning to speak with his dad. Her heart was beating fast, and she was sure that her cheeks were on fire.

How was it that her crush was starting to not feel quite so crush-like anymore?

That was a question to be contemplated at another time when Gareth wasn't sitting right next to her.

It wasn't too long before Wilder and Kayleigh showed up. Wilder smiled at Aria as he sat down on Gareth's other side. Kayleigh made her way along the row in front of them, then took Charli's hand to help herself up to sit beside her.

Janessa leaned closer to Aria. "Ready for a wild night?"

"Is Wilder performing?" she asked. After a beat, Janessa grinned, and they both laughed.

Music began to play in the gym, and the cheerleaders of both teams started to hype up the crowd. By the time the teams were introduced, those seated in the bleachers were cheering and clapping loudly. Aria immediately spotted Cole amongst the players, while Jay stood with an older man beside a bench across the gym from the bleachers.

Every seat around them was filled, mostly by people wearing the same maroon and gold T-shirts that they had all worn. When Skylar sent Layla back up to them, the little girl chose to sit with Gareth. She was absolutely glowing with excitement. Aria was pretty sure that she was looking at a future cheerleader for the school.

It was a good thing that Gareth didn't have to explain things to her like he had the previous week, because she wasn't sure she would have been able to hear him. The previous week's team might have been their biggest rival in terms of skill, but this smaller crowd was definitely a rival for noise.

Gareth and his siblings were even more engaged in this game, no doubt egged on by the spectators around them. Aria had noticed one thing about the Halversons that set them apart from many of the fans and that was that they never booed the refs or other players. She never heard any of them shout anything negative. They simply cheered loudly for their team without running their opponents down.

There were a few fans on both sides that did, however. It made her glad to be a part of a group that didn't do that. The players were just teens, and no matter which side they were on, they should only be offered encouragement. Even though she'd never been interested in sports herself, she'd heard about how far some parents of players could take things, creating tension and hurt.

Jay also appeared to keep a pretty level head, even as he was yelling out instructions to the players. At times, he and Gareth seemed to yell the same thing, making Aria wonder if they were aware of what they were doing.

When halftime came, each cheerleading team put on a performance, then people got up and milled around. When Janessa stood up, so did Aria.

"Do you need to get by?" Aria asked.

"No. I just need to stand up for a moment. I don't have enough padding in my behind to sit on these bleachers without a break."

"You could always bring a pillow," Gareth said as he stood up as well. He stretched his arms above his head and leaned side to side, just barely missing Aria's head with his elbow.

"Looks like you need a pillow too, old man," Janessa said.

"We should get one of those body pillows," Aria suggested. "Then we could share."

"Or you could just bring seats like we do," Mr. Halverson said from behind them.

Aria and Janessa turned around, and Mr. Halverson got to his feet and shifted enough so that Aria could see that he had some sort of seat that wasn't just padded but also had a back to it.

"We're not old enough for those yet, Dad," Janessa protested.

"So you'd rather be uncomfortable?" He nodded his head as he sat back down. "Makes total sense."

Gareth chuckled. "Never try to beat Dad with logic. He'll win every time."

"Why do you think we're still happily married after all these years?" his mom asked.

"I dunno." Gareth shrugged. "I thought maybe you loved each other."

"Well, there is that." Mr. Halverson looped his arm around his wife and pulled her in for a quick kiss. "Definitely, there is that."

"Abort. Abort." Janessa turned back to face the court. "We can't pay them too much attention when they get lovey-dovey. They like to get all mushy and gross us out."

"Gross you out?" Aria asked. She happened to think their affection for each other was really sweet. It was the type of relationship she'd love to have one day.

"No kid wants to see their parents being too physically affectionate," Gareth said.

"Oh. I get it now," Aria said. Not having had two parents, she hadn't witnessed anything like that. The few boyfriends her mom had had over the years hadn't been the super affectionate sort.

Gareth leaned closer to her. "We don't really mind it. It's just a game that's carried over from our teen years."

Having Gareth that close let her get a whiff of his cologne, and when she glanced at him, she could see the dark flecks in his brown eyes. She couldn't let her gaze linger, though, so she looked back out on the gym floor.

"It seems like a cute little game."

"It is, actually," he agreed.

The Halverson family was so different from anything she'd experienced before. And Gareth... well, she wasn't sure how to react to him in such a way that she didn't reveal her growing feelings. The last thing she wanted was to make things awkward, so she had to keep them under wraps as best she could.

CHAPTER TWELVE

Gareth walked to the reception area with the last patients of the day, a little boy and girl who had come with their single mom for a well-child visit, which had included some vaccinations for the kids. There had been a steady stream of patients that morning, but that wasn't unusual for the Saturday morning clinics.

"Thanks, Doctor Halverson," the woman said.

"You're welcome. If any issues crop up, just give the clinic a call."

The kids waved to him with the hand that wasn't clutching the stick of the lollipop they'd each chosen. Gareth locked the door behind them, then headed back to his office.

"Everything good?" he asked when he ran into Janessa coming out of one of the exam rooms.

"Yep. No issues."

"Is everything going okay with Aria?"

"I think so," Janessa said. "Do you have concerns?"

"No. She seems to fit in well here."

Janessa nodded. "I hope that she'll be up for helping with the Saturday morning clinics eventually, but I don't want to pile that on her just yet."

"That would be good," Gareth agreed. "But don't schedule her with Nora, at least not at first."

His sister grimaced. "Yeah. I would say that if there's an issue anywhere with Aria, it's with Nora. She definitely wants to put Aria through her paces."

"Hopefully it will get better." Gareth wasn't sure if there was a real chance of that, but he prayed it would. "I would recommend just leaving things as they are. Keep Aria on reception for now."

"I agree." Janessa headed into the supply room. "I've been happy that Aria seems to be settling in at home, too."

Gareth was glad to hear that. He'd seen it as well. Her willingness to join the family for meals and the basketball games seemed to show that she was embracing her new life in Serenity Point.

"What are your plans for the evening?" Janessa asked as she took supplies off the shelves in the room.

"Nothing too exciting." Gareth pulled off his white coat. "I have worship team rehearsal at four, then I'll probably head home."

"Not hanging out with Wade and Jackson?"

"Nope. Wade's still working on a project that's tying up a lot of his time, and Jackson has a date."

"Serious?" Janessa asked.

"You know Jackson," Gareth said with a huff. "He doesn't take a whole lot seriously."

Janessa snorted. "So true."

"How about you? Plans?"

"I think we're doing pizza and movie night," she said. "Want to join us?"

Gareth thought about it for a moment. "Are we talking about a princess movie here?"

Janessa laughed as she left the storage room. "What do you think?"

As Gareth followed her, he had to wonder why he was even considering her invitation. Watching the princess movies his niece favored was the punishment—uh, the privilege—of babysitting Layla. Outside of that, those types of movies were definitely not what he chose to watch.

"I might come for the pizza," he said. "But not sure about the movie."

"Well, be there by five-thirty. We'll have a pizza for you."

"Sounds good. Do you want me to pick up the pizza, or are you getting delivery?"

"You can pick it up. I think the pizza shop employees like it when you come around."

Gareth chuckled. He was sure they did because he always tipped well, remembering what it had been like to earn a living as a teen. "Okay. Let me know what time it's ready, and I'll grab it on my way over."

He headed into his office while Janessa went into another of the exam rooms they'd used. After hanging up his white coat, he settled into his chair at the desk to work on his reports from the morning. Janessa peeked her head in to say goodbye, then it was just him in the clinic.

His phone rang just as he was finishing up his work, and when he saw Nora's name on the screen, he debated not answering it. He had a feeling that no matter what reason she had for calling, she was going to be disappointed with his response.

With a sigh, he tapped the screen to accept her call.

"Hi, Gareth," she said when he answered. "How did the clinic go this morning?"

"It went well." He was more than happy to have a discussion related to the clinic. "It was busy, as usual, of course, but there was nothing out of the ordinary."

For the next couple of minutes, they discussed specific patients that they'd both treated with some concern over recent months. One was a young man suffering from something that caused him chronic pain. He refused further testing, wanting only the drugs that would ease the pain. Gareth had warned him that morning that he wouldn't prescribe any further painkillers beyond what he did that day until he got some testing done.

The man hadn't been happy when he'd left, so Gareth had no idea if he'd return. Thankfully, Nora agreed to follow through with that should he show up again the following Saturday. It didn't sit well with Gareth to use up a spot in their free clinic for someone who clearly had no interest in actually getting better and seemed to only want the drugs.

"Are you busy tonight?" she asked once their discussion about the clinic was over.

"Yep. I have worship team practice for church, then I'm meeting family for dinner." He was careful to not mention which family that was exactly. "How about you?"

"Well, I didn't have plans, so I was thinking of suggesting that we grab dinner," she said. "But I guess I need to get my request in sooner for Doctor Popular."

Gareth made a non-committal response. "I hope you have a good weekend. I'll see you on Monday."

Their conversation ended without her getting upset—at least that he could hear—so Gareth took that as a win. After he shut everything down, he headed for home to change out of the clothes he'd worn to the clinic and into something a bit more comfortable.

His home was an older Craftsman style house that had been completely renovated before he'd bought it. Though the house was nice, he loved the fact that it had a view of the mountains in the distance and that it sat on an acre and a half, so he wasn't right on top of his neighbors.

It had more bedrooms than he needed, but he hoped he *would* need them in the future. In the meantime, the bedrooms were there for any friend or family member who needed a place to crash.

The basement was set up with his drums as well as a large television where he usually watched sports, and where the men sat on the comfy couches he had there when he hosted their men's group, which would be the case that next week.

After he'd changed, Gareth grabbed his drumsticks, preferring his own to the ones they had at the church. With them in hand, he left the house, moving off to the next thing he needed to do.

Weekends were rarely restful for Gareth, especially when he worked at the free clinic, but he didn't mind. The things he chose to fill his time with were, for the most part, things he enjoyed.

Plus, he had a job he really loved, so he rarely felt like he needed a break. When he did, he wasn't foolish enough to ignore it. He'd book time off from the clinic, then spend the day working on the land around his house or sometimes, if it was nice weather, he'd go for a hike.

That day, he was going to go play some drums with people he liked, then go eat pizza with people he loved and maybe… just maybe… he'd watch a princess movie.

A couple of hours later, the aroma of pizza permeated the interior of his car, making his stomach growl in longing. Janessa had ordered a stack, which made him wonder who all was going to be there. At this rate, there was more than one pizza per person, and he was pretty sure that Layla couldn't eat a whole one by herself.

When he pulled up to the curb in front of the house, he spotted Kayleigh's car, but that was the only one he recognized. Lights were on in the other houses on the street, and he knew a couple of the families who lived there. Janessa and Charli were friendly with all their neighbors, but Gareth only knew them through the clinic.

Steam rose off the pizza boxes as he lifted them out of the car, exposing them to the cold early evening air. He shut the door, then headed for the house. Before he even reached the top step, the door swung open to reveal his niece.

"Uncle Gare!" Layla called out. "You brought pizza again!"

"I did bring pizza. Again." he agreed. "Just for you."

"Momma and Auntie Nessa are making food, too."

"More food?" he asked as he stepped into the foyer. When Aria appeared from the kitchen, he smiled at her.

"Let me take those so you can take off your jacket," she offered as she approached him.

Gareth handed the boxes over, waiting until she had a firm grip on them before letting go. As he unzipped his jacket, he watched her walk away, noting that she dressed much like Janessa in her off-time with leggings and large sweatshirts. Charli, on the other hand, seemed to prefer baggy sweatpants and T-shirts.

After he hung up his jacket in the front closet, he followed Layla into the kitchen. She was happily chatting about a play date she'd had with someone from school that afternoon.

Gareth loved that his niece was such a happy child, and he tried to step in to help fill the lack of a father in her life, as did his brothers and his dad. She would never lack for male role models in her life.

"How are you doing?" he asked as he dropped his arm around Kayleigh's shoulders. She was the shortest of his sisters. Well, unless she was wearing her ridiculously high heels.

She leaned against him for a moment. "Lovely day fielding rich people's complaints."

"Bunch of them show up for the weekend?"

"Yeah. There were a few familiar friendly faces, so that was nice," she said. "But then a large group of lazy-gen wealth showed up."

Gareth knew who she was talking about because of the nickname she'd given them when she'd started working at the resort. They were the kids of ultra-wealthy families who had never worked a day in their lives and could be super demanding. Some of them weren't above trying to get employees fired during their time at the hotel. They certainly gave their families a bad name for not having raised them better.

His own family could be considered rich, but his parents had made it quite clear that they would not be handed anything in life except an education. And even then, it wasn't going to be a frivolous one. They had been allowed to pursue any career they wanted, so long as it would support them.

"Are they just there for the weekend?" Gareth asked, watching as Aria helped Janessa open the pizza boxes on the counter.

"Nope. They're staying for a week."

"Sorry to hear that. I'll be praying you have patience."

"Oh, I'll need a good dose of that, for sure. All we need is for any of the Cattaneos to show up. That would be just great."

The owners of the resort, which was comprised of a large hotel and a bunch of smaller lodges, were rarely around. Which was a good thing for the staff. Stress levels shot through the roof whenever any of them showed up.

"Can we eat?" Layla asked as she climbed up on a stool, bracing her arms on the counter as she leaned over to peer at the pizza. "I'm hungry."

"I am too," Gareth told her as he leaned down beside her on the counter. He looked up at Aria and Janessa. "Can we eat?"

The smile that appeared on Aria's face was beautiful, and it made Gareth smile in return, his heart feeling lighter at the sight of it. Aria's interactions with Layla were sweet, and seeing the affection on her face as she helped his niece get a piece of her favorite pizza, touched Gareth. Anyone who treated a family member that way was definitely okay in his books. Maybe better than okay.

"What's your choice?" she asked as she handed him a paper plate.

"I go for the all-meat ones," he said. "How about you?"

"I'm pretty easy when it comes to toppings. I'll eat most things, though I'm not a fan of mushrooms or pineapple. They shouldn't even be an option."

"Right?" Gareth grinned. "I agree with that."

He put a couple of pieces of pizza on his plate, then added some salad to make him feel better about indulging yet again. Soon, they were all seated in the breakfast nook.

Gareth was glad he'd come, and he realized that he'd probably stay for the movie. Just so that he could hang out with his sisters...

and yes, Aria. The more time he spent with her, the more time he wanted to spend with her. Especially outside of the office.

For the first time in a long time, his heart demanded he get to know all he could about a woman, and he wasn't sure what to do about it. Aria was still settling into her life in Serenity, so he didn't want to complicate the situation. However, it was hard not to ask her out and then spend their time together getting to know her more.

The problem was... would she think she had to say yes to spending time with him since he was her boss? Her job wasn't in any sort of jeopardy, but she might worry that it would be.

Maybe he should talk to Janessa. If there was one thing he could count on, it was his sister being totally honest with him. She knew Aria well, so she'd know if this was a totally bad idea. He really hoped it wasn't.

"You're on the worship team tomorrow, Gareth?" Charli asked.

"Yep. We had practice right before I came here. I'm filling in for Steve, so I'm on three weeks in a row."

"You didn't swap weeks with him?"

Gareth grimaced at Janessa's question. "My usual group prefers not to work with Steve. Plus, I don't mind doing it."

"You're a good drummer," Aria said, making Gareth want to grin, since he very much liked that she thought that.

"He's the best," Charli agreed. "He should do it every week, to be honest."

"Steve's fine," Gareth said. "He's just young, and he likes to have some attention on himself."

Charli laughed. "Yes. Yes, he does."

"I wish I played an instrument," Aria said.

"You didn't want to take lessons as a kid?" Gareth asked, taking the opportunity to learn a bit more about her.

"No. We moved a lot." Aria hesitated. "And I doubt Mom had the money to spare for lessons."

"You know you can take lessons as an adult," Gareth told her. "It's never too late to learn to play whatever instrument you want."

She seemed to consider that before she said, "I never really thought about it."

"Our music teacher has retired from teaching now, but she might make an exception for you." Janessa smirked. "Especially if Gareth asks her. He's her favorite."

"Gareth was *everyone's* favorite," Kayleigh groused. "He set the bar way too high for the rest of us."

"Not my fault," Gareth said with a laugh. "I was just doing my best."

"You could have done just a little worse," Janessa told him.

Gareth shrugged. "I liked school."

"Aria always did better than me at nursing school," Janessa said. "She was more interested in studying than partying."

"You didn't party *that* much. Plus, it didn't seem like you needed to study as much as I did. Even without studying as much, your grades were fine."

Janessa grinned. "I was lucky. Mom and Dad would have gotten after me if my grades weren't good, and they'd have made me stop socializing so much."

After they finished their pizza, Charli and Janessa got out all the fixings for sundaes. Ice cream was a weakness for Gareth. And if he had to watch a princess movie while he ate his sundae, he'd happily do so.

Once Layla had her bowl of ice cream, Charli went with her down to the basement where the large television was.

"You sticking around for the movie?" Janessa asked as she handed him a bowl.

"I guess I am if I want to have ice cream."

"Do you want a banana?" Aria held one out to him.

"Yep. Thank you." He smiled. "I'm going to take it all."

Aria's brows lifted slightly. "Ice cream fan?"

"Gareth loves ice cream," Kayleigh said. "When we were kids, he used to bribe us for our ice cream when we'd have it for a treat."

"What sort of things would you bribe them with?" Aria asked.

"It depended on who I was talking to." Gareth put two scoops of ice cream in his bowl. "Most of the time it was doing their chores. I washed lots of dishes and took out a ton of garbage when I was a kid."

"Was it worth it?"

Gareth winked at Aria. "When it comes to ice cream, it's always worth it."

Aria's cheeks pinked slightly as she gave him a shy smile. "I'm more of a brownie or cookie person myself."

"Which is why we have brownies here too," Janessa said as she slid a container toward Aria.

Gareth noticed that Aria didn't pile ice cream on her brownie, so it was clear she wasn't perfect. However, he could deal with that particular flaw.

When they went downstairs to watch the movie, Aria settled onto the large, overstuffed loveseat, and after a moment's hesitation, Gareth approached her.

"Do you mind if I set here?" he asked, wanting to give her the chance to say no.

Without hesitation, she smiled up at him and said, "Nope. Not at all."

That was good enough for him.

CHAPTER THIRTEEN

Aria wasn't sure what to make of Gareth's request to sit beside her. There were plenty of other seats in the large rec room. The space held a couch, a couple of love seats and two armchairs. Layla had a special chair that was decorated with the figure of her favorite princess. It was front and center, facing the television where the movie she'd chosen was playing.

Janessa was in one armchair, sitting with her legs drawn up and her heels on the edge of the cushion. Her bowl of ice cream balanced on her knees. Kayleigh and Charli sat on opposite ends of the couch.

"How are you finding the clinic?" Gareth asked, then pointed at her with his spoon. "Be totally honest."

"I think it's really going well," she said. "I'm feeling more comfortable with the appointment software. I'm placing a stock order this week, so we'll see how I manage that."

"Just remember that if Jay gives you a hassle over anything, it's not personal. And if you need someone to battle him for you, go to Janessa. Or, alternatively, you could come to me. It wouldn't be the first time I've had to wrangle over the budget with him."

Aria didn't want to have to butt heads with Jay, but she really didn't think there should be much to debate over ordering stock. After all, she wasn't trying to order a new x-ray machine or anything. Since she'd started working there, she'd become familiar with what supplies the clinic was using. She would order based on what they needed and hope that Jay understood.

Because Jay spent most of his day in his office, Aria hadn't interacted much with him at work. From what Janessa had explained,

Jay handled all the billing and administrative stuff. She also hadn't socialized with Jay since he hadn't come to the house like Gareth and Kayleigh had. Getting to know him would come in time, she was sure, but she didn't feel the intense desire to know more about him like she did with Gareth.

Aria had no idea what his actions meant. Was he just being friendly because she was a new employee and a friend of Janessa's? That would make the most sense, because Aria wasn't sure she could believe that Gareth would have any interest in her beyond either of those reasons.

Though she might have wished differently, Aria would assume that Gareth's overtures were for friendship, and she'd respond in kind. She still wasn't sure she was ready for another relationship, regardless, but it was nice to know that she could feel something for a man.

After she finished her ice cream, Aria glanced over to see Gareth had finished his, too. He'd had twice as much as she'd had, making it clear just how much he really liked the treat.

"Let me take that upstairs for you," Aria said, holding out her hand for his bowl.

After a moment, he handed it over to her. "I'll come up with you. I need to get a drink."

Aria collected empty bowls from the others while Gareth took orders for drinks from the others. Together, they climbed the stairs and went into the kitchen. While Aria rinsed the bowls and put them in the dishwasher, Gareth pulled glasses down from the cupboard and started to fill them.

"Do you enjoy living here with Janessa and Charli?" Gareth asked as he set a full glass on the counter.

"I really do," Aria said. "Since I can be a bit of a loner, living here ensures that I get some socialization. I mean, I deal with people all the time at work, but that's in a professional capacity. I'd probably just stick to my home if I lived on my own."

Gareth leaned a hip against the counter, crossing his arms as he abandoned the water glasses. "Do you not like being around people?"

Having his attention so intently focused on her made Aria want to squirm. His brown eyes were warm, though, not at all judging.

He had obviously changed after work since he now wore a pair of loose worn jeans and a dark blue T-shirt with long sleeves. He didn't look much like a doctor in the casual wear, but Aria found this version of him just as attractive.

"I don't mind being around people I know," she said. "Like these get-togethers. Since I know you—or I'm getting to know you—I feel more comfortable. That's why Janessa was good for me when we roomed together. She'd take me along to parties where she knew people, and she'd introduce me to them. When I don't have to rely on introducing myself, it's a lot easier."

Gareth nodded. "I have a couple of siblings that are like that."

"You do?" Aria asked, because she hadn't gotten that feeling from any of the ones she'd met so far.

"The two that are off at college are more like that. You'll see that when they come home for the summer."

"Are you close to them?" Aria asked.

Gareth nodded. "Now that I'm done with med school and residency, I've tried to cultivate a relationship with each of my siblings, though admittedly it's harder to maintain that when they're not here."

Aria had no idea what it must be like to have so many people in a family. She would have been happy with just one sibling who would have been able to help her shoulder the burden of her mom's sickness and the financial debt she had been left with after her mom had passed away.

Her thoughts went briefly to the test she'd taken at one of the DNA sites. She'd received notification that her results were back, but she hadn't gone to the site to check what they were. Though she'd continued to receive emails from the company, she'd ignored them all without checking to see if they were actually notifications of a DNA connection or just generic emails about their services.

"I'm surprised you all seem to get along so well," she said, pushing aside those thoughts. "With so many different personalities, I would think there'd be more conflicts."

"Oh, there are," Gareth said with a laugh. "You're right. We do have a lot of unique personalities. Mom and Dad didn't always step in to separate us when we argued or fought. They said we had to learn how to deal with our differences, and to work through whatever we were arguing about, making sure that when all was said and done, we were each in a good place."

"Who did you fight with the most?"

Gareth grinned. "I bet you think I'm going to say Jay, but that wasn't the case. We did have conflict, for sure, but I think Kayleigh and I argued the most."

"Really? Why's that?"

"Since we were barely two years apart, she often felt that she should get things at the same time I did. She'd also get mad if I was allowed to do things, and she wasn't. Sometimes, she'd take what I'd been given without asking, then she'd use it or hide it. So yeah, we had a lot of fights."

"You seem to get along fine now," Aria said. "From what I've seen, anyway."

"We do," Gareth agreed. "I think we worked out most of our differences growing up. Once I left for college, we began getting along much better."

"Who are you closest to now?"

Gareth seemed to consider the question, which surprised Aria. She'd have thought he'd have an answer right away. "Really depends on the situation. I find I spend the most time with Kayleigh, Charli, and Janessa, so I'm probably closest to them."

Though Aria already had a friendship with Janessa, she found that she really liked Charli as well. She was grateful that she got along well with the woman, since she was living with her. Hopefully, Charli also liked her and didn't mind her presence in the big house.

"Guess we'd better get these drinks back downstairs," Gareth said, turning his attention back to the glasses on the counter. He picked up the one empty glass and filled it. "Do you want to grab a couple of these?"

Aria came to the counter and managed to pick up three of the glasses. Gareth had less trouble picking up the remaining three in his larger hands.

"Lead the way," he said with a nod toward the stairs. "And I'll try not to trip and give you an inadvertent shower."

Aria grinned as she headed for the stairs. Since she didn't want to trip either, Aria kept her gaze on the carpeted stairs that led to the basement.

"Were you fetching water from the lake?" Kayleigh asked as Gareth handed her a glass.

"Or digging a well?" Janessa added when Aria gave her one.

"Or..." Charli began, then laughed. "Never mind. I can't come up with anything."

"How about *did you have to melt ice cubes*?" Gareth suggested, as he gave Layla a glass.

"You should come to school with me and hand me lines when the kids start acting crazy."

Gareth returned to his seat beside Aria. "You need help to outsmart a bunch of elementary kids?"

Charli sighed. "Some days. Yes."

Aria wasn't sure why Layla wasn't shushing them all so she could hear her movie, but the little girl seemed able to tune out the adult conversation around her. For the rest of the movie, Aria didn't talk much, preferring to listen to the others interacting. The more insight she gained into this family, the more she was so very grateful that her road had led her to Serenity Point and the job at the Halversons' clinic.

She wondered if her mom would have agreed to move with her if she'd still been alive when this job offer had come to her. It would have been so wonderful to have her mom there with her.

Aria stared unseeing at the cartoon characters on the screen, thoughts of her mom flooding her mind. It had been over a year since her mom had passed away, and while she missed her every single day, she'd definitely felt her loss more acutely when her circumstances had been so terrible.

Now, though, Aria missed her in a different way. She wished her mom was there with her, not just for her own sake, but also for her mom's. After the rough life her mom had had, Aria felt like coming to Serenity would have been so wonderful for her.

There was no chance for that now, and Aria mourned the loss of what might have been for them. In the months following her mom's death, when things had fallen apart at her job, she hadn't been sure that she'd ever be happy again. Having lost her fiancé, mother, and her job within such a short period of time had almost killed her.

But now, she felt like happiness was seeping back into her life. A small trickle of it, coming in unexpected ways through unexpected people.

"Everything okay?"

Gareth's quiet question drew her from her thoughts. She looked over and gave him a small smile. "Everything's fine."

His smile at her words was bigger than hers had been, crinkling the corners of his brown eyes. She'd always liked blue eyes, but for some reason, Gareth's brown ones seem to glow with a warmth that made her feel like he really cared.

"Princess movies can make me space out, too."

"Do you watch them frequently?" Aria asked.

"Anytime I babysit, which, admittedly, isn't very often. But even though Layla likes to watch these movies over and over, she seems to understand that the adults in her world aren't as big a fan of princesses as she is."

"I don't recall being obsessed with princess movies as a kid," Aria said.

"What were you obsessed with?"

Aria thought back to when she'd been a kid. "Books. Mom used to take me to the library every week, and she'd let me check out as many books as I was allowed."

"I've always been a fan of books, too," Gareth said. "Which was a good thing, as I spent a lot of time reading them for college."

"So you don't read fiction?"

"I do, but my preference is non-fiction. Now most of my reading time is focused on medical journals. My curiosity about medical stuff is always quite high. How about you?"

"I've read a lot of true crime books, but I also like suspense fiction." She'd spent a lot of the past year reading to fill her spare time. Since she had basically been confined to her room in the apartment, reading had been the only thing she'd had to do.

She could hear the other three women talking amongst themselves, and she wondered what they thought about Gareth conversing with her the way he was. He could have sat anywhere in the room, so it was a bit odd that he'd chosen the seat next to her.

Given the questions he'd been asking about her, she got the feeling that he was just trying to get to know the person who'd taken up residence with his sisters and niece and had also taken a job in his family's clinic. He probably wasn't one to just take his sister's word that Aria was a good person.

Jay didn't appear to have the same concern, since he hadn't pursued any type of conversation with her beyond what they'd exchanged at work. She just hoped that nothing she said would be a red flag for Gareth. There were red flags in her life, but as long as she wasn't put in a nursing role, they wouldn't matter.

She had no desire to share what had happened with anyone. That whole ugly chapter needed to be firmly closed. She'd embraced the role of receptionist and was happy to work in a medical environment again, even if it wasn't in the role she'd studied so hard to achieve.

Charli asked Gareth a question about the service the next day, shifting his attention away from Aria. The discussion between them carried on until the end of the movie.

"I guess I'd better head for home." Gareth got to his feet. "Thanks for letting me hang out."

"And eat our pizza," Janessa said.

He pointed a finger at her. "That I paid for."

"You make the big bucks, bro. It's only fair you pay."

Gareth laughed. "Well, just for that, I'm going to take my pizza home with me."

"That better only be a threat about the pizza you liked best and not all of it," Charli said. "I was counting on some for breakfast tomorrow."

"I love pizza for breakfast." Layla went to Gareth and looked up at him with wide eyes. "Please don't take it all."

Gareth reached out and ruffled her hair. "I see that your aunts have been training you well. For your sake—and your sake only—I will leave everything but the all-meat one."

"Oh, thank you, Uncle Gare," Layla said as she flung her arms around his waist. "You're my favorite uncle."

The three women snickered at Layla's words, while Gareth said, "You are a fickle little child. I don't believe I'll be your favorite anymore when you want to wear your cheerleader outfit. Then Jay and Cole will be your favorites since it's for a basketball game."

Aria watched as Gareth swung Layla up onto his hip to give her a hug. Her ex had agreed that they'd have children one day, but she'd never really seen him interact with kids. When there had been children around, he'd been more apt to focus on the adults than the kids.

It hadn't really bothered her because she hadn't been around a lot of kids, either. She'd just assumed that when the day came for them to have a child of their own, they'd know what to do. Watching Gareth with his niece was like a glimpse of how he'd be as a father. It was definitely an appealing sight.

As Gareth headed to the stairs, still carrying Layla, the rest of them got up and followed him. In the kitchen, Janessa identified which box of pizza was his favorite. Then they all went to the front door. Kayleigh pulled on her jacket while Janessa held the pizza box so Gareth could put on his.

"See you guys tomorrow," Gareth said as he took the pizza from Janessa. "Don't be late."

"We're never late," Charli scoffed. "We're always there in time for the sermon."

"But then you miss my wonderful contribution to the worship time."

After a little more joking around, Gareth turned to Aria and smiled. "It was nice chatting with you tonight. See you tomorrow."

Aria nodded. "I'll be there."

Cold air rushed into the house as Kayleigh opened the front door. Gareth followed her out onto the porch, pulling the door shut behind him.

Janessa turned to Aria, one of her dark brows slightly arched. "Looks like maybe Gareth has taken an interest in you."

CHAPTER FOURTEEN

Aria froze, then frowned at Janessa. "Um... What?"

Janessa turned to Charli. "What do you think? Am I wrong?"

Charli shrugged. "It seems like a definite possibility."

"I don't understand why you'd say that," Aria said, her stomach in a knot. As much as she might have wished that to be true, there was a moment of panic that it might be a wish that could come true.

"Let's get something to drink," Janessa said as she turned toward the kitchen.

"Make me a cup of tea, please." Charli held out her hand to her daughter, who grabbed it without hesitation. "I'll be back once Layla's in bed."

"Will do."

In the kitchen, Janessa grabbed the kettle and filled it with water. Aria settled on a stool at the island counter, nervous about the conversation yet to come. She had no idea how Janessa felt about the pronouncement she'd just made.

Janessa had definitely warned her about Gareth appearing interested in someone when he was actually just being friendly. Aria had taken that warning to heart. But was Janessa now saying that wasn't the case?

Working in silence, Janessa pulled mugs down from the cupboard and got out the basket of assorted teas. After removing two tea bags, Janessa slid the basket across the counter to Aria. Though she wasn't a big tea drinker, Charli and Janessa had a large selection of teas, and in the time since she'd moved in, she'd found a couple of flavors she enjoyed.

After finding one of those flavors, Aria turned her attention back to her friend. "Did I do something wrong?"

Janessa finished pouring the hot water into the last mug, then looked over at her. "No. Not at all."

Relief spiraled through Aria. She couldn't lose this job, and she didn't want anything to jeopardize the home she'd found in Serenity Point. Whatever Janessa suggested she do in this situation, she would do. The last thing she wanted to do was upset her friend.

Janessa set a mug in front of Aria before she put the tea bags in each of the other two mugs. Once that was done, she moved to stand on the other side of the counter, lifting the mug to her lips. Her dark eyes regarded Aria as she took a sip.

"Can you explain what you meant about Gareth?" Aria asked. Normally, she wouldn't be so bold, but too much was at stake for her to not try to figure out where Janessa's mind was.

"I've been watching Gareth with you," Janessa said before taking another sip. "I wasn't sure, at first, if he was just wanting to get to know you as a new employee."

"That's what I assumed," Aria said, cupping her hands around the mug. She appreciated the warmth that soaked into her hands and also kept her from scratching her arms as anxiety crawled beneath her skin. "It made sense since I'm not just living with his sisters, I'm working for him."

"You're not really working for *him*," Janessa clarified. "You're working for the clinic. As the receptionist, you fall more under Jay's supervision since you do admin work. As a nurse, I fall under Gareth's supervision."

When Janessa put it that way, it made sense, though Aria looked at all three of them as her supervisors. She'd definitely take advice or guidance from any of them. Nora was the only one she wasn't entirely comfortable dealing with.

"Why don't you think that he's just getting to know me as a new employee?" Aria asked.

Janessa gave a short laugh. "Have you not seen how he looks at you?"

Aria lifted her mug, inhaling the aroma before taking a sip. She was trying to figure out how to answer Janessa. Had she seen how he'd looked at her? Sure. But she didn't know how he usually looked at people since she didn't know him very well.

"He's looking at you like you fascinate him," Janessa said when she didn't respond. "And he gravitates to you like he just can't help himself."

That would explain why he'd chosen to sit next to her downstairs, even though there had been plenty of other seats available. She supposed that if anyone would know what Gareth was thinking, it would be one of his sisters. Did the others see the same things Janessa did?

"Are you sure?" Aria couldn't help but ask. "I mean, I'm no one special."

Janessa frowned. "We're all special."

Since her mom had died, Aria hadn't known anyone who made her feel like she was special. Even her fiancé had never made her feel as special as her mom had. It was hard to believe that Gareth—or any of Janessa's family—really thought she was all that special.

Though Janessa had offered her a place to live, Aria hadn't assumed that she'd have any sort of presence in her friend's family. All she'd wanted was a steady job and a safe place to live. Everything else was gravy.

Charli walked into the kitchen and joined Janessa at the counter, picking up her mug to take a sip. After humming in appreciation, she said, "Where are we?"

"I'm telling her that Gareth is acting differently with her than he usually does with women."

Charli nodded. "He does seem to be."

Aria continued to grip her mug, really at a loss as to what to say in response to Charli and Janessa's observations. She and her ex had met when his mom had been a patient on the ward where she'd worked. His mom had introduced Aria as her favorite nurse, and she and her ex had chatted whenever he'd come to visit his mom.

The day after his mom had been discharged, he'd shown up at the hospital with a bouquet of roses and a request for a date. They'd dated for over a year before he'd proposed. And then six months after that, he'd decided that he was done with her, leaving her alone to deal with the weight of her mom's illness and eventual passing.

If Aria was a little leery of trusting her own judgement when it came to men, she hoped people would understand. Plus, after her ex had walked away from her so easily, it was hard to believe that a man of Gareth's stature in his community and town would be interested in her, of all people.

Especially when he had women like Nora wanting his attention. While it was clear that Nora wasn't his choice, there were plenty of women out there who might be.

If Janessa was right, what was it that Gareth saw in her? Or would his attention eventually wane the same way her ex's had?

"I guess the question is," Janessa began. "Do *you* have thoughts on Gareth's interest in you? Is he barking up the wrong tree? Is he not your type?"

Aria's brows lifted. Not her type? Whose type *wasn't* a friendly, smart, good-looking man? That he was a doctor and had a great family was just the icing on the cake.

"He's very... nice," Aria said slowly.

Charli frowned. "That doesn't sound like a good thing."

"Oh. It's a very good thing," Aria hurried to reassure her. "Dating Gareth would be a dream for a lot of women."

"So why do you sound so reluctant?" Charli asked.

"What happens if, after we date for a bit, Gareth decides he's not interested in me anymore? Do I lose my job? Do I lose my place to live? Will I have to leave?" Aria cleared her throat, letting go of her mug in order to wrap her arms across her waist. "I don't want any of that to happen because I really like it here."

Janessa's expression softened as she leaned forward on her forearms. "I get that."

Charli nodded. "That is a valid concern. I guess the best thing we can do is perhaps let Gareth know you're not interested, so he doesn't get caught up in feelings for you when there isn't a chance for anything more."

Charli's words sank into her heart and filled Aria with a sense of loss. She wanted to protest telling Gareth she wasn't interested. She stared down at her mug, wondering if it was worth taking a risk.

Her heart was saying it was absolutely worth it. That she needed to take the risk on a man who had shown himself to be wonderful in so many ways.

Her mind, however, remembered what it was like to love and lose. To be stuck in a job that barely paid her rent and bought her food. To be living in an apartment with drug users and never feeling safe enough to sleep soundly. She remembered how much pain she'd suffered over and above her grief because the man who should have been there to support her had left her on her own.

"Are you okay?" Janessa asked.

Aria looked up and took a deep breath, realizing she'd started to scratch at her arm. "I don't really know what to say. Part of me wants to see where things go, but another part just doesn't want to take the risk."

"As you might have guessed," Charli said. "I've had a negative experience with a guy. The man who fathered Layla left me heartbroken, and I've been leery of giving any other guy a chance. Janessa has mentioned that you had a broken engagement."

"Yeah. He wasn't terribly keen to stick around when I couldn't devote all of my time to him after my mom got sick."

"Is *that* why he ended the engagement?" Janessa said. "You didn't tell me that. You said your lives were just moving in different directions."

"They were." Aria clenched her hands into fists. "His was moving in a direction that didn't involve a fiancée with a dying mom."

"That's just terrible," Charli said with a frown. "No wonder you're wary of this."

There were a lot of reasons to be wary, but Aria couldn't share all of them with the two women. She didn't want to talk about why she'd lost her job and everything that had followed and why she feared losing the security this job offered her.

"If it helps you at all, Gareth wouldn't abandon you if you needed him. As a friend or something more. That's not the sort of man he is."

Janessa nodded in agreement with Charli. "If he ever did that, he'd have my parents—and all of us siblings—to answer to."

"We're not saying you have to jump into a relationship with Gareth, but maybe just be open to getting to know him as a... friend," Charli suggested. "At this point, Gareth is just wanting to get to know you. If you don't want it to go further than friendship, he'll understand."

"Maybe we should just let things ride for a bit," Janessa suggested, then tilted her head slightly, her brow furrowed. "Unless you want to shut it down altogether. Just keep things professional between you."

Aria relaxed her hands, then lifted her mug and took a sip, trying to figure out what she should do. This conversation had certainly not been something she'd thought she'd have that day. Or any day, really.

With her heart and mind at war, it was hard to come up with a definite answer. Fear definitely had a tight hold on her. Prior to her engagement and everything that had followed, she would have embraced the opportunity to get to know Gareth and possibly pursue a relationship with him.

"Let's just leave things for the time being," Aria said. "Because I still don't believe he's actually interested in me."

"Okay." Janessa smiled. "And I think you might be surprised."

The expression on her friend's face actually bordered on a smirk, for whatever reason. Still, Aria trusted Janessa to be honest with her.

As she finished her tea, Aria listened to the sisters chat about their plans for the next day after church. As she talked, Charli puttered around the kitchen, breaking down the pizza boxes and putting them in the recycling bin. Janessa pushed herself up to sit on the counter, off to the side, so she didn't block Aria's view of the room.

"We'll be at Mom and Dad's for supper tomorrow night since they're leaving Monday morning," Charli said.

"What are we having?" Janessa asked.

"Mom said she was making stew," Charli said. "I told her that we'd bring dessert, so I'm going to make something after we get home from church tomorrow."

Aria had no idea if she would be invited to the meal, but she'd probably decline to go if she was. It seemed to be a farewell dinner for Janessa's parents, and that felt like something that shouldn't include outsiders. And she had no problem with that.

After having shared an apartment with a couple of drug addicts, Aria didn't take for granted being able to just enjoy the quiet of her home. And though being alone wasn't quite the relief that it had been in that rundown apartment, she still appreciated it.

The next morning, as they sat in church, Aria couldn't help but see Gareth through new eyes. She'd never thought that the crush she'd been harboring on the man would be given the chance to grow into something more. *Maybe.* She still wasn't convinced.

While Janessa spoke to some people in the row behind them, Aria watched Gareth as he shook hands with the man who had preached the previous week. He spoke to him for a minute before climbing the steps to join the other musicians on the stage.

After greeting each of them with a handshake and a smile, Gareth sat down at the drums behind the plexiglass shield. He held a pair of drumsticks in his hand, but he didn't start to play immediately.

She waited for him to look out across the congregation like he had the previous week, but he didn't. The man with the guitar standing next to him strummed his instrument, but he also continued to speak to Gareth. As the two men conversed, Aria recalled that this wasn't Gareth's normal worship group, so that might explain why he didn't seem to be as relaxed as he'd been the previous Sunday.

Remembering how she'd felt when his gaze had found her and he'd smiled, Aria wanted that again. However, his attention stayed mainly on the worship team.

When he did look away from them, his gaze landed on someone near the front, and he smiled at them before focusing back on the worship leader. In that moment, Aria was convinced that Janessa and Charli were wrong. Gareth was nice to everyone. There was nothing special about how he looked at her.

She'd spent the previous night reminding herself not to get her hopes up. Apparently, she hadn't gotten the message because she felt acutely disappointed at that realization.

Lowering her gaze to her lap, she clenched her hands together. Aria shored up the defenses around her heart and tried to refocus her thoughts. Gareth and his interest in her, or lack thereof, didn't matter right then. It wasn't why she'd come to church that morning.

Despite her best intentions, it took a real force of her will to keep her attention from constantly drifting in Gareth's direction. The struggle was worst during the singing since he was on the stage.

But thankfully, once the pastor got up to preach, she could focus better.

She listened as the man spoke about the blessing of brokenness. Through all the struggles that had broken her over the past year, Aria had never viewed any of them as a blessing. More often, she'd thought of those struggles as a punishment of some sort.

"The Bible says that God does not despise a broken and contrite heart," the man said. "In fact, it says in Psalm 34:18 that the Lord is near to those who have a broken heart and saves such as have a contrite spirit."

Since coming to Serenity, she'd seen in others an approach to church and faith that made her really think about her own relationship with God. As her health had failed, her mom had been almost fanatical about making sure that Aria had accepted Jesus into her heart. She'd told Aria to read the Bible and pray. But following her mom's death, Aria had done neither of those things.

The near constant ache in her heart soaked up the pastor's words. The idea that God wanted to be close to her, even though she was struggling so much, seemed foreign to her. But, oh, how she wanted God to be near to her, to heal those parts of her that still hadn't fit back into place.

Regardless of how things might or might not work out with Gareth, Aria wanted to be the best version of herself as she built a life in Serenity Point. She wasn't sure exactly how to make that happen, but the sermon that day gave her hope.

When the service was over, Aria turned to Janessa. "I think I'm going to head home."

"Uh..." Janessa's brow furrowed, then she said, "Okay. We'll see you there in a few."

She'd brought her own car to church that morning, telling Janessa it was because she didn't want her to feel like she had to leave when Aria wanted to. And even though she'd enjoyed the service, Aria was ready to leave as soon as it was over.

The sun was shining brightly as she left the church, but the air held a chill, causing her to hurry across the lot to where she'd parked earlier. It took her a few minutes to exit the parking lot since many were leaving at the same time.

She made it home without getting lost, where she was greeted by the aroma of chicken that Charli had put into the oven before they'd left for church. Since Janessa and Charli would be having a big meal with their family later, they'd decided to use the chicken to make sandwiches for lunch.

Aria went to her room to change out of the clothes she'd worn to church into something a little more comfortable. She had no plan to go out again that day, so comfy clothes were where it was at.

Once she was dressed in warm leggings, a sweatshirt, and thick socks, she headed back down to the kitchen. While she waited for Charli and Janessa, Aria set the table in the breakfast nook.

She was actually looking forward to a quiet evening. She had never needed time alone when living with her mom, but after acquiring her druggie roommates, she'd been desperate to be by herself. She'd been forced to spend time in her small room since she had nowhere else to go in the apartment. Now she didn't mind spending time in her room because it was a beautiful, safe place, and she was choosing to be there instead of being forced there.

And it was the perfect place to get a little space to clearly think about how to deal with this Gareth situation. If Charli and Janessa hadn't said anything, she could have just continued on with her little crush that no one else knew about.

But then Charli and Janessa had shared their thoughts, which complicated everything, and Gareth was ignorant of all of it. Which was definitely for the best. Unfortunately, it didn't help the feeling that her little crush had grown by leaps and bounds over the past day, just because of the little bit of hope the two women had offered her.

Frankly, her feelings were a mess, so she needed some time and space to figure out how to deal with it all, especially since she'd be seeing him at work the next day.

CHAPTER FIFTEEN

Golden light spilled warm and inviting from the windows of his parents' home as Gareth pulled his car to a stop. He was looking forward to spending time together with the family in anticipation of his parents' departure the next day. They would only be gone a short time because they planned to be back for Cole's state championship game—provided his team made it.

Cole would be going to stay with Jay, while Skylar and Bella would end up with Janessa and Charli. The teens protested that they should be allowed to stay by themselves at the house, but that hadn't happened yet. And he wasn't sure it ever would.

Gareth jogged up the steps and opened the front door of the house. He stepped into an aromatic warmth that embraced him and filled him with a sense of home. He quickly closed the door to keep the cold from sweeping into the house, then hung up his jacket.

"Hello, son," his dad said when Gareth walked into the kitchen. He wore an apron and was washing up some dishes in the sink.

"Hey, Dad." Gareth approached him and draped his arm over his dad's shoulder for a quick hug.

His mom joined them a moment later, also wearing an apron. "Gareth! I didn't hear you come in."

She greeted him with a tight hug, then pulled him down to kiss his cheek.

"What can I help with?" Gareth asked as she left him to go to the two large crock pots that sat on the counter.

"You can fill the pitchers with water," she said, gesturing to the glass jugs that sat on the counter next to the water dispenser.

Gareth picked up the first one and began to fill it. "Everything ready for leaving tomorrow?"

"Yep. We've got packing for these trips down to a science," his mom said.

"We received word from Jacques that the order of meds and supplies we had arranged to have shipped over to the clinic arrived safe and sound."

Gareth glanced up at his dad and straightened with the half-filled jug in his hand. "That's amazing, and what an answer to prayer."

"It sure is," his dad agreed as he put the large bowl he'd been washing onto the dish drainer. "We asked a lot of people to pray for the safety of this shipment since we've lost a couple recently."

"Where do you think they ended up?"

His dad shrugged as he reached back to untie his apron. "Since the shipments never arrived, your guess is as good as mine. When Jacques went to the harbor to check the ships they were supposed to arrive on, the shipments just weren't there."

Gareth returned to filling the pitcher he held. "Here's hoping those supplies at least reached people who needed them."

His mom scoffed. "I doubt that, but it sure would be nice if they did. We know that there is some corruption, as well as some opposition to us being there, so who knows. We're just grateful that *this* shipment reached the clinic. They need those supplies and medicines desperately."

"Everything else okay at the clinic?" he asked. "Or will you be running into issues when you get there?"

"Nothing major," his dad said, coming over to take the full pitcher from Gareth. "But there are a few personnel issues we need to address."

"Well, we'll pray as we always do that God will go before you and smooth the way so that you're able to work without incident while you're there."

"The weather looks good," his mom said. "We'll definitely get rain, but it shouldn't be excessive."

Gareth was glad to hear that. His parents had been on the island during both an earthquake and a hurricane. It had been nerve-wracking since they'd tried to contact them and hadn't been able to. After the first incident, Gareth had insisted that they invest in a satellite phone, so even if cell service went down, they'd have a way to stay in touch.

Part of Gareth wished he could travel with them, but it just wasn't possible. His role for the moment was to be in the clinic in Serenity, so his parents could do this work. None of them had gone with their parents on these trips yet, but hopefully that would change in the years to come.

When the door opened again, Gareth glanced over his shoulder as he finished filling the second pitcher. Hearing Wilder's voice, he focused back on his job, swapping out the full one for an empty one on the counter. Skylar and Cole appeared from upstairs, greeting both of them before going off to set the table at their mom's request.

Kayleigh arrived next, with Jay not far behind her. Last to show were Charli, Janessa, and Layla, but no Aria.

Gareth was disappointed not to see her with them. He hadn't had a chance to talk to her at church because she'd scooted out right after the service was over. He'd thought he'd be able to chat with her at dinner, but apparently not.

"Aria not coming?" Gareth asked as he greeted Janessa.

"Nope. She said that since it was a family dinner, she didn't want to crash it."

Gareth frowned. "She would have been welcome. You told her that?"

Janessa gave him an exasperated look. "Of *course* I told her that. But just because she's living with us doesn't mean she has to come to every Halverson family event."

"I know that." Gareth set the final pitcher on the counter, then crossed his arms. "I just don't want her to think she's not welcome."

This time, she rolled her eyes. "Yeah. I'm sure that's what you meant."

Gareth frowned at her. "What are you talking about?"

"I'm sure that was all that you wanted. It had nothing to do with the fact that you wanted to talk to her."

What could he say to that? It wasn't like he could deny it. Apparently, at least one of his sisters had picked up on his interest in Aria. "Sure. I enjoy talking with her."

"So do I," Janessa said, holding up her hand. "She spent the afternoon giving us manicures."

"Looks like she did a great job."

"She did. She said that she learned how to do it because her mom loved to have pretty nails, but she couldn't afford to go for regular manicures. Aria ended up buying the supplies and learning how to do her mom's nails."

"That's cool." Gareth was happy to gain some new insight about the woman, even though she wasn't there.

"She painted Layla's nails, too." Janessa called for the little girl to come over.

Layla skipped over to them, then held up her hands even before Janessa asked her to. "Look at my pretty fingers, Uncle Gare. Aria did them for me."

Gareth bent to inspect the light pink nails, then smiled at his niece. "They are very pretty. Just like you."

Layla's smile widened even further. "I love them. They're the prettiest things ever. She even drew some nice designs on them. And she did Momma's nails too."

"They look like a professional did them," Gareth said, although realistically, he wouldn't know for sure one way or the other.

"Yeah, they do," Janessa agreed.

"I'm going to need to get in on the nail action," Kayleigh said as she approached Gareth and Janessa. She took Janessa's hand and bent to admire her nails. "Aria did a great job on you guys. I'll need to talk to her about getting mine done." She glanced around the room. "Where is she?"

"She didn't come tonight," Janessa said.

Kayleigh frowned. "Why not?"

Gareth wasn't sure if his sister was just disappointed because she couldn't get a nail appointment lined up, or if Kayleigh really liked Aria. His sister had always been a bit more stand-off-ish with new people in their lives. If Aria doing her nails helped Kayleigh warm to her, that could only be a good thing.

"She felt that since this was a family dinner, she'd sit this one out."

"Oh." Kayleigh shrugged. "I appreciate that she respects that even though she would have been welcome."

Gareth tried to set aside his disappointment at not seeing Aria and focus on the dinner ahead. At some point in the evening, they'd video call with the two siblings who were away at school, so they'd feel like they were part of the evening.

They'd eat some good food and laugh and talk together. They'd also spend some time in prayer for their parents' trip. It was an evening he looked forward to, though he wished Aria was there to be part of it all.

Early the next morning, Gareth let himself into the clinic. Jay would be late coming in as he had volunteered to drive their parents to the airport. There was a familiar uneasiness within Gareth that came whenever his parents set off on one of their trips.

He knew that they viewed what they did as service and a way to share God's love with the people they helped. He even accepted that this was their mission. But it was the knowledge that if anything happened to them, the responsibility for the family would fall on his shoulders that weighed down on him. The will made him guardian of any underage children—which was just Skylar now—and he would be responsible for executing their will.

So far, nothing had ever happened to them beyond the storms and struggling with stomach issues as they adjusted to new food and water. Other than that, they'd been safe and healthy during each of their trips.

But Gareth never took that for granted. He accepted the uneasiness he felt as a reminder to keep them in his prayers during their trip.

In the quiet of the clinic, Gareth spent some time in prayer for them, as well as the patients who had appointments with him. By the time he heard the back door open an hour later, he was ready for his day.

Getting up, he retrieved his white coat and put it on. He slipped his pen into the pocket, then left his office, turning to the left to head to the front of the clinic and the reception area.

The lights were all on, and he could hear the murmur of conversation as he approached. Sometimes Janessa took part of Monday off after helping with the free clinic on Saturday. But other times, she saved up the time and took off a full day at some point.

He hoped that eventually Aria could take over some of the Saturday clinics so that Janessa didn't have to work them as much. They had a semi-retired nurse who was willing to work one or two free clinics a month, but having a third person to help would be even better.

Gareth rarely took off time to account for his hours spent at the free clinic. He enjoyed doing it, and since it was only every other Saturday, he didn't have a problem with just absorbing the hours into his work week.

"Good morning," Gareth said as he joined the two women at the reception desk.

Aria looked away from the monitor and gave Gareth a quick smile. "Morning."

"Did you have a good weekend?" Gareth asked. "I didn't get a chance to talk to you yesterday."

"I had a great weekend. Yesterday was very relaxing, which was nice."

"I hear you did some manicures. Layla was quite proud of her pretty nails."

She smiled at his words. "Yep. I put my mediocre skill to work."

"Mediocre?" Janessa scoffed. "You did a great job. I'm not one to go for manicures very often because I never seem to have the time. Having it done in my own home was a treat."

Gareth enjoyed seeing the flush of joy on Aria's face. "Kayleigh said she'd like you to do her nails too. You should start charging."

"I wouldn't do that," Aria said with a shake of her head.

"You're using up your nail polish on us, and I checked last night and that polish you used isn't as cheap as the normal stuff," Janessa said. "I think we should each buy a set of colors we like for you to use on us."

"If you want," Aria agreed amiably. "The colors I have were ones my mom picked out, so fresh colors might be good."

Gareth never in a million years would have thought that he'd enjoy a conversation about nail polish, but he was talking with Aria. He would happily talk with her about anything her heart desired.

"Maybe tonight we can look online for some colors for me and Charli," Janessa suggested.

"You need to talk about this later," Nora said from the hallway, where she stood with her arms crossed. "I don't think this is the right time or place for conversations about frivolous things like manicures."

Gareth was glad to see that Aria didn't cower under Nora's derisive comments. She didn't say anything, but she sat with her chin up and shoulders squared.

"Good grief, Nora," Janessa said. "It's not even time for the first patient yet. And it may be frivolous, but no more so than people who put on makeup."

"But I'm not talking about it in my workplace."

Gareth sighed. "This is not a big deal, Nora. We're ready for the day and were just chatting about our weekends."

He was so, so tired of the pettiness he was seeing in Nora. So far as he knew, she hadn't been that way with any patients, so that was good. If only she'd back off with Aria so that things in the clinic would settle down. That would be the best solution for all concerned.

"I'm going to unlock the door," Aria said, getting to her feet.

Though Gareth stepped aside so that she could move past him, her arm brushed against his. He wanted to watch her, but that would likely draw Nora's ire. When he saw his sister glaring at Nora, and that Nora was glaring back, he wanted to sigh.

This was going to be a *great* Monday. It was too bad that he couldn't have been the one to take his parents to the airport. Maybe then they would have all had a better start to the week.

"I'll be in my office, Janessa," Gareth said. "Let me know when my first patient is here."

"Gareth," Nora called after him as he strode down the hall back to his office.

He did sigh then as he turned to face the woman. "What's up?"

"Maybe we could talk for a moment," she suggested before sweeping past him, headed for his office.

Left with no choice but to follow, Gareth trailed her into his office, skirting around his desk to reach his seat while she settled into one of the chairs opposite him. He grabbed a pen from his pocket and leaned back in his chair, clicking it as he regarded Nora.

"What did you need to talk about?"

"I would like to once again address the possibility of bringing in a new receptionist." She sat with her back straight, hands folded in her lap, looking for all the world like she'd just made a reasonable request.

"No." Gareth clicked his pen again.

Nora's brows drew together as she frowned. "You haven't even heard my reasoning."

"Aria has done nothing to warrant losing her job here at the clinic," Gareth said calmly. "So, my answer is no, and Jay's answer will also be no."

"You've only hired her because she is Janessa's friend," Nora said, so determined to beat a dead horse. "I feel that is a bad precedent to set."

"I was hired here because I am my parents' son. Jay was hired because he is my parents' son. Janessa was hired because she is my parents' daughter. I think a precedent has already been set. The fact that she's a friend of the family is a definite point in her favor. Janessa has vouched for her character and ability, so my answer with regards to firing Aria—unless something truly egregious happens—will be no."

Nora stared at him with narrowed eyes for what felt like forever before she got to her feet and left the room. As Gareth watched her leave, he hoped that was the last conversation they had about Aria. But somehow, he doubted it.

Her attitude toward Aria was ridiculous. It was bordering on obsessive, which was a bit concerning. Not for the first time, he wondered if they had missed something about Nora when they'd interviewed her. None of her references had indicated that she had any kind of issues like they were seeing.

His parents had been present with him and Jay at that interview, and they'd made it clear then that while they would take her input into consideration, the final say for most decisions would come from Gareth and Jay. She'd seemed fine with that. At the time.

The whole issue with hiring a receptionist had taken on a life of its own. It seemed as if she thought that because she'd brought them a couple of recommendations for the position, one of them should have been selected for the job. They'd been fine with her contributing, but aside from Janessa's determination that her friend would get the job, neither of Nora's suggestions would have worked out. And they'd told her that.

After a moment's hesitation, Gareth sat forward and brought up the email program on his computer. Janessa tapped on the door as he typed.

Glancing up, he said, "I'll be right there. I just need to finish this email."

He kept the message relatively short as he reached out to yet another former colleague to ask them to put out feelers for a female doctor. Clearly they needed to expand their search, and if it meant reaching out to people he hadn't talked to in awhile, he was more than happy to do it.

After every discussion with Nora about replacing Aria, the need to replace her increased. And now it was getting even worse because he'd become personally invested in keeping Aria close. He wanted a chance to see if there could be something between them, and if Nora chased her away, that could never happen.

CHAPTER SIXTEEN

Aria stared at the order form on the computer monitor, making sure she had included everything they needed. Once she was confident it was complete, she printed it off, then took the paper to Jay's office. The clinic had just closed, so they were all still there.

At the door to Jay's office, Aria paused for a moment and took a deep breath. She'd had relatively few interactions with the man since starting to work there, so she hoped that this went well.

She knocked on the door frame, waiting until he looked up to say, "Janessa said I needed to run the supply order by you before I submit it."

Jay nodded. "C'mon in."

As she approached the desk, she held the paper out, then sat down on the chair opposite him. Jay focused on the order for a minute before looking up and pinning her with his dark gaze.

He laid the paper on the desk in front of him. "How are you finding the job here?"

"Oh. It's fine. Now that I'm getting the hang of things, I'm feeling more confident."

"Janessa seems to feel that you're doing well."

"I'm glad to hear that. I really didn't want to disappoint her after she convinced you to let me work here."

Jay's smile grew. "Oh, it was more like demanded than convinced."

Aria shifted in her chair. "Well, I don't want anyone to regret giving me this opportunity."

"I really don't think you need to worry about that," Jay assured her with a smile. "As long as you do your job, everything will be fine. And from what I've seen and heard, you are doing well in learning your responsibilities."

Aria smiled in relief. She was doing the job to the best of her ability, so it was good to hear from Jay that he thought she was doing fine. Janessa and Gareth had both said that, too. The only person who seemed to have chronic complaints about her was Nora. Apparently, she had either not gone to Gareth or Jay with her complaints, or if she had, they'd ignored her.

It was probably petty of her, but Aria hoped it was the latter.

"So is the order okay?" she asked, gesturing to the paper.

"Yep." He scribbled something on it, then handed the paper back to her. "When you submit it, make sure that you record the order number on this paper and then file it. Janessa will show you where."

"Okay. Thanks."

Jay nodded, then turned his attention back to his computer. Aria took it for the dismissal it was and left his office.

She nearly bumped into Nora as she stepped out into the hallway. "Oops."

"You need to watch where you're going."

"Yep. Sorry about that." Aria stepped around her and made her way back to the computer at her desk.

As she sat down, she frowned when she glanced at the monitor. The order she'd printed off had disappeared from the screen. She brought up the website again and clicked on the basket, her heart sinking when she saw it was empty. Leaving it the way she had, the order shouldn't have disappeared like that. Was it a deliberate action or a glitch in the system?

Aria glanced down the hallway. Had Nora done something? It seemed unlikely. So far, the woman had just been all talk and no action. But who else would have done it? Janessa certainly wouldn't have, and Aria doubted that Gareth would have either. Since she'd been with Jay when the order had disappeared, she knew he hadn't touched her computer.

Rather than dwell too much on the irritation of the moment, she got to work remaking the order.

"Still working?"

She looked up to see that Gareth stood next to the desk, now without his white coat on. "Just finishing up an order for supplies."

He came and sat down on the other chair at the reception desk. "Did Jay give you any hassles?"

"Nope. He signed off on it and everything," she said, pointing to the scribbled signature on the paper.

Gareth leaned back in the chair and stretched his legs out, crossing them at the ankle. Aria turned her attention back to the screen where she was trying to input the items again, though she was acutely aware of Gareth's nearness.

"Didn't you already input the order?" Gareth asked.

She glanced at him, then back to the monitor. "I did, and then I printed it off to take to Jay. Something must have happened since when I came back, the order form was blank."

"Like a glitch or something?"

She nodded. "Most likely. I don't know why else it would have disappeared. So now I'm having to input it all again."

When Gareth didn't reply, Aria looked over at him. He had a frown on his face as he stared in the direction of the hallway. She wondered if he might suspect what she did.

"I've never heard anyone complain about issues with ordering supplies, but maybe Jay knows more."

Aria shrugged as she typed in the amount for tongue dispensers. "It's not a big deal. It should only take me a few minutes to get it inputted again. I just won't leave the order up on the screen next time, in case there's something that automatically happens when you do that."

"Ask Janessa if she's ever had that happen. She was doing the orders before, so she would know."

"I will," Aria said, though if Janessa said that nothing like that had happened before, she might also get suspicious. The last thing Aria wanted was more conflict with Nora, and that would inevitably happen if anyone confronted her about it.

For now, she just wanted to get the order done and off her plate. Thankfully, it wasn't a daily or weekly event, so whatever had happened wouldn't have the chance to happen again for another couple of weeks. She only had three more rows to input, and she'd be done... for the second time.

"Would you be interested in going out for dinner sometime?"

Aria froze, then turned her chair to face him, heat rising in her cheeks. "Out for dinner? With you? Just you?"

Gareth grinned. "Yes. Yes. And yes."

Butterflies erupted in Aria's stomach as she realized that Charli and Janessa had been right. At least, she assumed he was talking about a date. Maybe he was just talking about taking her out so that he could get to know her better as an employee or a friend.

She wasn't opposed to that. Honestly, she wasn't opposed to the date idea either, but that was a lot scarier for her. And if word got back to Nora that she'd gone out for dinner with Gareth—whether or not it was a date—she would probably lose her mind and make Aria's life miserable.

Would Gareth step in to make sure that didn't happen?

When Gareth said, "You don't have to let me know right now. And there's absolutely no pressure for you to go if you don't want to," Aria realized that she'd hesitated too long.

"It's not that I don't want to," she told him.

"Are you worried that it might make things awkward here at work?" Gareth asked, his expression turning serious.

"Maybe. I'm also wondering how Nora would react if she got wind of the fact that we'd had dinner together."

Gareth nodded, obviously taking her concern seriously. "I understand that, and I certainly wouldn't tell her, and I don't think any of the others would either."

Aria didn't doubt that at all, but it wouldn't surprise her if Nora had spies spread around Serenity to report on Gareth's activities. The woman was intently focused on the man, and if Aria agreed to this dinner, that focus would land on her with none of the fondness that Nora held for Gareth.

Even without time to think about it, Aria wanted to say yes. To embrace yet one more opportunity. To see if the feelings she had for Gareth might be returned.

"In that case, I would love to go for dinner."

This time, his smile lit up his face. "Wonderful! Do you have a preference on where to go? Type of food?"

"I don't know anything about restaurants around here, so I'll leave that up to you."

"What about the type of food?" Gareth asked, his relaxed body posture making it seem like he did this kind of thing all the time.

Only Janessa had said that he wasn't a big dater, and that too often, women misread his interest in them. Aria needed to keep that in mind until she got a clear sign one way or another.

It would probably have been wiser for her to say no and keep her distance from him in all but a friendly or professional manner. This situation held so much potential... for hurt, definitely, but there was also the possibility that something might grow between them. And she desperately wanted that.

"I like most types of food," Aria said. "Though I have to say I'm not a huge fan of seafood."

Gareth nodded. "So no shrimp or lobster."

"Yep. And no fish."

"You're in luck in that I have a seafood allergy, so I won't risk taking you to a restaurant that only serves something that's going to cause me great discomfort."

"I don't have any food allergies, though being around cats can have me sneezing my head off."

"Too bad you're not allergic to dogs," Gareth said. "Then Charli could use that as an excuse when Layla bugs her for a dog."

"Charli doesn't want a dog?"

"Charli and Janessa don't want a dog," Janessa said as she approached the desk. "I don't mind Bella coming over temporarily, but I don't want a dog full-time."

"You're such a mean aunt." Gareth's grin took the sting out of his words. "You're probably Layla's favorite aunt, and still, you're willing to break that little girl's heart."

"Shut up." Janessa grabbed a piece of paper from the printer and balled it up before quickly tossing it at Gareth. When it bounced off his forehead, she yelled, "Score!"

Gareth chuckled as he leaned over and plucked the ball of paper from the floor. "Now try to get it into the garbage. Jay could do it."

"But not you?" Aria asked.

"I need a set of goalposts or an end zone."

"And still you didn't score as often as I did," Jay remarked. "Is there a meeting going on?"

"There wasn't," Gareth said as he tossed the paper ball at Jay, who easily snagged it out of the air, then pivoted and tossed it into the garbage can. "But perhaps there should be one."

"If it's about Nora, I'm out." Jay leaned back against the wall and crossed his arms.

"Don't tell me you don't have an opinion," Janessa said as she pushed at his arm. "Because I know for sure that you do."

"Oh, I do," Jay agreed. "But there's nothing we can do about the situation at the moment. Until she does something that warrants firing, it's a waste of time to keep discussing her. I'm not a fan of going in circles."

"Mark this on your calendar," Gareth said. "I agree with Jay."

"Creating a hostile work environment should warrant a firing," Janessa grumbled.

"And it does." Jay straightened, bracing his hands on his hips as he directed his gaze Aria's way. "Has she made work horrible for you?"

"Not... horrible," Aria said. "Just uncomfortable, sometimes."

"If that changes or things get worse, you be sure to tell one of us."

"I'm pretty sure it will be my word against hers." And Aria was also pretty sure they wouldn't choose to keep a receptionist over a doctor.

"You let us decide that," Gareth said. "Just let us know what she's done, and we'll discuss the situation and make a decision."

"I know you wouldn't fake something just to get rid of her." Janessa gave her a smile. "We trust you to be honest about what's going on. Just keep this." Janessa gestured between Aria and Gareth. "Out of the office or it will be a hostile workplace for *all* of us."

"What's this?" Jay asked, a frown furrowing his brow.

Aria froze, not wanting to be the one to answer Jay's question. That was mainly because she wasn't sure *how* to.

"I asked Aria out on a date," Gareth said without hesitation.

Well, that answered her question on whether or not his invitation to dinner was a date. Warmth swirled through her at the thought that Gareth—the man she had feelings for—actually liked her enough to want to go on a date with her.

"Oh." Jay glanced between them. He didn't seem upset, so that was a good thing. "Well, then I definitely second what Nessa said. Keep it out of the office for sure. And please, if it doesn't work out, stay friends so things don't get messy."

"You mean like you do with your exes?" Janessa asked.

"Exactly."

Given how badly her relationship with her fiancé had ended, there had been no possibility of remaining friends. It had never really entered Aria's mind that a couple could remain friends after breaking up. She wasn't sure how a person could have feelings for someone and then go on to be friends when things didn't work out romantically.

If that was actually possible—and from what Jay indicated, it was—maybe she didn't have to worry as much about losing her job if this attempt at dating Gareth fizzled out. Though she had a hard time believing that if she still had feelings for Gareth and he broke up with her, that she'd be able to handle seeing him day in and day out, possibly moving on with another woman.

But she was borrowing trouble from the future, so Aria set those thoughts aside for the time being.

"We were just discussing where to go for dinner," Gareth said.

"Are you going tonight?" Janessa asked.

"I was thinking tomorrow or Wednesday. I have Bible study on Thursday, and we have another of Cole's games on Friday night." Gareth looked at Aria. "Would either day work for you?"

"Yes. I don't have any plans." Aria glanced at Janessa in time to catch her smirk.

"Don't go anywhere in Serenity," Jay said. "Not unless you want everyone to be talking about you by the next day."

"Yeah. That's true. Do you have any suggestions, Jay?" Gareth asked. "You've been on the most dates."

Aria listened as the three siblings debated the restaurant options for the surrounding towns. Since she hadn't explored much beyond the town of Serenity, she had no opinion. The furthest she'd gone was to the nearby town for Cole's basketball game.

"Is Indian cuisine okay with you?" Gareth asked. "Do you like spicier food?"

"Not super spicy," Aria said. "But I like butter chicken and rice."

"That restaurant has the best Indian food," Jay said. "You'll enjoy it."

Janessa hummed. "Now I want to go there."

"Find a guy to tag along with you, and we can double-date," Gareth said.

That suggestion made Janessa groan. "I just want the food. Not a guy."

"Sorry." Gareth grinned at her as he shifted his chair back and forth lightly. "Date night only."

"You're mean." Janessa turned to face Aria. "But *you're* not. Will you bring me some food?"

"Sure. I suppose I could do that."

"See, Gareth?" Janessa flicked her hand in his direction. "That's how a nice person responds to a desperate plea for good food."

As usual, Aria enjoyed watching the siblings interact. She was also excited about the plans for her date with Gareth, but she just hoped that she didn't screw anything up.

So many wonderful things had happened over the past few weeks, and she was worried that maybe there had been too many. It was like waiting for the other shoe to drop, but maybe there was no other shoe. Maybe this was going to make up for the absolutely horrible two years she'd had to endure.

"Well, I'm heading out," Jay said with a salute. "I need to get to the school for practice."

"Are you ready to go?" Janessa asked Aria as Jay disappeared down the hall toward the back of the building.

"I can give you a ride if you're not ready to go yet," Gareth offered.

"That sounds perfect," Janessa said before Aria had a chance to respond. "I'll see you at home."

With that pronouncement, Janessa gave a wave of her hand, then followed Jay.

Gareth chuckled. "That one has never been subtle."

"I just have to finalize this order, then I'll be ready to go."

"No rush." He pulled his legs in and got to his feet. "I'll be in my office. Just come get me when you're ready."

Aria nodded, then watched as he walked away from her. She still had a hard time believing that a man like Gareth would really be interested in someone like her. Of course, he didn't really know her all that well yet, so he might change his mind once they'd spent a little time together.

Shaking her head, Aria tried to rid herself of the negative thoughts so she could focus on the order. It was important that she do this correctly so Jay wouldn't have any reason to complain about her work.

Once the order was submitted, she wrote the transaction number on the paper copy of the order, then put it in the file Janessa had shown her. She'd use it to verify they got everything when the order came in.

After that was done, she made sure everything was ready for the next day, then she shut down the computer. The clinic was eerily silent as she left the reception area, shutting off lights as she moved toward the hall. She knew the cleaner would be in shortly, but for the time being, it was just her and Gareth in the building.

As she passed Gareth's office, she paused and knocked on his door. "I'm just going to grab my coat and purse, then I'll be ready to go."

"Perfect." Gareth pushed back from his desk. "I'll be there in a minute."

In the small staff room, Aria pulled on her warm jacket. She met Gareth by the back door, where he set the alarm before holding the door open for her.

The sun had already set, and the air held a chill, making her doubly glad for the thick jacket she wore.

"We might end up with some snow," Gareth said as he started the car. "They've been forecasting it, and it feels like maybe they're right."

"I don't suppose that you shut down the clinic for a little snow."

Gareth laughed. "Nope. We don't shut down much of anything around here for a little snow, and it's been a while since we've had a snowfall that did shut things down."

Aria angled herself in her seat so that she could watch Gareth, but she wasn't able to see him well in the dimly lit car. "I wasn't sure if you were actually asking me on a date earlier."

"But you said yes," Gareth said. "So, what did you think you were agreeing to?"

"I thought maybe it was just a desire on your part to get to know me better as an employee."

"Huh. I guess I should have clarified. Maybe if I hadn't asked you at work, it might have been clearer." He paused, then looked over at her as he pulled to a stop at a red light. "Would you have said no if you'd known it was a date? I mean, I don't want you to feel like you have to go if you'd prefer not to."

"I *do* want to go," Aria hurried to assure him. "I would have happily accepted either reason for a dinner with you."

Gareth put the car in motion again, and in the flashes of light from the lampposts as they drove, Aria could see a smile on his face. "I'm glad to hear that."

Gareth actually seemed to be excited about it, which made Aria both excited and nervous. She hadn't felt like that since her first few dates with Tim. Hopefully, this wouldn't have the disastrous outcome that her engagement had had.

CHAPTER SEVENTEEN

Gareth paused for a moment in front of the mirror on his closet door to check how he looked. Since they were going to a casual restaurant, he could get away with a pair of jeans and a white cotton collared shirt. It was long-sleeved, but he'd rolled the sleeves up to his elbows.

After making sure that he looked okay, Gareth made his way to the front door. He grabbed his wallet from where he'd left it on the small table by the front door and shoved it into his back pocket. After pulling on his jacket, he picked up his keys and left the house.

Though he'd just seen Aria not that long ago, he was excited to pick her up. Word had spread fast through the family that he'd asked her out. It wasn't a surprise because he wasn't sure that any of the family could keep a secret to save their souls.

Well, they could keep professional secrets because they would have been out of a job pretty quickly if they couldn't. But when it came to family related stuff, they were quick to share news.

Gareth wasn't upset about his plans being known by all his siblings, especially since no one seemed concerned by the prospect of him dating Aria. He'd even gotten a message from his mom around lunch. As she was inclined to do, she'd offered both encouragement and advice, reminding him to be sensitive to Aria and to take things slowly, among other things.

He understood why she cautioned him to take things slowly. She knew his tendency to get very focused on an issue, which made him move more quickly than perhaps he should. While that could be a good trait for certain things, like tackling medical school, his mom had told him that when it came to dating and relationships, moving too quickly wasn't always beneficial.

Considering he'd only known Aria for a few weeks and that already he had feelings for her, his mom's caution might have arrived a little too late. He didn't want to reveal too much to Aria just yet, in case he scared her off.

When he pulled to the curb in front of the large house, Gareth grinned, even though he was alone in the car. He got out and headed for the front door. When it swung open, Layla stood there with a big smile.

"Uncle Gare!" she called out. "We've been waitin' for you!"

"Have you?" He closed the door, then swung her up into his arms and rubbed his cheek against hers, sending her into gales of laughter.

"You're cold and prickly!"

"You're not going with him, Layla," Charli said as she joined them.

"I want to, though," Layla whined as Gareth set her back down. "Why can't I go too?"

"This is just a special dinner for Aria and Gareth," Charli told her. "No one else allowed."

Layla crossed her arms and frowned. "That's not fair."

"You need to stop with the attitude, Layla Marie," Charli cautioned. "We told you why you can't go. Your whining isn't going to change that. If you keep it up, there will be no television or movies for you tonight."

That clammed Layla right up. She pursed her lips but didn't say anything more.

Gareth felt a little bad that his niece was so disappointed, but he didn't feel bad enough to take her along with them. "We'll do dinner another time. Okay?"

"Okay," Layla murmured, then she headed for the kitchen with slumped shoulders and dragging feet.

"Next time, we won't discuss your dates around her," Charli muttered with a shake of her head. "And I'm going to remember this when she starts dating. I'll throw a tantrum when she won't take me with her."

"Oh, that's a great idea. I'll be happy to beg her to go along, too."

That made Charli laugh. "You'd probably be a lot scarier for a guy dating her than I would be."

Movement caught his eye, and Gareth turned to see Aria and Janessa coming down the stairs. Aria was dressed in a pair of fitted jeans and a dark green, oversized sweater. She looked ready for a relaxed evening, much like he was.

When she glanced up and their gazes met, she gave him a smile that seemed to be a little shy. Gareth smiled back at her, eager to get their evening underway. Since they both had work the next day, they wouldn't be able to stay out super late, which was why he didn't want to waste any time.

"You look beautiful," he said, unable to keep that observation to himself.

"Thank you." Her cheeks flushed even as her smile grew. "You look very nice as well."

"You two are adorable," Janessa said. "I'm so glad I'm getting to witness this."

"Me, too," Charli said.

"And now we're going to go." Gareth turned to Aria. "Are you ready?"

She nodded. "Just need to get my jacket and boots."

He stepped to the side so that she could get to the closet near the door.

"Are you sure I can't come with you?" Janessa asked.

"Good grief," Charli exclaimed. "Do I have to threaten you with punishment, too?"

"You're not the boss of me," Janessa told her, sounding amazingly like Layla.

"I'll tell Mom you're trying to sabotage Gareth and Aria's date."

Telling Mom was the one threat that would pull most of them back into line.

"You did promise to bring me food, Aria," Janessa said, turning her back on Charli.

Aria nodded as she zipped up her jacket. "I will."

"Perfect." Janessa grinned. "I'll text you my order."

"Text it to me," Gareth said. "I'll just order it along with our food."

"Did you want anything, Charli?" Aria asked.

Charli hesitated, then said, "Sure. I'll have Janessa add my order to hers."

"We'd better scoot before they decide it would just be easier to come with us," Gareth said as he moved to where Aria waited by the front door. "Let's make our escape."

Aria grinned as he opened the door and motioned for her to precede him out onto the porch. Once he pulled the door shut behind him, he breathed a sigh of relief.

"Your family is so wonderful," Aria said as they walked to the car.

Gareth opened the passenger door for her. "Are you being sarcastic?"

"Not at all."

He closed the door for her, then went around to slide behind the wheel. "I happen to agree with you. However, just because I think they're wonderful doesn't make them less annoying. We're just lucky there were only three of them there. If Wilder and Jay had been present, the banter would have been much worse."

The drive to the nearby city that had the best Indian restaurant took about half an hour. There wasn't a huge variety of authentic cuisine like Chinese or East Indian in Serenity. During his medical school days, he'd been introduced to a variety of cuisines that he hadn't grown up with, and he'd grown to appreciate the broad diversity offered in Seattle.

"Do you like different cuisines?" Gareth asked as he drove along the dark highway.

"Mom and I didn't eat out much," she said, her voice soft with an edge of sadness that made him want to pull her into his arms and hold her close. "So we didn't have much opportunity to try different types of food."

"But you're okay with Indian?"

"Yep. I worked with a lovely East Indian woman, and she would bring food to work that her mom had made. I wasn't a fan of the curry. It was a little too spicy for me. But the butter chicken and naan were wonderful."

Gareth was glad to hear that. Even though she'd said she liked it when he'd first asked her, he wanted to be sure that she was going to enjoy every part of their time together. Since food was a big part of the evening, if she hated that, then it would put a damper on their time together.

"What types of food did you and your mom like?" Gareth hoped that asking about her mom wouldn't upset her. He wanted Aria to know that he wanted to hear about her mom, knowing that she had been so important to Aria.

"Mom loved potatoes in any form, though mashed were her favorite."

"Oh, I really like mashed potatoes too, especially when served with gravy from a roast. What's your favorite?"

"Type of potato?" Aria asked.

"Sure. Or just food in general."

"I like French fries, but I didn't eat them too often. As far as other food, my mom made the most amazing homemade mac and cheese. I think I could have lived on that and just swapped out the accompaniments. You know, bacon with it for breakfast. Hamburger for lunch. Chicken for supper."

Gareth laughed. "It must really be amazing if you'd eat it that frequently. Did she teach you how to make it?"

"Yeah, but I haven't made it since she passed away."

"Well, if you do make it, please invite me to try it."

"I will. The main reason I haven't made it yet is because it's not much fun making it for one, you know?"

"Yeah. I get that."

"Do you know how to cook?"

"Yep," he said. "Mom tried to teach all of us at least the basics. So I can cook for myself, though I do try to catch a meal with one of the siblings as often as possible. I get the best food at Charli and Janessa's, though if I go to where Kayleigh works, it's pretty good food too."

"I enjoy cooking at Charli and Janessa's," Aria said. "That kitchen is amazing. I've only been helping them with meals so far since I don't think I'm as good a cook as either of them."

"We aren't fancy eaters," Gareth assured her. "As long as the food tastes good, we'll eat it."

When they reached the restaurant, he found a parking spot close to the building, then they got out and headed for the door. Gareth hadn't been to the restaurant in a while, but he was quite sure the food was still good.

A smiling woman greeted them upon entering the restaurant, and it took only a moment to be seated. It was a small restaurant, focused more on takeout than dine-in, so the atmosphere was cozy and intimate, the air richly scented with spices, promising a tasty meal.

The server who came to take their order greeted them with a warm smile. Considering his earlier conversation with Aria, it was no surprise that she ordered butter chicken. He ordered curry since he did like spicier food, and it was rare that anyone in the family made it. They also requested rice and naan bread.

Once they were left alone, Gareth floundered for a topic of conversation. It wasn't that he had nothing to say; it was that he had *so much* he wanted to learn about Aria that he didn't know where to start.

"Do you miss living in a big city?" Gareth asked. "I know that moving to a smaller city can be a bit of an adjustment."

Her expression seemed to freeze for a moment before she shook her head. "I didn't mind living in the city while I was there, but I'm happy with the change of scenery. It isn't like I've moved to the middle of nowhere. As long as I'm within driving distance of a store or two, I'm happy."

"How about working in a hospital?"

Again, she seemed to pause for a moment before answering. "I actually like the slower pace of the clinic and knowing that I'll become familiar with people over time."

"The clinic is definitely slower paced. It was a bit of an adjustment for me when I came back here after doing my residency."

"Was it always your plan to return?"

"Yep. I always knew that I'd come back and work alongside my folks. But not long after I came home, they decided to semi-retire from the clinic and do medical missions work."

"Did that happen right away?"

Gareth shook his head. "It was about a year after I got back, though they told me about their intentions sooner. They wanted to make sure I was confident in running the clinic alongside Jay. He'd been doing the admin work for a couple of years by that point. Most importantly, though, was my mom's desire that we have a female doctor to work with me before they completely left the clinic."

"That's where Nora comes in, huh?"

"Yep. It took us almost the full year to find someone who was willing to move to Serenity."

"Why was Nora willing to move when others weren't?"

"That's a good question," Gareth said with a shrug. "Perhaps she had issues in previous workplaces. We've had no problems—for the most part—with her patient interactions. The issues have definitely been centered around her perceptions concerning my relationships with other women."

"Jealousy?"

"I guess. The problem is that it's usually just her imagination. She seems to think any woman I have a conversation with, I'm interested in dating." Gareth frowned as he recalled some of the conversations he'd had with Nora that had no basis in reality. "I've only dated one woman since Nora came to work with us."

That made Aria frown. "Did you stop dating her because of Nora?"

"No. Carly ended up getting a job offer in another state, and neither of us wanted to do long-distance."

"Do you..." She paused, her brow furrowing. "Do you think it will be different with us? I mean, are we going to have to... to date in secret?"

"I know that doesn't sound like fun," Gareth admitted. "But thankfully, because you're a friend of Janessa's, and a family friend now too, it will make sense for us to hang out together."

The server returned with their food, interrupting their conversation. After she had set down their plates and a small basket that held several pieces of naan bread, Gareth said a prayer of thanks for the food. Their conversation focused on the food for a few minutes, before Gareth turned it back to the former topic.

"I'd understand if you'd rather keep your distance than deal with Nora."

"She's already been a bit difficult," Aria said, rubbing her free hand against her opposite arm. "And that was before you asked me out. I doubt her meanness would stop, even if we weren't dating."

"I don't think she'd stop even if she and I dated because she wouldn't trust me. Interaction with any other woman on my part would signal cheating to her. I couldn't deal with that."

"So you were never interested in her?"

Gareth shook his head. "I wasn't going to date her just because she thought we should be a medical couple like my parents were. Jay and I have been searching for a doctor to replace her, but it's not been easy."

"So you're really going to replace her?"

"It's not that I want her gone on a professional level," Gareth said as he ripped a piece off his naan. "But I've spoken to her plenty of times about not interfering in my personal life. How am I ever supposed to have a relationship if she's right there interfering and stalking me? It's just not normal."

"There was no sign that she'd done this in her past?" Aria asked.

"Nope. Personally, I think that perhaps none of her previous workplaces said anything because they just wanted her gone. It's too bad, really, because she's smart and dedicated to her work. She just needs to pull back on the personal stuff and focus on her own life."

He had a feeling that she was going to interfere with Aria, whether or not she was aware that they had started dating. It bugged him that he would have to police his interactions with Aria just so that Nora wouldn't pick up on anything.

"Anyway, enough about Nora," Gareth said. "Although you need to tell us if stuff gets too bad with her."

"I will," Aria said, but Gareth wasn't reassured. Aria didn't strike him as the type to make trouble for someone, even though they might make trouble for her.

Gareth steered the conversation away from Nora and on to more pleasant things as he told her more about his life in Serenity. She seemed more interested in talking about him than talking about herself. Gareth would give that to her for their first date, but in the future, he wanted to know everything about her.

He wanted to ask how she was dealing with her mom's passing, but that seemed heavy for the first date. And on the off chance she was really sensitive to the topic—which he completely understood—he didn't want her to start crying.

So he kept the conversation light, taking great delight in making her smile and laugh as he regaled her with tales of things he'd done with his siblings and his friends. He knew he'd been blessed with his large family and his friends, some of whom had been with him for most of his life.

It seemed that perhaps that hadn't been the case for Aria. She hadn't mentioned having any other friends, but surely, she'd had at least one in Sacramento. She struck him as someone people would enjoy being friends with.

He was aware that not everyone had a large circle of friends. Even in his family, there were some who were happy to have just one or two close friends.

It had been a while since Gareth had been on a first date, but as far as he was concerned, this first one was going great. He suspected that was because he was drawn to Aria in a way he hadn't been to a woman before.

Her smiles seemed genuine, and they made him smile. He hoped that it meant she'd consider a second date, even with the specter of Nora hanging over their heads.

He'd always been attracted to quiet women. It wasn't that he didn't want them to talk, but he liked a woman who had a calming effect on him. With a job that could be stressful, he needed someone who wasn't focused on drama or was demanding of his time.

Aria's presence in the clinic and in his life so far had shown her to be calm and efficient. Even the patients' comments had turned from her relationship status to how sweet she was, and how much they appreciated her. She'd definitely been the positive addition that Janessa had promised she'd be. In the clinic and in his life.

When Janessa had mentioned wanting to offer the receptionist position to her friend, Gareth had never imagined that she'd fill a spot in his personal life as well as his professional one. He was so thankful that he and Jay had finally agreed with Janessa, even if they'd had their doubts. The thought of never meeting Aria hurt his heart, and Gareth was glad that he didn't have to consider life without her.

CHAPTER EIGHTEEN

Aria welcomed the heat that enveloped her as she sank into the heated seat in Gareth's car. The cold seemed to have intensified while they'd eaten dinner, and she'd gotten chilled even though it had only been a short walk from the restaurant to the car. Since Gareth had placed the bag with the takeout order for his sisters on the back seat, the aroma of their dinner followed them into the car.

"Thank you for dinner," she said as she watched Gareth guide the car out onto the street. "It was wonderful."

"I'm glad you enjoyed it." Gareth glanced over at her. "Maybe we could do it again sometime."

Warmth flooded Aria that had nothing to do with the heat spilling from the vents or the heated seats. That Gareth had enjoyed their time together enough to want to do it again made her so happy.

And hopeful... Probably more hopeful than she should be.

Her confidence had taken a huge hit after Tim had ended their engagement. He'd made her feel like she hadn't been worth the effort of going through the hard times with her. Even in the short time she'd known Gareth, she'd seen that he was different. That he would be a solid rock if someone needed that strength in their life.

"I'd love to," she told him.

"We can try another restaurant next time. Maybe one of those Korean barbecue places. Although we might have to drive a bit further for that."

As far as Aria was concerned, the farther the drive, the better. Not just because it lessened the chances of Nora seeing them together, but also because she'd enjoy spending extra time with Gareth.

Cocooned in the warmth of the car, with Gareth sitting next to her, Aria felt happier than she had in a long time. Was it really possible that she could finally leave the horror of the past two years behind? She'd never leave the memory of her mom. But everything else that had happened? Yeah, she wanted all that to be gone from her memory.

"Have Janessa and Charli talked to you about their small group at church?" Gareth asked.

"They've mentioned it in passing." Aria wasn't sure that she was ready to be part of a group like that just yet, so she was glad that they weren't pressuring her.

"I hope you know you'd be welcome to join them if you ever want to."

"Yes. Janessa mentioned that." She hesitated, not sure if she should talk about her previous non-involvement with a church. But she wanted to. Even though she couldn't tell him everything about her past, she wanted to tell him a bit about it. "My mom and I moved around a lot during my growing up years, so we never really got involved with the small groups in the churches we attended. Mom also always seemed to prefer large churches."

"Did you have any kind of support from the church you were attending when your mom passed away?"

"No." Aria turned her gaze to the road in front of them. "Even though we'd been attending that church regularly for a couple of years, we hadn't really made any friends there. It was easy to blend in and get lost in the crowd. My mom seemed to want that, and to be honest, at the time it was easier for me, too."

"So, no one from the church was there for you when your mom died?"

Aria clenched her hands together, trying not to let her heart return to that time, though her mind did. "Not really. No. But it was okay."

Even as she said the words, she was certain that Gareth saw them for the lie they were. Losing her mom—her only family—like that had broken her in so many ways, and there had been no one there to hold her as she'd tried to put her life back together again. She still clung to some broken pieces of herself, trying to figure out how to fit them into the new shape that her life had taken after she'd been left alone.

"I know that it's probably not a time you like to dwell on," Gareth said, his voice low and soft. "But just know that you can talk to me about it, if you need to. I'm sure you already know that Janessa would always listen, but so would I and so would Charli. Any of our family would, actually."

Aria did know that, but the last thing she wanted was to weigh them down with all her emotional baggage. She didn't want to be a burden to anyone. She wanted them to see her as a positive addition to their lives. None of them seemed to struggle the way she did.

"Thank you. I appreciate that. I'm doing okay, though, and most days it's just easier to keep focused forward."

"I get that," Gareth said. "But I also know that sometimes our emotions can take us in a different direction. Which is why I want you to know that you're safe to share your heart with us."

He might think he was safe, but there were things Aria wasn't sure she could ever share with any of them. She was aware enough about mental health to know that she should probably have gone to counseling after everything that had happened, but she hadn't had the money to spend on that. Her anxiety, though better since coming to Serenity and leaving behind the toxic situation in Sacramento, had still not completely vanished. She hoped that in time it would, but something told her it wasn't likely.

"Has your family lived here your whole life?" Aria asked, ready to turn the focus back on Gareth.

He hesitated for a moment, and she wondered if he wanted to question her more about her past. Thankfully, when he replied, it was to tell her a little about the history of his family.

"My dad's family is from here, but my mom's from Washington State. They met in medical school, then when they got married, they came back here and took over the clinic from my grandfather. He and my grandma live in Florida now. A few years ago, my mom came into a significant inheritance from her grandparents, and it gave her and Dad the opportunity to get involved in the medical mission work."

"I'm sure they're happy that you are carrying on their work at the clinic."

"They would have continued to work there if none of us had been interested in the medical profession. As it is, it's just me and Janessa who have gone that route."

"I'm glad Janessa became a nurse," Aria said as she angled herself toward Gareth again. "If she hadn't, I never would have met her, and I wouldn't have come to Serenity."

"That would definitely have been our loss." Gareth glanced over at her. "My loss, especially."

Aria couldn't keep the smile off her face. His words were like a balm on the parts of her heart that were still bruised and broken.

"It would have been my loss too," she told him. "Being able to come here has been so wonderful. I'm very thankful for this opportunity."

"We're very blessed to have you," Gareth said. "The patients also really like you. More than one has mentioned how much they enjoy you being at the front desk. The kids especially like you."

"I like them too, and I'm glad I'm able to help them not be so scared of the big bad doctor."

Gareth chuckled at her words. "Is that what they call me?"

"No, but judging from how scared some of them are, you'd think that was who they were going to see."

"Maybe I need to hand out the lollipops instead of you."

"Maybe, but then they wouldn't like me as much."

As they neared Serenity, disappointment filled Aria that their evening was almost over. At least she knew that she'd see him the next day at work, and it sounded like they'd be going out again soon, so she could look forward to that.

"Are you planning to go to the basketball game on Friday?"

"Yep. I've become a bit of a fan of the game now," she said. "I enjoy the atmosphere at the games and being able to cheer on someone I know."

"Would you like to go out for dinner on Saturday?" he asked. "I'm tied up for the rest of the evenings this week, but we could go out after I finish practicing with the worship team on Saturday afternoon."

"Saturday would be great."

"We can decide if we want to eat Korean barbecue or something else later," Gareth said. "Or we can do something else. Like go to a movie."

"I enjoyed our dinner. I liked being able to talk to you, which wouldn't be possible if we went to the movies."

He glanced over at her, and as they passed under a streetlamp, she could see the smile on his face. "I enjoyed talking with you, too."

For a moment, Aria wondered if she was dreaming. She'd come to Serenity in search of a new life. With no job, no fiancé, and no family, she'd come hoping to escape the pain and the hurt. A new job—even if it wasn't what she'd trained for—and a safe place to live were all that had mattered to her. And yet it seemed like she was going to gain so much more.

New friends, and possibly... hopefully... a new love.

When Gareth pulled to a stop in front of the house, Aria wanted to tell him to keep driving. She didn't want the evening to end. But since they both had work the next day, it was inevitable.

Gareth fell in step beside her, his arm brushing hers as they walked toward the house. When they got to the door, he grabbed hold of the doorknob, but didn't open the door right away.

The sconces on either side of the door cast soft pools of warm light around them as they stood there. Aria didn't know what to say. Didn't know how to end their time together, especially since she didn't want to.

Tim had moved in for a kiss at the end of their first date, but something told Aria that Gareth wouldn't do that. And she was okay with moving a bit slower.

"I'll see you tomorrow, which makes me very happy." The smile on his face was soft, and Aria's heart melted a little as he reached out and took her hand, holding it gently in his. "I know that we have to interact as co-workers at the clinic, but just know that in my heart, you're so much more."

Her heart stuttered at his words, finding that they were true for her as well. "I feel that way, too. But even though we have to hide our relationship at work, I'm glad I get to see you there every day."

Gareth's smile grew as his fingers tightened slightly around hers. "I totally agree."

When the sconce lights flickered, Aria looked at them in concern. Meanwhile, Gareth chuckled.

"That would be Janessa or Charli," he said when she looked at him. "Just being a sibling."

Letting go of her hand, Gareth opened the door, then motioned for Aria to precede him into the house. As she stepped into the foyer area, Aria spotted Janessa leaning against the wall next to the light switches with her arms crossed, a broad grin on her face.

Bella lay on the rug behind her. The dog lifted her head briefly, and her tail gave a thump on the floor before she settled back down again.

"We should have taken bets on which one of them it would be," Gareth said as he closed the door.

"I think we both would have guessed Janessa."

"True," Gareth agreed. "Charli would probably have just opened the door."

"How did it go?" Janessa asked, her grin settling into a genuine smile.

It made Aria feel good that her friend seemed to support Aria dating her brother. A small voice reminded her, however, that there were things that should Janessa learn of them, she might not be so keen on them dating. She ignored the voice, hoping it would fade away and never come back.

"We had a great time." Gareth held out the bag from the restaurant. "Here's your food."

"Oh, thank you. Thank you." Janessa took the bag from him. "Dinner is sorted for tomorrow night. I hope you got lots."

"I got plenty. No worries." Gareth turned to Aria. "I'd better get going. I'll see you tomorrow."

Aria nodded. "Have a good night."

After he said goodnight to Janessa, he gave Aria one last lingering look before he opened the door and stepped out onto the porch. Aria stood in place, watching until the door closed, blocking off her view of him.

"So you really had a good time with my boring older brother?" Janessa asked as she wrapped an arm around Aria.

Aria glanced over to find her friend staring at the closed door. "He's not boring."

"Maybe not to you," Janessa said. "But give it a few, and he will be."

"I somehow doubt that."

Janessa looked over at her, dropping her arm as she grinned. "Well, it's good to see that you're already so enamored with him."

"He's very nice," Aria told her. "And I very much enjoyed spending time with him."

"Are you going out again?" Janessa asked as she turned and headed for the kitchen with the bag of food. "Just wondering where I might get food from next."

Aria laughed and followed her, then settled on a stool. Janessa investigated the contents of the bag before putting the food into the fridge.

"We're going to go out on Saturday," Aria said. "But we haven't decided where yet. He did mention something about Korean barbecue, though."

"Oooh, that sounds yummy," Janessa said as she folded up the takeout bag and put it in the recycling bin. "I'll have to figure out what I want."

"Are we going to have to bring you food from every restaurant we go to?"

"Of course. Consider it payment."

"Uh... for what, exactly?" Aria asked. "It's not like you're babysitting for us or anything."

"Oh. Babysitting for you guys? This is definitely moving faster than I had expected."

Aria sputtered out a laugh at her friend's over-the-top reaction. "Good grief. That was just an example. There was no talk of kids or anything like that tonight."

"Whew. I thought for a minute I was going to have to lecture Gareth about not rushing into things."

Aria thought back over the years she'd lived with Janessa, trying to remember what she might have said about Gareth. He'd been in medical school and doing his residency for much of that time. Janessa had talked more about Jay and Charli, though she'd shared bits about all her siblings. It just seemed she was closest to those two, which made sense since Jay was her biological brother and Charli was closest to her in age.

"Are you really okay with me dating Gareth?" Aria asked, hoping that she would not regret asking the question. What would she do if Janessa said no?

"I'm fine with it," Janessa said. "From a strictly personal standpoint, he's great, and you're great. I think you could be great together. I just don't want anything to go wrong, that would mess with the environment at work."

Aria nodded. "I understand that. But I really do like Gareth, from almost the moment we met. I just didn't think he'd like me back."

"I was a bit surprised, but honestly, I shouldn't have been." Janessa leaned over the counter on the other side of the island. She braced her arms on it, interlacing her fingers as she regarded Aria. "You *are* very much his type."

"He likes blondes?" she asked.

Janessa laughed. "No. He doesn't seem to have a physical type. You're his type, personality-wise. He's always liked quiet, more introverted women. High maintenance or extremely extroverted women are not his thing."

Would wanting a significant other to support her through something like she'd gone through be considered high maintenance? Tim had made it seem like it was. "Well, pretty sure I've got the quiet and introverted part down pat."

"I know that from personal experience," she said with a wink. "You would have thought I was suggesting torture when I'd try to encourage you to socialize."

"Sometimes it *was* torture," Aria said. "I found some of the people around us to be incredibly juvenile. Not you, though. I respected that you knew when to work hard and when you could let loose. Some of the people at school seemed to only be there for the parties. Since I'd worked so hard to get scholarships, I couldn't afford to mess around."

"I understood that, but I also thought it was important that you take the time to relax occasionally. That's why I only dragged you out once in a while and not all the time."

Aria traced a pattern over the smooth surface of the counter with her fingertips, keeping her gaze lowered. "Will your parents care if we're dating?"

"If they had concerns, they would have voiced them to Gareth," Janessa said. "But ultimately, they will leave the decision up to him. We're adults now, and while they might not agree with all our decisions, they still support us. They just don't bail us out of the consequences that might come from any bad decisions we make."

Aria looked up at her friend. "Would Gareth tell me if your parents had concerns?"

"Probably. If you asked him. He wouldn't lie if you came right out and asked him. However, he probably wouldn't volunteer the information unless he felt that you needed to know."

Aria wasn't sure she had the nerve to ask him. At least not yet. Maybe if they kept dating, and things were more solid between them.

The front door opened, and soon Skylar appeared in the doorway. She wore a pair of skinny jeans and a baggy sweatshirt with the high school logo on it.

"You made it just under the wire," Janessa said, straightening up from the counter. "Even Aria beat you home."

Skylar wrinkled her nose. "The important part was that you said be home by ten, and here I am."

Charli joined them in the kitchen a couple of minutes later, and Aria listened as the three sisters discussed the plan for the next day. Skylar didn't look thrilled to have to be staying with her sisters while her parents were away, but she didn't argue with them.

After a bit, Aria excused herself and went up to her room, eager for a few minutes alone to think over her evening with Gareth.

Ever since everything had gone wrong in her life, Aria hadn't really asked God for much.

When Tim had broken things off, she'd asked God to make him reconsider. That had been a solid no. Not only had he not been willing to reconsider, he'd refused to even talk to her again.

Then it had felt like God had turned a deaf ear when she'd pleaded for healing for her mom, and her reaction had been to make some terrible decisions.

When the situation had arisen with her job, she'd prayed that they would be lenient with her, considering the circumstances, but they'd still fired her.

As she sat on her bed then, her heart full of emotion and her mind set on Gareth, Aria sent up a prayer, begging God to allow them to build a relationship together. Tears fell as she pleaded for something that had become so important to her.

Maybe... hopefully... God would grant her one more thing, in addition to the new job and a safe place to live.

Or maybe she was being selfish in asking God for something more, and Gareth wasn't meant to be hers.

Aria's heart hurt at that prospect, but she had to prepare herself, because there was just as much chance that their relationship would crash and burn as that it would succeed.

CHAPTER NINETEEN

Friday afternoon couldn't come soon enough for Aria. Though her date with Gareth wasn't until Saturday, she was looking forward to spending some time with him later at the game.

"So, I suppose you'll be going to the ball game tonight."

Aria looked up from her computer to find Nora standing next to the desk, her expression impossible to read.

"Yes, I think so," Aria said, though she really didn't want to give Nora any insight into her plans.

"I suppose you go so that you can get close to Gareth."

That comment struck close enough to the truth that Aria couldn't exactly deny it, but that wasn't the whole truth. "I go because Janessa invites me. I don't have any friends here yet aside from her and Charli, so I enjoy hanging out with them."

"Don't you hang out enough with them since you all live together?" Nora asked.

"Not really. Plus, I really enjoy the games."

Nora crossed her arms. "I only went to one game shortly after I started to work here. Gareth invited me."

Aria ignored the comment about Gareth. Not because she thought Nora was lying, but because it just wasn't relevant anymore. "Did you enjoy it?"

"Not really. The benches were hard. The gym was noisy. And the food was terribly unhealthy."

"All of that is true," Aria agreed. "But I still think it's fun."

"Perhaps I should give it another shot."

Aria wanted to discourage Nora from coming, but she had a feeling that would only make the woman more determined to go. "Perhaps you should."

Nora's brows drew together as she stared at Aria. "You wouldn't care if I came to the game?"

Aria shrugged. "I mean, if you think you'd enjoy it, why would I tell you not to come?"

She looked skeptical at Aria's reply, but all she said was, "Maybe I'll see you there."

Aria smiled brightly at her, which Nora didn't return before she turned and left. Aria's smile slid into a frown as she watched the woman walk away. She really, really hoped that Nora didn't show up at the game. It would definitely put a damper on the evening for her. But at least Nora didn't know about Saturday evening.

At work, she and Gareth had kept their relationship professional, making sure their conversation was focused on their work. They'd agreed that would be easiest, rather than having to remember to make sure Nora couldn't hear them before having a more personal conversation.

That didn't mean they hadn't spoken. Gareth had texted her on Wednesday to see if she'd mind if he called. Her immediate reply had been that she'd mind more if he didn't. They'd spent time on the phone the past two nights, talking about life—both personal and in general. It was the most time she'd spent talking to a guy about stuff like that... ever. And she'd loved it.

She'd been looking forward to spending time with Gareth at the game, but if Nora did show up, they might have to hold off conversing much until a phone call later in the evening. It would be disappointing, but she knew that they'd have plenty of time to talk on their next date.

After finishing up her work, Aria shut down everything at the front. She did a quick restock of the rooms with Janessa to prepare for the Saturday morning clinic.

Jay had left earlier to meet with the team, and Nora had left shortly after her conversation with Aria, so it was just her, Janessa, and Gareth in the clinic.

"Nora said she might come to the game tonight," Aria informed them.

"What?" Janessa demanded. "Why on earth would she say that?"

Aria gave them a quick recap of the conversation she'd had with Nora. "I just didn't want to protest too much."

"You did the right thing," Gareth said. "I kind of doubt she'll show up. She really didn't enjoy it the one time she came."

"Yeah. I remember that." Janessa frowned. "She seemed more interested in impressing you and our parents than watching the game."

"But if she does show up, just act like you normally would." Gareth smiled at Aria. "It'll be fine."

Aria couldn't help but smile back, all the while hoping that Gareth was right. It rankled her that by showing up Nora could force her and Gareth to keep their distance from each other. She wondered how long they'd have to structure their interactions around the other woman's presence.

"Are you coming by the house?" Janessa asked. "Or are we meeting you at the game?"

"I'll come by," Gareth said. "I just need to run home and change."

"We're doing sandwiches as usual," Janessa told him. "Charli's stopping to pick up stuff."

"Sounds good."

The three of them left the building and walked to the cars in the back parking lot. As they neared Janessa's car, Gareth took Aria's hand. When she turned toward him, her heart skipped a beat at the affection in his gaze.

"See you in a bit," he said.

The frustration she'd felt toward Nora faded away. "I can't wait."

He gave her hand a light squeeze before letting go to open the passenger door of Janessa's car for her. Aria slid into the seat, then watched as Gareth shut the door, then stepped back. He didn't go to his car right away, and Aria could see him in the mirror on her side, standing with his arms crossed as Janessa drove out of the parking lot.

"You two are so sweet," Janessa said. "I'm worried I'm going to end up with cavities."

Aria blushed, then gave a laugh. "Sorry. Hope you have good dental insurance."

"Luckily, I do." Janessa chuckled as she turned the car in the direction of the house. "Are you worried about Nora showing up tonight?"

"Not worried." Aria sighed. "Just frustrated because she seems determined to keep me from having any opportunity to spend time with Gareth. I understand why we have to be careful at work, and I have absolutely no problem with that, but it seems like she's going to show up whenever there's a chance the two of us will be in the same place."

"If she goes that far, we'll have to fire her for sure. We can't have a doctor on staff who is stalking people."

"I don't want to cause any problems," Aria said.

"You're not. Nora is the one causing problems. She's had an issue any time she's seen Gareth talking to a woman for longer than just a couple of minutes. Nora is going to stalk anyone she sees as competition, not just you."

"I'm just trying to keep my interactions with her calm."

"You're a better woman than I am. You've seen how she frustrates me. That was going on even before you showed up."

"Well, maybe when I've been dealing with her as long as you have, I'll also be more easily frustrated."

Once they got home, Aria hurried up to her room to change into a pair of jeans and the T-shirt with the team's logo on it. Though they always wore them at away games, Aria liked to wear the T-shirt at home games too. She had to wear a long-sleeve T-shirt underneath it, though, because she was still barely tolerating the cold.

When she walked out of her bedroom, Janessa was coming out of hers as well, dressed in almost identical clothes to Aria. They went back down to the kitchen and found Charli and Layla preparing sandwiches while having an argument about Layla eating any vegetables with hers.

Aria would never have thought she'd enjoy the sometimes-hectic environment of a family home. When it had been just her and her mom, their apartment was usually quiet. Sometimes the television was on, but more often than not, soft music was the background to their conversations and the games they'd liked to play together.

Given how stressful her job at the hospital could be, Aria had always appreciated the calm atmosphere her mom had created in their home, especially in later years. It was an atmosphere that she'd tried to continue to create even as her mom's health had deteriorated. She'd needed the peaceful environment as much as her mom had. Maybe more, considering that her anxiety and worry over her mom had been almost debilitating.

Now, though, Aria found that she enjoyed Layla's chatter and Charli's and Janessa's responses. Even though she didn't always participate in their conversations, they still made her feel welcome.

When the doorbell chimed, Layla abandoned her sandwich and veggies to go answer it. Aria had worried, at first, about the little girl answering the door by herself, but she'd seen that they only let her do it when they knew who was coming. Security cameras were discreetly positioned around the house, so Charli could quickly check them and remotely unlock the front door if it was someone that Layla knew.

"Hello, lovely Layla."

Hearing Gareth's greeting, Aria turned her attention from the sandwich she was preparing to the doorway of the kitchen. When he appeared with Layla in his arms, his gaze found her. A smile grew on his face, and it made her want to run and fling her arms around him.

"Hello, brother," Charli said. "Do you want a sandwich, or are you just going to stare at Aria all evening?"

Heat rushed into Aria's cheeks as Gareth chuckled. "Much as I'd love to do that, I guess I'd better get a sandwich."

He approached the counter, taking a second to settle Layla back on the stool she indicated was hers before coming to stand beside Aria. She glanced at him, giving him another quick smile.

"Nice to see you in the school colors," Gareth said as he took a couple pieces of bread from the bag that Charli had set on the counter.

"I like people to know who I'm cheering for, especially since I'm not one of the loud fans."

"Unlike me," Gareth said with a laugh. "Not sure why Janessa is wearing the school colors. She's even louder than I am."

That set off another session of banter between the siblings. Aria continued to make her sandwich, her arm brushing Gareth's as he did the same. Once she was done making her sandwich, she didn't move away, and neither did he. Side by side, they stood at the counter eating their sandwiches.

Aria didn't have much of an appetite. Her nerves, along with flutters of excitement, had robbed her of much of her desire to eat. She'd had similar feelings when she and Tim had started dating, but never to this extent. And weirdly, a lot of her emotional response had to do with Gareth's choice to cross the room to stand beside her.

Tim had always seemed to expect her to come to him. If he entered a room after she did, he wouldn't come to where she was. He'd wait for her to join him. She hadn't figured it out at first, but then he'd told her that she needed to come to him, regardless of who arrived in the room last.

But here was Gareth, seeming more than willing to come to where she was. And that warmed her, making her feel like he saw her as important.

Once they'd finished eating, they quickly cleaned up the remnants of their meal. Then, after a brief discussion, Charli decided to take her car with Layla while Janessa said she'd ride with Aria and Gareth.

"Unless you'd rather I didn't come with you," Janessa said as she bumped Aria's arm with her elbow as they got ready to go.

"It's fine with me," Aria assured her.

And that was the truth. She and Gareth might still be getting to know each other, but the ride to the school was so short, having Janessa with them wouldn't interrupt any sort of intimate conversation.

The noise that greeted them as they walked into the gym made Aria smile since it was just a taste of the excitement to come. It didn't take them long to find the other members of the Halverson family, though the parents were missing from the bleachers for the first time since Aria had arrived in Serenity.

As they filed into the row Wilder and Kayleigh had saved for them, Aria wondered if it was a good idea for Gareth to sit next to her. Well, it was an excellent idea, if not for the possibility of Nora showing up.

Once they were seated, Aria turned to Gareth and said, "Do you think it's okay for us to sit next to each other?"

He obviously hadn't heard her question over the noise because he slid his arm around her shoulders, then bent his head closer to hers. His cologne teased her nose, and she fought the urge to inhale more deeply. And more than anything, she just wanted to lean into his strength and nearness.

But instead, she repeated her question. He gave a small nod, then turned so that he could speak closer to her ear. "I think it will be fine."

When he sat back a bit, his arm slid from around her shoulders, leaving Aria feeling bereft. He lifted his brows, and she nodded, agreeing with his response.

She wanted to enjoy the evening without worrying about how she was acting toward Gareth in case Nora happened to show up. Since Gareth didn't seem concerned, she'd take her cues from him.

And throughout the game, Gareth's cues were definitely that he wanted to be close to her, and he didn't really seem too worried about who might see them. Aria let her own worries fade away under the excitement of the game and cheering Cole and his team on to victory yet again.

"Do you want to get some ice cream or maybe some hot chocolate?" Gareth asked as they walked out of the high school after the game.

"I could definitely go for a hot chocolate," she said. "I'm not sure about ice cream when it's this cold."

Gareth laughed. "If we waited until it was warm to eat ice cream, we'd be deprived for at least three or four months."

"You are definitely an ice cream fan."

"Aren't you?" Gareth asked as he opened the passenger door of his car.

Aria stepped into the opening between the car and the door, then turned to face him. "Is it a deal breaker if I'm not?"

Gareth pressed a hand to his heart. "I don't know. Not like ice cream? That might be a serious incompatibility."

"But wouldn't that mean there would be more ice cream for you?"

"I suppose that's true." Gareth grinned at her. "Do you really not like ice cream?"

"It's not that I don't like it," Aria said. "It's just not my favorite sweet treat."

"I guess I can live with that."

"I'm so glad to hear it."

Aria was still smiling as he slid behind the wheel and started up the SUV. Though there were so many things she found attractive about Gareth, his lighthearted interactions with her lifted her spirits. She had never been with a guy who made her smile or laugh the way Gareth did.

Gareth drove to a small, warmly lit building and parked in the lot next to it. "This is my favorite place to get ice cream, but they have plenty of other sweets for those who have no taste for ice cream."

They continued their lighthearted teasing as they made their way into the building. Inside, it was warm, and a sweet smell lingered in the air. There were a few people seated at the small bistro style tables that were scattered throughout the room.

Together, they approached the counter, where a young woman greeted them. Her braces flashed as she gave them a wide smile.

"Hi, Doctor H," she said, her curious gaze moving between the two of them.

"Hello, Jeannie," Gareth responded. "How's life going?"

"It's going good. Were you at the game tonight?'

"I was. We won."

"Yay! That's great," she said with a broad smile. "I wanted to be there, but I agreed to cover this shift for a friend to help her out."

"There's always next week," Gareth said. "No shortage of games now that the season is underway."

"Yep. I've been to a few already." She glanced at Aria, then back to Gareth. "What can I get you tonight?"

Aria looked at the menu that was written on the board behind the young woman. When she spotted a variety of cheesecakes, she quickly decided to get a slice of one to go along with her hot chocolate.

It didn't take long to get their order, then Gareth led the way to one of the tables in the back corner of the room. Aria was glad to be away from the windows because the last thing they needed was for Nora to drive past and spot them sitting together. Obviously she could still come into the restaurant, but hopefully that wouldn't be as likely to happen that late in the evening.

"Cheesecake, huh?" Gareth asked as he dipped his spoon into the banana split he'd gotten. "That's also a great choice here. They make wonderful desserts."

"I enjoy cheesecake. My mom loved it too. We'd get some once or twice a month."

Gareth's expression softened. "That was nice you had a treat you both enjoyed."

Aria nodded, but when she felt the sting of tears, she looked down at her cheesecake. She used her fork to scoop off a piece and took a bite.

The creamy sweetness with just a bit of tartness was delicious, but it took some effort to swallow past the tightness in her throat.

Trying to focus on the delicious cheesecake instead of the memory of her mom, she said, "This is really good. Probably better than your ice cream."

He chuckled at that. She was grateful when he went on to extol the greatness of his ice cream rather than asking her more about her mom. There would come a time when she was sure that she'd be able to talk more about her, but it wasn't that night.

They ended up staying at the restaurant until almost closing time. Gareth had nodded at a few people as he and Aria had talked, but no one had approached their table. Perhaps they'd correctly assumed that he was out on a date and so gave him space.

Though she'd heard lots about the family from Janessa when they'd roomed together, there was plenty that Gareth shared with her that Janessa hadn't. Especially since she and Janessa hadn't talked as much once they were done school. They'd kept in sporadic contact, but they'd both been busy with their jobs and life in general to allow for long conversations.

Aria told him bits about herself, but she found herself thinking over her words before speaking. The last thing she wanted was to talk about the previous two years. If she had her way, she'd rather pretend that everything with Tim, her job, and the past year had never happened.

It was almost eleven-thirty by the time Gareth pulled up to the house. There didn't appear to be many lights on, so maybe everyone was in bed.

Gareth walked with her to the door, then unlocked it to let them into the house. No one was waiting for them in the foyer this time.

"Thank you for a lovely evening," Aria said quietly as they stood in the foyer. "I really enjoyed myself."

"I did too."

"Even if I don't like ice cream as much as you?" she asked.

"Even then," Gareth murmured. He hesitated for a moment, his gaze on hers, and Aria held her breath.

For a moment, she thought he might kiss her, but instead, he reached out and ran his fingertips lightly over her cheek.

"Have a good night. I'll be by here around five-thirty tomorrow to pick you up."

"I can't wait."

"Me, either." The smile he gave her held an emotion that made her heart skip a beat.

After Gareth left, she went up to her room, praying as she climbed the stairs that she didn't do anything to mess up their growing romance.

CHAPTER TWENTY

Gareth struggled to quell his irritation at having to curtail his interactions with Aria at work, to be strictly professional. However, he couldn't deny that it had had the desired effect. Aria had mentioned that Nora seemed to treat her with less derision over the past couple of weeks, ever since that day she'd threatened to attend Cole's game.

And it hadn't just been how she'd treated Aria. She'd stopped making overtures to Gareth as well. It was like she'd accepted that he and Aria were simply co-workers, so she didn't feel like she needed to continually stake the claim she thought was hers.

It was probably just as well that they were learning early on how to put boundaries in place between their personal and professional lives. Still, at this stage in their dating relationship, he would have loved to be able to have the lighthearted flirtatious moments during their workday that they had outside of the office.

But regardless, he had plans for Valentine's Day, which was that day, and those plans included making sure that she knew how he felt about her. He had the whole day planned, ending with a romantic dinner at a cozy restaurant in a nearby town. He'd made reservations a couple of weeks earlier to make sure he'd get a table.

He would still respect the boundaries they'd put in place for work, but that didn't mean he couldn't have things delivered to her. She would know who they were from, even if he didn't sign his name to anything.

As he let himself into the clinic, Gareth smiled at what was to come that day. After two weeks of talking each evening as well as spending time together when their schedules—his schedule, really—allowed, he was quite confident that she also had feelings for him.

He'd never imagined what it would be like to find a woman he was so in tune with. Over the years, he'd been witness to his parents' relationship, and he'd seen how they handled their differences of opinion. They'd never had screaming fights like he'd heard some of his friends talk about their parents having. That didn't mean his parents hadn't argued, but he'd seen how they would work through whatever it was they were dealing with.

In fact, whenever he and his siblings had squabbled, their parents had guided them through their disagreements in much the same way they settled their own. He and Aria hadn't argued yet, but he knew that if—when—that day came, he'd do his best to make sure that they moved past it with their love for one another intact.

He'd been in the office for about fifteen minutes when he heard the back door open. Though he wanted to go see if it was Aria, he stayed at his desk. It was a good thing he did because when someone appeared in his doorway, it wasn't the woman he wanted to see.

"Happy Valentine's Day," Nora said as she came to stand in front of his desk.

"I guess it is Valentine's Day today, isn't it?" He wasn't about to wish the same to her in case she read something into his response.

She frowned for a moment. "You didn't remember?"

Gareth didn't want to outright lie, so he had to choose his words very carefully. "Valentine's Day hasn't exactly been a holiday that's demanded my attention in recent years."

"That will change once you get into a relationship," she said with a flirty smile.

So much for her not being focused on him. "Yep. I'm sure it will change once I've met the right woman."

That was absolutely the truth, since he was more focused on Valentine's Day that year than he ever had been in his adult life.

Nora, however, didn't appear to appreciate his truth. A frown chased the smile from her face, and her flirty attitude disappeared.

He hoped that Nora's reaction to his comment didn't ruin the day for everyone. If Nora was upset, it was possible she would take out her feelings on everyone else.

No doubt the gifts he'd arranged to be delivered for Aria were going to upset Nora more, even if she didn't know they were from Gareth. It was too late to change anything now. But regardless, Aria deserved to know that she was special to him on this day.

The next person to appear was Jay, who paused in Gareth's doorway. He looked between Gareth and Nora before he said, "Did I miss that we were having a meeting?"

Gareth and Jay might knock heads at times, but Gareth knew that the other man would always have his back, particularly when it came to Nora. "Nope. Nora just stopped by to remind me it's Valentine's Day."

Jay grimaced, no doubt recalling that he was once again broken up with his long-time girlfriend. "The holiday devoted to torturing all the single people? Who wants to be reminded?"

"That's been my philosophy," Gareth agreed.

"That might actually be the reason the two of you don't have girlfriends," Nora announced as she swept out of the room, forcing Jay to take a quick step back so she didn't mow him down.

Once she was gone, Jay grinned at his brother. "Pretty sure you didn't need a reminder this year."

"You'd be right, but I'm not about to tell her that."

"You got plans?" Jay asked as he dropped into the chair across from Gareth.

"I do."

"I wasn't sure how I felt about you and Aria dating, but it seems to be going okay."

Gareth nodded. "It is."

"I'm happy for you," Jay said.

"Thanks." Gareth paused, then said, "Do you think you and Casey will manage to get things worked out?"

Jay frowned. "No. I think we're over for good this time. We've talked a few times, but it's just not going to work out."

"That's too bad," Gareth said. "I really thought you two were in it for the long haul."

"That was only going to be possible if I agreed to leave Serenity. Casey has her heart set on a bigger city where she'd have better opportunities for her law career."

"You could have left if you'd wanted to," Gareth said. "You know that Mom and Dad would never say you had to stay here."

Jay nodded. "I know that."

Gareth waited for him to go on, but instead, his brother just sighed, then got to his feet. With a wave of his hand, Jay walked out of the office, leaving Gareth to stare after him.

He wanted to press Jay for more information but doing that had never ended well in the past. Their communication was always better if Jay initiated their conversations.

Leaning back in his chair, Gareth clicked his pen as he considered his morning so far. Hopefully Jay's day would look up. And hopefully, Nora would leave him alone.

Movement in the doorway pulled Gareth from his musings, and he looked over to see Janessa coming toward him with something in her hand. When she set it on the desk in front of him, he saw it was a container. "What's this?"

"Just a little sweetness for your Valentine's Day from you-know-who."

Gareth couldn't help the smile that came in response to her revelation. "Oh, nice."

"Enjoy," Janessa sang out as she left his office.

Oh, he most definitely would. Aria had taken to giving him baked goods that she'd made. His favorite so far were the double chocolate chip cookies. As he cracked the lid on the container, he saw she had once again made them, but these were in the shape of hearts.

Even though he hadn't had breakfast that long ago, Gareth slipped a cookie out of the container and took a bite. Humming appreciatively, he put the container in the drawer of his desk, not wanting anyone else to steal its contents.

If Janessa was in the building, that meant that Aria was too, so it took all of Gareth's willpower to not get up and seek her out. Instead, he focused on his appointments for that day, trying to put aside his excitement over his plans for later. He still had a full slate of appointments that he needed to get through before he could focus on Aria.

He was coming out of one of the exam rooms an hour and a half later when Nora approached him with a smirk. "Looks like Aria has an admirer."

"Really?" he asked, assuming that the first of his gifts had arrived. "Why do you say that?"

"She received a delivery of flowers."

Gareth turned his attention back to the paper he'd jotted down some notes he wanted to look into regarding the patient he'd just seen. As he walked toward his office, he murmured, "That's nice."

He wasn't completely sure what she'd hoped to accomplish by telling him about the flowers. Did she expect him to react with jealousy? Truthfully, if the flowers had been from someone other than him, he probably would have been jealous.

Though he really, really wanted to head out to the reception area to see Aria with the flowers, he knew he couldn't do that. It was enough to know that she'd received them.

He'd just settled behind his desk when his phone vibrated in his pocket. Gareth fished it out, smiling when he saw the text on the screen.

Aria: *The flowers are beautiful! Thank you so much.*

She included a selfie of herself with the bouquet, her smile beaming and beautiful.

Gareth glanced at the door, then took a minute to send her back a response. *I'm glad you like them, though their beauty doesn't come close to yours. Thank you also for the cookies. Happy Valentine's Day!*

Aria: *You're welcome. Happy Valentine's Day to you too!*

Aria: *Your next patient is here. Chat later!*

Gareth smiled as he sent her back a thumbs up. He hoped that she enjoyed the rest of the things she'd be receiving from him that day.

***

Aria stared at the young man who stood on the other side of the reception desk. He held a basket wrapped in clear cellophane with a large bow made of red ribbon.

"That's for me?" she asked.

He grinned at her. "If your name is Aria, then yes."

"Well, yes, it is."

"Then it's definitely for you."

"Oh, thank you."

"Enjoy!"

As she perused the contents of the basket, Aria was quite certain that she would. And given that each item appeared to be something she'd mentioned to Gareth during their conversations, it was obvious he'd curated the basket contents himself.

She moved the basket to the side, but when she sat back down on her chair, her gaze kept going to it and the beautiful bouquet of red roses that sat next to it. When the roses had arrived, she'd been surprised, though maybe she shouldn't have been. Gareth had shown himself to be attentive in the times they'd been together, seemingly devoted to making her feel special.

Though they had plans later in the day, she'd wanted to give him something special, which was why she'd had Janessa give him the cookies she'd baked the night before. Those cookies felt so insignificant now when compared to the flowers and the gift basket. She hadn't expected him to do so much.

"Who is the gift basket for?" Nora's gaze was laser-focused on it as she approached the desk. "You should really call to let someone know that there's a delivery for them."

"The gift basket is for me," Aria said.

Nora frowned as she shifted her attention to Aria. "You never mentioned that you had a boyfriend."

"I don't really feel like I should discuss my personal life here at work," Aria replied, turning her attention to her monitor.

"Is he from around here?" Nora asked.

Before Aria could reply, the door opened, and a middle-aged woman walked in.

"Hi, Doctor," she said with a smile at Nora before turning to Aria to check in.

Nora spoke with the woman for a moment before heading back to the exam rooms. Aria breathed a sigh of relief to not have to discuss that topic any further with Nora. When Janessa came to get the next patient, Aria told her to come back when she was done.

"What's up?" Janessa asked when she returned.

"Uh... I've received another delivery," Aria said, gesturing to the gift basket.

Janessa didn't look at all surprised as she grinned at her. "I see that."

Keeping her voice low, Aria said, "Nora is giving me the third degree over the deliveries. She thought the basket was for someone else and that I hadn't called to let them know. Then she wanted to know if my boyfriend was from around here."

Janessa sighed. "Trust her to spoil your Valentine's Day."

"Would Gareth be upset if I put the basket out of sight?"

"Of course not," Janessa said. "Especially if Nora's giving you hassles."

Aria reached out to turn the basket around so she could see everything in it. "I can't believe he got me this."

"I have to say that I'm a bit impressed by what he's done," Janessa said. "I wasn't sure he could be romantic. Apparently, he just needed the right inspiration."

"I feel bad that I didn't do any grand gestures for him." Aria glanced at her friend. "I hope he doesn't think that means I don't care for him."

"Don't worry about that," Janessa told her. "Gareth is doing this because it makes him happy, and he hoped it would make you happy, too."

"It certainly does."

"How about I take the basket and put it in the stockroom?" Janessa suggested. "And I'll lock the door."

"Thank you." Aria got up so she could hand her the basket. "I want to keep the flowers here, though. They're beautiful."

"One of these days..." Janessa let out a long sigh. "Maybe I'll get a chance at love."

"Hopefully, you will. I didn't see this happening when I moved here."

"Neither did I," Janessa said with a laugh. "Happy surprise all around."

Aria hoped everyone thought it was a happy surprise. Well, she knew it wouldn't be a happy surprise for Nora, but hopefully everyone else that it mattered to was happy about her relationship with Gareth.

Janessa headed to the stockroom with the basket, leaving Aria alone with her thoughts. She struggled, at times, to accept that what she had with Gareth was real.

After her engagement had ended so painfully, she hadn't thought she'd ever be interested in another relationship. But she hadn't anticipated someone like Gareth coming into her life.

Over the past several weeks, Gareth had proven just how into her he was. Though he had a fairly busy schedule most days, he *always* made time for her. Even if it was just to call her for ten minutes to talk before they fell asleep.

Aria had been used to hearing from her ex when it was convenient for him. He'd been busy with his career, as she had been with hers, so a couple of days could go by without them talking. But she'd been ok with that, not realizing that it could be so much better.

Her life was already so intertwined with Gareth's that it would be weird to not hear from him each day. The nice thing was that it wasn't just her wanting to hear from him, but that he also wanted to hear from her. He'd told her she could call him anytime, and if he couldn't talk, he'd get back to her as soon as he could.

She still hadn't seen him that day, which was probably just as well, since right then, she felt like she wouldn't be able to keep her feelings hidden. However, she could still thank him for the basket.

The basket!! It's amazing. Thank you so much!

She knew he was with a patient, which meant it would be a little bit before he got back to her. After sliding her phone into the drawer so she wouldn't check it obsessively, she spent a few minutes making phone calls for appointment reminders for the next day.

Just before noon, the last patient of the morning left. Janessa had asked Aria to place an order at a nearby restaurant for lunch for everyone, so Aria waited at the front desk for the delivery.

"Janessa said to come help you with the food."

A smile formed on Aria's face before she even turned to see Gareth. "That was nice of her, and of you."

Gareth grinned, but then winked at her before schooling his expression. Aria wanted to say something more to him, but she knew she didn't dare.

"When we get back to work after lunch, could you phone the lab and see about blood results for Mrs. Stanton?" Gareth asked. "I checked, but they're not online yet. I'd like to have them for her appointment, if possible."

"Sure. I can call over now while we wait for the food."

"Thank you," Gareth said with a smile.

Aria placed the call, hoping that someone would answer even though it was close to noon. When a woman answered, Aria asked about the lab results while Gareth went to wait by the door. Before she was finished, the food delivery man showed up.

Gareth took the order, then locked the door and gave her a smile before he carried the food to the staff room. When Aria finished the call, she got up and left the receptionist's desk, eager to spend a little time with Gareth.

When she got to the room, her stomach twisted at the sight of Nora sitting beside Gareth, leaning into him. Knowing that she couldn't react or sit beside him, Aria slid onto a chair beside Janessa, leaving one empty between herself and Gareth.

He glanced at her, a quick smile crossing his face. It was a safe smile. One that Nora couldn't read anything into, though it was likely she still might. The one consolation was that it was the same smile he gave Nora. The smiles Aria loved the most from him seemed to be reserved strictly for her.

And she had something very special to look forward to that would more than make up for the distance they needed to keep right then. Since she'd woken up that morning, she'd had a low-level hum of excitement in anticipation of their dinner.

"Since you don't have plans tonight," Nora began, leaning against Gareth's arm. "How about we grab some dinner?"

Aria stared down at her food, trying not to react to Nora's words.

"I never said I don't have plans tonight," Gareth replied, his tone even. "It's not like all other plans stop just because it's Valentine's Day."

"They don't for me," Janessa said.

"Me either," Jay added. "In fact, I actually try to have some sort of plans on this day, just so I don't feel sorry for myself and eat all the ice cream in the house."

"You don't keep ice cream in your house," Janessa said.

"It's one way to make sure Gareth never shows up uninvited. He's more likely to go where they have ice cream."

"I feel very attacked," Gareth protested. "Just because I like a little ice cream."

"A little ice cream," Jay scoffed. "You never eat just a *little* ice cream."

Aria managed to keep from laughing, appreciating how Gareth's siblings were, in their own crazy way, circling the wagons around her and Gareth.

Nora didn't appear to appreciate the joking, though she did use it to her advantage. "I have ice cream. You're more than welcome to come by and have a bowl."

"Nora, I'm going to say what Gareth appears too nice to be able to," Jay said, leaning forward to rest his arms on the table, bracketing his food. "He's not interested in dating you. He's tried to let you down nicely, but you're not getting the message."

"And how would you know that?" Nora demanded.

"I'm his brother. We talk."

Tension built in the room, and Aria didn't dare to even breathe since she didn't want to draw Nora's attention to her.

"You just don't realize how perfect we could be together," Nora said as she got to her feet. She grabbed her container of food, then left the room.

"Don't say I never did anything for you," Jay said as he pointed his fork at Gareth.

With a smile at Aria, Gareth said, "I will never say that. You've definitely saved my bacon."

"Unfortunately, now she's going to hate me, too."

"Welcome to the club," Janessa said. "It's about time you joined."

Aria felt a little bad for Nora, but from things Janessa had said, the woman had brought this on herself by being unwilling to back off with the flirting around Gareth. Still didn't mean that she and Gareth could be open about their relationship, though, which was too bad. But she was okay with that as long as Nora didn't keep trying to hit on Gareth.

CHAPTER TWENTY-ONE

Gareth was glad that the workday was over, and he could finally just focus on his evening with Aria. He'd hoped that Nora would just keep things professional throughout the day, but apparently that had been expecting too much.

He realized belatedly that he'd done her no favors by trying to be subtle in his rejection of her advances. The way Jay had done it might have been a bit harsh, but Gareth had no doubt that Nora had gotten the message. The other thing he'd realized was that if he and Aria could keep things professional at work, then so could Nora, regardless of her interest in him.

They needed to get the personal stuff out of the clinic, since it was causing issues. Maybe he needed to just have a very frank conversation with Nora, letting her know that there would never be anything between them and that they needed to maintain a professional relationship at work.

But that was a problem for another day.

Gareth pushed open his door and got out of the car. The sun was setting, so the sky had taken on the colors of twilight, and there was a bit of a chill in the air. No snow was in the forecast, and he hoped there would be no more snow for the season.

He jogged up the sidewalk toward the house, eager to pick Aria up and get their date underway. Surprisingly, the door hadn't already been opened by the time he reached it, so he rang the doorbell, then waited for someone to answer it. When the door finally swung open, Janessa stood there.

"Sorry, we're not buying," she quipped, then made as if she was going to shut the door.

Gareth braced his hand on the door. "Do you really want to sleep with one eye open if you keep Aria from our Valentine's Day date?"

Janessa sighed as she stepped back, opening the door wider for him. "No. I suppose that wouldn't be a good call."

Gareth glanced around as he stepped into the foyer. "Where's Layla? I thought she'd be answering the door."

"She had a bit of a melt-down, so Charli took her to their rooms."

"Oh boy. What caused it?"

"Bad Valentine's Day at school."

"Oh bummer."

"And, as you know, Valentine's Day isn't great for Charli either, so I think I might go get some fast food for us and call it a day."

Gareth felt for his sister. It wasn't easy being a single mom on the best of days, but combined with Valentine's Day. "Anything I can do?"

"Nope. Just go enjoy your date with Aria. I know she's looking forward to it."

That made Gareth happy. "I am, too."

They chatted for a few minutes before Aria came downstairs. She wore a black skirt that ended just above her knees over the top of black tights, and her light pink shirt was fitted, ending with a curved hem at her hips.

"You look beautiful," he said.

Her cheeks flushed. "Thank you." Then she gave him a shy smile. "You look very handsome."

"Yeah. Yeah. You make a lovely couple." Janessa made shooing motions with her hands. "Now go enjoy yourselves."

Gareth helped Aria with her coat, then they went out to the car.

As he pulled away from the curb, he said, "Do you know what's up with Layla?"

"Something happened at school regarding Valentine's cards that were given out. Sounded like some little boy liked another girl's card better than the one Layla gave him."

"I'm not sure that celebrating Valentine's Day at that age is a good thing. I have never really enjoyed the day in the past, to be honest. And I never saw the sense in it when I was Layla's age. Mom would make me sit and address cards to all the kids in my class. Even the ones I didn't like. It was a pain."

Aria laughed. "I didn't mind doing the cards. Mom would help me glue chocolate kisses to them, which meant that everyone liked mine best. Unfortunately, I haven't really enjoyed the holiday much as I've gotten older. This has been the best one I've ever had, and it's not even over yet."

Gareth loved that he had done that for her. "Weren't you engaged?"

This was the first time they'd ventured into past relationships, but Gareth felt like maybe it was time. Though he didn't like to imagine Aria with another man, he knew it was important to understand how she'd felt about that relationship. It had been serious enough to have turned into an engagement, so clearly that man had played a significant role in Aria's life.

"Yes. I was engaged for about eight months. My ex broke it off not long after my mom was diagnosed with cancer."

Gareth frowned, unable to keep from asking, "He broke it off *because* your mom had cancer? Or was that just bad timing?"

"Because of my mom's diagnosis," she said. "I was spending a lot of time taking care of her, and between that and my job, I didn't have much time for our relationship."

Gareth felt a surge of anger toward the man who had abandoned Aria during a time when she'd needed him most. "And he didn't understand that?"

"He tried to at first, but then he said that he needed more from me."

"I'm sorry you had to deal with that while also helping your mom."

"It was difficult," she said. "But now I'm glad that it didn't work out with him."

Her words made Gareth smile. "Maybe it's selfish of me. But I'm glad too."

"He was my first really serious boyfriend," she revealed. "Honestly, I didn't know much about how romantic relationships worked, since my mom never had a boyfriend. So I know I played a role in its demise, too."

"But you should be able to count on someone who says they love you," Gareth said. "I understand that relationships don't work out, but it shouldn't be because someone doesn't want to stick around through the rough patches."

Aria fell silent, and Gareth regretted having delved into the topic with her. He didn't want her to be thinking about a relationship that had failed when he hoped to cultivate a serious relationship with her himself.

He reached over and touched her hands where they rested in her lap. "I'm sorry to have brought up a bad time in your life."

She flipped her hand over and interlaced their fingers, then put her other hand on top of their joined ones. "It's a part of what brought me here, so even though I was upset when it happened, I can see now that it was for the best."

Gareth definitely agreed with that, and he was glad that she viewed it that way, too. He didn't want to be second best to the man she'd been engaged to. He didn't want to be the man she settled for because she couldn't have her ex.

"I've never been engaged," he said, feeling like he needed to share his romantic past in the same way she had. "I never had a serious enough relationship. I was too focused on school, then on my residency. Plus, I knew I was coming back to Serenity Point, and none of the women I was interested in had any desire to move up here."

"Were the women you were interested in doctors?"

"No. Not all of them. If the main thing I wanted in a woman was that she have a medical degree, I would have gotten involved with Nora. I need a connection that goes beyond our professions."

"And you feel we have that?"

"I do feel that," Gareth said, rubbing his thumb over her fingers. "Though I'm not happy about the hassles Nora has caused, I have to say that having a clear line between our work and personal life because of that, hasn't been an entirely bad thing."

Aria was quiet for a moment before she said, "I hadn't thought of it that way."

"I wasn't actively looking for the silver lining around the cloud that Nora has brought upon us," Gareth said with a chuckle. "But it seems that God was determined to give me one, anyway."

As they approached the town where the restaurant was, Gareth had to let go of Aria's hand. The small parking lot beside the restaurant was almost full, so he was glad he had made a reservation.

Once they were out of the car, Gareth held out his hand, which Aria took, falling into step beside him as they walked to the building. He hadn't been to the restaurant in a long time, so he hoped that the food was as good as the last time he'd been there with his family, celebrating his parents' thirtieth wedding anniversary.

Gareth opened the door and held it so that Aria could walk in first. A smiling woman greeted them as they stepped into the foyer.

"I have a reservation for Halverson."

The woman nodded as she picked up a couple of menus. "Please follow me."

Gareth waited for Aria to go ahead of him, then he followed them to a round table set against the far wall next to a high narrow window that looked out on the hedges around the building. It wasn't much of a view, but he wasn't there to stare out the window when he had Aria sitting across from him.

Once they were at the table, he held Aria's chair as she sat down, then went around to his seat. The woman handed them each a menu before leaving them alone.

"Is there something you'd recommend here?" Aria asked as she looked up from her menu.

"Well, I'm going to be unoriginal and order steak," Gareth said. "But honestly, I think anything would be good. When we all came here a few years ago, we each ordered something different, and I don't remember anyone complaining about their food."

"I think I'm in the mood for pasta and maybe chicken."

They talked about other things on the menu, eventually deciding to get an appetizer as well as their main courses.

"And of course, we'll get dessert," Gareth said with a grin.

Aria laughed. "Ice cream, right?"

When Aria laughed, Gareth's heart skipped a beat. The joy on her face filled him with joy as well. He'd never had feelings like that for a woman before. Sometimes, he wasn't sure what to do with all the feelings he had for Aria, and he wondered if she had them too. Or was he the only one feeling things so strongly?

Hopefully, this time together might help to clarify things for him... for them.

***

Aria's nerves had settled now that she was sitting with Gareth. She hadn't known what to expect for their date, but like the gifts he'd given her that day, the restaurant he'd chosen was perfect.

Soft jazz played in the background, with the muted sounds of conversation and the clink of dishes layered over it. The restaurant was decorated in a rich burgundy, and the wood accents in the space were dark and shiny. The chairs were styled to look antique, but since they were all the same, Aria doubted they were authentic.

Still, they looked appropriate to the décor, and the padded seats were comfortable.

She'd gone to fancier restaurants with Tim, but this one seemed nicer than any of those. That was due, no doubt, because of who she was with.

The conversation they'd had so far had mainly been light, and she appreciated that. Their date that night didn't feel like a place for really heavy topics, even though they'd already touched on the end of her relationship with Tim.

There was really only one topic she didn't want to discuss, but thankfully, there wasn't much chance of him bringing it up.

"You don't talk about your dad," Gareth said. "Is he not around?"

Well, this would be a brief topic of conversation. "I actually don't know who he is."

Gareth's brows rose. "You don't?"

Aria shook her head. "My mom was only fifteen when she had me. Over the years, she refused to talk about her family or my dad. Even when she was dying, all she'd say was that I was better off without them all."

"Have you ever thought about doing one of those DNA tests to see who might show up?"

Aria finished chewing the bite she'd taken. "I did take one, actually, but then I never followed through on the results. It kind of felt like it would be disrespecting my mom, since she obviously didn't want me to know about any relatives."

"Yeah, I get that," Gareth said. "Though I'm just not sure I could handle the insane curiosity I'd have to know about that side of my family."

"I asked Mom about it a lot when I was younger, and since she never budged on her position, I eventually just let it go." Aria took a drink of her water. "I guess I'm also afraid of discovering things that will make me have more questions for my mom, only she's not around to answer them for me. I think that would be harder for me to deal with."

During the times they'd spent together already, they'd only talked about her mom briefly. He hadn't broached her death specifically, though, and Aria hoped that he didn't that night. The last thing she wanted to do was to start crying over their dinner.

Their server interrupted them, checking to see if they needed anything, and when the woman left, Gareth didn't continue that direction of conversation. Someday she wanted to tell him about that horrible time, but not that night.

After the server returned a short time later with their dessert, Gareth reached out and rested his hand on the table, palm up. When Aria looked up at him, his expression was serious. She set her fork on the edge of her plate and moved her hand so that she could hold his.

"Since our first meeting, I have enjoyed the time I've spent with you," he said, a small smile tipping up the corners of his mouth. "Whether we're actually together or just talking on the phone."

"I've enjoyed it too," Aria assured him. She'd actually more than enjoyed it. She'd *loved* their times together.

"All the times we've talked and shared stuff about ourselves has only reinforced the feeling that I want to be with you. I'd love for us to date exclusively."

Until he said the words, Aria wasn't aware of how much worry she'd carried that Gareth would decide that she wasn't worth the effort of a relationship. She knew it was stupid, since Gareth had proven over the past several weeks that he actually enjoyed being with her. And everything he'd done for her that day had reinforced that.

Still, having him put his thoughts into words went a long way to soothing her worries.

"I want that too," Aria said, unable to keep from smiling at Gareth as happiness spiraled through her.

"We still need to keep things professional at work, of course. But I want to hold your hand outside of work hours. I want to hug you when I see you. I want people to know that we're together."

Emotion welled up inside Aria. Gareth could have had any woman, and yet, he wanted to be with her. She didn't know how to put her feelings into words. How to share the overwhelming love she had in her heart for him.

Of all the things she'd hoped to gain in coming to Serenity Point, a man like Gareth had never even been on her radar.

When they finished their meal, Gareth paid for it, then they left the restaurant. Aria took Gareth's hand, enjoying his nearness as they walked through the chilly evening to his car.

The drive back to the house seemed to go by a lot faster than the one to the restaurant had. Or maybe it was just that she didn't want the evening to end.

When he pulled up to the house, Aria looked over at Gareth. "Thank you so much for this evening. This whole day, actually. It's been wonderful."

"I'm glad you enjoyed it," he said with a smile. "That was my goal."

"You definitely achieved it."

She wished she could see him more clearly, but they weren't sitting close enough to the streetlamps to have the interior of the car illuminated.

Gareth reached out, running his fingers along her cheek. Aria couldn't keep from pressing into his touch. When Gareth shifted closer, leaning across the console between them, her heart began to pound.

But then he paused, and Aria realized he was waiting for her to make the final move. To be the one to initiate their first kiss. This close, she could see him a bit better. The strong outline of his features. She let her fingers drift along the firm edge of his jaw.

She wanted this physical connection with him to go along with the emotional connection they were already building. This man was everything she'd never known she wanted in a man.

Leaning forward, she brushed her lips against his. Lightly at first, then with a little more pressure. She slid her hand around the back of his neck as he returned her kiss.

Though she'd obviously kissed a man before, this felt different. Momentous. Precious. The start of something more than she'd ever experienced before.

When their kiss ended, Aria moved back from him slightly. Words hovered on the tip of her tongue, but she held them back. The feelings were too new, and she wasn't sure about giving voice to them yet. About setting them free into the world.

"I guess we'd better go in," Gareth said softly. "Though I wish we didn't have to."

Aria nodded reluctantly, but she finally shifted back into her seat, letting her hand slip from his neck. "There's always next time."

"Definitely," Gareth agreed with a quiet laugh. "And then the time after that."

Smiling, Aria got out of the car, then walked hand in hand with Gareth to the front the door. He stepped inside with her, but he didn't take his jacket off. The house was quiet though, so they stood uninterrupted near the front door.

"It'll be hard not to hug you when I see you in the morning," Gareth said. "But I guess we'd better continue to keep that kind of thing outside of the clinic."

She felt exactly the same way, but the kiss they shared already would have to tide them over until they could be together again.

Up in her room, Aria flopped back on her bed with a happy sigh. It had been the best day she'd ever had. And now that she and Gareth had decided to take their relationship to the next level, she couldn't wait to see how life unfolded for them.

It felt so freeing to be moving toward something wonderful, leaving behind the horrible turn her life had taken over the previous year.

CHAPTER TWENTY-TWO

Aria frowned as she took in the pathetic sight of her friend slumped at the counter in the kitchen. "You're not feeling any better?"

"I'm feeling *worse,*" Janessa groaned as she laid her head on her arms. "And I didn't think a person could feel this bad and still be alive."

Janessa had been sick for the past two days, and it didn't appear that she was going to get better in time to work her shift at the free clinic the next day.

"So, can you cover for me tomorrow?"

Nerves fluttered in Aria's stomach. Over the past two days, she had covered part of Janessa's responsibilities at the clinic. She'd juggled directing patients to exam rooms along with her usual duties, but Gareth and Nora had taken over the rest of what Janessa usually did.

Aria wasn't sure if that would be the case at the Saturday clinic. Though she really didn't want to take on actual nursing duties, it seemed like she wouldn't have a choice. Everyone thought she was able to perform the duties of a nurse, but that she was just filling in the role of receptionist because that was where they needed her.

She would prefer to not have to explain why she didn't want to do the nursing side of the job. At least not yet. Because of that, she either had to just do what was required of her or tell them why she wouldn't do it.

But since everything was still so new, she just didn't want to tell them why she didn't want to perform nursing responsibilities and jeopardize any of it. Her job. Her home. Most especially, her and Gareth's relationship.

That couldn't happen.

"Sure. I'll cover for you."

"Thank you," Janessa moaned. "I don't think I'm ever going to feel human again."

"I'm sorry you're feeling so badly," Aria said.

"I just want some water, then I'm going back to bed."

Aria went to the fridge and pulled out a bottle of water. "Just one?"

"Maybe two. Then I won't have to come back down."

Aria grabbed another bottle and set them both on the counter in front of Janessa. "Do you want something to eat? I can bring food up to you."

"I'm not sure I'll ever want to eat again." Janessa dragged herself to her feet, then picked up the water bottles.

"Anything else I can do for you?" Aria asked.

"Nah. I'm just going to try to get some sleep."

"Call me if you need something. That way, you won't have to come back downstairs."

"I will."

After Janessa left, Aria took the disinfectant spray that Charli had been using since Janessa had gotten sick and sprayed down the spot where she'd been sitting. Aria understood Charli's concern, since it seemed to be a particularly virulent bug. The last thing Charli wanted was for Layla to catch it.

After she'd wiped everything down, Aria checked the crock pot of soup that Charli had put on before going to school that day. She had hoped that Janessa might want some, but it seemed her appetite still hadn't returned.

Charli and Layla had gone to a dance class after school and would be home later. Though there was usually a basketball game on Friday night, the team had travelled farther than normal for their game, so only Gareth and Jay had gone. Aria had considered going, but since the guys were staying overnight, and it had been likely that she'd need to cover for Janessa, she hadn't been able to go.

Gareth had promised to call, and sure enough, just before ten that evening, her phone rang.

"Hello, sweetheart," Gareth said when she answered.

"Hi." Aria settled on her bed, crossing her legs. "How was the game?"

"It was great. They're going to the championships next weekend."

"Was there any doubt?" Aria asked.

Gareth chuckled. "Not really. They've had a great season. But you never know. Just need enough players to have an off-day, which they do sometimes, and they could have ended up with a loss."

"It would be a shame for them to get all the way to the championships and then not win."

"Yes, it would be." Gareth's voice was serious. "And since it's Cole's last year, he will be devastated if they don't get the title."

"Is everyone going to the game next week?"

"Yep. Nora has agreed to work at the clinic two weekends in a row."

"Janessa asked me to cover for her tomorrow."

"She's still not feeling well?"

"No. She looked pretty bad earlier."

"Are you okay with working tomorrow?" Gareth asked.

"I guess. I'm not thrilled to be working with Nora."

"I wish we could get someone else, but the nurse that we usually get to help with the Saturday clinic isn't available tomorrow."

"It'll be fine." Aria wasn't sure that it would be, but over the past week, Nora had been surprisingly professional.

Aria had no idea if Nora had heard from anyone that she and Gareth were dating. If she had, she was taking the news remarkably well. Working alone with her the next day could indicate how she really felt.

Best-case scenario, Nora kept things professional.

However, things had been going so well that Aria figured she was due a worst-case scenario moment, and that could definitely come from Nora.

"If you have any issues, let me know."

"I will, but I think it'll be okay. From what I've heard, it's a pretty busy time, so it's not like we'll have opportunity for much interacting."

"True."

Aria didn't feel as confident as she was trying to convince Gareth she was, but she wanted to prove that she could handle the situation with Nora. She couldn't expect Gareth to constantly come to her rescue, even though that was appealing from a romantic viewpoint.

"I have worship team practice tomorrow afternoon," Gareth said after they'd talked for a little while. "Do you want to come with me?"

"The other team members won't mind?"

"Nope. Not at all," he said. "And maybe afterwards we can go get supper somewhere."

"Sure. I'd like that."

"Practice is at four. I'll come by the house around three or three-thirty."

She heard the murmur of conversation on Gareth's side, then he sighed. "For some reason, these two are hungry at ten o'clock at night, so I guess we're getting some food."

Aria laughed. "Well, Cole, at least, is a growing boy."

"And if I don't want to hear a bunch of whining, I'd better get going. Have a good night."

"You too," Aria said. Again, the words revealing her feelings were on the tip of her tongue, but she held them back. They weren't something to be uttered over the phone. "I'll talk to you tomorrow."

After they said goodnight, Aria put her phone on the nightstand, then went to get ready for bed. She fought against the anxiety that was fluttering to life inside her, and it wasn't just because of Nora.

The next morning, Aria was up and ready to go when she'd normally have been sleeping in. After she drove to the clinic, she let herself into the dark and quiet building. Aria had just finished making herself a cup of coffee using the single serve coffee maker instead of the big pot when the back door opened.

Aria braced herself for Nora's appearance, hoping that her prayers would be answered, and the next few hours would go smoothly.

"Aria?" Nora said from the doorway. "What are you doing here?"

"Janessa is still sick, so I'm covering for her."

She just nodded, then turned and headed down the hallway.

Aria blew out a breath, then lifted her mug to take a sip, grimacing when she realized Nora had interrupted her before she had added the sugar. After stirring in a teaspoon of the sweetener, Aria took her mug to the desk at the front.

Janessa had said that they opened the door at eight. It was an earlier start than their weekday hours, but since they closed at noon, it allowed for four hours of appointments.

A few minutes before eight, Aria unlocked the door and held it open for a young woman with a baby in her arms who had been waiting. She greeted her with a smile, then went to the desk. After the woman gave her name, Aria dove into the day.

Just before ten, Nora appeared at the desk. So far, they hadn't had many interactions. Since Nora was only using two exam rooms, she just went from one to the other.

"Aria, can you please give the baby in exam one her six-month vaccines? She's up to date on her protocols, so it's just a standard set."

Aria clenched her hands as her heart began to pound. She had no choice, though. "Sure."

She knew where the vaccines were kept, and thankfully, Janessa had made a list of the specific protocols by age. Because Aria had worked on an adult ward at her most recent nursing job, she hadn't given pediatric vaccinations in a while.

The medications were stored in a small, locked room with its own alarm. Janessa had given her the code in case she ever needed to get in, and here she was, needing that access. Once inside the room, Aria took a moment to calm herself, then read through the list of vaccines that Janessa had posted. Once she'd prepped the shots, she went into the exam room, where a mom with two small children waited.

Aria greeted her as she sat down on the stool at the desk, then she looked over the file, verifying Nora had recorded her request. She made note of the previous vaccines, just to confirm what had been given already, then wrote down the ones she would be administering.

The toddler watched with wide eyes as Aria quickly gave the shots to the baby. Despite her anxiety being at an all-time high, her training had kicked in, and she was able to do what she needed to.

The baby hardly cried at all, and the mom smiled at her. "Thank you so much."

"You're very welcome," Aria told her. "Were you supposed to see the doctor again?"

"No. She just said to sit in the waiting room for fifteen minutes after Miley got her shots to make sure everything was okay."

"Okay. I'll help you out there." Aria took the large diaper bag and carried it out to the waiting room for the woman.

She checked the next person in before going back to prep the room the woman had just left. Doing so many things kept her busy, and the rest of the morning flew by.

Once the last patient was out the door, Aria locked it and returned to the desk.

"Well, I'm off," Nora said. "Enjoy the rest of your Saturday."

"Uh, you, too."

Aria slumped back in her chair once she was alone in the building. While it was great that she and Nora had gotten through the morning without any issues, she wasn't calm inside. There were still things she needed to do before she could leave the clinic, but she just needed a moment to catch her breath.

Even though everything had gone okay, her panic over administering the shots still hadn't dissipated. Her confidence was still shaky, and she wasn't sure when or if that would change.

Logically, her reluctance to carry out nursing duties made no sense. She'd definitely made a bad decision that had resulted in her losing her job, but her skills hadn't been called into question, and she hadn't injured a patient. She *should* have been able to do something like give a baby a shot without any nerves.

However, what she *should* be able to do versus what she *could* do were two completely different things when factoring in her confidence and anxiety. Would she ever get to a point where the events of that time didn't cause her panic? Panic that wasn't actually rooted in reality?

Finally, she got up from her chair and went to clean the exam rooms and restock where necessary. It was close to one by the time she let herself out the back door of the clinic once she'd locked everything up. Aria was desperate to put the morning behind her and get on with the rest of the day.

Aside from that one little blip, being able to meet the people who came for the free clinic had been lovely. She'd spoken to most of them when they called to make an appointment, so putting faces to names had been good. However, she was worried that they'd ask her to do more Saturday shifts, now that she'd done this one.

How was she going to say no without giving an explanation?

Back at the house, she checked on Janessa, who was sound asleep in her bed, then went to her room. Charli and Layla weren't around, so the house was quiet.

Knowing that Gareth was due to show up in a couple of hours, Aria took the time to try to calm herself, then freshened up. She wanted to just enjoy her time with Gareth, but she had a hard time getting rid of the pit in the bottom of her stomach.

This was supposed to have been a new chapter. The old one was closed. It should have stayed that way. It might still stay closed if she just made sure she didn't get herself into a position like she'd found herself in that morning.

Shame swept through her as her thoughts went back to her previous job and everything that had happened. With her mom gone, Aria had been all alone in the world and that knowledge had definitely done a number on her. She'd made some bad decisions while mired in her grief and heartache.

Aria slumped down on her bed again, regret weighing her down. However, she couldn't change the past. She couldn't change how she'd reacted and the decisions she'd made.

The distance she'd put between herself and that mess over the past several weeks had seemed so vast that all of it had barely been in her mind anymore. But now, everything was front and center of her thoughts and emotions once again.

Part of her wanted to text Gareth and tell him she wasn't feeling well and wasn't able to go with him. But there was another part of her that hoped being with him might help to shove the past back to where it belonged.

When her text alert sounded, she stared at her phone for a moment before picking it up. She almost wished that it was Janessa texting her for something.

Gareth: *On my way! See you soon.*

The heart emoji he tacked on to the end of the message soothed some of her anxiety. She just needed to spend time with Gareth, watching him do something that he enjoyed.

She sent him back a heart, then got up and went to check on Janessa one more time.

Her friend was awake this time, laying curled up with a miserable look on her face.

"Hey," Aria said softly as she approached the bed. "How are you feeling?"

"So achy and just... blah." She sighed and turned onto her back, staring up at the ceiling.

"I was going to go with Gareth to his practice, but I can stay if you want."

Janessa turned her head to the side and looked at her. "No. I'll be fine."

"Can I get you anything before I go? Water? Meds?"

"Both please."

"Sure. I'll be right back."

Aria hurried downstairs to get another bottle of water, then returned to Janessa's room. She handed her the water before going into her attached bathroom to get the meds Janessa had been taking.

Janessa had pushed herself up to sit propped against her pillows and held the water bottle in her hands. "Thanks so much, sweetie. I don't think I've ever been this sick before. I really hope that no one else gets this bug."

"So far, so good," Aria said. "Charli has pulled out all the disinfectant stuff. We're fighting the germs one spray at a time."

Janessa lifted the water bottle in a toast. "Keep up the good work."

Aria smiled as she put the medicine on the nightstand. "Charli and Layla aren't here. If you need something, text me. I'm sure Gareth will let me drive his car back."

"Okay. But I think I'll be fine. I'll try to eat something in a little while."

"At least keep drinking."

A small smile tipped the corners of Janessa's mouth. "Yes, Nurse."

Aria's stomach twisted a bit at the inference, but she still smiled. "The doctor will be here any minute if you think you need to see him."

Janessa waved her hand. "Nah. No need to expose someone else to this nastiness."

"Okay. Well, I'd better go. Gareth will be here soon."

"Have fun," Janessa said.

Aria left the room, then went downstairs. She washed up at the sink, then used some hand sanitizer, just to be safe.

She was drying her hands when the doorbell rang. Her heartbeat accelerated as she hung up the towel, then went to open the door.

"Hey, sweetheart," Gareth said with a smile as he stepped inside.

Aria accepted his hug and lifted her face for his kiss. As she leaned against him, Aria took a moment to appreciate his nearness. His strength. His gentleness in dealing with her.

He was a light out of the darkness of grief and heartache. Her reason for focusing forward.

"Everything okay?" Gareth asked as he looked down at her. "You seem a little tense."

"I'm fine. Just worried about Janessa," she said. "Plus, I didn't realize how busy the Saturday morning clinics are."

Gareth gave a huff of laughter as she turned to grab her jacket from the closet. "Yeah. They can be a bit hectic. Did Nora give you any trouble?"

Aria zipped up her jacket. "Nope. She arrived, saw patients, then left."

"Good. I'm glad to hear that."

They left the house and walked to Gareth's car. As Aria slid into the passenger seat, she hoped Gareth wouldn't ask any more questions about the morning.

The drive to the church didn't take long, and soon they were walking into the church hand-in-hand. New nerves flared up at the thought of meeting these people who knew Gareth well. What would they think of her?

"Hey, man!" a man called out as they entered the sanctuary and headed down the aisle. "Heard they won last night."

"Yep. It was a great game," Gareth said, leading Aria to where the man stood. "They definitely had to fight for the win, though."

The man turned to Aria, holding out his hand. "I don't think we've met. I'm Travis."

Aria shook his hand. "I'm Aria."

Travis' smile grew. "The girlfriend. He's told us about you."

Gareth slid his arm around her waist and smiled down at her. "All good things."

"Definitely all good things," Travis agreed with a nod.

Two more people walked in, and Gareth introduced Aria to them. The women were both friendly and greeted her with smiles. The apprehension she'd felt at meeting them eased as they stood chatting.

The final two people arrived a few minutes later, and after one last round of introductions, Aria settled on the front pew while the worship team members went up on the stage to the instruments.

Gareth smiled at her from his place at the drums, spinning the drumsticks in a way she knew he wouldn't during a worship service.

It was a move that made her smile, especially when he winked at her.

As she listened to them rehearse familiar songs, many of which she and her mom had sung together at church, she began to relax. The stress of the morning faded, and her anxiety lowered to a more manageable level. She hoped that once Janessa was back to work, she wouldn't have to think about the past anymore and could focus on the future.

A future that she hoped included Gareth in an even more important role.

CHAPTER TWENTY-THREE

That hope buoyed Aria, and her sense of calm lasted until Thursday. When she got home from work that day, there was a brown envelope waiting for her on the small table in the foyer. She picked it up and searched for a return address, but there was none.

Janessa had finally felt well enough to go to work the day before, but she'd gone right up to her room to lie down for a bit. Aria followed more slowly, curious about what was in the envelope. She didn't remember ordering or signing up for anything.

Up in her room, she changed, then settled down on the bed with the envelope. It felt like it held more than just a single piece of paper. Sliding her finger under the flap, she worked it open.

She pulled out the sheets of paper, frowning as she read the top sheet of paper. Dread slowly filled her stomach with each word.

Aria ~ Do you know what Gareth values above everything else?

His family's clinic and its reputation.

What would the patients think about the clinic if they found out that the Halversons had hired a nurse who was fired from her job for showing up drunk? Her job at a hospital... where she took care of patients?

You haven't told Gareth, have you?

Do you think he'd be happy to find out about the horrible decision you made? One that would reflect poorly on his family and their precious clinic. One that could jeopardize his patients if you made another bad decision.

Aria felt like she was going to be sick. With trembling fingers, she looked through the papers, her breath coming in rapid and shallow pants.

There was a report of her dismissal from the hospital. All the horrible details of that day. Then there was a picture of the information she'd put in the baby's file about the shots she'd administered. Her signature was highlighted on the paper. The last page continued the message from the first page.

Do you want Gareth to see this? To know that you were willing to put his beloved clinic at risk? How will Janessa feel? How about their parents? No one would want someone working for them who has shown that they have the poor judgment you do.

Aria blinked rapidly, trying to clear the tears from her eyes. The ones that escaped dropped on the papers in her lap. She didn't know what to do.

You have three days to leave the clinic and Serenity Point. Otherwise, I will share all of this information with Gareth, and you'll be leaving anyway, only with your tail between your legs.

There was no signature, but Aria didn't need one to know who had sent everything. It all made sense now. The reason Nora had been professional with her over the past couple of weeks. Also, why she'd asked Aria to administer those shots to the baby.

It had all been a set-up, and Aria had been lulled into a false sense of security. Stupid... so very stupid.

She hadn't *technically* done anything wrong in giving those shots, since her nursing license hadn't been revoked. The hospital hadn't reported her for showing up drunk because she hadn't actually begun her shift or treated any patients. Plus, they'd taken into account her work with them up until that point, which had been—according to her supervisor—exemplary.

However, they'd still had to fire her because they'd recently had a high-profile situation where a patient had died as a result of negligent care by an impaired nurse. Her impairment had been because of drugs, but still, a nurse impaired by anything was a bad thing.

So she still had her license, and it was valid in Idaho.

It wasn't the legality of what she'd done in giving the shots. It was that she hadn't told anyone about what had led to her dismissal. She hadn't given the Halversons the chance to make an informed choice in hiring her. Even though she knew how important their clinic was, she'd come anyway because she'd been desperate.

Desperate and selfish.

And so... so... so stupid.

Panic tightened around her chest as Aria tried to figure out what to do. How was she going to leave within three days? If she had lived by herself, she could have just packed up and left. But if she started to carry stuff down to her car, Janessa and Charli would know that something was up.

She was supposed to go with them the next evening to the championship basketball game. How was she going to be happy and excited at the game the way she should be when she was in a state of panic?

Every bit of happiness she'd found since coming to Serenity Point evaporated.

Aria shoved the papers under the pillow, then curled up on her side, wishing she could escape the panic, the heartache, and the pain that were battling inside her. They were familiar feelings. Ones that had taken hold of her after her mom's death, sinking into her with a ferociousness that had been hard to shake.

The joy and peace she'd embraced lately disappeared, and Serenity Point suddenly didn't feel like the safe place she'd thought it was. In fact, with the arrival of Nora's letter, it felt even less safe than her apartment with drug-addicted roommates had.

A knock on her door jerked her from her thoughts. Aria rubbed her hands over her cheeks to make sure there weren't any signs of tears, then sat up as she called for her friend to come in.

"Oh no," Janessa said as she approached her. "You're getting sick, aren't you?"

Aria stared at her friend, trying to figure out what she meant.

"I recognize that glassy-eyed look," Janessa continued. "I saw it in the mirror for more days than I liked. And you're flushed."

Her brain caught up with what Janessa was saying, and Aria grabbed it for the opportunity it was. "Yeah. Just sort of landed on me."

"I get that." Janessa frowned. "Gareth is going to kill me because you're not going to feel well enough to go tomorrow night unless you managed to catch a less awful version of whatever I had."

Aria slumped back over onto her pillow. "If I'd understood how horrible you really felt, I would have felt even more sorry for you."

"Ah, sweetie, I'm so sorry." Janessa sighed. "Why don't you get into bed? I'll go grab you some water and meds."

Aria did as she said because, honestly, being in bed was where she wanted to be. Plus, she really did feel horrible. Her heart hurt terribly, which led to an actual physical ache throughout her body. Unfortunately, she doubted that the meds Janessa had gone to get for her would help with that pain.

Thankfully, she'd seen enough of how Janessa had looked and acted over the course of her illness that Aria felt she could fake the symptoms in order to get out of the events planned for the next couple of days.

Aria was trying to keep her mind from touching on the huge loss that would occur in her life when she left Serenity Point. But if she stayed, the loss would still be the same. Gareth wouldn't want any association with her once he knew what she'd done.

Tears stung her eyes as she imagined how empty her life would be without Gareth. How empty her *heart* would be. And she was going to lose her friendship with Janessa, too.

"Hey." Janessa's voice was gentle, and Aria realized tears had escaped through her closed lids. "Are you in a lot of pain?"

Aria sighed as she scrubbed at the tears. "Just being a weepy baby. I miss my mom when I'm not feeling well."

"Oh. I'm sorry, sweetie."

"I'll be okay."

So many lies... If they ever found out, it would just reinforce to them that she was a liar.

"Do you want something to eat?"

Aria shook her head, positive that if she ate something right then, she would throw it all back up. "Just water. Then hopefully, I can sleep."

"I'll let Gareth know you're not feeling well," Janessa said. "And don't worry about work tomorrow. I'll cover for you. After all, you covered for me."

"Thanks." She hadn't felt tired when she got home from work, but she definitely felt exhausted right then. Part of her wanted to tell Gareth, but she knew that the sooner she distanced herself from him, the better.

"You just rest," Janessa said as she moved around the room, closing the blinds. "I'll come back and check on you later. If you need anything, text me. You have your phone?"

Aria lifted it so Janessa could see it, then set the phone on the bed next to her. Janessa turned off the overhead light, which left only the light from the lamp on the nightstand.

"I'll see you later."

"Thanks." Once Janessa left the room, Aria snapped off the lamp, then pulled the covers up to her face.

Grief at the loss that was to come swept over her. She should have known that things wouldn't stay good for her. After everything that had happened over the past two years, she should have been prepared for this. But she wasn't, and it felt like someone had taken a sledgehammer to her heart, shattering it.

She'd had time to prepare for her mom's death, to brace herself for the change it would bring to her life. But this... in one fell swoop, she was losing everything. Her home. Her job. Her friends—both old and new. And worst of all, the man she loved.

The love might have been new, but it had held a potential that she hadn't felt with Tim. A potential and a hope that now had been completely shattered.

If she'd been honest from the start, Nora would have had nothing to threaten her with. But she'd compounded that initial bad decision, by making another bad decision in keeping it all a secret.

She had no one to blame but herself for where she'd ended up, and Aria needed to accept that so she could do what she needed to in order to leave everything behind.

Tears fell heavily, and Aria buried her face in her pillow to muffle the sobs that welled up from the depths of her soul. She didn't know how she was going to move on from this. Right at that moment, she didn't even want to.

But she couldn't stay, so it was necessary for her to pull herself together enough to pack up her life and leave.

***

"I'm so sorry," Janessa said. "If she hadn't done such a good job of taking care of me, she never would have caught what I had."

Gareth felt so bad that Aria was sick. He'd heard how horrible it had been for Janessa, and he hated that Aria was experiencing that now.

"I told her I was going to stay home this weekend and take care of her, but she is insisting that I go."

Gareth nodded as he helped Janessa finish up. Even though it was Friday, the clinic had closed at noon, since they were heading to the game in a city four hours away. Nora could have worked the rest of the day, but it would have been difficult for her without someone to handle the reception desk.

"I texted her that I'd stay too," Gareth said. "But she was very insistent that she'd be okay."

"I mean, I was okay, too, for the hours I was on my own while she and Charli were at work. So I think she will be, but I just feel so bad."

"Stuff happens," Gareth told her. "And honestly, Aria doesn't seem to blame you at all."

He'd talked to her the night before, and she hadn't sounded great. They'd texted off and on that morning, and he planned to see her when he went by to pick up Janessa, Charli, and Layla.

Janessa sighed. "I just know how much you and her were looking forward to this weekend. I feel like I spoiled all that. Especially since it's Cole's last big game."

Gareth laid an arm around her shoulders and gave her a squeeze. "There will be lots of big events to come."

Janessa gave him a sly grin. "You looking that far into the future?"

"I am," he said confidently. And there was something in his heart that told him that Aria was too. "So yeah, lots of events we can attend together in the future."

That seemed to be the right thing to say because Janessa's shoulders lowered, and she moved a bit faster as she went to finish up the last few things before leaving. Thankfully, Nora and the other nurse were covering the free clinic the next day.

Nora had gone above and beyond lately, taking care of the Saturday clinic three weeks in a row now without complaint. He'd thought there would be some sort of repercussions following Jay's blunt statement, but it was like she'd finally accepted that there was no future for the two of them.

Once the clinic was closed up, Gareth headed to his place to change and pick up the bag he'd packed for the trip. Kayleigh had booked them into a short-term rental place for the night. It was large enough for them all to stay there, so they'd have a quick meal together before going to the game.

He didn't linger long at his place, hoping he'd be able to spend a few minutes with Aria before they left.

When he got to the house, he jogged up the walk, then took the steps two at a time to the front door. He'd barely rung the doorbell when it swung open, and Layla stood there with a grin. She wasn't dressed in the cheerleader outfit that she'd no doubt wear to the game, but she was clearly ready to hit the road.

Gareth stepped inside, closing the door behind him. After he took off his boots, he followed Layla into the kitchen. Aria was there at the counter, sitting on the stool furthest away from everyone, while Janessa and Charli discussed the snacks they'd bought for the trip.

Aria looked as bad as Janessa had when she'd been battling the bug, and it made Gareth's heart hurt. She gave him a weak smile when she saw him, but as he walked toward her, she held up her hand.

Shaking her head, her expression turned regretful. "I'm not going to be responsible for you getting sick."

Gareth stopped in his tracks with a frown, realizing she was right. "This sucks."

She nodded, looking as miserable as he felt that he couldn't hug her. "I just don't want to take the chance of any of the rest of you getting sick."

"So far Layla and I are feeling fine," Charli said. "But admittedly, you were around Janessa more than we were."

"Let's keep everyone as healthy as possible." Janessa grimaced. "Trust me—and Aria—this is not something you want to get."

Aria nodded, her gaze lowering to her hands. She wasn't even touching the counter beside her, so Gareth knew she was taking spreading the germs seriously.

It was frustrating, though. He wanted to hug and kiss her before going. However, if she was well enough to hug and kiss him, she'd be coming with them.

"Let's go! Let's go!" Layla jumped around, clapping her hands. "Let's go watch Cole win!"

Charli chuckled. "Okay. Let's make one last bathroom stop before we leave."

"Guess I'd better do that too," Janessa said. "Don't want anyone to yell at me if we have to make a bathroom stop halfway there."

After she left, Gareth said, "I'm really sorry you're feeling so badly. Is there anything I can do for you before we leave? Do you need anything?"

"I'm fine. They stocked the fridge with lots of food and water for me. I think I'll be able to survive the next twenty-four hours."

"I can video chat with you if you want to watch the game," Gareth offered, wanting to take away the miserable look on her face.

"That would be nice, but it seems like all the body wants to do with this bug is sleep. Janessa slept a lot, and I feel like I could sleep forever."

"It is best to get rest," Gareth agreed.

"Just send me pictures and videos," she said. "And I'll look through them when I wake up. Send stuff of everyone. Especially you."

Gareth laughed. "Okay. I'll do that."

"I'd send you pics of me, but this..." She waved a hand at herself. "Is as good as it's going to get. Plus, I don't exactly want this preserved for posterity."

"I'm ready to go," Layla announced as she skipped into the kitchen.

Charli and Janessa followed more slowly, each carrying a duffle bag. Gareth was torn between wanting to get on the road because he was as excited as Layla for what was to come, and putting off leaving so he could spend more time with Aria.

He knew he just needed to go. They'd be back in less than twenty-four hours, so his reluctance to leave was a bit ridiculous.

He was sure part of that, though, was just seeing how miserable Aria looked.

"Okay. We're going." Gareth turned back to Aria. "Consider yourself hugged and kissed. We'll make up for all the hugs and kisses we've missed when you're better."

Her expression seemed tremulous for a moment before her mouth tipped up into a small smile. "Definitely."

With one last look at her, Gareth followed his sisters and Layla out of the house to his SUV. He loaded their things into the back while Charli retrieved Layla's booster from her car. Once everyone else was in the car, Gareth looked at the house one last time, lifting his hand when he saw Aria standing in front of the living room window.

After she waved back, he slid behind the wheel. "Let's hit the road."

The four-hour drive could have been a headache with a child of Layla's age, but Charli always made sure she came prepared to entertain her for the duration of the trip. They did stop halfway through to get gas and use the bathroom. Gareth grabbed himself a coffee, then sent a quick text to Aria, attaching a selfie he'd taken as he'd pumped gas.

She didn't respond right away, but by the time they arrived at the house where they'd be staying the night, she'd sent a text back.

MyHeart: *Looking good! Hope everything is going well so far!*

Once they'd carried their bags into the house, Gareth took the time to send her a reply. *Just arrived. Trip went great. Smells like supper is ready, then we're heading off to the game.*

Gareth greeted his parents, who had returned for Cole's game and planned to spend a couple of weeks at home before heading back to Haiti.

"I heard that Aria was too sick to come," his mom said, concern on her face.

"Yeah. She got the bug Janessa had and is just miserable. It's too bad because she's really become a basketball fan, so it's sad she has to miss this final game."

"You and me are sharing a room, bro," Wilder said as he dropped his arm on Gareth's shoulders. "I called the top bunk."

"We're on bunk beds?" Gareth asked. "I might need to find a hotel room."

"C'mon. Let's check it out."

Gareth picked up his duffel. "I'll see you in a few, Mom. Gotta go see what Kayleigh has stuck me with."

His mom laughed as Gareth trailed after Wilder. The house Kayleigh had rented was huge, with plenty of bedrooms, which was necessary whenever their family showed up. Of course, the two family members in school were absent, but he was pretty sure that one of them was going to video call them so they could watch. They didn't do that for every game, but this was the big one.

When he got to the bedroom, he discovered that, as usual, Wilder was joking around. The room had two double beds in it, so they'd have plenty of space. He had a king-sized bed at home, which was way more space than he needed, but he'd bought it hoping that some day he'd share it with his wife.

"I grabbed the bed by the window," Wilder said.

"Frankly, I should have a choice of the beds since you lied to me."

Wilder crossed his arms. "You want the bed by the window?"

"No. I just wanted the choice."

"Goober," Wilder said as he reached out and punched his brother's shoulder.

They left their bags on the beds, then went back to the main area. Food was spread out over the large island counter. Once he had filled a plate and sat down at the enormous table, Gareth took a bunch of pictures of the people there and sent them off to Aria.

That continued as they finished eating and went to the building where the championship game was being played. The noise level was high as they found seats, which were close to their team's bench.

Gareth spotted Skylar standing with the rest of her cheerleading squad, but the players weren't out yet. They were going to have a good vantage point for the game, and Gareth's excitement grew.

He sent another batch of pictures, even though Aria hadn't replied to the last set yet. It was such a shame that she couldn't be there. He would have loved to share this experience with her. They wouldn't have many opportunities to go to basketball games with as much significance as this one.

Cole's college career was going to take him away from Idaho, so attending any of his games was going to be much more difficult. But hopefully he'd get to a few, and he couldn't wait to take Aria with him.

CHAPTER TWENTY-FOUR

The next morning, Gareth frowned down at his phone. He'd sent a ton of pictures to Aria throughout the game and after the win, but she hadn't replied to any of them. Nor had she replied to the message he'd sent to say goodnight.

Putting his phone in his pocket, he lined up to get some of the breakfast that was spread out on the island. Once his plate was full and he had a cup of coffee, Gareth sat down next to Janessa at the table.

They were getting off to a slow start that morning with some of the family still not having put in an appearance. Since they didn't have to be out of the house until noon, he knew some were going to head home a bit later. He had planned to leave around ten, but now he wanted to head out as soon as he finished eating.

"Have you heard from Aria?" he asked Janessa after he'd said a prayer for his food.

"Just a message last night, saying goodnight right at the beginning of the game. She said she was tired and might not wake up again until late."

That was around the time she'd last texted him, too. "I just thought maybe I'd have a message from her this morning."

"If she's feeling anything like I did, she's probably just getting up to use the bathroom, grab some water and meds before falling back into bed to sleep. It's a crazy bug, I have to say. I've never had something that made me feel so bad. Just completely wiped out with lots of aches and pains. I'm sure she's just sleeping."

Gareth hoped so, but he was worried. "I think I might leave as soon as I'm done eating. Do you want to go with me?"

"Sure. I don't need to hang around here."

"Charli," Gareth said, trying to get her attention where she sat across the table. When she looked over at him, he said, "Janessa and I are going to leave when we're done eating. Do you want to come with us?"

"Yep. I'm ready to go as soon as Layla's done. I'll just go pack the rest of our stuff while she finishes up."

With that decided, Gareth finished his breakfast and poured a second cup of coffee while he waited for his sisters.

Gareth breathed a sigh of relief when they were finally on the road. It was hard not to floor the accelerator, but he managed to keep to the speed limit. When they reached the house, the first thing Gareth noticed was that Aria's car wasn't there. Given how miserable she'd looked the day before, it surprised Gareth that she wasn't holed up in bed.

The house was quiet as they let themselves in, but it also felt... empty. Which made sense since it was clear that Aria was out, but Gareth felt something deep inside him. The emptiness felt ominous when combined with her lack of response over the past several hours.

Gareth followed Janessa into the kitchen while Charli and Layla went to their rooms with their bags. "Aria didn't say she was going out?"

"No. Maybe she went to buy some medicine or something."

"But why wouldn't she respond to texts?" he asked.

"Did you try to call her?"

"I didn't want to wake her up if she was sleeping. I guess I could try now since that's clearly not the case." Gareth settled on a stool at the counter and brought up Aria's contact information. He tried to quell the worry that was growing inside him. He tapped the screen to place the call, then lifted the phone to his ear. It had barely rung before going to her voicemail.

Lowering the phone, he stared at it. Had she sent his call to voicemail? Or was her phone off?

"Gareth?"

He looked up to find Janessa removing a piece of paper from under a magnet on the fridge. She turned to face him, her dark eyes wide and a worried look on his face.

Getting to his feet, he rounded the counter to where she stood. "What's wrong?"

She shoved the paper at him and headed out of the kitchen. Gareth watched her for a moment before turning his attention to the paper.

I had to leave. I'm so sorry. Thank you for everything. You'll never know how much it all meant to me. Aria

The air was sucked out of Gareth's lungs as he read the message. She was gone? His heart pounded hard within his chest for several beats before it shattered at the realization that Aria had left them. Left him.

The paper slipped from his fingers as he turned to follow Janessa out of the kitchen. She had already disappeared by the time he reached the top of the stairs. He knew which room had been Aria's, and he headed toward it.

Janessa stood just inside the doorway, staring at the room. The *empty* room.

As he stepped around his sister, he took in the full scope of the emptiness. There was nothing on any of the surfaces, and the bed was neatly made. It looked just like it had when he'd seen it before Aria had moved in. Though he hadn't seen it after she'd settled in, he knew that the starkness he saw right then was in direct contrast to how it had been when she'd called it home.

"What happened?" Janessa asked. "Why would she leave? I don't understand."

Gareth rubbed his fist against his chest, trying to ease the pain that pulsed inside him. "I don't understand either. Was she actually sick?"

"She looked sick. Pale. Tired. I just assumed..."

"Something happened," Gareth said. "Something happened that made her leave. We just have to figure out what that was."

"It might not be something here," Janessa said. "She had a life before she came to Serenity. Maybe something happened from that."

"We'll never know if we can't get her to talk to us." Gareth pulled his phone out again. His pain demanded that he try to figure out what was going on.

He couldn't believe that he'd held Aria for the last time. That he'd never again kiss her. It was inconceivable. Being with her had brought with it the hope of so much more. The hope of forever.

What happened? Please talk to me. I need to understand. If you're in trouble, we can help.

Gareth knew he sounded desperate, but that's because he was. He'd never felt for anyone else the way he felt for her. Words of love might not have been spoken between them, but the feelings had been there. For him, at least. Now he had to wonder if she'd felt anything for him.

"Can you try calling her?" Gareth asked. "My call went right to voicemail, and she's still not answering my texts."

"I already did. It went straight to voicemail, too." Janessa covered her mouth with her fingers, her brows drawn tightly over her worried gaze. "I just don't get it. She didn't say anything to me. I thought she was happy here."

"What's going on?" Charli asked from the doorway.

"Aria left."

Charli frowned as she came further into the room and looked around. "Why?"

"We don't know," Janessa said. "She just left a note that said she had to leave."

"And she's not answering our calls or texts."

Charli turned to him, her gaze sympathetic. "Ah, Gare. I'm so sorry."

He wanted to reject her sympathy, because that meant everything was truly over. But until he knew more, he refused to accept that. "We need to find out what happened."

"How can we do that?" Janessa demanded, frustration edging her tone. "She won't talk to us. She's gone. What are we supposed to do?"

Gareth had no answers for her. Helplessness filled him, bringing with it a frustration that mirrored Janessa's.

If she'd gotten into trouble, why hadn't she trusted him enough to come to him for help? It really hurt to realize that perhaps she *hadn't* trusted him at all.

"I'm going home," he said, suddenly needing to be by himself as he dealt with all the emotions drowning him. As he walked past Janessa, she reached out to grab his arm. He stopped, taking a moment before he turned his head to look at her. "I need to go, Nessa."

Her eyes grew damp, then she nodded. "Please call me if you hear anything."

"I will. And you let me know if she contacts you, too."

After Janessa agreed, she released his arm, and Gareth made his way to his car, detouring for only a moment to grab Aria's note off the kitchen floor. Though he wanted to crumple it up and throw it away, he carefully set the paper on the passenger seat before starting up the car and driving home.

He'd been worried about her being sick, but now he wondered if she'd been sick at all. Looking back, he thought of how she'd held him off from hugging her before he left. If she hadn't really been sick, had she just not wanted to hug him one last time?

The thought made him sick, and the conflicted feelings inside him grew. He honestly didn't know what to feel. All of this felt like he'd been alone in his feelings and like such a betrayal.

When he got to his house, he sat in his vehicle for a moment, suddenly feeling completely drained. All the exhilaration he'd felt from Cole's team winning the state championship was gone.

Finally, he got out of the car and headed inside, determined to get some answers, though he had no idea how.

***

Aria might not have actually caught the bug Janessa had, but she felt as tired and achy as if she had. After leaving the house in Serenity, she'd headed south and just kept going, driving for ten hours before exhaustion had forced her to find a place to stay.

Now she was sitting on a lumpy mattress in a cheap motel room, too tired to even think. Which was fine, because for the past ten hours she'd done nothing *but* think.

She hadn't wanted to dwell on what she was leaving behind. All the hopes and dreams that had grown in her new life in Serenity. The friendships. The love...

Gareth.

She'd tried to listen to audio books or podcasts to distract her from her thoughts and feelings, but to no avail.

Before she'd left Serenity, she'd turned off her cell and data service so that she wouldn't receive anymore of Gareth's or Janessa's texts or phone calls. She didn't think she was strong enough to resist reading and responding to them.

Looking at the pictures they'd sent had been hard enough. The desire to be with them had been so strong. And when she'd read the one about Cole's team winning, tears had come to her eyes, and she'd wished more than anything that she could have been there to celebrate with all of them.

Her favorite pictures, however, had been the ones of Gareth. In them, he'd been grinning, and her heart had cracked a little more with each one he sent. Then he'd sent her a video of him in the midst of all the celebrations.

I miss you so much and wish you were here. I can't wait to see you tomorrow. Sleep well. I hope you're feeling better.

He'd blown her a kiss, then the video had ended, and the pain in her heart had taken her breath away.

She'd spent some time wondering if there had been another way to handle things. But the bottom line was, that by not revealing her past, she'd shown a lack of honesty that could have negatively affected the clinic. Plus, it shamed her to have to admit her poor judgment in not only drinking far more than she should have, but in going to work in that state.

It was easy to blame her actions on her grief, but even her mom wouldn't have accepted that excuse. It had been so much more than her grief that had propelled her to make those poor decisions, but nothing changed the fact that, even though she hadn't treated anyone before her supervisor realized she was drunk, she had been prepared to put patients at risk.

Getting to her feet, Aria went to the desk and picked up the chair. She carried it over to the door and hooked it under the doorknob. Though the motel looked run-down, it hadn't looked super sketchy, so she hoped her car was safe for the night.

Come morning, she'd have to make a plan. She couldn't just keep driving aimlessly, though that was tempting. But making plans was like acknowledging she was never going to see Gareth again, and her heart didn't want to accept that yet.

A short time later, she slid beneath the covers on the bed, hoping that they were at least clean. They smelled like they were, so hopefully that wasn't just some air freshener they'd sprayed on dirty sheets.

In the darkness of the room, Aria gripped her phone, wanting more than anything to turn it on. But she knew she couldn't. She wasn't strong enough to read the messages or listen to the voicemails she undoubtedly had. Not just from Gareth, but likely from Janessa as well.

Her heart hurt at the knowledge that she'd caused them both pain. The relationships she'd been forging with them had been genuine on all their parts, so she knew they would be hurt by her actions. Not just in choosing to leave, but also in not revealing what she'd done.

Tears slipped free from her eyes, soaking into the pillow. The memory of being in Gareth's arms and now realizing that would never happen again hit her hard, and her tears turned to sobs.

How was she supposed to survive this? She'd tried so hard to hang on after her mom had died, but for what? Just more and more heartache?

When would it end?

When would God give her a break?

She'd thought Serenity had been that break, but she'd been so wrong.

In the morning, she would try to gather herself together. But that night, grief once again demanded its pound of flesh from her broken heart.

When morning came, Aria's eyes were gritty and swollen from crying, and she was a mess. She laid there for a moment, hoping that everything had just been a bad dream, but the lumpy mattress beneath her squashed that thought pretty quickly.

As she lay under the thin blanket, Aria stared at her phone where it lay on the worn nightstand. She'd plugged it in, so it was fully charged, but she still hadn't turned on the cell or data.

She still wasn't sure that she had the strength to listen or read the messages on it. Or maybe she was afraid that there wouldn't be any messages once they'd discovered she was gone.

Aria's chest tightened at the thought. She pulled her arms in tightly, curling into a ball. Fresh pain flooded every cell in her body, layering over the existing pain of losing her mom.

For a brief moment of time, she had felt like she had a place in the world once again. That she had people she could rely on. The Halversons had welcomed her into their world without hesitation. She wanted to go back to Serenity. She wanted to see Gareth and explain everything.

But she was too ashamed of herself and her actions.

Gareth was such an amazing man, and the last thing she wanted was to see the disgust on his face when he found out what she'd done. There was no way he'd want to be with her after that.

Aria couldn't help but wonder if Nora planned to tell everyone what she'd done. Or maybe Nora would pretend that she had no idea why Aria had abandoned her job at the clinic.

Those thoughts did nothing to ease her pain, and she knew that she needed to accept that her employment in Serenity had been granted under false pretenses. It had never been truly hers.

And yet, she couldn't seem to move further away from the place that held her heart. So when it neared checkout time, Aria crawled from the bed and got dressed to go to the office to let them know she was staying an extra day.

Given that there weren't many cars in the parking lot, it wasn't a surprise when the college-aged woman in the office said it was fine for her to stay in her room for another night.

"There's coffee and muffins if you'd like some," the young woman said with a friendly smile. She had also been working the day before when Aria had checked in. "And there are cookies, too. We get all of it fresh from the bakery in town."

Aria glanced at the cute setup on the buffet against the wall. Her appetite was non-existent at the moment, but Aria was sure that at some point, she'd need to eat.

"Take as much as you'd like," the woman said as Aria walked over to the buffet. "We didn't have a lot of people here last night."

"Thank you." Aria poured some coffee into a large disposable cup that came with a lid. "This is very nice."

"We try." The woman paused, then said, "Are you okay?"

Aria looked up from where she was doctoring her coffee. "What do you mean?"

"You look... sad," she said. "Is everything alright?"

Aria hadn't expected a stranger to pick up on her emotional state. "Oh... uh... Life has kind of kicked me over the last few days."

"I'm sorry to hear that. I hope you feel better soon."

Aria tried to give her a smile, but it felt like too much effort. "Such is life, huh?"

"That's true," the woman said as she got up and came over to the buffet. She reached out and grabbed a cookie. "But that doesn't make it any easier. I lost my mom five months ago, and it's been hard not to let my grief drown me. Thankfully, I still have my dad and siblings."

"You're very fortunate," Aria said, clutching her cup in both hands. "When my mom passed away a year ago, I had no one else."

The woman's brow furrowed. "Is that what you're struggling with?"

Aria shrugged, then lifted the cup to take a sip, savoring the warmth. "It will always be something I struggle with, and it has certainly compounded other struggles recently."

The woman nodded. "My mom's death has made everything harder. Situations I could deal with before are more complicated now. I was away at college, and I had to come home after she died. School was too hard. Life was too hard."

Aria understood that feeling, but at least the young woman had family around to share the weight of grief. "Is this motel owned by your family?"

"Yep. We were planning to do a bunch of renovations before Mom got sick, but all those plans have kind of been put on hold for now. I'm sorry that it's so rundown."

"That's understandable," Aria said. "I'm glad that I ended up here."

Even though it hadn't been the most comfortable bed to sleep in, knowing about the family who owned the motel and the tragedy they shared, she was now glad that she'd stopped there.

Someone came into the office, drawing the woman's attention away from her. Aria freshened her coffee, then picked up a couple of muffins and a cookie before she smiled at the woman, then headed for the door.

There was an icy wind blowing as Aria made her way back to her room. She felt it in her bones, and it reminded her of when Gareth had found her walking in the cold, underdressed for the weather in Serenity. He'd been so caring and compassionate right from the start. It was just one of many reasons she'd fallen for him.

Tears pricked at her eyes as she let herself into her room. And the brief reprieve she'd had from her heartbreak ended as she closed and locked the door. Setting the baked goods and her coffee on the nightstand, Aria crawled back under the covers, seeking the oblivion of sleep.

CHAPTER TWENTY-FIVE

Gareth's emotions had swung from hurt to anger over the course of the past two days. It hadn't helped when, at the church service the previous day, the pastor had spoken about dealing with the unexpected turns life took and how to use them to bring glory to God.

It wasn't that he wanted to hang onto the hurt and anger indefinitely, but it was still too soon to be looking for the silver lining. As far as his heart was concerned, there was no silver lining.

"Good morning, Gareth," Nora said as she stepped into his office, a folder in her hand. "Do you have a moment?"

Nora was the last person he wanted to deal with in his current mindset, but they were at work, so he had to put aside his feelings and be professional. "Sure."

She gave him a smile that seemed to border on smug and sent a frisson of unease through him. As she sank down on one of the visitor chairs across from his desk, she set the folder on the desk.

"I'm very sorry that Aria didn't do the right thing."

Gareth frowned, the unease inside him growing. "What are you talking about?"

"Information came to me that Aria was fired from her nursing job at the hospital where she worked."

The statement took Gareth off-guard. "And I suppose information also came to you about why."

Nora nodded. "She went to work intoxicated."

"What?" That didn't sound like the woman he'd come to know and love. "That makes no sense."

"That's what I heard, and it's what was given as the reason for her firing." Nora frowned. "If I had known about this, I wouldn't have asked her to help me at the free clinic by giving vaccinations to a child."

Gareth's anger grew, eclipsing his unease and hurt. In that moment, he was mad at Aria along with Nora. Why was he hearing this from Nora? Why hadn't Aria told them about this? Such information might have played a role in their hiring of her.

When they'd initially mentioned her helping with the free clinic, she'd had the perfect opportunity to share why she'd rather not. Instead, she'd brushed it off, saying she enjoyed the lower-pressure position of receptionist. And when they'd asked her to help when Janessa was sick, she could have told them then. *Should* have told them then.

But she hadn't. She had agreed to step in and do Janessa's job as receptionist *and* nurse. How had she not been aware of how bad that was for the clinic?

"And she was also living with drug addicts before moving here," Nora added.

Gareth stared at her, that latest revelation confirming that this wasn't information that had just fallen into her lap. Though he hadn't really believed that to begin with. Clearly, Nora had gone looking for information on Aria.

The words *you're fired* were on the tip of his tongue, but he couldn't say them. He needed to speak with Janessa to find out how much of this she knew before they could move forward.

Once his sister found out that Nora was behind Aria leaving, he wasn't sure what she would do. He really hoped that Janessa hadn't known about all of this when she'd convinced him and Jay that hiring her friend was a good thing.

"Thank you for bringing this to our attention." He turned back to his computer, hoping she'd get the point that their conversation was over.

Nora gave an annoyed exhale before she got to her feet. "You know I only have the best interests of the clinic in mind."

Gareth was quite sure that *wasn't* true. She'd had it out for Aria from day one, and he suspected that she'd somehow gotten wind that he and Aria were dating. Had been dating.

Had been dating... The past tense of that statement was a punch to his stomach.

Pushing aside the hurt, he said, "I'm sure you do."

Her brief hesitation before leaving the office likely came from her realization that this might not end the way she intended. He watched her go, then glanced at his watch. He didn't have time to talk to Janessa before they started to see patients. It would have to wait.

He didn't want to think about it. He didn't want to deal with it. The pain that came from discovering he didn't know Aria the way he thought he did was nearly crippling.

But now he had answers, and that's what he had wanted.

However, he was really having a *be careful what you wish for* moment.

With a sigh, Gareth closed his eyes and said a prayer for strength to get through the day with this new information weighing down heavily on him. He couldn't be distracted while he tended to patients. They were coming here for his professional attention, and he owed that to them.

He spent time doing what he usually did, perusing the files of the patients he'd see that day, while he waited for Janessa to let him know his first patient was there. All the while, he ignored the file that Nora had left on his desk.

It wasn't until Janessa tapped on his door that he reached over and picked it up, sliding it into the drawer of his desk before he left the room.

"Can we eat lunch in my office?" Gareth asked Janessa after he'd stopped her in the hallway when his last patient of the morning had left. "I need to talk to you."

She frowned but nodded. "I'll just go grab our food. I put it in the break room already."

Gareth didn't much feel like eating, but he knew he should have something. He hadn't eaten anything yet that day, and the countless cups of coffee he'd already drunk ate at his stomach.

When Janessa walked in, she carried two wrapped subs. She closed the door, then handed him one before sitting down on the chair opposite him.

"What's going on?" she asked.

After a moment's debate, Gareth pulled the file Nora had given him out of the drawer and leaned forward to set it on the desk in front of her. He hadn't read through it, but he was pretty sure it contained everything Nora had told him earlier. Possibly even more.

Janessa's brow furrowed as she picked the file up. "What's this?"

"The reason Aria left."

"Really?" She quickly flipped the file open and sat back to read it.

Gareth unwrapped his sub but left it sitting on the desk while he waited for Janessa to react. He really hoped that she hadn't known about any of it.

"She was *fired*?" Janessa asked, her voice pitching higher. "For *drinking*? That makes no sense."

"What do you mean?"

"Aria never drank. When we were in college, people would try to get her to drink at parties, and she never indulged. At least not that I ever saw." She looked back down at the file. "This happened a few weeks after her mom died. Before she came here, she'd been working as a cashier."

"What about the drug addicts for roommates?" Gareth asked. "Did she ever mention that to you?"

"No. She didn't. She mentioned moving, but she said it was to a smaller apartment since she didn't need a two bedroom one after her mom died."

Gareth was relieved that Janessa hadn't known about any of this before asking them to hire Aria. Still, it really hurt to realize that the woman he'd come to love had lied by omission to all of them.

"So you didn't look into her background before asking us to hire her?"

Janessa's shoulders slumped. "I didn't think I had to. She was at the top of our class and took everything so seriously. I mean, I did too, but she was so much more focused than anyone else. So I had confidence that she would be a great addition here. I made assumptions that I guess I shouldn't have."

The pain on his sister's face fed the anger that brewed inside Gareth. He struggled to reconcile the woman he'd fallen for with the one that was coming to light now. That struggle also fed his anger.

Gareth didn't get mad very often. Sure, he had occasional bursts of temper, but this prolonged forest fire of anger wasn't common for him. He had no idea how to extinguish it. So far, everything seemed to feed it rather than help to extinguish it.

"I'm sorry," Janessa said, her shoulders slumping. "I thought I was doing a good thing."

"You were. This is not totally your fault. Aria should have told you about the firing, at the very least."

Janessa opened her mouth, then closed it and sighed. "I hate that this has happened, not just because of the ramifications for the clinic, but because Aria is all alone again."

"Because of her own actions," Gareth reminded her, trying to squelch his own concern for her. "If she'd just been honest, we could have worked with her."

Janessa regarded him for a moment before she said, "Would you have? You and Jay weren't really on board with hiring her. If I'd told you that she'd been fired for going to work drunk, would you have considered allowing her to work here at the clinic? Even just as a receptionist? I'm pretty sure you wouldn't have."

Gareth couldn't argue that point with her. His need to make sure that the clinic only had the best employees would have meant he'd object strongly to someone with a black mark like that on their employment record. And Jay would likely have felt the same way.

"She probably assumed that too, which was why she hid it from us. I don't think it's wrong to assume that she was desperate."

Gareth frowned, blocking out the attempt by his heart to feel sorry for Aria. He wasn't going to let that happen. She had *lied* to him. She had put his clinic at risk. She'd agreed to a relationship with him, all the while hiding something very significant.

"This is not the time to see things in such black and white terms," Janessa said. "You need to be more empathetic."

It wasn't that Gareth didn't have empathy. He did, especially when dealing with his patients. He didn't have as much empathy, though, for people who ended up in bad situations because of their own decisions.

"Your hurt is making you angry." She picked up her sub, then got to her feet. "My heart is with Aria. If I'd known what was going on, I would have had her come and stay with me, even if we hadn't offered her a job. You know she's special. You're just letting your hurt and anger tell you that she's not."

With those words, Janessa left the office, leaving Gareth with the thoughts generated by her parting shots.

It was more than his hurt making him angry. It was also just not understanding how a person could be in a relationship with someone and not be honest about something like what had happened to Aria.

Maybe this would be easier to accept if it didn't feel like a double whammy. Her dishonesty was impacting him on both a personal and a professional level.

He wasn't sure how to get over it. As he thought it all over, Gareth felt like he was justified in how he felt. He wasn't the person who had screwed things up.

The anger was easier to deal with than the hurt and heartbreak, so he chose that. Chose his anger to be where he funneled his emotional energies.

Ignoring his food, he turned his attention to his computer, needing a break from the situation. It wasn't to be, however, because there was a knock on his door, and he looked up to see Jay coming into his office.

Gareth let out a sigh as he leaned back, watching as Jay settled into the chair Janessa had just vacated.

"So I hear we need a new receptionist," Jay said, his expression unreadable.

The idea of seeing someone other than Aria sitting at the reception desk was like a stab to his heart, piercing through the thick layer of anger. Shoring up his defenses against the hurt, Gareth said, "Guess so. Were there any other potentials among the applications we received?"

Jay's brows drew together, and his dark gaze held Gareth's. "No."

Gareth sighed. "I suppose you have an opinion about all of this, too."

Jay crossed his arms over his chest and shrugged. "I can't say I'm happy to find out that Aria wasn't honest with us about what had happened with her previous hospital employment."

"Nora certainly was pleased to share the information with me."

"Well, of course she was," Jay said with a snort. "She's been dying to get rid of Aria."

"I'm concerned that unless we get a receptionist she doesn't feel threatened by, we're going to keep having issues." Gareth sighed and reached for his pen, clicking the end of it several times. "Although, honestly, I don't much care about Nora at this point. We just need to find a capable receptionist."

"Aria definitely was that."

"Janessa can't handle it all on her own again," Gareth said, ignoring Jay's comment. "So we need to put out an ad."

"Are you sure that Aria isn't coming back?"

"You'd give her back the job, knowing what you do?"

"The issue wasn't her work as a receptionist. We just wouldn't use her as a nurse."

"Putting aside everything else," Gareth said, ignoring the ache in his chest. "Aria's return would cause huge issues with Nora."

Jay nodded. "It would be something we'd have to deal with."

"I think it's a moot point. She hasn't even been in contact with Janessa. I don't think she's coming back."

"I guess we'll see," Jay said as he got to his feet. He hesitated a moment, looking like he was going to say something else, but then he turned and left the office.

Gareth stared at the empty doorway. Jay hadn't reacted like Gareth had assumed he would. He either had other stuff on his mind, or he just didn't care. Gareth was going to go with the former because it was rare that Jay didn't care about something that impacted the clinic negatively.

When Janessa knocked on his door to let him know his first patient of the afternoon was in an exam room, Gareth realized he hadn't eaten his lunch. He still wasn't hungry, so rather than force himself to eat, he took his sub to the break room and put it in the fridge. He wanted a cup of coffee, but that would have to wait until he had some time between patients.

"Hello," Gareth said with a forced smile as he walked into the exam room. "How're you doing today?"

"I'm okay," the elderly woman said. "Just here for the follow-up you wanted on my blood pressure."

Pushing aside all his thoughts and emotions, Gareth focused on his job. It felt like the one stable thing in his life right then.

"What happened to Aria?" the woman asked once they were done discussing her health concerns. "Is she sick?"

Gareth hadn't anticipated dealing with patient inquiries about Aria, though he probably should have.

"She's moved on," Gareth said.

The woman frowned. "She left? Why would she do that?"

"Yes. She had to leave for personal reasons."

That was true enough, though it didn't seem to appease the woman.

"I really thought she'd stick around. She seemed to like it here."

Gareth had thought that, too. "Apparently, she changed her mind."

The woman peered at him with sharp blue eyes. "You didn't do anything to chase her away, did you?"

"No. I can honestly say that this had nothing to do with me."

"Well, it's a real shame that she left."

The woman stood and reached for her coat. Gareth helped her put it on, then walked with her to the front. "Take care of yourself."

"You too, young man."

His gaze landed on the empty chair behind the reception desk, and his heart ached. He might want to hold tight to the anger, but there was no denying—to himself at least—that beneath it all was the hurt... so much hurt. Its presence just added to his anger because he didn't want to feel it.

She was the first woman he'd ever felt such depth of emotion for—had ever really loved—and now he didn't trust his feelings because it felt like they'd been for a different person.

When he went home later, Gareth busied himself with stuff around the house. Though he had someone who came to do a general cleaning of the home, he did his own dishes and laundry. So after putting on his favorite medically-oriented podcast, he threw in a load of laundry, then wandered into his garage.

He opened the overhead door to let in some fresh air as he worked to organize his tools. They weren't necessarily messy, but he had a tendency to put tools he used on the workbench instead of back on the wall or in the spaces he'd set aside for them. Sorting them out was never his favorite thing, but right then, he needed the distraction.

A hand landed on his shoulder as he worked. Startled, Gareth jerked around, sighing when he spotted Wade.

Pulling one of his ear buds out, Gareth said, "What are you doing here?"

"Something is obviously wrong, so I'm here to see what's up." He put his hands on his hips as he glanced around. "What's going on?"

Gareth turned his attention back to his tools. "Nothing."

"You lie," Wade said without heat.

"I don't want to talk about it," Gareth told him.

He heard shuffling behind him and glanced over his shoulder to see that Wade had taken a seat on one of the stools Gareth kept in the garage. Wade didn't say anything, just sat there with his arms crossed, watching him expectantly.

If Jackson had been there, he would have pestered Gareth until he spilled everything. Wade's silence was weighty, and Gareth knew he was going to end up sharing all the details.

"We found out that Aria lied to us," he said, reaching to hang the trimming sheers on the hook above the worktable. "She left without saying a word to anyone."

"I thought she was sick."

"That was all a ruse, apparently. When we got back to the house on Saturday, she was gone."

"And she didn't tell you anything? How did you find out she lied?"

"She left a note saying she was sorry." Gareth dropped a pair of pliers into a drawer. "But Nora was the one who gave us all the details."

"Well, that's not suspicious at all," Wade said with a snort.

"I would have agreed with you, except she had proof. Her jealousy of Aria led her to try to find some dirt on her. Unfortunately, there were things Aria had hidden that gave Nora all the ammunition she needed."

"And Aria didn't stay to defend herself?"

"Not much she could defend against," Gareth said, turning to lean back against the workbench. "If it had been faked, Aria could have stayed and defended herself. She had to know that we'd give her the benefit of the doubt against Nora's charges."

"What did she do?"

For a moment, Gareth found that he wanted to protect Aria. He didn't want people to know what she'd done, even though she wasn't there. But he knew he could trust Wade with the information. The same couldn't be said for Jackson, as the guy liked to talk, and not everything he said passed through his brain first.

Staring at the floor, he slowly shared the details with Wade.

"How are you doing?" Wade asked when he was done.

"The clinic is suffering without her," Gareth said. "Janessa too, since Aria wasn't just another employee to her. She's lost her friend, and she's having to cover the receptionist job as well as her own again."

"How are *you* doing?" Wade repeated.

Gareth pushed down the ache that tried to swell up inside him. "I'm fine."

"You lie *again.* Don't do that, bro," Wade said quietly. "I've never seen you so gone on a woman the way you are over Aria. Tell me how you're really doing."

"I'm angry," Gareth finally said. "If she'd felt anything for me like I feel for her, she'd never have been able to leave the way she did. It was like she just didn't care about any of us."

"I know that hurts. But from watching you two together, I honestly think she does care for you."

Gareth frowned. "She has a very funny way of showing it."

"I would think that she's probably ashamed and embarrassed," Wade said. "I know I would be. And telling people I really cared about that I hadn't been truthful would be super hard."

Gareth understood what Wade was telling him, but it didn't ease his anger and hurt. He wanted her feelings for him to have been strong enough to risk telling him the truth. He wanted her to have trusted him.

Knowing that he'd had neither her love nor her trust made pain pulse deep in his heart.

"God wouldn't want you to carry anger or hate in your heart for her," Wade said.

"It's been *three days.*" Gareth glared at his friend. "I think it's unrealistic for you to expect me to be beyond the hurt and anger already. How long did it take you to get over your divorce?"

Wade regarded him with a calm gaze. "I'm just saying that if you're presented with the opportunity for a second chance and your heart is full of anger, you may screw it up."

Gareth didn't want a second chance. The intensity of his emotions since realizing that Aria had left scared him. If nothing else, he'd learned that he needed to get to know someone much better than he had Aria before getting involved on a deeper emotional level with them.

CHAPTER TWENTY-SIX

Aria's stomach trembled as she guided her car past the outer limits of Serenity Point. Gripping the steering wheel tightly, she fought the urge to turn the vehicle around and head in the opposite direction.

The decision to return had been a difficult one. She'd ended up spending three nights at the small, rundown motel. The young woman—who she'd learned was named Jasmine or Jassy for short—had befriended her and talking with her in the quiet of the motel office had been refreshing.

In the middle of nowhere, she'd found someone who understood the depth of her grief and how it impacted everything. She'd listened as Aria had poured out everything that had happened, then she'd encouraged her to go back.

If you tell them everything and they reject you, then you can move forward with your life. But if you don't give them a chance, you'll always wonder what might have been.

Aria had realized that Jassy was right. If this was a chapter in her life that was closing, she needed to know that all of it had been written. And if there was any chance things could be worked out, she knew she wanted that.

What worried her, though, was that while Janessa might listen to her and give her a second chance, Gareth might not. Aria knew that there was every possibility that he would be so angry about everything that he wouldn't be willing to even listen to her.

But Jassy was right, she had to do this in order to move forward.

During the trip back to Serenity Point, in between spikes of anxiety, Aria had formulated a plan of action. She didn't feel comfortable going to Janessa's house. It wasn't her home anymore. It had ceased to be that the moment she'd carried her last suitcase out the front door.

So instead, she drove to the motel she'd found on the internet that was within her limited budget. She'd broken the trip into two days, so she was arriving early afternoon, giving her time to check in and try to settle her anxiety before going to talk to Gareth.

She planned to talk to him and then to Janessa. However, if Gareth wasn't receptive to what she had to say, her conversation with Janessa would also include a goodbye.

The motel, though small, was in better shape than Jasmine's, but Aria found that she missed her new friend. In the room a short time later, Aria sat on the edge of the bed, trying to quell her anxiety, tapping out a message to Jassy to let her know she'd arrived.

She didn't know if Gareth would go home after the clinic closed, but she hoped he did. Her nerves and anxiety were becoming unbearable, and she had to keep her hands fisted so she didn't scratch at her skin.

As the clock clicked toward five, Aria got up and went to the bathroom to make sure she looked okay. The dark circles under her eyes were impossible to hide, so she didn't try too hard.

At five-fifteen, she took a moment to pray, though she wasn't sure that God was listening to her. Finally, she got to where she just wanted to get the apology over with, so she left the room and headed for her car.

She'd only been to Gareth's house once, but she remembered where it was. After parking down the street a ways from his property, she saw that his driveway was empty.

It was possible he had parked in the garage, but Aria decided to wait a few minutes before going to the house. Just in case he still wasn't home from work.

As every minute passed, her anxiety continued to climb. As she swallowed against the nausea intensifying in her stomach, Aria began to question her plan. Maybe she *didn't* need to know. Maybe she could move forward without talking to Gareth.

She closed her eyes and said another prayer for calm. After several deep breaths that did little to ease her nerves, Aria opened her eyes just in time to see Gareth pull his car into the driveway.

He didn't park in the garage, so maybe he planned to go out again. That meant she didn't have time to waffle around now that he was home.

With her heart pounding in her chest, she watched him walk around his car and head for the front door of his house. It was a home that she'd occasionally allowed herself to imagine what it might be like to live in one day.

That hadn't been in her thoughts since Thursday... when her dreams of a life in Serenity had died.

Aria fought to make herself pull the handle to open the car door. If she waited any longer, her anxiety would force her to drive away and leave Serenity without accomplishing what she'd returned to do.

Grabbing her keys from the ignition, Aria got out of the car. She headed to the sidewalk, and though it felt like her shoes weighed a hundred pounds, she tried not to dawdle. It would only prolong the inevitable, which she was quite sure would be Gareth sending her on her way.

But at least she would have apologized. They deserved that much after all they'd done for her.

When she got to the steps, she paused for a moment before climbing them, gripping the railing tightly as she went. Once at the door, she took one final deep breath and pressed the doorbell.

It took a minute before the door swung open. Gareth had changed out of his work clothes into a pair of worn jeans and a T-shirt with a faded picture on the front.

"Can I talk to you?" she asked, clenching her hands together to stop them from trembling.

Gareth frowned, but he moved back. Aria tried not to let his lack of welcome dissuade her from her purpose. She stepped inside, then moved to the side so he could close the door.

His frown was still in place as he turned to face her, crossing his arms over his chest. His expression was one she'd never seen before, and there was no sign of the affectionate smile he always gave her.

"I want to apologize," Aria said, needing to get it out before he told her to go. "I shouldn't have left the way I did without explanation."

"Oh. We know why you left."

So even though Nora had told her she would tell them about her past if she didn't leave, she'd gone on to tell them even after she'd done what Nora had asked.

"I'm sorry that I didn't tell all of you what had happened at my old job," Aria said, then swallowed, her gaze dropping to her hands. "I just really needed to leave Sacramento, and honestly, I was embarrassed by everything."

"You put our clinic at risk." The coldness of his voice killed her a little inside, though she had to admit to herself that he was definitely entitled to his anger.

"I understand. I just wanted to apologize." As her worst fears were realized, Aria turned to the door and opened it. "Thank you for everything."

When he didn't stop her as she stepped out onto the porch and closed the door softly behind her, Aria knew that she'd lost everything where Gareth was concerned. Tears clouded her vision as she made her way back to her car.

There would be no future for her in Serenity. She'd gone to Gareth first because she'd been desperate to see him, but also because she knew that if he couldn't forgive her, there was no way she could stay.

Settling behind the wheel, Aria blinked back tears as she started up the car and pulled away from Gareth's house. If she allowed herself to cry, she wasn't going to stop, and she still had one more person to see.

It didn't take her long to get to the house she'd shared with Janessa and Charli. Her anxiety wasn't as high as it had been prior to seeing Gareth because she had nothing left to lose. Regardless of how things went with Janessa, she already knew she'd be leaving.

Still, she sat for a minute after parking. And even though her prayer hadn't been answered with Gareth, she tried again, asking God to help her get through this next conversation without breaking down completely. She grabbed a tissue from the box and blew her nose, trying to edge back from the weepiness that wanted to grab hold of her.

When she finally got out of the car, pain and weariness seemed to drain all the life out of her. But pushing through it, she put one foot in front of the other.

Both Janessa's and Charli's cars were there, so she knew they were home. She kind of hoped that Layla would be the one to answer the door.

Instead, Janessa opened the door. Her eyes widened, and then she flung her arms around Aria. Her friend's hug soothed some of the hurt Aria was carrying, and she clung to her, trying not to break down, but desperately needing the comfort.

"I can't believe you're here," Janessa said, stepping back and gripping her arm to pull her into the house. Janessa led her into the living room and pushed her down onto the couch before she sat down beside her. "Why did you leave?"

"Nora said that if I didn't, she'd tell you about what happened with my last nursing job."

"You should have told us," Janessa said. "We would have understood."

"I was struggling," Aria confessed. "And I'd dealt with the end of my engagement and my mom's death really badly. I was working as much as possible to escape my grief, and when I wasn't working, I was drinking. When they called me for the extra shift that day, I said yes because I'd rather have been working than sitting home alone. I called for a ride and off I went."

"So you didn't drive drunk?"

"No. Of course not." Aria sighed and looked down at her hands. "Which sounds ridiculous because I was prepared to work drunk."

"What happened?"

"As soon as I got to work, someone noticed I appeared intoxicated and confronted me. My supervisor got involved, and they fired me. They were actually really good to me, all things considered, taking into account my previous record and what I was dealing with personally." As Aria explained what had happened, the memory of that time brought with it so much pain.

"So they suspended your license and fired you?" Janessa asked. "That doesn't sound like they were really good to you."

Aria shook her head. "They didn't suspend my license. Just fired me."

"Huh." Janessa frowned. "We thought you'd lost your license. So that was why we got upset about you having given shots to a patient."

"My license is still valid," Aria said. "I was just so... ashamed of the bad decisions I'd made that I didn't want to tell you."

"Are you not wanting to work as a nurse anymore?" Janessa asked.

"It wasn't that I didn't want to," Aria told her. "It was that I would have had to share about my last job before anyone would hire me. It felt easier to just... do something else. Plus, my confidence in myself and my abilities was shaky."

"What did you do after you were fired?"

"Got a job as a cashier at a big box store. I had to get a cheap apartment and a roommate. I didn't realize at the time that she was a drug addict, and she came with a boyfriend who also did drugs. It was horrible. When you contacted me about coming to work here, I was so grateful." She sighed. "And then I messed it all up."

"You didn't," Janessa said, reaching out to grab her hand. "Yeah, things got a little crazy with you just leaving instead of talking to us."

"I'm sorry. I just couldn't stick around and see the disappointment, because if I stayed, Nora was going to tell everything." Aria rubbed her hands on her thighs. "I couldn't do it."

"Why did you come back?"

"I needed to apologize," she said. "And say goodbye."

"No. You're not saying goodbye. We can work through this."

Aria shook her head and gave her a sad smile. "I've already talked to Gareth. I can't stay if he doesn't want me here. And it's clear he doesn't."

Janessa gave a low growl and shook her head. "He's hurt and mad. More hurt than mad, but I think he's choosing to embrace the anger. He doesn't get mad easily, but when he does... he can carry a grudge. But he *does* get over it."

"I understand why he's upset," Aria said. "I don't blame him at all, which is why I need to leave."

"Please don't," Janessa pleaded in a way that Aria wished Gareth had. "Where would you go, anyway?"

Aria tried to give her a reassuring smile, but it felt really weak. "I'll figure it out."

"Don't go yet. Give Gareth a chance."

It wasn't that she didn't want to give him a chance, but he didn't give her the feeling that he wanted that. Though that hurt more than anything, Aria accepted that this was her fault. If she'd been honest from the start, she wouldn't be in this position.

"Ariaaaaa!" Layla came running into the living room and hopped up onto the couch between Janessa and Aria. She flung her arms around Aria's neck and gave her a tight squeeze. "I'm so glad you're back!"

As Aria hugged the little girl, her gaze met Janessa's. "It's good to see you again, Layla."

The little girl sat back and grinned at her. "Your room is so empty."

Your room. She wished that it was still her room.

When Charli came into the room, her eyes widened, and then she smiled. "It's good to see you again, Aria."

Though she was sure that Charli had thoughts and feelings about what Aria had done, she didn't seem to be mad at her. "It's good to see you again, too."

"Layla, sweetie, let's let Janessa and Aria talk. You can help me get supper ready."

Layla didn't look pleased, but she slid off the couch and followed her mom out of the room, glancing over her shoulder once before she disappeared. The hole in Aria's heart grew at the thought of not having the bright little girl and her friendly mom in her life anymore. Charli had become a friend, just like Janessa was.

"You can stay here," Janessa said. "Even if you're not working at the clinic, you can still stay here."

"This is somewhere Gareth enjoys visiting. I'm not going to make it uncomfortable for him to come here."

"Where have you been staying?"

"At a motel about ten hours from here."

"You really did leave," Janessa said. "But then you decided to come back?"

"I met someone there who listened to me spill everything, and she helped me realize that I needed to come back to apologize before moving forward."

"Don't move on just yet. Please. I know we weren't in close contact over the last year, and I'm sorry for that. You needed me, and I wasn't there. Give me... give us... some time."

"I don't want your pity, Janessa," Aria said. "I'm not entitled to it. Every decision I made—good or bad—is my responsibility. My mom would have been so disappointed in how I reacted. She would say that she raised me better than that, which she did."

"I know about grief, Aria. I remember how lost I felt when my mom died, even though we had a supportive family ready to take us in. If I'd been all alone as an adult, I'm not sure I would have made good decisions."

Aria appreciated Janessa trying to excuse her behavior, but there really was no acceptable excuse. She hadn't taken any accountability for her actions at the time, even though she'd accepted the consequences. Now, however, she was trying to do that, and she couldn't take the easy way out.

"If you won't stay here, at least stay in Serenity for a couple of days. Give us a chance to talk to Gareth. I think he just needs a little bit of time."

Janessa obviously knew Gareth better than Aria did, but Aria understood that she'd hurt Gareth, and not everyone was willing to forgive that. And even if he *did* forgive her, it didn't mean he'd want to be in a relationship with her anymore or would even want her around.

"I can stay, I guess." It wasn't like she had a plan of where to go next. She'd be staying in cheap motels for the time being, so staying in one in Serenity didn't make any difference.

She'd use the time to figure out where she was going to go next. Because even though she wished with all her heart that Gareth would accept her apology and want to get back together, she could not allow that hope to grow inside her.

For some reason, losing Gareth hurt worse than her engagement to Tim ending had. Gareth was a different kind of man, one who had resonated strongly with her heart. She had been able to imagine a future with him so vividly. He'd brought joy and happiness into her life, and in return, she'd broken his trust and hurt him.

She'd also hurt and broken Janessa's trust, but they'd been friends longer and perhaps their shared parental loss had made Janessa more willing to forgive. Though the best-case scenario would have been Gareth and Janessa both forgiving her and accepting her back into their lives, at least still having Janessa's friendship helped soothe a bit of her pain.

As long as she didn't think about Gareth.

Unfortunately, his hard gaze when she'd last seen him was a memory she couldn't shake, and she was sure that would be the case for months to come. That thought made her heart pulse with hurt.

"I need to go." She'd spent so much time crying over the past few days, that holding back the tears was getting more and more difficult.

"Can't you stay for dinner?"

"I'm not really hungry, to be honest."

"And you don't want to stay here? I mean, your room is still empty."

Aria got to her feet. "I've already checked into the motel."

Janessa sighed as she got up. "I don't like this."

"I'm sorry. I think it's best for now."

"Just don't leave town."

"I won't."

"Keep your phone on and answer it."

"I will."

When they reached the front door, Janessa pulled her into a hug once again. "Thank you for coming back and explaining."

"I shouldn't have left," Aria said. "I realize that now. Thank you for listening to me and forgiving me."

Janessa smiled at her. "Always."

Tears pricked at her eyes as she walked away from the place she'd come to consider her home. She slid behind the wheel of her car, once again having to blink rapidly to clear her vision. Her tight hold on her emotions was slipping away. She just had to make it back to the motel, then she could break down.

CHAPTER TWENTY-SEVEN

Gareth stared at the closed door, trying to sort through all his emotions. He'd been shocked to find Aria standing on the doorstep. Shocked and angry.

Why hadn't she returned any of his calls? It had been four days, and she hadn't been able to call him back? But she could just show up on his doorstep?

His anger, which bubbled furiously just below the surface of his emotions these days, had definitely overridden his common sense. He knew he should have reacted differently, but the hurt/anger combination didn't lend itself to rational reactions.

Gareth turned and went out the back door to his deck. Bracing his hands on the railing, he stared at the mountains in the distance. There was a bit of a chill in the air, but he ignored it, seeking the peace he often found when looking out over nature.

Unfortunately, it didn't work this time.

He knew he had to get past his hurt and anger. Neither emotion was doing him any favors.

But seeing Aria again... he was reminded of all the reasons he'd fallen in love with her. Every moment they'd spent together flashed through his mind. The joy and happiness he'd experienced when she'd look at him, her smile, gentle and disarming.

His biggest struggle was to not feel like she'd duped him. To not think that the gentleness and joy she'd exuded had masked her lies. Would she ever have told him what had happened? Or would she just have carried the lies through the duration of the relationship?

The longer he stood there, the more he wished he'd been able to formulate a better response to Aria when she'd come. His anger upon seeing her had faded a bit, and he could accept that she had appeared to be genuine in her apology.

Gareth knew he had to forgive her, even as God had forgiven him... that's what the Bible taught. His forgiveness had nothing to do with how he felt or how genuine Aria's apology was. However, offering forgiveness had always been a struggle for him. From the time he'd been young, if someone did something to make him mad, he had struggled to forgive them. Even if they'd said they were sorry.

How did he get over his anger at her for withholding vital information from them? How did he get past his hurt that even though she'd agreed to be in a relationship with him, she hadn't trusted him enough to share her past?

Gareth didn't know how much time had passed as he stood out there trying to sort through his emotions, but the sun had fully disappeared behind the mountains. Unfortunately, he still didn't know how to move forward.

He had questions that he wished he had asked Aria earlier. But he wasn't sure that her answers would have made any difference with his anger. In fact, they might have made it worse.

As he turned to go inside, his doorbell rang. His heart gave a hard thump in his chest, though he was quite sure it wasn't Aria. Most likely, it was Wade and/or Jackson.

"What are you doing here?" Gareth asked when he saw Janessa and Jay.

"Can we come in?" Janessa asked.

Gareth didn't feel like company, but he stepped back and fully opened the door to allow them inside. Because he wanted their visit to be quick, he didn't offer them coffee.

Even without his invitation, however, they went right to his couch and sat down. With a sigh, Gareth closed the door and went to join them.

"What can I do for you?"

"I've spoken with Aria," Janessa said. "She came to see me after talking to you."

"Oh?"

"*Oh?* That's all you have to say?" Janessa demanded, anger flashing in her eyes.

Jay reached out and put a hand on her arm. "That's not going to help."

Janessa frowned at Jay before she let out a huff and turned back to Gareth. "Did you even *talk* to her? Or did you just let her leave?"

Gareth narrowed his gaze at her, trying to keep from getting angry at yet another person in his life.

"Aria is determined to leave Serenity. In fact, she'd already left, but then came back to apologize." She stared at him for a moment before taking a deep breath. "Listen, I'm not sure if she told you this, but if she hadn't told me, I'd be operating under a wrong assumption."

"What's that?"

"That her nursing license had been suspended."

Gareth frowned. "Considering the offense, I would have thought that a suspension was a given."

Janessa shrugged. "I assumed the same. She said that she hadn't treated any patients while she was intoxicated, plus they took into account her previous work for them as well as the circumstances she was dealing with at the time."

"But they still fired her," Gareth said. "Why didn't they just put a reprimand on her file?"

"Apparently they'd had a recent huge issue with a previous situation involving someone coming to work high. In that case, the person had gone on to treat patients, and someone had died. After dealing with a suit from that patient's family, they couldn't be seen not taking harsh action on something like that again."

While Gareth was glad that she had retained her license since she'd treated a patient in their clinic, he still thought that she should have told them about everything before agreeing to take the receptionist job with them. If she'd explained all that, they would have been sympathetic and probably still would have hired her.

"I want her to come back to work at the clinic," Janessa stated. "And Jay is also willing to have her back on the job."

Gareth glanced between his siblings. Janessa had a determined look on her face, while Jay's expression, as usual, was pretty much unreadable.

"Why do you think it's wise to bring her back?" Gareth asked, directing his question to Jay. "Is it just because it's the easiest thing?"

Jay shrugged. "I'm not going to deny that is part of my reasoning. However, I do think she was doing a good job. She fit in well with us. I like her. Plus, we could use her skills as a nurse for real this time."

"And you don't care that she didn't reveal her past to us before she took the job?" Gareth demanded.

"I do care, but situations aren't always so black and white," Jay said. "I know you tend to see things that way, but in this case, it's doing you a disservice. Grief can make a person do things they might not normally do. It clouds everything. And I'm sure that's what happened to Aria."

"She's ashamed of what happened, Gareth," Janessa said earnestly. "If you'd just taken time to talk to her, you would have seen how torn up she is over everything."

When she'd come to talk to Gareth, she hadn't seemed terribly upset. However, it was possible she'd managed to keep her emotions under control for the few minutes she'd been in his home.

"I'm not saying you have to get back together with her," Janessa said. "But let us hire her back. You two kept your distance at work before, you can do it again. Just for different reasons this time."

Gareth knew he had to set aside his emotions in order to consider what Janessa and Jay wanted. He wasn't sure he could handle seeing Aria on a daily basis, but it seemed he was going to have to.

"I guess I'm outvoted here," Gareth said with a wave of his hand.

Jay and Janessa exchanged a look, then Jay said, "If you're definitely opposed to it, we won't force the issue. I just want you to make the decision without your emotions being involved."

"How exactly are my emotions supposed to *not* be involved?" Gareth demanded. "We were in a relationship. I cared for her... a *lot*! And then I find out that she lied to us... to me. Didn't she trust me? How can we be in a relationship if she doesn't trust me? And if we can't be in a relationship, how can I be around her when it *hurts* me and makes me so angry just to see her?"

Janessa's expression softened. "Don't write her off, Gareth. Surely you can see that she's a good person who made a mistake. She's hurting too."

Gareth didn't respond to that, just said, "Let her work at the clinic again, if that's what you want."

"She might still say no and choose to leave Serenity," Janessa said with a sad frown. "But I hope that knowing that you're... okay with her working there, she might stay."

"We'll see what she says," Jay told her. "We have to accept whatever answer she gives. I'm not going to guilt her into staying. And neither will you."

"I won't."

Jay got to his feet. "We'll let you know her decision."

Gareth stood up, shoving his hands into his pockets. "I'll see you tomorrow."

Once the pair had left, Gareth stood in the living room, staring blankly out the front window. Would he be able to work alongside Aria? Would he be able to get over her if they worked together again? Somehow, he doubted it.

Feeling like he'd been forced into accepting Aria's presence in the clinic didn't help lessen his anger. He just wanted a chance to take a breath and not have everything keep smacking him in the face.

There was no way he could deal with any of the situation with Aria because he just couldn't escape it. Even being in his home by himself didn't mean he could get away from everything because he couldn't escape his thoughts.

The next morning, Gareth dragged his tired self into the clinic a little earlier than usual. There were no cars in the parking lot, which was exactly what he'd hoped for.

Before going to his office, he made a pot of coffee, then, when it was ready, poured a good amount of it into his large, insulated mug. He took his first sip of the hot liquid while standing in front of the coffeemaker, relishing the bitter bite of it.

Carrying his mug in one hand and his briefcase in the other, Gareth made his way through the quiet clinic, turning on lights as he went. He had no idea if Aria was going to be in that day, but he went ahead and closed his door, just in case. The last thing he wanted was to get an unexpected glimpse of her.

He tried to do his usual morning routine at work, but it was a struggle. Though he wanted to pray for each of the patients who were on his schedule of appointments for the day, his heart and mind just weren't in it. Finally, he just prayed for the day as a whole, including his own mindset, which he knew wasn't so great.

As he continued to sip his coffee, Gareth checked through his email, then read a few articles that had been forwarded to him by a guy that he'd done some of his residency with. It helped to keep him from focusing on everything else, but that reprieve came to a screeching halt when there was a knock on his door.

When he called out for the person to come in, Janessa opened the door and poked her head in. "I just wanted to let you know that

Aria said that she needed a day to think things over, so she won't be in today."

"Thanks for the head's up," Gareth said. "Let me know when my first patient is in."

Janessa hesitated, then nodded before closing the door again.

Relief helped wash away some of the tension he hadn't realized he'd been holding in his body. He slumped back in his chair and blew out a long breath, thankful for the reprieve he'd been given.

Now, if only he could get a reprieve from Nora. She was still strutting around the clinic like she owned the place. No doubt she'd feel differently if Aria showed up again. He had a feeling that if she saw Aria in the clinic again, Nora would lose her mind.

By the end of the day, Gareth was grateful to be going home, even if it meant he was once again alone with his thoughts.

He'd just finished making himself some supper when his phone rang. Seeing Janessa's name on his screen, Gareth hesitated to answer it. However, he knew she would just keep calling.

"She said she'll come back," Janessa said once he answered. "As long as you're really sure it's okay."

"I'm not sure that it is, but it's fine."

"That... That makes no sense."

It made perfect sense to him, but he didn't try to explain it to Janessa.

"I know this isn't easy," Janessa said softly. "It's not easy for Aria either. She knows how you feel about her."

Gareth doubted that. How could she, when he didn't even know how he felt about her? "But she's still coming back to the clinic."

"She found something here that she desperately needed. It goes beyond just you," Janessa said. "She has no one, Gareth. She needs a job, and she needs a home."

Gareth knew that, and it would make him selfish to deny her those opportunities.

"I said it was fine," Gareth said, keeping his tone firm so that it gave away none of the conflict he felt. "If you think this is the right thing to do, then stop trying to convince me."

Janessa let out a big sigh. "Fine. I'll see you tomorrow, and Aria will be in too, because I could really use the help."

After they said goodbye, Gareth gripped his phone. He barely had time to collect his thoughts when his phone rang again. Recognizing it as a video call, he frowned, since it was usually only his parents who liked to see him while they talked.

Sure enough, it was his mom calling. He'd been a bit surprised that they hadn't contacted him yet to share their thoughts on the situation with Aria.

"Hello, darling," she said when he answered. "You look tired."

"I am. A bit." He knew better than to deny something his mom observed.

"We had a conversation a few minutes ago with Jay," she said as his dad moved into view behind her. "How are you doing?"

Gareth rubbed his forehead. "I've just been trying to deal with my own personal emotions about everything."

"I understand and let me say that I'm sorry about what's happened with Aria."

"It was a bit of a shock to discover what she'd kept from us."

"Are you willing to forgive her?" his dad asked. "Or has your anger gotten the better of you?"

His parents had known him the longest, and they knew his strengths and weaknesses. "I'm struggling."

The love in the smile his mom gave him pulled emotions from deep within him. Emotions he'd been trying to ignore.

"We're praying for you," his dad said. "And we've been talking since Janessa told us what had happened with Aria, trying to figure out the best course of action for the clinic. You know we prefer to let you and Jay handle things there now, but this seems to be a situation that requires involvement from all of us."

"We'll be in the office tomorrow morning to speak to Nora." His mom grimaced. "We've decided to let her go."

"Really? You're going to fire her?" Gareth asked. "I would have thought you'd see her actions as protecting the clinic."

"I might have seen it that way if I didn't think she had ulterior motives," his mom said. "This was not about the clinic. This was about her feelings regarding Aria. If she'd truly been concerned about the clinic, she would have approached the situation much differently."

"We can't be without a female doctor," Gareth reminded them.

"We understand that, so your dad is going to return to Haiti for another month," his mom said. "I'm going to stay here to help out in the clinic."

"Are you sure they don't need you in Haiti?" Gareth asked.

His mom smiled. "It'll be fine. We have two more doctors scheduled to go to the clinic in two weeks' time. Your dad will overlap with them for a couple of weeks, then come back home. The clinic there is taken care of."

"Thank you," Gareth said, not realizing until that moment how much he wasn't looking forward to continuing to work alongside Nora.

"Please keep us up to date," his dad said as he leaned closer to the camera. "And we'll be praying for you, son. Don't let your anger rob you of your happiness. Make sure you're seeking God's purpose in all of this."

"We saw the happiness you had with Aria," his mom added. "Pray hard before you give that up."

Gareth nodded, though he wasn't sure that he could do what they wanted him to. At least not yet. "Love you both."

"And we love you too, darling. See you tomorrow."

After the call ended, he tossed the phone onto a dishtowel on the counter. He rubbed his forehead, trying to massage away the tension there. An ache was slowly blooming in his head, and he had a feeling no amount of medication would wipe it out.

He had to admit that he was glad his parents were going to take care of Nora. While at one point he had thought he'd enjoy being the one to fire her, in this particular situation, it was better that it wasn't him, Jay, or Janessa. Nora would have had plenty to say about them caring more about their friend than the clinic.

Gareth didn't think she'd say the same things to his parents. But he could be wrong. After all, he hadn't imagined the lengths she'd go to in order to get rid of Aria, especially after Jay had made it clear that Gareth wasn't interested in her.

The idea of being in the clinic with Aria again filled Gareth with a mess of emotions, and he had a feeling his sleep that night would be as restless as every other one had been since discovering Aria had disappeared. And the next night was also his men's group, and for the first time in a very long time, he had no desire to go.

Thankfully, it wasn't at his place, so he wasn't forced to attend. Jackson and Wade could cover for him, just like he'd covered for them on the occasions they'd been unable to attend. He'd only have to endure a million questions from Jackson about why he couldn't be there.

CHAPTER TWENTY-EIGHT

When Gareth arrived at the clinic the next morning, his parents and Jay were already there. He dropped off his jacket and briefcase in his office, then he joined them in the break room.

"We would like you both to be present at our meeting with Nora," his dad said. "I want her to see that we are united in our decision. Plus, if she makes any accusations about the two of you, we want you to be able to defend yourselves."

Gareth would have rather avoided the confrontation, mainly because his headache hadn't gone completely away. The meeting with Nora would no doubt ratchet it up.

"I don't think she's going to take this well," Gareth said as he filled his mug at the coffeepot. "She's been far too happy about what she managed to accomplish with her machinations."

Jay nodded. "I think she figures there's no way we'd be anything but grateful to her for sparing the clinic a potential problem."

"She definitely seems to have been able to kill two birds with one stone in her favor," his dad mused as he lifted his mug.

"What if she spreads rumors about the clinic and Aria working here?" Gareth asked. "How do we defend against that?"

"If necessary, we present the facts. Aria never lost her license, so any medical work she does here in a nursing capacity is legal," his mom said. "Most people see her strictly as a receptionist, so would likely be confused by Nora's accusations."

"Don't worry about that right now." His dad set his mug back down on the table. "We'll see what Nora says, then prepare ourselves for moving forward."

Gareth didn't think his parents truly grasped how conniving Nora had been since Aria's arrival. But his head—and heart—hurt too much for him to press for them to consider it more right then.

"Why don't we spend a little time in prayer for this meeting?" his dad suggested.

Though Gareth didn't feel like praying, he knew better than to argue with his dad. Leaning forward, he braced his elbows on the table and rested his head in his hands. Over the next few minutes, his mom and dad both prayed. They must have suspected that he wasn't in the right frame of mind to pray, because his dad ended the prayer time without waiting for him to join in.

Then they sat in silence, drinking their coffee, waiting for Nora to show up. She usually arrived right before it was time to see patients, unless they had a meeting scheduled.

"I asked Janessa to tell Aria to wait to come in until after we're finished with the meeting and Nora has left the building," his mom said. "That way, she doesn't have any sort of run-in with her. Janessa can handle the reception desk until then."

Gareth didn't relish starting the day late, but it couldn't be avoided.

When they heard the back door open, his mom got to her feet and left the room.

"Good morning, Nora," Gareth heard her say. "We're just having a quick meeting, and we'd like to have you join us."

"Oh. Sure."

A moment later, Nora breezed into the break room ahead of his mom. Nora's brows pulled together briefly as her gaze swept over the men, then she settled into the chair beside Gareth.

"I wasn't aware we had a meeting this morning," Nora said, holding herself stiffly.

"It was a last-minute decision in order to address the situation with Aria," his dad told her.

"More information has come to light regarding what you shared with us," his mom said.

"Really?" Nora asked, sounding far too excited about the prospect. "What information?"

"Information that has made it a non-issue that Aria administered shots."

Nora frowned. "What?"

"I'm not sure if you didn't receive the information or if you just failed to pass it on, but surely you had to realize that we would do a little more investigating ourselves."

"What are you talking about?"

"First, Aria didn't lose her nursing license because of what occurred," his mom said.

"She didn't?" Nora stopped, then cleared her throat. "I mean, yes, it's true she didn't. However, she showed remarkably poor judgment in what she did."

Nora was showing poor judgment herself by making it seem like she knew about the license issue.

"This is true," his mom agreed. "But there were extenuating circumstances. I called Aria's previous supervisor yesterday, and she spoke very highly of her, and she wished that they could have given Aria a second chance."

Gareth was surprised to hear that his mom had called the supervisor, though perhaps he shouldn't have been. She always liked to gather all the information she could before making a decision.

"Still, the whole situation wouldn't reflect well on the clinic," Nora said defensively.

"Except that we hired her as a receptionist, and she was living with Janessa, who would have seen any sign of excessive drinking being an issue for her. If that was still a problem for Aria, she wouldn't have agreed to live with someone she worked with."

Nora crossed her arms as her frown deepened. "What exactly is this meeting about?"

"We feel that you gathered this information for your own benefit, not the benefit of the clinic."

"I don't *think* so," Nora barked.

"From the day Aria stepped foot in the clinic, you have been after Gareth to get rid of her. You then went digging for dirt on her, and I have no doubt that if you hadn't found anything, you would have continued to try to get Gareth or Jay to fire her."

"We do not tolerate harassment of our employees," his dad said, his voice firm. "Your determination to get Aria fired for no reason is unacceptable."

Nora glanced at Gareth, then glared at his dad. "It wasn't for no reason."

"It was," Jay said. "You haven't been happy with her in the clinic from day one. So yes, it was for no reason."

"Unfortunately, all of this has led us to decide that it would be best for the clinic if we parted ways with you."

"You're *firing* me?" Nora demanded. "You can't do that."

"I think you'll find that we can," his dad said. "This is our clinic, and we can decide who we feel is the best suited to work here."

"How are you going to run this place without a female doctor?" Nora scoffed.

His mom smiled at her, though it was a smile that made Gareth exchange a look with Jay. They both knew that this didn't bode well for Nora.

"Oh, that won't be a problem," she said. "After all, I'm still a female doctor. Initially, I had hoped you could fill my shoes, but this situation has made it apparent that's not the possible."

"You've worked your last day here," his dad said.

Nora swung to face Gareth. "You honestly would rather have a woman working here who thought it was okay to go to work *drunk*?"

Gareth sighed. "At this point, for me, it's less about that and more about not wanting to deal with your attitude toward other women. If I so much as look at, let alone talk to a woman, you're jealous. I'm tired of dealing with that, so yes, I believe letting you go is the right decision."

"The patients *like* me," Nora insisted.

"This is true," Jay said with a nod. "And it's the only reason we haven't let you go sooner. However, they also like our mom, so I think we'll be fine."

"You'll regret this," she assured them.

"If you want a reference that has a hope of getting you a job in the future, you'll think twice about threatening us. As it stands now, we'll tell anyone who calls that you were good with the patients, but that you had personality conflicts within the clinic," his dad said sternly. "If you say anything more regarding the clinic, Aria, or any of us here, I will happily share *all* the details of what has gone on here with anyone who calls for a reference."

"I would strongly recommend you reflect on this experience and make some changes before you move on to your next place of employment or you'll be facing this type of dismissal again," his mom added. "I have a feeling that if your previous references had been more forthcoming, we wouldn't have hired you."

When Nora didn't respond to that, Gareth realized that perhaps they'd been right all along with that assumption. With jerky movements, Nora shoved to her feet and stomped out of the room.

Gareth sighed, wishing that her departure had lessened the tension in his head. Unfortunately, that lingered even as she didn't.

"Well, that... went," his mom said. "I'm a little surprised that she persisted as long as she did."

"It might not be over," Jay cautioned. "Though I sure hope she'll just leave Serenity and set up shop somewhere on the other side of the country."

"I'm going to go make sure Nora is leaving the building," his dad said as he got to his feet. "I'll let Janessa know you'll be ready for patients shortly."

Gareth wasn't sure he was actually ready, but he pushed to his feet, anyway. Before leaving the break room, he refreshed his coffee, then headed for his office.

He knew the tension still lingering in his head came from the knowledge that he and Aria were soon going to be in the same building. And while he'd like to believe they could avoid each other, he wasn't sure that would be possible.

***

Aria stared at the back door of the clinic, knowing she needed to go in sooner rather than later. Janessa had told her that she needed to wait for her call before coming in that day. Aria wasn't sure why, but she'd stayed at the house until her friend had called and said to come to the clinic.

When Janessa had talked to her about staying and continuing to work at the clinic, her optimism had been infectious. Aria had grabbed onto the hope that her friend offered her, that it was just a matter of time before Gareth would come around. That he'd get over his anger and be willing to give her another chance.

She'd moved back into the house with Charli and Janessa, but unlike last time, she hadn't unpacked. The suitcase with her clothes sat on the floor with the lid open, and the bags containing her other things remained zipped in the closet.

The closer the time came for her to go to work, the more doubts had crept in. And as she sat there staring at the building, unease made her want to run away again.

Though she'd been praying about the situation, Aria hadn't felt a lot of peace, and she couldn't help but wonder if that was because this wasn't where she was supposed to be.

But she'd promised Janessa she'd at least try.

Pushing open the car door, Aria got out, then tugged the edges of her jacket close. There was a bit of a chill in the air, though it wasn't nearly as cold as it had been when she'd first arrived in Serenity.

As she reached the door, Aria took a deep breath and blew it out. And though she wanted to see Gareth more than anything, she prayed that for this first day, she wouldn't. Not for her sake, but for his.

Aria could hear voices as she stepped through the back door, and she quickly made her way to the break room to hang up her jacket. Her heart was pounding as she walked down the hallway to the front. Thankfully, she made it without running into Gareth or Nora.

Where Nora was concerned, Aria figured it was only a matter of time before the woman sought her out. With that fear looming in her future, the unease she felt about being back at the clinic continued to grow.

Janessa was standing at the reception desk and absolutely beamed when she saw Aria. When Aria reached her, Janessa grabbed her into a tight hug.

"She. Is. Gone!!"

"What?" Aria mumbled against her shoulder.

Janessa moved back, holding Aria at arm's length, her eyes sparkling. "Mom and Dad fired Nora this morning, and she's gone!"

Aria blinked at her. "She's gone? For real?"

"For real," Janessa said with a nod.

"But what about her patients?"

"Mom is going to take over until we find a new doctor."

Aria's already nervous stomach twisted. "Does your mom know that I'm working here again?"

"Yep, and she was glad to hear that you had agreed to come back."

Aria had a hard time believing that. But just in case Janessa's parents weren't entirely convinced that her being there was a good idea, she planned to work hard and give them no reason to regret her return.

"I can't believe she's gone," Aria said. Her emotions in that moment were a mess. She was happy and relieved that Nora was gone, but that didn't ease the anxiety and nerves still inside her.

"We'll celebrate later," Janessa promised, and though Aria didn't feel much like celebrating, she nodded.

It didn't take long for Aria to fall back into her role at the front desk. People greeted her with smiles, many not even realizing that she'd been missing for a week.

Their friendliness went a long way toward calming her nerves, though she remained on edge, waiting for that first time her path crossed Gareth's. She was going to do what she could to postpone that inevitability.

"You're going home?" Janessa asked when noon rolled around.

"I think that would be for the best."

Janessa looked like she was going to argue, but then she just nodded. "I think Gareth is in his office at the moment."

Aria appreciated the head's up and quickly made her way to the break room to grab her jacket and purse, then left through the back door. When she got to the house, she went to the kitchen, but wasn't sure what to eat given that she had absolutely no appetite.

Her anxiety always stole her appetite, and it had been particularly bad following the death of her mom, which had made her drinking that much worse. There had been plenty of times when she'd wished that her way of coping was to eat her feelings, but the opposite had always been true. Her feelings had eaten her, and she'd done her best to drown them in alcohol.

Aria knew that if she didn't want Janessa to become overly worried about her, she needed to eat. With that in mind, she pulled out some bread and put it in the toaster. When all else failed, she fell back on the meal she and her mom had shared plenty of times.

Thankfully, Charli kept them well stocked in peanut butter and a variety of jams.

Once she'd spread peanut butter and raspberry jam on two slices of toast, she poured herself a glass of milk, then sat down at the counter to eat. Eating wasn't easy when she felt like anxiety was choking her, but she managed to get both slices down with the help of the milk.

After going upstairs to wash her hands and brush her teeth, Aria took a minute to sit on her bed and just... breathe. In her room, there was no chance of running into Gareth nor was there a need to keep up the façade that she was fine.

She was becoming less convinced that staying in Serenity was a good idea. It seemed that hanging around would feed into a hope that would never be realized. She hated to disappoint Janessa, but if Gareth wasn't ever going to forgive her, sticking around was just putting off the inevitable.

His reaction to everything—though expected, at first—made her wonder if she'd been more emotionally invested in their relationship than he'd been. All she knew was that if he'd apologized to her for a similar situation, she'd like to think she'd have accepted that apology.

While there were clearly some issues that would be deal-breakers for her in a relationship, she didn't think that if the roles were reversed, she would toss away what she had with Gareth. Especially given how she felt about him.

Aria decided she'd give the situation another week before deciding whether she could handle working alongside Gareth if he never forgave her. And in the meantime, she'd start looking at options for where to go next.

Unfortunately, it turned out that Aria didn't need to wait a full week to realize that the situation was untenable. It wasn't fair to anyone working at the clinic to have to tiptoe around her and

Gareth, and her anxiety while in the building spiked. It was so unlike how things had been prior to her running away.

By Wednesday afternoon, Aria knew she needed to move on, but she also didn't want to leave them in a lurch. Even though things weren't working out, the Halversons had been good to her, and she didn't want to leave them without someone to fill the vacancy she'd leave behind.

Once the clinic closed on Wednesday, Aria made her way to Jay's office. Now that the basketball season was over, he didn't leave the office as early, so he was still there.

She knocked on the door to get his attention. When he looked up from his computer, he smiled and motioned for her to come in.

After a moment's hesitation, she closed the door behind her. Jay's smile faded as she sat in the chair across from him.

"What's up?" he asked.

"I want to give my notice," she said. "I don't think it's going to work out for me to keep working here."

Jay sighed as he nodded. "I wasn't sure that it would, but I wanted to give it a chance."

Aria clenched her hands in her lap. "I'll work until you can find someone else."

"I appreciate that," Jay said. "But if you feel that you need to leave sooner, we'll understand."

"I'm sorry to have to put you in this position."

Jay leaned back in his chair. "We all make mistakes. What you did wasn't unforgiveable." He paused, a frown forming on his face. "Or it shouldn't be."

Like his sister, Jay seemed more than willing to move past everything. If only Gareth felt the same way.

Jay's gaze was assessing as he said, "Did you tell Janessa yet?"

Sadness swept through Aria as she shook her head. "I figured you'd be less likely to try to talk me out of this decision."

The man's brow furrowed at her words. "I hope you don't think that I don't want you to be here."

"No," she assured him. "It's not that. It just seems that you have a more... pragmatic view of what's happened. You've been willing to give me another chance, but you're also realistic enough to realize it probably wouldn't work for me to stay on."

"I really did hope that it would," Jay said. "You've fit in really well here, and being able to use you as both a receptionist and a nurse would have been a benefit to the clinic."

What he described sounded so appealing, but it wasn't to be. "Thank you for giving me this opportunity in the first place. I know that Janessa kind of forced the issue."

Jay nodded with a wry smile. "Yes, she did, but she was also right. I hope you can see that."

"Being here has helped me gain some breathing space and showed me that I can move past what happened in Sacramento."

"I know you feel you can't continue to work here at the clinic, but you don't necessarily have to leave Serenity."

"I think I do. Everything that I've loved about being here is also tied up with Gareth. I won't be able to get over him if I have to deal with that, even if I'm not working here."

"I understand. Just know that you can use me as a reference. I'll have no problem telling anyone how much we have appreciated your work."

Tears pricked at Aria's eyes. She hadn't expected this conversation with Jay to be emotional at all, but underneath his often-unreadable facial expressions was a heart filled with kindness.

"Thank you."

Aria left Jay's office with a mix of emotions. There was a gut-wrenching sadness that she would have to leave behind the man she loved, as well as the friends she'd made. But there was also relief. She couldn't live with the tension and anxiety that being so close to Gareth created.

It was time to move on... yet again. And she prayed that wherever she landed next, God would help her find friends and a job that she enjoyed, like what she'd had in Serenity. What she didn't want was another romantic relationship. The ones she'd had had come at too high a price, and she didn't think she could handle any more heartbreak in her life.

CHAPTER TWENTY-NINE

Gareth was hanging up his white coat in his office when he heard movement behind him.

"Got a minute?" Jay asked before Gareth had even turned around.

"Sure." Gareth finished putting his coat on the hanger, then moved to sit behind his desk. Jay had already settled into his usual seat. "What's up?"

"Aria came to see me yesterday after work." He leaned back and crossed his arms. "She asked me to put out an ad for the receptionist position."

Shock gripped Gareth at his brother's words. "What?"

Jay stared at him for a moment before he said, "She's put in her notice, though she said she'll work until we find someone to replace her."

"But I thought she'd agreed to continue to work here."

"She had," Jay said with a nod. "But she's realized that it's just too difficult."

"Too difficult?" Gareth knew he was just parroting what Jay had said, but his mind was whirling with the idea of Aria leaving the clinic. Of disappearing once again.

"Don't be stupid, Gareth. Figure it out."

Gareth frowned at his brother. It was true that he hadn't particularly enjoyed working the past few days, but a lot of that was because of the constant war going on inside of him. Now that his hurt wasn't so fresh, his anger had faded some, but not completely. It festered inside him still, and he knew it wasn't healthy.

He'd never been so angry. But then again, he'd never been so deeply hurt.

"So she's leaving the clinic."

"She's leaving *Serenity*," Jay stressed. "She said staying here would make it too difficult to move on from your relationship."

Gareth's stomach clenched at the thought. Rather than responding to that, however, he just said, "Thanks for letting me know."

Jay gave a huff of frustration as he got to his feet. "I don't know about you, man. Give your head a shake and get over your pride before you lose something that could be great."

As parting shots from a basketball pro like Jay went, it was pretty much a three-point dunk from the other end of the court. And it was in Jay's words that Gareth gained the clarity he'd been lacking.

Pride.

He'd thought it was all about hurt and anger, but the firm foundation under both those emotions was pride.

Though he'd assumed the hurt had come because she hadn't trusted him, the fact was that it was his pride that had been hurt. Instead of thinking more about why she'd done what she had, all he'd focused on was why she hadn't trusted him. Why she hadn't seen him as trustworthy.

He'd made the situation about himself, not her.

Gareth frowned. But he *hadn't* just been thinking about himself. He'd been thinking about the clinic, and how Aria had put it at risk by not revealing what had happened at her previous job. That wasn't about him. That was about protecting the clinic. Protecting the hard work that had built it.

However, Gareth had to admit that Jay and their parents were as protective of the clinic as he was, and yet they'd been willing to let Aria continue working at the clinic. They'd been willing to accept her apology and move forward.

His anger had been a more comfortable emotion for him since it was focused outward. He'd clung to it to mask the hurt of Aria not trusting him. Of her not feeling as strongly for him as he felt for her. He could see now, however, that the anger was also hugely damaging.

While the hurt from Aria not trusting him caused *him* pain—which was why he didn't want to dwell on it—the pride and anger were causing pain to those around him. Especially Aria.

Especially Aria.

Gareth's shoulders slumped, and his head dropped forward. He could have protected the clinic and still had empathy for Aria and what she'd gone through. Instead, he'd chosen anger and pride. Only caring about his own emotions. About how he felt.

Though his plan had been to avoid the men's group again that night, Gareth knew he needed to go. For advice, but more importantly, for prayer.

Pulling his thoughts together, Gareth tried to focus on what he needed to do before he could leave the office for the day.

When he pulled up at the apartment block where the men's group was being held that evening, Gareth sat in his vehicle for a couple of minutes. His earlier conversation with Jay and the situation with Aria continued to weigh heavily upon him.

He'd made a huge mess of everything, and he had no idea how to fix it. Or if it was even possible to fix it. Aria might not want anything more to do with him after how he'd treated her, and he could hardly blame her. No, he had no one to blame but himself for the hurt he felt more acutely now that he'd let go of the anger.

A rap on his window made him jump, and Gareth looked over to see Wade peering at him. With a sigh, he grabbed his keys from the ignition and pushed the door open.

His friend stepped back, giving him space to join him outside the car. "Good to see you, man."

If it had been Jackson who'd said that, Gareth would have assumed he was being sarcastic since he'd been avoiding them lately. However, he took Wade's words at face value and gave him a nod.

Together, they walked into the building. As they waited for the elevator, Wade talked about the project he'd been working on, thankfully not asking how Gareth was doing. He wasn't sure he'd have an answer that didn't reveal his true state of mind.

Jackson was already there when they walked into the apartment, and he immediately headed their way.

"Good to see you finally showing up, bro." Gareth grimaced as Jackson thumped him hard on his back.

"Lay off, Jack," Wade said.

Jackson lifted his hands. "Hey. Just glad to see him."

"Sure. But still, chill out," Wade said, then turned toward their host as he approached the three of them.

Gareth made small talk as the rest of their group gathered. After a short time of socializing, Wade led the group in prayer, then began the study.

When the study and discussion portion of their evening was over an hour later, Gareth said, "I could use some prayer."

He sat with his head bent, staring at his hands as he recounted what had happened over the past couple of weeks, being vague when sharing the details of what Aria had done at her job. It wasn't his desire to have people know her business, but they needed to know enough to understand why he'd reacted the way he had.

"I don't think your immediate reaction was out of line," one guy said. "But if you actually want to have a relationship with Aria, you need to get your head straightened out."

"And your heart," Wade added.

"Do you want this relationship with Aria?" Jackson asked. "I mean, it seemed like the two of you were getting pretty serious."

Gareth interlaced his fingers and squeezed them at Jackson's words. They *had* been getting serious. Or at least he'd felt like they had been.

"Regardless, I think you need to speak to her," another of the guys added. "It doesn't sound like you've had an actual conversation with her about what happened."

The man was right, which filled Gareth with shame. After telling Aria about how they solved conflict in their family, he'd failed to do it with her. A conversation was the very least that he'd owed her.

"I'm sure we've all had struggles in relationships," Wade said. "And I'm a clear example of not being able to successfully resolve them. But Tom's right. You need to at least have a conversation so that if you really don't feel like a relationship between you is going to work, you've at least cleared the air. You'll struggle to move on if you don't."

"It seems like she's willing to talk to you, considering she came back," Jackson said. "Maybe she even wanted to give the relationship another shot. I doubt she'd turn you down if you asked to talk with her."

"You're all right," Gareth told them. "I just got so angry, which I see now was because my pride was hurt."

"Anger, especially resulting from hurt pride, rarely steers a person in the right direction." This came from one of the older guys in their group who had spoken frequently about his struggles with anger over the years.

Gareth had never thought he had a problem with anger because he rarely got mad, but clearly, infrequent bouts of anger could still be damaging to a relationship.

"If you want another chance, you're gonna have to show her that this reaction will not be the norm when you get angry," Jackson told him. "I mean, we learned early on that if you got mad, you just needed time to cool down and you'd come around. Just took you longer than usual this time."

For all that Jackson could come off as shallow and flippant, he could also be remarkably perceptive. "Thanks, man."

"You know I love you," Jack responded. "And I like Aria too. She seems really sweet and perhaps a bit too good for you."

Even though Gareth knew the man was joking around, right then, it seemed like Jackson was also right.

It felt like a fog was lifting from his mind, giving him the clarity that had been lacking over the past couple of weeks. Everything he knew about how God viewed pride and anger flooded into his heart, and he wanted to weep. So far, he hadn't cried over the situation, but the stark realization of what he'd done to Aria broke him.

"Why don't we spend some time in prayer for Gareth and Aria?" Wade suggested, briefly rubbing a hand on Gareth's back. "Are there any other requests?"

As the men prepared to lift one another up in prayer, Gareth's grief mired him down in regrets and self-recrimination. He was grateful for the support and prayers of his friends, but it didn't stop him from beating himself up.

From his conversations with Aria, he'd picked up on the fact that, while she was a Christian, she hadn't seemed to put a strong focus on her spiritual life beyond going to church. As the more mature Christian, he should have set the example. Instead, she had been the one to return and ask their forgiveness. He should have given it to her immediately, even if he hadn't completely felt it in his heart yet.

Now he needed to ask Aria's forgiveness and hope that she would give it to him and not tell him to leave her alone. Even though that was absolutely what he deserved.

The next day, Gareth tracked Janessa down where she was cleaning up one of the exam rooms. "Are you doing pizza tonight?"

She glanced over at him, a frown on her face. "Probably, since none of us want to cook. Why?"

"Can I come over?"

That got her attention more fully, and she turned from her task to face him. "You do know that Aria is living at the house, right?" Gareth nodded. "So why do you want to come over, then? I thought you were avoiding her."

"I know, but I don't think that continuing to do that is going to work."

Janessa nodded. "Though I don't think it makes any difference at this point. She's leaving."

"Jay told me."

With a sigh, Janessa turned her attention back to what she'd been doing. "I hate this. I hate all of it. But most of all, I hate myself for not having done more to keep in contact with her over the past year. I checked in with her regularly, but didn't press when she said she was fine. I should have pressed. I mean, who, after losing their mom, is *fine*? I'm a horrible friend."

It seemed like they both had a multitude of regrets regarding everything that had happened. Somehow, they needed to move past it, and he hoped that the change would start with the conversation he hoped to have with Aria. But if she brushed him off, he would have to accept it.

"I'll phone in the order, and you can pick it up," Janessa said. "Same time as usual."

"Okay."

He returned to his office, planning to work until he received Janessa's text to let him know the pizzas had been ordered. It seemed to take forever, but finally his alert went off. After checking the message on his phone, Gareth grabbed his things and left the building, locking it up behind him.

The number of pizzas waiting at the restaurant indicated that more than just the three women and a child were going to be in attendance. But maybe that wasn't a bad thing.

When he got to the house, he saw that Wilder's and Jay's cars were both parked on the street. His younger siblings weren't likely to be there since they were back to living at the big house, and besides, Friday nights were for friends now that basketball season was over.

Balancing the boxes on his arm, he locked up the car and headed for the house. Once inside, he was quickly relieved of the pizzas.

"How's it going?" Wilder asked, thumping Gareth on his back. "Gotten over your temper tantrum yet?"

Gareth would have snarked back at him if his younger brother wasn't speaking some truth. "Working on it."

"Glad to hear it," Wilder said. "I'd liked this all resolved before I pull out of town."

"Is that happening soon?" Gareth asked with a frown. "Don't you usually wait until April to leave?"

Wilder shrugged. "Yeah. But the slopes just aren't speaking to me right now. I'm ready for something new."

"Where are you headed next?"

"Not sure yet. But I'm sure I'll figure something out."

Gareth had never been able to understand his brother's lackadaisical approach to life. It would drive Gareth crazy not to have a plan in place. If he hadn't been focused and determined, he never would have made it through med school and his residency. It almost seemed like he'd gotten Wilder's share of those two qualities.

"Have you told Mom yet?"

"Of course not. She'll just nag me and nag me about making a detailed plan so she knows exactly where I am every single day I'm away."

"She's your mom. Of course, she wants to know those things. But even a general schedule would probably make her happy."

"Well, I can't even give her that at the moment, so I'd rather wait to tell her."

"Probably a good idea," Gareth said as he followed Wilder into the kitchen.

It only took a moment for him to glance around the room and see that Aria wasn't there. He wasn't surprised, but he was still disappointed.

As he thought of speaking with her, his nerves flared to life. The next few minutes might very well decide the direction in which his life moved. With Aria or without her.

Either way, he'd learned an important lesson. Unfortunately, it might have taken him too long.

The thing was, going through his residency especially, he'd bumped up against plenty of pride and ego, and he'd likely responded with ego and pride himself without even realizing it.

Since the study the previous night, he'd prayed and spent a lot of time in introspection. It had brought to light plenty of examples in his life where his pride had come into play strongly. Each time, he'd attributed his success to his hard work. And he'd taken pride it in, feeling like he deserved his successes because of his own efforts.

But he had discounted so much. Not the least of which was his incredible support system. That hadn't come just in the form of his family. He'd had financial support that most didn't. And on top of all that, he'd had people praying for him.

Would he have had the drive and perseverance if he'd had to accomplish it without all of that?

He remembered what Janessa had said about Aria studying so hard at school because she'd been there on scholarships. It had been just her and her mom, which meant that when her mom passed away, she'd been all alone. And she hadn't even had a spiritual support system from the church she'd been attending.

Aria may have looked fragile, but in order to have accomplished what she had, she was so much stronger than she appeared. She was definitely stronger than he was. Even her decision to leave everything and come to Serenity showed strength. He realized now that it was that quiet strength that had drawn him to her.

Gareth approached Janessa. "Is Aria around?"

"She's upstairs in her room."

"Thanks."

Gareth didn't want to have this conversation with an audience of his siblings, so he headed up the stairs to the second floor. Hopefully Aria would be willing to sit with him on the landing and listen to his apology.

Outside her door, he paused to pray that God would guide his words, and that he would accept whatever her response was with grace. He couldn't remember ever feeling so nervous. Even going into important exams, he hadn't had a case of nerves this bad. He'd always been fine when taking those tests, confident in what he knew.

But with this situation, he had no confidence in himself. Which was why he needed God's help.

When there was no response to his knock, he tried again. Still, no answer. With a frown, he went back down to the kitchen to find Janessa.

"Back so soon?" Janessa asked when he approached her.

"She didn't answer the door."

"She didn't?"

Gareth shook his head. "Would you mind going up with me and maybe opening the door to see if she's okay?"

At Aria's door a couple of minutes later, Janessa knocked firmly on the wood. Gareth stood off to the side, waiting to see if his sister got a response. When there was no answer, Janessa slowly opened the door and poked her head inside.

"Aria?" She went into the room, closing the door behind her.

Gareth walked over to stare out the large window that faced the front street. The sun was setting, casting the town in gray shadows, with splashes of light spilling from the windows of the houses and businesses. Normally, it would be a sight that calmed him, but not that day.

When the door to the bedroom swung open again, Gareth turned to face it. Janessa came out of the room with Aria following more slowly behind her, her face expressionless. Seeing her again filled Gareth with emotion, and he longed for the right to hold her in his arms again.

Janessa approached Gareth and gave him a hard look before muttering, "Don't mess this up."

"I won't." He hoped he could keep his word.

She gave Aria a quick hug before she went back down the stairs, leaving the two of them alone. Gareth's heart was thumping so hard in his chest, he was sure that Aria could hear it.

Clearing his throat, he said, "Can I talk to you?"

CHAPTER THIRTY

Aria sat on the loveseat in her room, an adult coloring book in her lap and an audiobook playing loudly in her earbuds. When Janessa had told her that Gareth would be coming for pizza, Aria had had no problem retreating to her room. When she'd decided to stay at the house, she'd accepted that there would be times like these.

So she'd pulled out the coloring book and colored pencils her mom had bought her one Christmas and settled down in her favorite chair in her bedroom, planning to keep her hands and her mind busy while Gareth was downstairs with his family.

When she sensed movement from the direction of her door, she looked over, surprised to see Janessa poke her head into the room. Pulling out one of her ear buds, she said, "What's up?"

Janessa came into the room, then closed the door behind her. "Gareth wants to talk to you. Do you want to talk to him?"

Aria's heart pounded at the question, and the anxiety that had calmed with her being tucked away in the safety of her room roared back to life. She scratched at her arm, then stopped when the pencil she held got in the way.

Despite her anxiety, Aria didn't hesitate to agree because she needed to know what he wanted to talk about now that she'd made her decision to leave. Her insides were trembling as she set aside her coloring book and earbuds to follow Janessa out of the room.

As soon as her gaze landed on Gareth, Aria felt her heart clench, and sadness swept through her. She still loved him and longed for what they'd once had, so it was hard to see him, knowing that he'd soon be out of her life.

"Can I talk to you?" Gareth asked after Janessa had left them alone.

"Uh... sure."

Aria made her way to the armchair, and once she was seated, Gareth sat down on the couch opposite. She perched on the edge of the armchair, hands clasped in her lap. She didn't relax back into its comfortable cushions like she usually did when she and Janessa spent time there chatting.

Gareth sat with his head bent for a moment before he looked at her. His gaze wasn't hard or angry like it had been the last time they'd talked, and hope tried to bloom inside her. Was he not mad at her anymore?

Her nerves morphed into a complex mix of anxious and calm, which shouldn't have been possible. She'd never experienced anything like it before. While her anxiety never completely went away, the calm mixing with it was new, and possibly came from having already accepted the inevitable.

"I want to apologize to you."

Aria stared at him, her eyes going wide in shock. "Apologize?"

At the most, she'd thought he had come to accept her apology. Essentially closing the chapter of their relationship before she left. But for him to apologize? She didn't know what that meant.

"I owe you an apology," Gareth said, his voice low. "I reacted badly when I found out what had happened."

"I understood why you were angry," Aria said. "I didn't blame you for that."

Gareth shrugged. "Maybe I had a right to be angry at first, but I shouldn't have let my anger take control of me the way I did. And when you came to apologize, I should have forgiven you right away."

Aria didn't know what to say to that. She wondered if she was actually dreaming because him accepting her apology had been a fervent hope that she'd come to accept would never be realized.

Apparently, he didn't need her to say anything because he kept talking. "When Jay told me you were leaving, the news was kind of like a smack to the head, knocking some sense into me. I was forced to take a hard look at myself and what I was feeling."

Aria wasn't sure what to do with that revelation. In her mind, she was responsible for everything that had developed over the past couple of weeks. If she'd only been honest about what had gone on in Sacramento, none of what followed would have happened. She might not have ended up getting the job, but at least she wouldn't have hurt Janessa, Gareth, and their family.

"I've learned some not-so-great things about myself," Gareth said with a sigh.

Aria knew that no one was perfect, but she'd thought that Gareth seemed pretty close. Janessa had told her about Gareth's tendency to hold a grudge when he got mad. She'd now seen proof of that herself, but she'd also felt like Gareth had a right to his anger. "I don't understand."

"I thought I was hurt because you hadn't trusted me," Gareth said. "But while that might have been a part of it, a large part was that my pride was hurt. I didn't understand how you couldn't trust me. I believed myself to be a trustworthy person, so it hurt my pride and made me angry that you hadn't seen that about me."

"It wasn't that you weren't trustworthy," Aria explained. "I was just so ashamed and embarrassed by what I'd done." She hugged herself, hunching her shoulders. "I didn't want you to know that I'd made such bad decisions. I didn't want Janessa to know that I wasn't coping well."

"I wouldn't have thought less of you," Gareth said. "Honestly, in discovering my own weaknesses, I've seen your strengths."

"What does that mean?"

Aria's face flushed as he explained what he saw in her. It almost sounded like he admired her, which Aria couldn't believe. Nothing he said changed how she viewed herself and what she'd done.

"I'm not strong," she told him. "I have anxiety so much of the time."

She'd tried her best to hide her struggle with anxiety from him when they'd been dating. But now, since she was leaving, it didn't matter if he knew.

"I suspected as much." Gareth leaned forward, his expression serious as he regarded her. "But having anxiety doesn't mean you're not strong. Anxious or not, you didn't give up on life after your mom passed away. You kept putting one foot in front of the other."

"I made some terrible decisions."

"You make it sound like you're the only one who's ever done that," Gareth said. "You've acknowledged what you did. You haven't made excuses for it."

But what good had that done? She was still going to leave Serenity. Sure, it would be nice to leave knowing that Gareth didn't think the worst of her anymore. She wished that their conversation was giving her a sense of closure, but all she felt was even more regret.

"Well, thank you for forgiving me," Aria said. "It will make leaving a little easier."

Gareth straightened, bracing his hands on his knees. "Why would you still leave? I mean, unless you really want to."

Pain squeezed her heart. Didn't he understand how hard it would be for her to stay around and have to watch him date other women? Clearly, he wasn't worried about her dating other men. It just reinforced her assumption that her feelings had run deeper than his.

"I think that I… need to leave."

"Oh." Gareth's shoulders slumped, and his gaze dropped.

"I've told Jay I'll stay until you've found a replacement."

Looking up again, he frowned at her. "To be honest, I don't really care about the clinic at the moment." He sighed. "I guess I shouldn't have expected that you'd want to stick around to see if we could work past this, given how badly I've acted. I just had hoped you might stay and give me a chance to prove that I can do better."

"Wait." Aria felt a brief surge of hope. "You... you still want to be with me?"

"Yes." He paused, his gaze dropping for a moment. "I guess I didn't really say that, did I?"

"I thought you were just apologizing."

"I am apologizing, but also, I'm hoping you'll forgive me and give me... give us... a second chance." Gareth grimaced. "I know that I hurt you badly with how I reacted, and I'm so very sorry about that. I'll understand if you don't want anything more to do with me."

Hope pushed its way up past her previous reservations. "I don't want that at all."

Gareth abandoned his seat, going to his knees in front of her. He reached out to cover her hands with his, gazing up at her with warmth and so much emotion in his beautiful brown eyes. "I promise that I have learned from this experience. I can't promise that I won't ever get angry again, but I won't let it linger like this. You can hold me accountable. Wade and Jackson will hold me accountable. I'll even tell Jay that *he* can hold me accountable."

Aria couldn't keep from smiling at that. "I'm sure he'll be happy to do that."

"Oh, he definitely will be," Gareth agreed with a grin that softened into a smile. "I know that my recent actions might not show it, but I love you, Aria, and I promise to do my best to prove that to you every single day."

Aria's heart skipped a beat, then began to pound rapidly. Gareth had said the words she'd longed to hear. Maybe she really was dreaming. "You love me?"

Gareth's fingers tightened over hers. "I do, and one day, I hope you'll feel the same for me."

She looked down at their hands, then relaxed her fingers and turned her hands over so that she could hold on to his. Clinging to the strength of his hands, she met his gaze. "I don't need to wait for one day, Gareth. I already know that I love you."

Emotion filled Gareth's gaze. "I prayed that you would, but I didn't feel that I deserved that. At least, not yet. Loving you makes me want to be a better man."

"I love you just the way you are," she told him.

Letting go of his hands, Aria cupped Gareth's face, then leaned toward him. Gareth rose up to meet her, and their lips brushed softly. The promise in that gentle kiss resonated deep in her heart, and when it ended, she had to blink back the tears stinging her eyes, nearly overcome by the emotion welling up inside her.

"Thank you, sweetheart," Gareth murmured, his voice rough. "Thank you for giving me a second chance. I love you so much."

Getting to his feet, he drew her up as well, then wrapped his arms around her. Aria sank against him as she gripped handfuls of the back of his shirt and hung onto him. As she inhaled the scent that she'd always loved and associated with him, Aria said a prayer of thanks. She'd thought he was lost to her because of what she'd done, but now he was there, holding her tightly like he didn't want to let her go.

Gareth picked her up and gently swung her around, making Aria let out a squeal before laughing when he set her back down. She gazed up at him and smiled, seeing a look in his eyes that she hadn't been sure she'd ever see.

Though she'd lost all hope for things to work out between them, she was now confident that their relationship actually had a great chance of succeeding. It hadn't been fun going through that horribly rough patch, but she felt like she'd learned a lot about herself,

Gareth, and dealing with issues within a relationship. Something told her that Gareth had learned a lot, too.

After sharing another lingering kiss, Gareth said, "Are you ready to go eat some pizza and deal with my siblings gloating?"

"I'd love nothing more."

Hand-in-hand, they walked down the stairs toward the chatter in the kitchen. Even knowing they were going to face some teasing, Aria didn't mind. Not one member of the family had been anything but supportive of her, even after her bad decisions had been revealed.

"Yay!" Janessa yelled when she spotted them. Abandoning her pizza, she hurried over and grabbed them both in a tight hug. "I'm so glad you two figured this out. I was afraid you wouldn't, and I'd lose you, Aria."

Aria hugged her friend back. "Thank you for caring so much."

"Of course!" Janessa smiled. "And now you're not allowed to leave. Ever!"

"I agree," Gareth said, slipping an arm around her waist.

"I have no plans to leave."

"That's a definite answer to prayer," Jay said from where he sat. "I wasn't looking forward to having to find someone to replace you."

"Receptionist problem solved," Janessa agreed. "Now we just need a doctor."

Gareth guided Aria over to the counter where the pizza boxes sat. He picked up a couple of paper plates and handed one to her. "I've reached out to more of my medical associates, so I hope something comes of those feelers soon."

Aria grabbed a couple of small slices of her favorite pizza and put them on her plate, then went to the table with Gareth. She glanced at Gareth, then took his hand as the conversation around the table quieted while he said a prayer for their meal.

With the situation between her and Gareth having settled, Aria found her appetite was better than it had been in recent weeks. She was full after the pizza, but she didn't hesitate to say yes when Gareth asked if she wanted to go for cheesecake and ice cream. Though she enjoyed being with all the Halversons, after everything that had happened, she wanted to spend some time alone with Gareth. And apparently, he felt the same way.

"I want to understand," Gareth said once they had chosen their desserts and were settled at a table tucked into the corner of the shop.

"Understand what exactly?" Aria asked. She would happily share anything with him now, but she needed to know what exactly he was talking about.

He hesitated. "I want to understand what life was like for you and your mom, and also for you after your mom was gone. But I don't want to pressure you to talk about any of it. Just know that if you ever want to share about those times—the good and the bad—I'm happy to listen."

Aria appreciated that more than Gareth would ever know. There were days when it felt like her mom was going to just slip into oblivion now that Aria was the only one with memories of her. Talking to people about her might bring tears, but then her memory would be alive in more than just Aria's mind.

"I think I've mentioned that my mom was young when she had me. She was, essentially, a baby raising a baby. I'm not sure how she did it, to be honest. But somehow, she raised me on her own with no support system. She still managed to be a great mom, and she was my best friend."

Gareth smiled, and for a moment, Aria could only relish the fact that he was sitting there with her again.

"I'm glad to hear that," he said. "And it sounds like she was a strong woman, just like you."

"I don't really see myself that way, but Mom was definitely strong." Aria smiled at him. "She would have loved you."

"I wish I'd had the opportunity to meet her and tell her what a wonderful daughter she raised."

Aria hoped her mom would have felt that way, especially considering the mistakes she'd made. Though she probably would have lectured Aria on what she'd done, she would have understood. Being completely alone was a hard thing for a person to truly understand unless they'd experienced it themselves.

"When we'd talk about what would happen to me after she passed away, Mom would remind me that even though she wouldn't be with me anymore, God always would be. I kind of forgot that when she died."

Gareth reached out and laid his hand on hers, squeezing gently. "I'm sure grief has a way of clouding your mind, especially at first."

Aria nodded. "I was mad at God too, though, so that didn't help. We prayed so hard for Him to heal her, but it didn't happen. I couldn't understand why He'd take the only person I had."

"There are some things that we'll just never understand on this earth. I know that Janessa and Jay struggled to understand that when their mom passed away. And it didn't seem to matter much that they had us. The loss of their mom eclipsed everything else."

Aria nodded. "For months, it was the first thing I thought about when I woke up and the last thing I thought about before falling asleep, and grief filled every second in between."

"How is it now?" Gareth's brown eyes held a wealth of concern and love, and Aria knew that if she didn't already love him, she would have in that moment.

"I can talk about her now without crying," she said. "Memories of her can make me smile, even though I still miss her tremendously."

"I know that none of us can replace your mom, but I hope you know that you're not alone anymore. With so many of us around, you can always find someone to spend time with, though I hope you'll come to me first."

Aria chuckled. "Pretty sure that's a given."

The conversation took a turn then, moving from the heaviness of her grief to some of the happier times she'd had with her mom. It was the first time she'd been able to share so much about her, and it was like she just couldn't stop talking.

Gareth didn't seem to mind, though. He smiled and laughed and made comments. She'd never expected that anyone would care that much about someone they'd never met.

When she asked him about it, Gareth said, "She was important to you." He lifted her hand and pressed a kiss to the back of it. "And you're important to me."

He was important to her too, but she didn't know how to phrase just *how* important. So she had to just settle for repeating his words back to him.

As Gareth drove her back to the house after the restaurant asked them to leave so they could close, Aria felt truly at peace. The burden of her secrets had weighed her down in a way she hadn't realized. Sharing the truth really had set her free.

She'd been so afraid that the truth would cost her everything. And while it might have felt like that at first, she could see now that it was not sharing the truth from the start that could have cost her everything. Ignoring the past hadn't made it disappear the way she'd hoped.

Like her, Gareth had made mistakes in how he'd dealt with the truth when it came out. Her hope and prayer was that they'd be able to leave everything in the past, while still remembering what they'd learned from it.

Standing at the door a short time later, Gareth pulled her into his arms, and Aria savored his nearness. After what they'd been through, it was something she'd never take for granted.

"I love you so much," he murmured after giving her a kiss.

"I love you too," she told him, so happy that she could share what was in her heart so freely with him and that he returned her feelings.

Epilogue

Phone in hand, Aria settled on the comfortable couch that was set up on the large landing that connected the rooms on the second floor. The fireplace on one wall was blazing, spreading warmth and the smell of burning cedar throughout the space. They were six days out from Christmas—the third without her mom and the first with the Halversons—and seasonal decor filled the large house.

For most of her life, Christmas had always been a special time. Though she and her mom had never been able to afford expensive gifts, they'd always loved the holiday. They had decorated their home with lots of dollar store decorations, and they'd gone to every free Christmas concert they could find and watched all the Christmas movies on TV. There had been nothing elaborate about the traditions they'd created over the years, but they'd found great joy in them.

Her first Christmas alone had come just a week after her mom's death. She had decorated the apartment at her mom's request since she'd wanted to enjoy the holiday, even in her weakened state. Which had meant that Aria had spent the first week of her grief surrounded by painful reminders of happier times.

The second Christmas after her mom had died had been a non-event. She hadn't decorated the apartment she'd shared with the drug addicts, and she'd done her best to just ignore the holiday.

This Christmas, however, she couldn't ignore the holiday if she wanted to. Thankfully, she didn't want to.

The holiday was different in Serenity, where snow covered the ground in amounts she'd never seen living in Sacramento. The town was also elaborately decorated. From the stores and businesses to the houses and apartment buildings, twinkling lights and beautiful greenery lined windows and was draped over doorways.

She had attended the church children's program with Gareth and the other Halversons, and she'd enjoyed it immensely. There had been a night market in the large community center, which had been festive and fun.

A constant longing to have her mom with her to experience it tempered the joy she felt in the season. Aria could so easily imagine the joy on her mom's face if she'd been able to be there with her. Maybe there would come a time when she'd experience new things without thinking about how her mom might have enjoyed it too, but she wasn't at that point yet.

Aria stared at the fire for a moment, the flickering flames going in and out of focus. The previous day had marked two years since her mom had passed away. It was hard to believe it had been that long because sometimes it felt like it had just happened a short time ago.

Her phone buzzed with an email notification, and she automatically looked down at her screen. She frowned when she saw it was from the DNA site she'd sent her sample to not long after her mom had passed away. This was the third email alerting her to a message that she'd received on the site in the past week.

It had been strange that after all these months, someone was contacting her. She'd ignored the first couple of messages because the anniversary of her mom's death was looming, and she just hadn't been sure she could handle whatever the news might have been. But now, that difficult day was over, and her curiosity grew as she stared at the message.

Was it really possible that she was related to someone out there?

After a moment's hesitation, Aria tapped on the link to the website. It took her a moment to figure out which password she'd used, then she navigated to the messaging section of the website. Sure enough, there were three messages waiting for her that showed they were from a DNA connection.

She didn't tap on the first message right away, knowing that once she did, things might change forever. Maybe not significantly if she chose not to respond to the person, but she'd have the knowledge that there was someone out there... family. She wasn't sure if she was ready for that.

Shifting her gaze from the screen to the fire again, Aria tried to figure out what to do. Her mom had definitely not wanted her to know anything about her family, but she wouldn't care now.

Hearing footsteps on the stairs, Aria looked over to see Gareth approaching her, two mugs in his hands. They'd been out for dinner, and when they'd come back to the house, he'd sent her upstairs to sit by the fire, promising to bring them some hot chocolate.

It had been something they'd started doing once the days had turned chilly. Fall in Serenity had been beautiful, and Aria had loved spending time in the evening with Gareth. They usually sat on one of the couches on the landing outside her bedroom. It gave them a bit more privacy than the living room, especially if Layla was still awake.

Gareth set the mugs on the coffee table, then sat down on the couch next to her. He wrapped an arm around her waist, and Aria cuddled against him.

"What's wrong?" he asked, making Aria realize she was holding herself tensely.

She blew out a breath and tried to relax before shifting so she could see him better. "I've been getting message notifications from the DNA site I submitted my sample to."

Gareth's brow furrowed. "What did they say?"

"I haven't read them."

Rather than ask why, he just nodded then said, "Do you want to?"

Aria sighed, then leaned her head against Gareth's shoulder. Gareth tugged her closer to his side, offering her the comfort and support she needed in the moment.

"I do," she said. "I think."

"You don't have to reply even if you read them, right?" he asked.

"No. But if they've already sent three messages, me not responding will probably just mean they'll keep sending more."

"Do you want me to read them for you?" Gareth offered.

Aria wasn't sure, but she appreciated his offer. Over the past several months, he had proven to be a protective, loving boyfriend. If situations arose that he could see were causing her anxiety, he tried to step in to help her. He hadn't always been able to do that, but she so appreciated that he cared enough to try.

"I'll read them." Without moving out of his embrace, she lifted her phone again. "I just hope that this isn't some weirdo. I don't want to be related to a weirdo."

Gareth laughed, and she joined him, the humor helping to ease the tension. "I don't know. I'm related to a weirdo, and it's not too bad."

She looked up at him. "Who are you calling a weirdo?"

With a smile, Gareth dropped a kiss on her nose, then said, "Who do you think?"

"Oh. I'm not going to go there."

"Frankly, we've all got a bit of weirdo in us."

"True. Some of us just flaunt it more than others."

"Well, let's find out who is claiming to be related to you."

Aria nodded and looked down at her phone again. She tapped on the first message and began to read it out loud.

Hi Aria ~ My name is Micah Ross, and I'm your half-brother. I have no idea if you know anything about your dad's side of the family, but I'm contacting you on behalf of my mother. She has been in declining health for the past year and asked me to help her find you. Apparently, she lost contact with your mom a couple of years ago and only recently found out that she had passed away. Mom is concerned about you, and she wants to make sure you're okay. After exhausting other options, I submitted to every DNA site I could find, hoping you had tried to find your family as well. I hope that you'll reply, so that I can give my mom some peace of mind about your well-being. Take care.

"Someone from your dad's family was in contact with your mom?" Gareth asked. "Did you know that?"

"I had no idea." Aria stared at the message. "Mom never said anything about her."

"What does the next message say?"

She clicked on it, both excited and worried about its contents.

Hi Aria ~ I hope you're doing well. I don't mean to pester you, but I want you to know that you have people who care about you. Are there questions you have about your past? We'd love to share with you what we know, but only if you're interested in that. I know it probably seems strange that our moms were in contact the way they were. My mom cared about both of you and was distressed to discover that your mom had passed away. Now, she is concerned about you. If you could just let me know that you're okay, I'll pass that on to her and not bother you again if that's what you want.

"Should I reply to him?" Aria asked.

The nervous flutters in her stomach were making her feel a little sick. Did she want to know the answers to her parentage? Honestly, the messages from this man had left her with even more questions. The biggest being why her mom had been in contact with the wife of her father.

"I can't answer that for you," Gareth told her gently. "But I'll support whatever decision you make. If you have questions, though, this seems like the person who can answer them for you."

"I can't decide right now. I think I need to pray about it."

"You know that I'll be praying about it as well. You're not alone in this."

And that reassurance from Gareth helped to soothe the upheaval in her heart. It was a reminder that she could count on him and his family to be there for her.

"Here." Gareth leaned forward and picked up one of the mugs. "Janessa helped me make it, so you know it's going to be good."

Aria cupped the mug in her hands, glad for the warmth that seeped into her palms. She took a sip and closed her eyes, pushing aside the thoughts of what she'd just learned and cherishing the nearness of the man she loved. The man she knew who would be by her side, no matter what decision she made. It comforted her more than she could ever put into words.

***

Gareth shook the pastor's hand as Aria moved on to speak to the man's wife. "Happy New Year."

The man smiled broadly. "The same to you, Gareth. Praying God blesses you greatly in the new year."

"You, too," Gareth replied.

His hope was that some of the blessing would start in just a few hours. They were headed to the big house for the rest of the evening, and the whole family was going to be ringing in the New Year together. It was something they did every year, though he'd missed a few of the celebrations while doing his residency.

"Is Janessa coming with us?" Aria asked as they moved away from the spot where the pastor and his wife were greeting people as they exited the sanctuary.

"I think so, but she's wandered off."

Aria slid her hand around Gareth's elbow, and he covered it with his own. He loved it when she reached out to initiate physical contact with him. It wasn't something she'd done initially, but as their relationship had grown, she'd gotten more comfortable with it. And now, she seemed to reach for him without even thinking about it.

"There she is," Aria said, pointing to where his sister stood talking to a group of her friends.

They were also friends of Aria's since she'd joined the women's group that Charli and Janessa were part of. But even though she enjoyed the group, she still seemed to prefer hanging out socially with just one or two people. Gareth's family being the exception. She seemed to like being with all of them. And thankfully, they liked her too.

"Do you need a ride?" Gareth asked Janessa as they approached her.

"Yep. Are you ready to go now?"

"I think so. Mom and Dad have left already."

Janessa turned to say goodnight to her friends, giving them hugs, as did Aria. He left the two standing just inside the door while he went to get his vehicle, sparing them the walk in the cold wintery night.

He let the SUV warm up for a couple of minutes, then pulled it up behind another car that idled at the bottom of the church steps. Janessa and Aria hurried to the car, slipping into their seats and pulling their doors closed without delay. Aria still didn't really enjoy the cold, so whenever possible, Gareth tried to warm the car up for her. She definitely loved the heated seats. Probably as much as she loved him. Maybe more on really cold days.

"That was a lovely service," Aria said as he pulled away from the church. "I've never been to something like that before."

"Ever since Pastor Ken arrived, he's had this type of service on New Year's Eve," Gareth said. "As you saw, it's not the most well-attended service, but our family always goes."

"It certainly seems like a great way to end off a year, reflecting on it, while also focusing on the next." She fell silent for a moment, then said, "This time last year, I would never have imagined this would be where life would take me."

"There's a few of us who can say that," Janessa remarked from her seat behind Aria. "It's just proof that we can start the year out with one plan or expecting certain things to happen and then God takes us in a completely different direction."

Gareth certainly hadn't started out that year anticipating that he'd get a girlfriend. Being in a relationship was always in the back of his mind, but he'd just assumed that the year would be like all the other ones with regards to dating and girlfriends, especially since Nora was there to chase off any potential girlfriends. Having Nora out of his life and the clinic had definitely helped his relationship with Aria flourish.

"I am ending this year with so many changes," Aria mused.

"Have you decided what to do about those DNA messages?" Janessa asked.

Aria shifted in her seat. "Actually, as I listened to the pastor speak tonight, I made a decision."

Gareth glanced over at her in surprise. The last time they'd talked about the messages from her half-brother, she still hadn't been sure about contacting him. He knew she struggled because her mom had never wanted her to know about her family. Finding out that her mom had been in contact with her father's wife had been a shock to Aria.

"What did you decide?" Gareth asked.

"I'm going to contact Micah." Given how uncertain she'd been whenever they'd talked about it over the past couple of weeks, her certainty now was surprising. "This has really been weighing on me, so tonight, when the pastor had us consider the burdens we carried and how we should hand them over to God, I knew I needed to do that with this." She sighed. "Honestly, I haven't prayed about it as much as I should have. I think I was scared of what God might want me to do about the situation."

Gareth had prayed about it plenty, concerned with how much stress it was causing Aria. Because of that, he was glad that she'd made a decision. He didn't have strong feelings about what she should do. He just wanted her to be happy with whatever she decided, and he'd support her in any way she needed him to.

"I don't know where that will lead, but I think it's time to find out more about my past and what my mom went through."

Reaching out, he gave her hand a light squeeze. "I'll be there whatever happens."

"I know." Her fingers tightened around his hand. "That is part of what gives me the strength to face the unknown."

As they pulled up to the house, Gareth felt a frisson of excitement. Though he'd rung in the previous year without much anticipation, that wasn't the case this year. Both his personal and professional lives were going well, and he hoped that the next year would be even better.

Once inside the large home, they were greeted with warmth, laughter, and the smell of amazing food. For the next three hours, they'd spend time eating, playing games, and then, as the new year approached, they'd spend some time in prayer.

The gathering there that night was a little larger than it had been in the past, but each person present was considered family, whether or not they were officially. And Gareth was glad that they were all there.

"Ten!" Everyone joined in the countdown to midnight, with Layla yelling the loudest. "Three! Two! One! Happy New Year!"

Gareth pulled Aria close, and they smiled at each other before sharing a kiss. There was lots of laughter and talking by the others in the room, but when he ended the kiss and lowered himself to one knee, everyone fell silent around them. He pulled the ring from his pocket, where he'd placed it earlier in anticipation of that moment. It had a simple setting, nothing too large or ostentatious, because he knew that Aria wouldn't want that.

"Sweetheart, I'm not sure you'll ever know how much you mean to me," Gareth began. "I find myself loving you more and more each day. You bring so much joy and light to those around you. Me included. I love your sweet spirit and how you care for others. Being able to spend every day with you has been a wonderful privilege, and there is nothing I'd like better than to spend the rest of my life with you. I love you, Aria. Would you do me the honor of becoming my wife?"

Aria's beautiful eyes had opened wide as she stared down at him, shock evident on her face. For a moment, Gareth wondered if he'd misjudged the seriousness of her feelings for him. But then tears welled up in her eyes and spilled over.

She grasped his hand in both of hers, gripping them tightly. "You want to marry me? Really?"

Gareth got to his feet and drew her into his arms. Holding her close, he whispered, "Yes, sweetheart. I love you so much, and I want to marry you more than anything else."

He heard Aria sniffle, then she lifted her face to look at him, a smile curving the corners of her mouth. "I love you too, and yes, I want to marry you. Being your wife would be a dream come true."

Relief filled him, followed quickly by a rush of love. Gareth moved back just enough so that he could slip the ring on Aria's finger, then he cupped her face gently in his hands and pressed a kiss to her lips. All around them there were cheers and clapping.

He'd planned it so that his family could participate in the happy occasion because he wanted Aria to know that they loved her, too. There wasn't a person there who wouldn't welcome her into the family, and she would never be alone again.

"Congratulations, my darlings," his mom said as she approached them and wrapped her arms around them. "I can't believe that I *finally* get to marry off one of my children. It's about time! And we couldn't be welcoming a nicer person into our family."

As other family members came up to congratulate them, Aria beamed at each of them. Gareth might not have known for sure what type of woman he'd eventually marry, but now that Aria had claimed his heart, he couldn't imagine loving anyone else.

Now that Aria had accepted his proposal, the new year held the promise of a deepening love and even more hope for their future as a couple. It made him excited to see what lay ahead for each of his siblings. Hopefully, if love was in their future, they would experience a smoother road than he and Aria had travelled.

But even if they didn't, he hoped they would look at him and Aria and remember that however rough a journey might be, with effort and God's guidance, they could make it through to experience the love of a lifetime.

ABOUT THE AUTHOR

Kimberly Rae Jordan is a USA Today bestselling author of Christian romances. Many years ago, her love of reading Christian romance morphed into a desire to write stories of love, faith, and family, and thus began a journey that would lead her to places Kimberly never imagined she'd go.

In addition to being a writer, she is also a wife and mother, which means Kimberly spends her days straddling the line between real life in a house on the prairies of Canada and the imaginary world her characters live in. Though caring for her husband and four kids and working on her stories takes up a large portion of her day, Kimberly also enjoys reading and looking at craft ideas that she will likely never attempt to make.

As she continues to pen heartwarming stories of love, faith, and family, Kimberly hopes that readers of all ages will enjoy the journeys her characters take in each book. She has no plan to stop writing the stories God places on her heart and looks forward to where her journey will take her in the years to come.

Made in United States
Orlando, FL
24 April 2024

46143799R00203